SUPERIOR TECHNOLOGY

A deep, shuddering breath, then, "What it was, going by the computer-corrected view of outside, looked like a huge ripple coming at us. Stars bouncing up and down behind a power boat—only they couldn't, of course; *space* moved, between us and them." Another pause. "The thing came so damn *fast;* then it hit and all hell popped loose."

In a soft, throaty voice with a trace of Boston accent, Nadine Potter spoke. "Do you agree with the consensus—that if Maggie was right about the chronometer reversing when the shock waves hit, it means something was moving faster than light?"

She was waiting for something, so Rance said, "By our books, FTL is impossible. It looks as if somebody hasn't been reading our books."

GW00722370

Please be sure to ask your bookseller for the Bantam Spectra Books you have missed:

The Trinity Paradox by Kevin J. Anderson and
    Doug Beason
Nightfall by Isaac Asimov and Robert Silverberg
Consider Phlebas by Iain M. Banks
What Might Have Been, Volume 3: Alternate Wars
    edited by Gregory Benford and
    Martin H. Greenberg
Rendezvous with Rama by Arthur C. Clarke
Rama II by Arthur C. Clarke and Gentry Lee
The Garden of Rama by Arthur C. Clarke and
    Gentry Lee
The Mutant Season by Karen Haber and
    Robert Silverberg
The Mutant Prime by Karen Haber
Raising the Stones by Sheri S. Tepper
Stranger Suns by George Zebrowski
The Next Wave #1: Red Genesis by S. C. Sykes
The Next Wave #2: Alien Tongues by Stephen Leigh

S L O W
FREIGHT

F. M. BUSBY

BANTAM BOOKS

NEW YORK • TORONTO • LONDON • SYDNEY • AUCKLAND

To Daryl and Betty Vincent.
We go back a long way.

SLOW FREIGHT

A Bantam Spectra Book / October 1991

ISBN 0-553-29110-6

Published simultaneously in the United States and Canada

*Bantam Books are published by Bantam Books, a division of
Bantam Doubleday Dell Publishing Group, Inc. Its trademark,
consisting of the words "Bantam Books" and the portrayal of a
rooster, is Registered in U.S. Patent and Trademark Office and in
other countries. Marca Registrada. Bantam Books, 666 Fifth
Avenue, New York, New York 10103.*

PRINTED IN THE UNITED STATES OF AMERICA

RAD   0 9 8 7 6 5 4 3 2 1

PROLOGUE

On the lab bench, frost covered the box. Keeping silent, Anne Portaris waited as Haal Arnesson stepped back from it. Senator Wallin cleared his throat. "What you're saying, Arnesson, is that this thing can *push* without having to expel reaction mass?" The Space Committee's chairman shook his head; with a slight phase lag his sagging jowls followed suit. "Space itself certainly gives nothing to push at; I don't see how such a gadget could work." The rich voice sounded amiable enough, but the heavy features showed signs of irritation.

Well, the senator wasn't noted for patience—back at Gayle Tech, though, the grants had run out; for Anne and Haal, NASA was the last opening and Wallin held the key. On the other hand, the agency itself could use a shot in the arm. So either way . . .

Looking like a slightly overweight blond Viking, Haal Arnesson said, "As our presentation digest indicates, sir, spacetime can be shown to have a vector structure. Our device produces artificial vectors; it's the interaction that produces thrust." The senator's nod was noncommittal; turning to Anne, Haal said, "Crank it up."

So this was it. Pushing dark auburn curls back off her forehead, Portaris reached across the box to the control console. "There's been no time to recalibrate since the plane ride; we may need to do a little tuning." Damned bumpy ride, too—but neither that, nor this chilly lab with the flickering light fixture, were Wallin's fault. On short notice he'd done the best hc could.

Carefully, in correct order she activated power to the exciter, the multipliers, and finally the vector dish itself. From that parabolic concavity came a flare of light, oddly shading down the spectrum as it spread.

"What . . . ?" As Anne moved back from the switch panel, a swelling fluctuation of the shimmering display grazed her hand.

"Oh my God!" Arnesson yelled. Then his voice trailed off as two small white bones struck the floor and rolled slightly. And white bone showed, too, at the stub where Anne's index finger had been.

Gasping, feeling the blood leave her face, Anne shook her head. Nothing hurt, exactly; the wound throbbed with numbness, dull ache, and nagging itch. She looked closely: dead bone—and near its tip, a narrow ring of flesh looked just as dead. "Let's get me to a doctor, Haal. Let's do it fast."

"I don't understand!"

"Neither do I, but gangrene I *don't* need. So turn off your death ray; we'll have to check it out later."

She turned to Wallin. "Sorry, Senator. Can we give you the test run tomorrow?" For a moment she clasped her good hand to her eyes, then uncovered them to look again, unwillingly, at her ruined finger. "Right now I wish I were the fainting type."

Next day, with a bandage covering the site of Anne's missing index finger, the three met again. As they watched the variegated light appear, Arnesson frowned and shook his head. "I can't account for this; we'll need to do some testing."

Picking up an insulated screwdriver, he poked its tip

into the coruscating display, then quickly pulled it back. And now that tip was rusted, corroded; it looked *old*.

"*Why?*" Anne said it.

"Not sure—but I have an idea. Let me turn the intensity down to minimum." That done, he hung his dialface watch over the end of the screwdriver and probed again. As the watch entered the field of light, its hands could no longer be seen. When he pulled it back they had changed position, and the case showed corrosion. The winding stem, when he tried it, was stuck solid.

Anne felt her brows rise; Haal said, "The light show— it has to be an area of accelerated *time*. Your finger was in it less than a second—or maybe more like several hundred years."

In momentary panic she gasped, "What if I'd stuck my stupid *head* in there?"

"Stupid doesn't apply. You didn't touch it on purpose —and besides, none of us could have known." He waved away her questions, and Wallin's. "We built this thing to push at space, right? But spacetime is all one package, phase-related." He looked at the senator. "All right so far?"

The heavy face smiled. "Don't talk math at me, son; mine's too rusty."

Snapping her fingers, Anne was surprised that her damaged hand could still do it. "Phase relations, Haal. The airplane did bounce around a lot, and we didn't rerun the adjustment sequence before we fired up. So . . ."

She waited until Arnesson continued, "Yes. What she's saying, Senator, is that the maladjustment has the unit making its push against *time*."

Some fast talk, then: any useful applications of this accidental side effect? A quick check, when Senator Wallin sacrificed his own watch, proved that the chronal effect tapered off with the inverse square of distance. "No death ray, then," Wallin said. "Not without a helluva lot of power to get any range at all. Just as well, too."

He grunted. "Now let's see what it's *supposed* to do."

The adjustment process seemed to take a very long time, Anne's own fidgeting made worse by the senator's obvious impatience. Finally, running closed waveforms around the phase circle on his 'scope's screen, Haal brought the pattern to a stop. "That should be it. Try it, Anne."

She nodded; keeping close watch on the power meter, slowly she turned the controlling knob. As before, the frost-covered box flared light, this time palely monochrome; then it quivered. Not fastened down as it had been at Gayle Tech, the unit made a brief, tiny lurch, as if to escape its own emissions.

The sudden movement caught Anne by surprise; her grip on the power knob turned it more than she intended, and the next jerk spun it fully.

"Hey!"

Too late! With its visual display trailing behind, the box shot horizontally off the bench, narrowly missing Wallin, and crashed against a wall. Connecting cables, ripped free, spewed sparks and smoke; static charges stood hair on end; the air reeked of ozone.

Choking back reasonless laughter, Anne said, "I think he's got it."

"Yes," said the senator. "I'd say the thing pushes against space, all right."

The report of Wallin's committee brought NASA back to life and health; within the year a manned spaceship, the *Jovian,* launched to explore those moons of Jupiter that lay outside the planet's major radiation belts. The ship's three propellant nodes formed an equilateral triangle, and a Tri-V news anchorman dubbed the Traction Drive "Three-fingered Annie."

Anne Portaris was not amused. When that anchorman's leading bird dog hailed her at a Congressional hearing, calling her by the nickname as he shoved a mike at her face, she was not overloaded with saintly patience.

"Now look, newsboy. I already gave one finger to this enterprise. But since you insist, here's another."

I

HABEGGER

Rance Collier never watched Tri-V news ("You can't turn the page"), but here at Gayle Tech he'd known Arnesson and Portaris quite well. So when Bowie Fleming told him about Anne's gesture on-camera, he laughed. "That's her, all right."

Squinting against glare from the Physics Department cafeteria's chartreuse walls, he said, "What's on my mind now, though, is today's demonstration. I'd trust old Habegger's math a lot better if I could follow it."

When Bowie smiled, her heavy lips lost their brooding look and made her a coffee-colored pixie; at such times he wished he had the nerve to try for more than casual-buddy status. She said, "In a few minutes we'll see, won't we?" And glancing at the wall clock, "About time to go?"

He nodded, and they stood: she dark and chunky, he tall, almost scrawny, pale-skinned with freckles. Rance didn't mind, he told himself, that she'd completed her Ph.D. in physics and was well along with an approved research project—while he, still nominally a doctoral candidate, had been sidetracked by lack of money. Now, under the guise of "liaison," he was doing more departmental PR than research. What did bother him was that if he couldn't respect his own shift of plans, how could Bowie?

Outside, in chilly air under pale blue sky, they walked toward the huge, boxy building that housed Dr. Habegger's experimental setup. "The gadget had *better* work," Rance said. "GIT's backed him solidly, even last year when the government grants people dragged their feet."

Bowie grinned. "Maybe the government types couldn't fathom Doc's brand of prose. Not that *I* do all that well on it."

"Modesty," said Rance, "is a snare and a delusion. Anyway, they can't expect him to come right out and say, in so many words, that he's invented instant Postal Service."

Bowie gripped his arm. "Do you think he really has? It's so hard to *believe.* "

"I know. Too bad there wasn't any money for preliminary small-scale tests, to confirm his computer simulations. Well, today's the day." As she let go his arm he patted her hand. "Let's go in. We're early, but I have a flyer to write for Habegger's press conference. And for background I want a last look around the machinery, before he cranks the juice up."

Except for a guard, who confirmed Rance's ID and then paid the two no more attention, the warehouse was empty of people. At one of the long sides a ten-meter strip of floor had been cleared; in two areas there, over the major equipment, lab-grade lighting replaced the original, dimmer illumination.

At the area's near end a conveyor belt sloped gently from the floor to an opening, its hinged lid raised out of the way, in the three-meter sphere that stood braced on insulating risers. At the far end stood a companion sphere, this one facing in the opposite direction with only an edge of its own ramp showing beyond. "This end's the transmitter," he told Bowie. "Assuming it works, that is."

Rance leading, they walked up the nearer belt, stopped at the opening, and looked inside. Bowie oohed. Rance had seen it before: a pattern of varicolored, anodized metal spikes studded the interior, including the inside of the raised lid. What he hadn't done was find words with which to describe it clearly.

He knew, because he'd been told, that different colors outlined esoteric polyhedrons in conjugate pairs, but phrases like "the perimeter of a tesseract rendered isometrically in three dimensions" didn't tell him much; his own work dealt with discontinuous boundary conditions in anomalous gradients and seldom required him to translate the math into English.

For Habegger's press debut, though, symbols on a screen wouldn't make it. Even if he knew the right symbols. "Synthesis of mass effect without mass," the Doc had said, and, "hyperrotation of the unmoving object"; after that, Rance lost track. He did understand that the efficiency of the multiphased fields generating those effects depended on their geometric properties and that high-temperature superconductors made the whole thing possible—but the press would want something more than that, and couched in layman's terms to boot.

Leading Bowie, he stepped inside the sphere, onto a nonconductive weblike grid, which looked fragile but did not sag. Actually it formed the upper surface of another endless belt, aligned to accept test objects from the entrance ramp. Pleased to recognize something he did understand, Rance explained how the weight of a specimen placed on the lower belt could activate both and also open the lid. "Once something's inside and centered, motion stops and the thing recloses. Transmission, then, can either proceed automatically or by using a switch on the console down there."

Looking around, Bowie shivered. "Let's go back out, before—"

"Before somebody hits the switch?" But seeing that her nervousness was real, he didn't laugh. "Sure." And hearing sound of movement and voices, "Here come the troops, anyway."

Trailing three assistants, Dr. Habegger entered. "Collier." As he nodded, the light caught glints from the clipped white fringe of his hair. "And Dr. Fleming? A pleasure. Not your field, this. But maybe a connection someplace. Take notes; anything you notice, might help."

As the older man turned aside, giving cryptic instructions to the man and two women who accompanied him, Rance drew Bowie out of the way; at the edge of the cleared area they found a stray, anonymous crate to sit on.

"Rance? How'd you get permission for me to be here?"

He shrugged. "Habegger likes me. Well, it's mutual, but also I've done him enough PR to be useful. So when I asked if I could bring an intelligent guest—"

Bowie snickered. "Long as he knows I'm housebroken."

Two of the helpers had gone to the far sphere and out of sight behind it; the third, a spare-featured, redhaired woman carrying a clipboard, hovered alongside Habegger as he sat before a small console near the belt ramp. As she read from a checklist he poked at switches, turned dials, and muttered—until gradually the installation came alive. A hum of power built; within the sphere, before its lid closed, Rance saw a brief glow of ionization—and then, outside it, a flickering halo. Leakage? He didn't know enough to guess.

The humming rose, fell, wavered, and then became steady. Around the sphere the ghost flickers died away. For a time, as nothing more happened, Rance felt the urge to fidget; a sidewise glance showed Bowie looking patient as a rock.

Then Habegger cleared his throat and stood; holding a small plaque, he stepped to the conveyor belt. "That's his international award, from five years ago," Rance whispered. "I wonder—"

Bowie squeezed his hand. "It's symbolic. He's putting his whole career on the line, right here and now."

Habegger set the plaque down; as its weight started the belt moving, the sphere opened to reveal a pulsing aura inside. When the plaque went out of view inside the sphere, its lid closed silently.

As silently as they all, now, waited.

"But where did it go, Rance? Where *could* it go?" The mood of the place—after Habegger found the plaque gone from the first sphere but also absent at the far end —was more than grim. Walking slowly but putting his feet down hard as he returned to the transmit console, Dr. Habegger showed no cracks in his surface calm. But if you punctured him, Rance thought, hot magma would erupt.

The man didn't give up easily. Adjusting power, fiddling with phase relationships, sometimes disabling the belt operation to walk up and deposit test objects by hand, he tried a variety of specimens, including a caged live gerbil.

With uniform results: twelve disappearances, no returns. "Batting a thousand," Rance commented, "but in the wrong league."

Eventually, looking like a man who had aged two decades since lunch, Habegger shut down the equipment. To standby, only: a safety interlock blocked any cutoff of the transmit function until receipt was signaled at the other end, and the installation drew power from its own self-contained reactor.

Leaving the place, as assistants gathered up the gear they'd brought with them, the doctor turned to where Rance and Bowie stood. When no questions came, he shrugged. "Drinks I will have, and some thought, and rest. And *more* thought."

As the man started to move away, Rance had a thought of his own. "If it's all right with you, Doctor, I'll skip making any report of this—uh—preliminary tuneup session." Nodding, Habegger made an effort to smile and walked away.

Unwilling to face the Physics Department's cafeteria again so soon, Bowie and Rance adjourned to the Faculty Lounge. "Should be serving drinks by now," he said.

Shortly, at a corner table, he and she nursed glasses of "rocks" floating in bourbon and Scotch respectively. Sipping, Bowie said, "What will he do now? What *can* he do?"

Rance considered. "On the experiment, I have no idea—and doubt that he has, either. Politically, though —the fundings and authorizations and all—the Board vote was last week. So the doc's solid for another year, anyway." He felt his forehead wrinkle. "Up in Admin, Elliott McCalder's been displeased for some time, I hear. Griping about the tie-up of *warehouse* space, if you can believe it. Not to mention Habegger's lock on a nuke box all his own, for one lone project."

"But if that one project should prove out—"

"If, yes. Earlier today, I think I'd have bet on it. Now all I know is, we can forget the press conference."

After half a week of gathering what he hoped would be newsworthy info on new refinements in radioactive dating, Rance spent the next day fashioning his notes into a presentable release. It didn't help that after he'd done the requisite jargon-filled version for the Physics Department's journal, the department head had him dumb it down to fill a half page in the alumni newsletter. "But that's how it goes," he said to Bowie at a chance-met lunch. And then, "Anything new with Habegger?"

"Nothing official," she said. "Nothing in print. But on the grapevine, word's getting around."

As they stood, ready to leave, Rance said, "I think I'll keep an eye on the project, look in once in a while."

"What good will that do?"

"Damn if I know. But it couldn't hurt."

Over the next few weeks, then, sometimes Dr. Habegger was at the warehouse and sometimes not; either way, Rance didn't learn much. One day he found the redheaded assistant—Cassandra Monlux, her name was—puttering around inside the sending sphere. When she came out, he asked, "How come it's safe to work in there? I thought the goojie was locked into Transmit."

"It is." She looked tired. "The linkage, if you follow me, won't deactivate. Nor the receptivity of the far unit.

But this terminal can't send until the cover's closed."
Someone called to her; she gave Rance a fleeting smile
and left.

Looking inside the sphere, then, he saw that some of
the metal spikes were missing from the complex array; a
pile of them lay at one corner of the grid, and the pattern was obviously in process of change. What this
meant, Rance had no idea, and Habegger wasn't there
to answer questions.

When Rance did find the doctor one afternoon, looking slightly less harassed than usual, he asked. Habegger
nodded. "In one equation there is a transformation;
quite early, I assumed that the solution of identities
would be the operative form. Seems not to be the case—
well, you've seen. So now I try the complementary solution." Dr. Habegger didn't seem to realize that he was
still nodding. Saying he hoped this answer worked,
Rance backed away and left.

While officialdom kept a tight silence regarding the entire expensive problem, unofficial parties began to take
an interest. Three students were caught trying to activate transmission with the complete undergraduate
transcript files piled on the conveyor belt. Some weeks
later, persons unknown did a more workmanlike job:
from the few items of clothing found scattered alongside the belt, campus police deduced that the entire
wardrobe of Gayle Tech's leading sorority, missing from
that house's closets, had gone wherever Dr. Habegger's
sphere sent test objects.

Elliott McCalder, administrator, had guards posted,
and for a time the pranks ceased. The next incident,
however, was hardly a joke. When the guard on duty
got up from a blow to the head and lurched into the
building to see what was going on, he was barely in time
to see the moving belt push a dead body into the
sphere's glowing interior. He knew it was a corpse, he
reported, because ". . . that dent in his head, you could
of hid a baseball."

The dent in the black-haired head, and the dark suit,
were all he could remember of the victim, even under
hypnosis. On that basis, Three-thumbs Dinotti would

have guessed right when the other stocking-masked man wanted the guard killed.

"Naw," Dinotti had said, "this pigeon can't ID nobody." But Three-thumbs wasn't entirely correct; hypnosis enabled recall of the dialogue, and more importantly, the right hand with two small thumbs side by side rather than the normal single larger one.

But as Dinotti put it in his recorded interview at the District Attorney's office, "Where's yer corpus derelicti? Without one a them, you ain't got doodly."

So except for the assault charge, a bailable offense, Three-thumbs was home free. The D.A. put surveillance on him, if only to show that he was willing, if not able, to pursue the case.

After McCalder added a second guard, the intrusions ceased.

From the Dinotti incident came one repercussion. At budget time, when individual fundings were chewed, hewed, and reviewed, in attendance was a representative of the State's Attorney. What she pointed out was that anyone who shut down power to Habegger's gear, thus cutting off all chance of access to the test specimen donated by Three-thumbs Dinotti, would be quite expensively in contempt of court.

So although Elliott McCalder frowned heavily, especially so since the termination of Habegger's grants meant that the doctor's expenses were now charged to McCalder's own budget, the project stayed minimally alive. Rance knew about that budget. The skimpiness of his physics fellowship had tempted him into the "liaison" work, and his departmental paycheck was hardly lavish.

Occasionally Rance looked in at the warehouse. As time passed, Dr. Habegger became more haggard and less talkative. The whole thing, Rance thought, was just too damn depressing. He wanted to talk to Bowie, but these days she was too busy, readying to leave Gayle for a position on the west coast. So the problem, the situation, just churned around in his own head.

It wasn't as though he could do anything to help. Still, as time passed, now and then he felt the need to look in and check up. Until one day, a little more than eighteen months after the original test, a guard told Rance that Habegger that same day had closed the control console and stalked out. "I asked when he'd be back but he just mumbled. 'Maybe never,' I think he said."

The next time Rance passed the warehouse, perhaps two months later, the doors nearest Habegger's input terminal had been torn out and replaced by a considerably larger entrance; as he watched, a disposal truck turned and backed inside. Elliott McCalder had found an economic use for Habegger's project.

With trucks and disposal-company employees in and out at all hours, security gradually became a farce. The first person to sprint up the ramp, and throw himself onto a load of garbage just as the lid closed, was a man of about thirty: white, average height, slim, with longish brown hair and short beard, nondescript soiled clothing, identity unrecognized during the brief seconds four witnesses saw him. No one fitting his description turned up in the Missing Persons file.

The second case was a young woman with a history of drug abuse and emotional disturbance. The third was Dr. Habegger; he walked in slowly, waving back the men readying the next load of garbage, and such was his presence that no one tried to stop him. Absolutely no one.

The day after the memorial service someone noticed a light blinking at the side of the farther sphere, and investigating, found that sphere open. Inside, the small conveyor belt began to move, and on it moved Dr. Habegger's award plaque. By the time others arrived, including Rance Collier, the sphere had opened and closed several times, ejecting individual test objects and groups. According to the log Cassandra Monlux produced from somewhere, these were the same items, in the same order, Habegger had used for his first tests, almost exactly two years ago.

Including the gerbil, alive and squeaking.

"You're not juicing me, Rance? This is *else*." Shaking her head, Bowie let him into her crate-cluttered apartment. Next day was her date of departure, so he'd brought along the makings of a going-away feast. Now, with the news he had, it could be a real celebration. For her, anyway; for him it meant the loss of a relationship he'd wanted but had never been able to speak for.

He refused to begrudge her achievement, though. While they fixed dinner and then ate and drank, in the talking he held his own, well enough.

The Habegger thing fascinated her. "Got so fed up, he tried *suiciding*? And then it turns out the machine works after all, only not exactly the way he figured?"

"That's about right."

"Just didn't wait quite long enough."

"No."

She shrugged. "Can happen to any of us, I guess. Even me."

"I—what do you mean?"

"This new job I took." He'd never seen her brown eyes widen so far. "Maybe if I'd waited longer, you'd have made your move."

"But . . ." He stood. "Bowie, I—we could still—"

"No. Just a one night stand. You wouldn't want that."

The hell he wouldn't! But since she'd put it that way, he couldn't possibly say so. "You're right, of course. We'll just have to drink to missed connections."

Later, going home, he settled for the consolation that he'd covered his feelings well enough to keep the party cheerful.

The press conference was going to be a bitch. With no overheating at all, Rance felt sweat tainting his shirt. Back at his desk he made several hurried phone calls and hoped he hadn't forgotten anything really important. What was all this going to *mean*? As yet he knew he hadn't guessed even a fraction of the possibilities.

Next day on Tri-V he saw that one of his phone calls had paid off. The D.A.'s people had caught Three-thumbs Dinotti at the airport and managed to convince a judge that under the circumstances the man could be held without bail for the requisite period. Assuming, of course, that everything came through on schedule.

At the warehouse, workmen were demolishing the rear wall, behind the receiving sphere and its ramp.

Well, all that garbage had *better* be out of there, before Dr. Habegger reappeared.

"Two years?" Rance thought. "That's not too many."

Elliott McCalder's memo came as part relief and part letdown. The administrator had postponed the press conference a month. Habegger's people, it seemed, wanted to make some tests first. What those might be, Rance had absolutely no idea.

II

CONFABS

Looking through old files, Rance found the notes he'd made, more than two years earlier, for the Habegger press conference that had never happened. Much of the material no longer applied, but a few items did; economically he excerpted those and fit them into the text he needed to finish in a hurry. For the official announcements tomorrow there'd be some big guns on hand, and Elliott McCalder had made it clear: now that the government people had given up trying to slap a security lid on the project, Rance had damn well better make his presentation both comprehensive and correct. Also, fast.

Looking down from his flyspecked monitor screen, Rance leafed through the papers Cassandra Monlux had given him. Helpful was the word for redheaded Cassie, who in Dr. Habegger's absence had settled in solidly as his surrogate. No two ways about it: with her specialized knowledge leapfrogging her above several who had departmental seniority on her, Monlux had a real opportunity here. If she could handle the pressure . . .

Scratching his head, Rance Collier scanned what he'd written: a brief, almost-shorthand summary of events to date. Now came the hard part. The *possibilities* of Habegger's device were simply too much to cover in detail; he'd have to stick to reminder notes. He began:

"Pipelines. Any application where you can wait two years for first delivery and then it comes solid." Cassie had assured him the input-output interfaces could be modified for continuous feed. So: "Oil. Alaska–Canada–U.S. pipe-tankers complex a leaky mess and getting worse. Two years to implement Habegger system, then drain pipelines and dismantle."

More oil notes. Soviet deposits, Arabian, Antarctic, or wherever—two neat terminals per route, no leaks, no biosphere damage. Hell on shipping interests, but that's progress for you.

The two-year delay, though. That's what we've got to sell them. Rance laughed. *We?* A PR flack from GIT, all that self-important? Still, right now it was his pitch that might steer what happened later.

All right—what other delivery networks could within two years be put on a pipeline basis, or equivalent? He needed someone from the Econ Department, but he didn't know anyone over there. So he'd have to generalize. Back to the keyboard: "Anything, any kind of transport, where steady dependability after a two-year wait would pay off. (Throw it open to audience to cite examples.)"

What else, what else? Hmm—the *Moon,* for Pete's sake! With a Habegger system in place, the shelved colony project could take off like billy-o. Still need the shuttles and transfer stages for personnel, of course; you couldn't ask *people* to trade two years for cheap transport. At such short distances . . .

Then his jaw dropped. The screen forgotten, Rance looked through his phone index and punched up a call.

The conference next day began well. Early on, after the history part but before Rance could even begin his listing of possible applications, someone asked the major question he needed: "Forty meters per year? That's not exactly high-speed transport, is it?"

Elliott McCalder, on the verge of becoming president of Gayle Tech, had wanted Rance to lead off, unasked, with the answer to that objection. But Rance said, "We've spent a lot of money getting that info; it'll have more impact if *they* bring it up." And he wasn't the best choice to tell it, anyway.

Second-guessing Habegger's equations in the face of the new developments, Cassandra Monlux and her two associates had found a set of terms, canceled by the doctor as indeterminate and redundant, which in their opinion didn't really cancel. And there, she swore, lay the source of the two-year delay.

She also swore the time wouldn't vary with distance —and when the government ponied up some money, she had set out to prove it. First move was to supply the receiving terminal with its own power source. Getting it to the nearest railroad spur, then, was no picnic, but mounted on a flatcar and covered against weather the terminal was shipped nearly two thousand miles south and west from Gayle Tech.

Now she stood, ready to report. Every time he saw her, Rance thought, her red hair got brighter and shorter, and though she couldn't have more than four or five years on him, her face showed gauntness and the first onslaught of lines. She said, "Our records don't include exact timing on the entrance of every test sample, but as near as we can tell there's no difference in transmission time: eighty meters or thirty-two hundred kilos."

She paused and had a sip of water; Rance took over again, to present his ideas on Earthbound applications. In a shorter while than he'd expected, he covered most of his reminder notes.

Going then to the audience for further suggestions proved to be a good move; out of it appeared several ideas he'd never have thought of.

One of these came as a question: given a number of Habegger systems in operation, how do we know where something will come out? And maybe in more than one place?

To his relief, Cassie fielded that one, too. "This isn't

the transmission of any kind of signal; it's transfer of mass in spacetime. And each pair of terminals is by its nature uniquely keyed, each to the other." In the face of her questioner's skepticism, she added, "Complex crystalline structures, split along the axis of symmetry and one half used in each terminal, constitute the equivalent of tuning devices. The odds against duplication make identical snowflakes look like a sure thing."

So much for that; time to get on. "So we see," Rance said, "that each transmission path is unique *and* that distance doesn't affect the time factor. Not in any Earthbound application, at least." He cleared his throat. "I suppose you've guessed the next step."

He waited, until someone shouted, "The moon!"

"That's being discussed in Congressional committees; we hope it's approved. Because that could be just for starters."

From the back of the hall a man yelled, "The new Jupe probe?"

Rance nodded. "Yes. If the moon works out, the other should follow." He shrugged tension loose. "Now then, do we have any more questions?"

From near the middle of the audience a woman's hand raised. Something about that hand didn't look quite right; suddenly he remembered his call to D.C. *So she did come!*

What with the distraction, he'd missed whatever she was saying. "Would you repeat that, please, Ms. Portaris?"

In her forties now, Anne Portaris could pass for somewhat younger; from this distance her curly auburn hair showed no gray. "I said, Mr. Collier, that after this shindig's buttoned up, we'd like to speak privately with you and Ms. Monlux."

Cassie looked puzzled; Rance nodded to her, then answered. "Of course. Come to the Liaison office, please." We? Oh yes; now he saw Arnesson sitting beside her. . . .

Then the open questioning began, and went on, and went on. Knowing the media's normal fact-to-frosting ratio, the inanity of some of the questions didn't surprise Rance. It was the intelligent ones that startled him—all three of them.

•   •   •

When the conference finally wound down, Rance and Cassie ducked out for Liaison. Slumping down into one of the big padded chairs, Cassie said, "Oh Jesus, Rance! I feel wrung out like a pair of stretch tights." She did a little stretching herself. "Those turtleheads! Do you think we made any dent?"

"Sure. You did great." He handed her a cup of coffee from the ever-replenished machine and sipped on his own. It tasted like last week's, but he needed it anyway. "And the first ones asking, who got their facts and then shut up, *weren't* dummies."

He sat behind his desk, where he felt most at ease, and they talked—sorting out points they might have handled better, but mainly winding down from pressure.

When the knock came, he realized he hadn't briefed Cassie for this appointment with Anne Portaris. Quickly he said, "You remember Three-fingered Annie?"

"Well enough not to ever call her that." She paused. "You used to know her fairly well, didn't you?"

"A while back; yes." His first year in grad school, when for a time she'd more or less taken him under her wing. And, to a degree, so had Arnesson. Thinking back, he smiled.

But that was then. "Right now, as I get it, she and Haal are either on loan from NASA to Senator Wallin's committee, or the other way around." Now his hand was on the doorknob.

"I'm not sure either. Doesn't matter; let 'em in."

Opening the door, Rance traded greetings with the visitors. Both met him warmly, Annie with a quick hug, but their serious expressions told him this was no time for Old Home Week. Then as Cassie stood, he introduced her also.

At closer view, Anne Portaris still held up in the looks department; she stood trim and moved well. Her blond Viking had curbed his weight problem and kept the youthful lines of his face, but not much hair to go with them. *Nobody wins 'em all.*

While the guests found seats, Rance offered drinks. On the bar's bottom shelf he noticed and mentioned a dusty bottle of akvavit. Haal Arnesson's expression brightened, and Portaris, who had first asked for wine, changed her mind. Surreptitiously Rance wiped the bottle free of dust, then presented it for inspection.

When the amenities were taken care of, he sat. "Okay, meeting's open. Who's first?"

"Are you familiar," said Portaris, "with the results brought back by *Jovian*?"

"Sure." Rance nodded. New data on Io's vulcanism, further anomalies of other major satellites and of Big Jupe itself—and the uncountable riches of the asteroids, still effectively beyond Earth's grasp because of gravity's fuel demands. Quickly he summarized these facts.

"Right," said Anne. "And you know that construction of *Jovian-II*, the improved model, is stalled for lack of funds." Another nod; still no news here. Portaris leaned forward. "Habegger's thingy may open up a whole new ball game."

"I know. Why do you think I called you?"

Arnesson cleared his throat. "Of course. But the point is, *how* new? Let's talk it over. If we come up with what I hope we will—Collier, I think we'll want you to change jobs. To do liaison between GIT and NASA. Plus PR, naturally. Since you're in on the ground floor already."

The discussion moved fast. The first *Jovian*, capable of extended acceleration with the Arnesson-Portaris Traction Drive, was basically limited by fuel supply and by the inevitable deterioration of its closed-cycle life-support systems. But *Jovian-II*, which even a Congressional blank check couldn't get off the pad within the next two years, could operate on a wholly different basis. Primed two years ahead of launch, Habegger "pipelines" could provide fuel, air, and other supplies, while a reverse system could return space-floating minerals to Earth for assaying—or, in emergency, a sick crew member for treatment. "If," said Arnesson, "the transport lag is experienced as stasis by the specimen in transit."

"Seemed to be, for the gerbil," Rance said. And then they got to the big stuff. In *Jovian-II* the space no longer needed for fuel, air, and food, etc., could be used to carry the components of *huge* Habegger terminals complete with power supplies, so that asteroid materials could be sent to Earth or Moon or to factories orbiting in cislunar space. A profitable venture, this version of *Jovian-II* looked to be.

Arnesson raised a cautionary hand. "What about energy costs? When it comes to potential energy, or conservation of momentum, does Habegger give us a free ride? Or do we pay the tab in power consumption? Until we've worked a system with one end off Earth, we won't know. Either way, of course, we still gain access to deep space. But—"

"Hold it," said Cassie. "We may have the answer already." She paused, the others silent and watching her, then said, "Our distance tests, remember? We've sent the receiving terminal, on a flatcar, down somewhere around Albuquerque. On the map, slanting, thirty-two hundred kilometers. Latitude and longitude giving changes of tangential velocity and also direction; right?" Rance nodded. She said, "And test objects, put in two years earlier, have been coming out on schedule. Plus, all received items were found, before the belt started moving them, sitting near the middle of the grid where they'd been placed, and certainly didn't look to have been bounced around at all."

She smiled. "I think the system disconnects objects from their initial frames of reference and connects them on arrival to the new ones." For a moment she frowned, then shook her head. "And the readouts show no spikes in the power drain."

"Over deep-space distances," said Anne Portaris, "there may be more pronounced effects. But so far, it does look good."

Arnesson spoke. "Well, Collier, do you think you'd like to change jobs a little and work with us on this? And you, Ms. Monlux. You'd still be primarily with Gayle Tech—but, of necessity, with a strong NASA tie-in. What do you think?"

Cassie shrugged. "Let someone else work out the administrative details. Just so nobody puts me in the middle, answering to more than one boss. In case they don't get along."

Arnesson laughed, but Rance knew she was talking about a very real problem. And maybe he had one of his own. "This is a temporary assignment you're offering. After *Jovian-Two* I look for a new job. Right?"

With her mutilated hand, Anne gestured. "That job's already looking for you." Rance blinked and she said, "Jove-two is only a trial run. For *Starfinder,* the manned interstellar probe. Because now, you see, that's feasible.

"If you can help us sell it."

As the receiving Habegger terminal made its long rail trip back to GIT, only one reporter rode with the tech crew. So when the sorority house wardrobe emerged, that woman had a scoop.

Everyone seemed to have forgotten that prank. Now of course the clothes were out of fashion, and meanwhile many of their owners had graduated, gained or lost weight, become pregnant. . . . Still, though, the whole thing made a good human-interest story.

When Rance read it, he got on the phone to the office of the D.A., who sent a wire ordering the flatcar shunted to a whistle-stop sidetrack, and then flew two detectives out to join it. They arrived in plenty of time; two days later the sphere produced the man with the concaved skull. The body, they reported, was still warm.

Faced with his recovered "corpus derelicti," Three-thumbs Dinotti's composure vanished. "He's singing grand opera," said one Assistant D.A., meaning that having first put the finger on his accomplice, Dinotti was now trying to nail him for the entire rap. On arraignment for Murder One, the two men fought to outdo each other in accusations. "Two biggest finks I've ever seen," said the Assistant D.A., and didn't bother to hide her laughter.

Before the hassle ended, Rance lost track of it. It wasn't that he lacked interest; he was simply too busy coping with the paperwork and priorities of changing over to his new job.

III

COMPLICATIONS

Before the paperwork had time to come to roost, Rance and Cassie were getting used to living out of suitcases. From GIT to D.C. and back, to the Cape—Traction Drive ships didn't need the isolation required by the huge old chemical rockets, but Canaveral had facilities, so why not use them?—and again to the nation's capital. Feeling a bit disoriented, Rance followed Cassie Monlux into Senator Wallin's office.

The man was thin these days; his former jowls hung in wattles. It wasn't age that had him in a wheelchair, though certainly he wasn't far from pushing eighty. But after fifteen years a "total hip" replacement had loosened, and he was delaying its revision (odd-sounding term) until the Congress adjourned.

After handshakes, Wallin gestured his visitors to seats. "All right," he said. "My staff's briefed me; I know at least part of what Habegger's mass squirter can do. And

I've skimmed your writeup, Collier, on its application to *Jovian-Two.* I expect my committee to have the project on the floor for vote before the week's out."

He leaned forward. "Now tell me about the interstellar probe. Keep in mind that I want it to go as much as you do, but don't spare me the limitations."

Well! Old and crippled Wallin might be, but his head still tracked. Rance nodded. "Ms. Monlux is the expert, so—"

Wallin shook his head. "No. Collier, you're the one who's supposed to sell this venture. So let's see you sell *me.* That is, assume I need selling. Ahumph! Go ahead."

"All right. For the public we have to recap from scratch, so bear with me." He began with the basic facts of Habegger's device, then its role in *Jovian-II.* "All right so far?" Wallin nodded. "These factors also apply to *Starfinder.* Continuous refueling will give the ship unlimited range and ability to maneuver—to accelerate or slow or turn—without regard to fuel limitations. And the same goes for life-support restrictions. Food, air, water, maintenance requirements—they're all renewable."

Fidgeting, Wallin mumbled something: if it wasn't "Get on with it," the intent had to be much the same.

"Sure. The big thing. Light speed's our limit, but we can accelerate as close to it as we choose. The trip to any of our best guesses for finding a habitable planet will take—oh, call it forty years, maybe more."

Now comes the good part. "But no *people* have to give that much of their lives to the venture. They can sign on for a tour of duty—one year, say. That's a year by ship's time; Einstein's figures say that here at home, depending on ship's velocity, five years could pass. Or ten, or twenty. Plus, each way in the pipeline, two years' transit time; that's a fixed quantity, but so far as we know, instantaneous to the transmitted object."

Pausing, Rance took a deep breath. "The point is, we can run the ship from Earth, with officers and crew serving relatively short hitches aboard. And once *Starfinder* reaches a good colony planet and sets up the larger Habegger terminal that makes up the major vital part of its cargo, that planet is no farther away from us than the other end of Habegger's warehouse!"

Silent and unmoving, Wallin sat. Rance said, "Did I miss something, sir? Do you have more questions?"

Headshake. "No, son, you got it all. I'm just sitting here, trying to absorb what it really means."

Besides *Jovian-II*, Congress authorized a Habegger-supplied revival of the moon colony. The president, chronically at odds with the Congress, quibbled a bit but signed the bills. For one thing, a moon base gave the stagnant military something to do.

By that time Rance and Cassie, having testified before the Congress in joint session, were traveling once more. First to GIT, assembling specs and notes, having them duplicated for distribution to contract bidders. Then again to the Cape, for Cassie to meet with the would-be design crews. Easier to figure things, Rance guessed, with *Jove II*'s half-completed hull at hand than relying wholly on drawings.

It was nearly all Cassie's show now; sometimes Rance felt he was merely along for the ride. Eventually he realized that at this stage of procedure he was the safety valve, taking care of perfectly legitimate questioners who would otherwise be wasting the attention of taut-featured Cassandra Monlux.

Oh, well; so be it. . . .

Losing track of time, it was all Rance could do to keep pace with developments. Some weeks after the event he learned what happened when the receiving terminal was returned to GIT's warehouse. Somehow, during the unloading at the railhead, the sphere had been disconnected from all power—yet it stayed "live" and continued to produce the test objects Habegger had fed it two years earlier. So it appeared that power as well as specimens was being transferred.

The trouble was, no one could determine whether that had been the case from the beginning or only following the original two-year transmission lag. In the case of *Starfinder*, it would pay to find out before that ship went anywhere.

Assuming it was ever built. Wallin was pushing, and pushing hard, with what was probably the final major thrust of his long political career. But politics being politics, the effort wasn't moving very fast. Though the senator got around rather well these days, Rance had to admit, on his new artificial hip joint.

He also had to admit that sheer accident could have strong consequences. A quick visit to D.C. ran into two major conventions and a mass protest. Rance never did know what the mass was protesting, but it clogged the city's accommodations badly enough that his and Cassie's room reservations were lost in the shuffle. And after midnight, following a ten-hour session of trying to make sense with unsympathetic bureaucrats, neither of them was in a mood to go find a cab, let alone vacancies.

Rance didn't like making scenes but he knew how. ("Hold your breath while you pound on the desk; it makes your face red. Speak slowly, through clenched teeth, just short of shouting." He'd read that somewhere; now he used it.)

Until the desk clerk, his own thin-lipped face mottled red and white, flipped through cards, punched desperately at his terminal's keyboard, and gave a sullen nod. "I can get you a room. Just one, though, not two. Not if you yell from now to breakfast."

Collier stifled a laugh; the clerk did have some guts to him! Then he noticed Cassie standing alongside, looking as if she weren't there and preferred it that way. "All right with you?" With no word she nodded, so he registered them.

Silently, carrying their gear, they rode the elevator and stalked the halls to 948. Rance opened the door and stood aside; as Cassie entered, she said, "You could have asked for two keys." She plunked her kit onto the desk-table across from the beds and rummaged in it while Rance took the foldout rack for his own bag. He didn't need much out of it, but by the time he found what he did need, she'd beaten him to the bathroom.

So he put the stuff on his bedside stand, sat, and removed his shoes. The room sported a minibar: Did he want a drink? Finding the ice machine seemed like too much work, but he was thirsty, and faucet water wasn't too good without ice, either. So he took the plastic "bucket," prowled the halls, and found the machine. When he returned, Cassie was lying on his bed.

She didn't have any clothes on.

Without smiling, she said, "If you don't like skinny redheads, I can move; just say the word. But you're the only man I see, nowadays, long enough to do more than say hello. It seems kind of a waste. And besides, I rather like you."

Except on the friendship level, which was usually fine, Rance was awkward with women and knew it. In his entire life he'd had only three affairs. The first was merely two kids trying to make love work but not doing very well; the girl got pregnant and her parents sued his. The second, actually more of an episode although it took place over several days, caught him squarely on his innocence and gullibility and dynamited what was left of his shaky self-esteem. So that later he was purely live bait for Charlyssa, who taught him every possible thing there was to do, then milked him broke and left him.

After that, he blew without fail every chance he might have had. Such as the latest one, two years back, with Bowie Fleming.

Now, feeling wooden and dissociated from his feelings, he gazed at Cassie. He'd known she wasn't busty; lying back, as she was, she showed large nipples on a near-flat chest. He looked farther down the length of her. "I never did figure you for a natural redhead," and silently cursed his gaffe in saying so.

She sat halfway up; now the nipples formed tips of small, unmistakable bulges. "I am, too!" She touched her head. "Not *this* red, but . . ." She shrugged. "It's the dim light."

The same dimness restored youth to her dry-skinned, lightly lined face. Hell, she couldn't be much past thirty; she'd done some of her aging early, was all. And come to think of it, hadn't changed much recently. If at all . . .

Details, though, were beside the point. Physically he wasn't at all aroused, and tired as he was, arousal might take some doing. But the way he suddenly *felt* about her . . .

Tangled in the shirt he was trying to shed, he bent down to her, and wasn't surprised that she did a fine grade of kissing. "Stay right there. I won't be a minute."

Actually he took longer in the bathroom, because he was scared, but when he came out she wasn't looking at her watch or anything, so he lay on the bed beside her, began a hug, and hoped for the best.

He was every bit as awkward as he'd feared he would be. Sheer excitement of the unexpected got it up for him, but fatigue and nervousness threw his rhythms off; he knew he wasn't doing much good for her, and he himself was much too tired to climax. When he gave up, though, panting and sweating, and began to pull free, Cassie gave him not only a kiss and hug, but also a very friendly-looking smile.

Saying, "It's okay to respect me in the morning, Rance—but don't carry it to extremes."

Next morning, somewhat short of sleep, Rance surprised himself. For starters, he wasn't nervous; Cassie had been so nice about his lousy performance, without making a big thing of it, that he simply wasn't worried. And everything *worked*!

From then on, they learned each other fast, and as the weeks passed, that learning continued. Now on trips they didn't bother to book separate rooms for propriety's sake; after all, this way the government saved money on their expenses.

Sometimes Rance Collier would give his harshfaced love a sidelong look and wonder: *Just how lucky can I get?*

Back at Gayle Tech, the enlarged rear entrance of its famous warehouse saw the coming and going of disposal trucks, to tidy up after Elliott McCalder's most notable miscalculation. The trouble, Rance saw when he and Cassie had occasion to visit the place, was that not all the garbage sat nicely atop the receiving terminal's wide-mesh grid and made neat exit to the bins outside. Instead, quite a lot of the repulsive stuff oozed down among the varicolored metal spikes and stuck there.

With pressure hose and vacuum sweep a crew worked at clearing the worst of it away. But every so often, when the lid began to close in preparation to receive the next load, the workers had to scamper out in a hurry. Rance knew it wasn't really funny, but couldn't help chuckling.

He wasn't present when the first live human emerged, but a Tri-V crew saw the lid lift to reveal a bearded young man enthroned on a pile of garbage, so Rance caught it on the news.

The man blinked, shut his eyes, and shook his head as the belts first moved to slide the major mass to its destination, then stopped. Eyes opened, he tried to stand but fell back, then sat up again. "What the hell! Where did all *you* bozos come from?" And plaintively, "But I thought this thing didn't work; it's supposed to be a one-way ticket to nowhere. That's why—"

They stood him up, brushed most of the detritus off his dirty garments, and perforce interviewed him. Name, Eldon Washougal; age, 31; status, dropout. Then things got out of hand, as Washougal saw his chance to tell the world (or at least the part of it that watched Newsbreaks on Channel 7) how the president and FBI were putting tiny microphones in his food. Everything he ate, he had to put through a blender and then a sieve. And even so, with the progress of miniaturization . . .

"Can you show us some of those microphones?"

"I haven't found any yet. That shows you how *clever* they are."

Marcie Caldwell, the next person to reappear, was an even more fractured personality. Watching on Tri-V, Rance thought that except for emaciation and the shakes, along with personal unkemptness, she might have been attractive.

Unlike Washougal, Marcie had not sought oblivion. She wouldn't say what she was tripping on—and obviously not even close to coming down yet—but what it did was let her talk with God. And God had told her that Habegger's apparatus was the means for transporting the Faithful (aside from herself, she wasn't too specific as to who the Faithful were) to Alpha Centauri. Since God wouldn't lie, obviously this place *was* Alpha Centauri.

Looking past the Tri-V crew, out through the enlarged rear doors, she said, "It doesn't look much different from Earth, does it?"

Then she smiled. "It will when the other sun comes up."

The main event, of course, would be Dr. Habegger's reentry. For that occasion, Rance made sure the schedule allowed Cassie and himself to be on hand. She had to be there because she'd been keeping the fires lit throughout Habegger's absence—and Rance also, because the two had become a true, interdependent team.

When the moment approached, they stood upfront of a fairsized crowd, flanking GIT President McCalder on one side while the local Tri-V anchor held down the other flank.

The time of Habegger's entry was known to within minutes; shortly before his expected emergence the reception committee moved back to allow removal of the penultimate pile of garbage before the doctor's arrival —on the final load, unfortunately.

They all waited—until Rance began to wonder whether, at this crucial point, the apparatus had failed. But then the sphere's lid slowly closed, paused briefly, and reopened. And there stood Habegger, bracing himself as the belt went into motion.

It was a measure of the man's stability that except for a brief widening of the eyes he showed no reaction. Nor did he speak immediately. After a moment the waiting crowd began to cheer. For a few seconds Habegger listened, then waved for silence and looked down to the people grouped around the end of the exit belt.

"Who fixed it?" he said. "You, Monlux?" As the belt brought him to ground he stepped off, just short of handshake distance with Elliott McCalder, and said to Cassie, "What was it I did wrong?"

"Nothing at all, Doctor. Here's how it is. . . ." Very quickly, in Rance's opinion, Habegger accepted the basic situation—including the fact that a truly thorough explanation would take longer than either McCalder or the Tri-V people would care to hold still for.

As McCalder's speechifying began, Rance nodded. Today was headlines and flashbulbs and champagne. Tomorrow was time enough to start work—but early tomorrow, so take it easy on the bubbly.

Well, not *too* easy . . .

IV

GOVERNMENT WORK

Once Dr. Habegger caught up with current happenings, he began to exert influence on them. Unlike Rance or Cassie, he wanted no part of split-allegiance employment; Gayle Tech was his domain and he liked it that way. Elliott McCalder looked relieved at that news; Habegger was his big drawing card these days, and McCalder didn't want to share him.

The doctor didn't mind lending expertise to NASA, though, on specific problems and for specific consultant fees. As Cassie put it, "Higher math's not his only forte; he's no slouch at accounting, either." Neither of them begrudged the man; for what he could contribute, he deserved all the payment he could get.

For instance, once he'd worked the bugs out of the continuous-feed terminals for pipeline applications, he showed how his improved design could be enlarged for deep-space work. "Opening-closing spheres, out there?" he said to Senator Wallin's committee in closed meeting. "Inefficient." And as the solons watched, Habegger blackboard-doodled a topological transformation of his spherical field into an open-ended cylinder.

"Here, and here. You see?" Probably no one did, except Cassie—Rance certainly didn't—but everybody nodded. "At the ends, boundary conditions. The disjointing of spacetime—an interface like that, you cross it, tear you apart; right?" He shook his head. "So we fool it." On a diagram that had long since left legibility behind, he doodled further. "At the ends, you see, asymptotic taper. The field pretends to be infinite, so you slide in or out nice and easy." He smiled. "But don't forget to stop in the middle, long enough for the transmit function to activate, or you pop right through and go no place."

As Rance noticed that Habegger hadn't drawn or mentioned the alternate loading ports at the sides of his pictured cylinder, Cassie raised a hand. "Do you realize, Doctor, that you've implied a much greater application here?"

Habegger laughed. "Who better?" He looked around the room. "For anybody didn't catch it, Monlux wants a thing said. Once your manned probe gets to Alpha Whatever, you set up one of these in space, to match one you already got here—and you send *ships* back or forth in two years. To those aboard, no time at all."

When that news hit Tri-V, Congress authorized building the starship without even waiting for *Jovian-II* to prove out.

By now that ship was somewhat misnamed; its mission had expanded to a tour of most of the major planets. The idea was to preview the crew-relief system for *Starfinder*.

That proposal had the project in trouble, because the military wasn't in it at all; these ships would be crewed entirely by civilians. And early on, the trainees organized the Astronauts Protective Association. If it wasn't exactly a union, it certainly quacked like one.

Cassie was away, down at the Cape, when Rance sat in on Senator Wallin's meeting with the APA's spokesman, Mike Horner. A chunky man with lots of black hair and even more energy, Horner managed, without loudness, to speak explosively. "The principle dates back to John L. Lewis and his mine workers, Senator: portal-to-portal pay. You're asking our people to sit two years each way in Habegger's pipeline on their own time, and—"

"No, I'm not," said Wallin. "Not personally." The old man was grinning; hard time or no hard time, he seemed to be enjoying himself and to rather like Horner. "But speaking for NASA, the case is simple: you want pay for time your people won't even experience, and the agency doesn't feel like paying it."

As Rance thought of the greater complexities inevitable in *Starfinder*'s case, Horner seemed to read his mind. "This agreement, Senator, will set precedent for the crews of the interstellar probe. I represent a protective organization, and I'm damned well going to do some protecting! So you see . . ."

Large or small, inflation was always present; delayed payment was essentially discounted payment, but money had no use in space. Compromise was needed, and now as Wallin took the discussion through various disputed areas, citing factors Horner hadn't considered but sometimes ceding a point without argument, Rance saw why the senator was considered a master of the art.

At the end of it, Horner read from his notes. "All time in space to be paid monthly at rates as agreed here, the wages to go as the crew member specifies . . ." For a moment he puzzled over a notation. ". . . support to family if any, the remainder to an investment trust jointly administered by APA and NASA for maximized capital gains in secure investment areas."

So far, so good; Horner continued. ". . . this mission or any other, time dilation notwithstanding, pay scale to be governed by passage of time *on Earth.*"

"Assuming," the senator put in, "that I can round up sufficient backing to get that one through."

"You'd better," Horner said. Then, with an apologetic gesture, "I know you'll do your best; all I meant was—"

"Of course," said Wallin. "If our agreement here isn't ratified all around, we're back to Square One."

"Right. Now then—time in the pipeline gets half pay.

I think I can sell that, though it's not what we'd hoped for." Horner closed his notebook. "Does that take care of it?"

Before Wallin could answer, Rance said, "Not quite, if you're including *Starfinder*." Both men looked at him as if he were a talking dog, but neither spoke. "Its first crew, getting the ship up to light speed, will work the same *subjective* time as any later relief crew, but Einstein won't dilate their paychecks to the same extent. I could show you the math, but—"

"But what?" Almost together, the two men spoke.

"It's irrelevant. On *Jovie* we're not into high-V; the problem doesn't arise. But on *Starfinder* I'd think the only fair way is to use the top, steady-state cruising velocity figure to determine wages for all onship time."

After a pause, Horner nodded. Wallin's forehead wrinkled; then he said, "Put it on paper, so I'm sure I understand."

When Rance had done so, once more the senator grinned. "All right. I knew I had you around here for *some* good reason."

Embarrassed, Rance parried the compliment with awkward thanks. Thinking that while wages were only a tiny part of a spaceship's costs, the astronaut business was certainly shaping up to be a well-paying one.

Regarding the tech side, Cassie Monlux reported that *Jovie* was on sked. *Starfinder*'s design phase had more problems, but in Habegger's part of it, nothing he couldn't handle.

On the sociopolitical front, though, things weren't so simple. As Senator Wallin said, "International pressure; we're doing the work but the UN wants in on the act." He shrugged. "Not on paying much of it, of course; as usual, we're welcome to that aspect. But five gets you ten that *Starfinder* will go with a UN crew aboard. We'll be lucky to keep command control."

Rance neatened the stack of papers he'd brought from Habegger. "*Jovie*'s planning's too far along, isn't it, for them to mess with?"

"Mostly. Except that we're stuck with a Soviet observer riding supercargo." Wallin shook his head. "I've met her."

■   ■   ■

The next time Rance's itinerary crossed Cassie's, she told him more. "Colonel Irina Tetzl. Old Iron Tits, they call her at the Cape. I don't think she's all that ancient—just prematurely gray and not bothering to hide it."

"But pretty well bulwarked in the chestal area?" Propped up on an elbow, he looked across the bed.

Cassie's smile only made it on one side. "Compared to me, isn't everybody?" He took her remark as cue to pay heed to the incongruously large nipples that sat so snugly to her rib cage. Maybe they weren't sitting on mountains, but their nerve endings were as rewarding as any he'd encountered.

So a time later he lay breathing hard, smelling the delicate perfume she dabbed behind her ears. For a change she'd let her hair grow a little, fluffed out into a soft mass. And hadn't used the red dye lately; the centimeter or so nearest her scalp showed brownish. Well, if she wanted to change her looks . . .

When they were dressed, he asked again about the Soviet woman. "Won't she throw a wrench into the compatibility setup?" Because duty on *Jovie Two* was no commuter hop; each relief crew would ride the ship for at least a year. Congress had some problems with that part; a surprising number of the legislators were thinking in *Skylab* terms, with celibate crews. While the would-be astronauts had no such idea. Nor did NASA; that agency's brass knew better.

Of course, the public image of morality needed stroking; John and Jane Q. Taxpayer mustn't think they were financing an orgy. Which, judging by confidential reports from the original *Jovian,* they probably weren't; that crew's behavior made no waves. But no matter what the news releases said, it hadn't been monastic.

The solution for *Jovian-II* lay in the Supreme Court's legalization of group marriage. Or rather, removal of Federal strictures; some states quickly enacted their own prohibitions, and it was a representative from one of those who learned of NASA's planning and made the fuss. Johnny Lee Devereaux was a thrice-risen former sinner ". . . and don't anybody ever forget it! I want to know—my church wants to know—my *people* want to know, just what kind of sinful goings-on we here in this Congress are being asked to put our blessing to."

Referring the Honorable Johnny to the Court's decision, the Speaker of the House was treated to a diatribe advocating impeachment of the Chief Justice. Rance Collier, waiting to testify on a technical matter, had never before seen anyone actually break a gavel.

His question now, to Cassie, was serious. Designed to be crewed by a minimum of six but providing living space for ten, *Jovie* would carry eight. The chosen octet had quietly, without publicity, joined in a group marriage ceremony. When it came to consummation the rite was merely permissive, not binding. But in that planned situation, where was Colonel Irina Tetzl going to fit? Having asked, Rance waited.

Cassie shook her head. "I don't think anyone's told her yet. In fact, I doubt anyone's had the *nerve* to tell her."

Rance shrugged. "Maybe they're leaving it for the Honorable Johnny Devereaux."

Informed or not, Irina Tetzl joined the previously chosen four men and four women for some quick last-minute training. Observer or not, *Jovie* couldn't afford layabouts. "So," Cassie told Rance as their plane began its landing approach, "she gets the crash course in procedures, communications, instruments: everything she can pick up in the time remaining. Once the ship lifts, it's all OJT anyway."

Rance agreed; for some time to come, in this new field, on-the-job training would play big. He said, "Does she have pretty good English?"

"Odd turns of phrase now and then. Accent, just enough to notice. You'll see when we get there." Lurching, the plane dropped through turbulent layers above Von Braun, the newest airfield near the Cape. Touchdown, when it came, was smooth.

On the ground, NASA took over; after a too-short refresher stop at their assigned quarters, Rance and Cassie were hustled to a pre-briefing buffet luncheon. The designated room, in a building within walking distance of Admin, was reasonably full but not packed: about sixty people, Rance guessed, and recognized not quite half the faces.

Worse luck, names were never his strong point. But across the room he spotted Cleve Rozanski, commander of *Jovie*'s launch crew, facing away and blocking view of whoever he was speaking with. Nudging Cassie, Rance said, "Let's go say hello."

She nudged back. "Get braced. Just past him, that's Old Iron Tits herself." So, to get a look at the Russian woman before meeting her, he steered them a curving course.

The gray hair lay smooth in a soupbowl cut that barely cleared eyebrows in front and a high blouse collar behind. Under pale, slightly tilted eyes, broad high Slavic cheekbones dominated the face. The nose was a straight blade; the wide mouth looked as if it should be mobile, but sat straight and inexpressive.

In a dark green tailored suit, like a uniform but lacking insignia, the woman's body pushed the sturdy side of slim. Hips adequate but not bulky, good waistline, calves and ankles muscular in an agile-seeming way.

But the nickname? Look as he might, Rance found nothing disproportionate about the tailored bustline; he shook his head. Then in conversational response the woman raised her chin, gave a half smile with brief glint of teeth, and with arms and shoulders made a small gesture. And suddenly Rance knew: grey hair and colonel's rank explained the "Old," but the spring-steel quality of her stance and movement had to be what sparked the adolescent-minded tag.

Working through the crowd gave him time to sort out his impressions of the Russian: admire but no desire, was how she added up. But if personality matched appearance, she could make quite a splash on *Jovie*. Or maybe waves.

Coming up to Rozanski, Rance and Cassie endured handshakes and introductions. Irina Tetzl's grip was firm but not demanding; at close range her fairskinned, almost pale face showed beginnings of the finelined wrinkles such skin is prone to. By a few years upward, Rance revised his first age estimate.

When the greetings wound to a close, he asked, "And what do you think of the mission so far, Colonel?"

Again came the brief half smile. "Irina, please." He nodded. "We would do it different, of course," and he noticed the slight accent: not "uff cawse" but a suggestion of it. "Nonmilitary, this mission—and rightly. Yet for such work your military organization is structured. To ignore that structure, to duplicate it . . ." She gestured: spring steel again, or maybe whipcord. "Wasteful. I would not think, in these times, any resource is to be wasted."

Cassie took the ball. "But Colonel—Irina—new resources are what this mission's *about.* It needs other kinds of specialists more than organizational experts. For instance, look at Cleve here—it's simpler to train a pilot in administrative skills than make a military administrator into a pilot." And what, thought Rance, of military pilots? *Oh, well.*

Rozanski spoke. "The organizing's going to be handled here on Earth, anyway. It can be, because *Jovian-Two* will always be in talking range. Until we butt out past Jupe, toward Saturn and farther, the one-way signal time is an hour or less. That's faster than people could communicate across a major city, say, a hundred and fifty years ago." He shrugged. "So what's our problem?"

Tetzl's answering shrug carried more grace. "My opinion was asked; I gave it." She turned away. "Shall we find us some good things for drinking?"

As the others drifted along with her, joining the larger group surrounding the buffet and bar, Rance was no longer within the woman's conversational orbit. But over the next hour, looking toward her now and then, he decided the Russian woman could put away one hell of a lot of booze without showing it.

When the buffet was cleared and the room set up for speakers, Rance carried only a slight glow from his own drinks. He felt relaxed, except for knowing that quite soon he was in for one prodigious burp; carefully monitoring his booze intake, he'd been less cautious with some of the more exotic dips.

Never mind. Escorting Cassie to the speaker's table he took the central position. She sat at his right, flanked by an empty chair; to his other side were Rozanski and then Colonel Tetzl.

With the audience seated but before chatter could build, Rance tapped the mike and introduced Cassie. Blessedly, the ritual applause covered his outsize belch.

By now he was used to these briefings. Part of any audience knew what Cassie was talking about and took notes; the rest might as well have made do with the packaged handouts. It was his job to field the really dumb questions.

As: After Cassie fully explained the time-and-place logistics, a gorgeous young Tri-V man stood and asked, "But you're sending fuel and supplies—and people—into the Habegger device, blind. How do you know where they'll come out?"

Cueing on Cassie's raised eyebrow, Rance said, "Heisenberg described the uncertainties of our universe. You're familiar with his theories?" When the man nodded, Rance knew he had him. "Since tests have shown that Dr. Habegger's discoveries aren't susceptible to Heisenberg's Principle, I'm sure you see why we have nothing to worry about."

As the young man sat, Rance saw stifled smiles on the faces of those who recognized his answer as double-talk.

So back to Cassie and on through the long, slow briefing. When the dinner break came, Rance had regained his appetite.

The meal was passable but not noteworthy. Rance and Cassie found a table with four foreign observers: a British couple, a man from France, and a German woman. As usual, dinner was no respite from shop talk. Rance wondered why, no matter how often the numbers appeared in print, only when inked on napkins did they convince some people that one gee of accel-then-decel could if necessary get *Jovie* to its namesake in about a week.

At the seminar's after-dinner session, the same question arose. Patiently he smiled and explained it once again, and then the corresponding data for planets farther out. "Keep in mind that with constant acceleration, transit time varies as the square root of the distance traveled. So—"

Cassie picked up for him. "Pluto, usually considered to be our outmost planet—although fairly recently it spent about twenty years inside Neptune's orbit—is roughly six times as far away as Jupiter is. So by the square-root law—"

Rance took it. "A straight one-gee shot to either Pluto or Neptune would require only about two and a half times as long as to Jupe." Then, as always, he had to explain why such an apparently quick-and-easy trip had a five-year schedule.

Part of it was, as Senator Wallin had predicted, the demands of other nations. Rance said only, "Some folks aren't willing to give up on Mars. We did scotch the idea of stopping to orbit and unload retrievable landers, which would have massed nearly half the mission's capability. But we *are* stuck with a slow fly-by to drop a one-way lander, and that concession costs us time."

Then the tricky part: why *Jovie* couldn't progress "straight out" past the planets in order of orbital distance. Pausing to put his explanation into mental order, briefly wishing the bar were still open, he explained that the worlds didn't *lie* in a straight line but were spread all around the ecliptic. "So it may be more economical in time and fuel to zig, say, from Saturn to Neptune and then back to Uranus." Fatigue was getting him; *wrap this up fast.* "The optimum routing is still being calculated; we expect to have those plans shortly."

Showing no strain at all, Cassie rode herd on the windup. The audience, straggling out to an announced social reception, seemed satisfied. *Another party? Well, why the hell not?* So, dragging a little, Rance followed along.

Outdoors, Cassie said, "I think I'll pass this. Okay?"

"Sure. I probably won't stay long. Just a little while, to unwind."

She pulled him to a stop and pointed off to their right. "Are you oriented? That's our quarters building, over there."

"Right; I've got it. Thanks."

"Good enough." She hugged him. "Give a kiss. Mmmmm. All right, go have fun. Just don't bring home a hangover."

"Wouldn't dare; I can't afford one."

As she walked away, he turned to overtake the group.

With dim lighting and loud music and a low ceiling, the party hall wasn't much to Rance's liking. Halfway ready to skip the whole thing, he heard Cleve Rozanski call his name.

So he followed the sound and sat down at a small table with Rozanski and Irina Tetzl. They had drinks and they talked; Rance figured why he half liked *Jovie*'s launch commander and half didn't: the guy was practically the archetype of the jocks who'd played *Homo Superior* in high school and junior college, before Rance escaped to Gayle Tech. But Cleve didn't *act* like a jock.

Oh, well, have another drink—*but take it easy*.

Still and all, it got a little blurry. Ol' Iron Tits was actually laughing, and then Cleve Rozanski was gone and the colonel was draped around Rance's neck while a waiter asked if they'd like another drink.

"Uh—don't think so," said Rance. "Should get home."

"And quite rightly." Tetzl helped him stand, then walk to the door and outside. "You will escort me, perhaps? My quarters and yours are not distant." Oh sure. Though by no means cool, outdoors the air came fresh; the longer they walked, the better Rance felt. And sure enough, when she turned him toward her own quarters, he saw his-and-Cassie's not fifty meters along the cobbled path.

At her door he mumbled good night, but she caught his arm. "A nightcap, is it? Yes." So he followed her inside. Sitting on a couch, shirtless and barefoot, Cleve Rozanski raised a glass in salute.

"Siddown, chum; take a load off. Drinks didn't run out; we got 'em here, too." As the woman disappeared behind a closing door, Rance found himself holding a full glass: straight vodka over ice, by the taste, so he barely sipped it. And listened, not paying much attention, to Rozanski's small talk, until the door opened and Irina Tetzl came out.

She wore only a towel. Rance blinked. The tits, now bare, sure as hell weren't iron.

Firm, though. Floating above them, to Rance's blurred gaze, her lips curved with a real smile. "No terrible hurry, gentlemen. But not *too* long, before you join me." She turned toward the bedroom; the towel dropped away to show lean buttocks surging with her stride. Then the door closed.

As he set his drink down, Rance knew his expression must be as blank as Rozanski's. "I—I'd better be going."

Cleve's gesture with his drinking hand didn't quite spill any liquid. "Stick around. You heard, she likes quantity."

"You've been with her that way?"

Headshake. "Not yet. Just us two. But she keeps *saying*, so I figured sooner or later. Well, it's sooner, so now—"

All Rance's inhibitions hit home. *"Not* now. I—"

"But what'll I tell her?"

"That—that I was too drunk." Not listening to Cleve's answer, its words only noise to him, Rance pivoted and ran outside.

Two steps past the door he heard it slam, knew he'd done the slamming, and walked fast enough to reach his own door winded; inside, he remembered to close that one gently. Dim light outlined the room; the bulge at the far side of the folddown bed had to be Cassie, and as he paused he heard her halfway-snore.

Careful not to wake her, he tiptoed toward the bathroom. And, tripped by an errant suitcase, fell flat.

"Oh, damn it *all* to hell!"

As he rolled over and started to rise, light came on; he saw Cassie, sitting up, reach to push her hair back from her forehead. He said, "Sorry. I fell over something."

"Not really!" She seemed awake enough. "I thought maybe you were practicing for the Olympics." Eyebrows reading 10:10 on a clockface, she leaned forward. "Rance, my dear boy—or should I call you Rancid? Did you forget not to get drunk?"

"No." As he stood he knew he spoke truth; the booze had worn off or burned away. But . . . "Long as you're awake, anyway, something I want to tell you." First things first, though. "Soon's I take a leak. Okay?"

She nodded. When he came back she was out of the bed, sitting on it. Taking her hand in both of his, he sat alongside. "The *funniest* damn thing happened."

He told it. For more than a minute she did not speak. Then, "You've never done any of that? Triads, or more?"

"No! Have you?"

"A few times. Long ago." Her brief laugh came shaky. "I think I know what our Soviet colleague had in mind, and it can be exciting. Physically fantastic. But—" She turned to hug him. "Emotionally I couldn't handle that scene, so I chickened out."

He considered. "Long time ago, huh?"

"Long enough that it doesn't concern you. All right?"

"Yes; sure. But—what bothers me—I mean, this woman's going on *Jovian-Two!*"

"So?" Her hand stroked tensions from his neck.

"Shouldn't somebody know what she's like?"

"Cleve knows, doesn't he? And he's in the command seat. Rancid—and please don't make me call you that again—why don't you and I just leave well enough the hell alone?"

He cleared his throat. "You think it'll be all right?"

Her nibble on his ear became a sharp, hurting nip. "We don't run the world. It is none. Of our damn. *Business.*" Bite! "Understand?" He nodded. "Like to come to bed now?"

"Yes. If you don't think it's too late, I'd like that."

The way things went, then, it wasn't too late.

V

QUESTIONS

Away from the Cape next day, Rance quit worrying. The colonel was Rozanski's problem—and Cleve, apparently, wasn't complaining.

At Washington, Cassie left for Gayle Tech while Rance kept an appointment with Senator Wallin. He found the old man using an aluminum hand crutch. Before Rance could say anything, Wallin waved his free hand. "My store-bought hip's just fine; it's the *real* one that's giving me a hitch in my get-along."

In Wallin's study, its dark wood paneling relieved by bright prints of prairie farms, they met with the senator's home state protégé, Congressman Bill Flynn. Rance knew him slightly: a stocky, freckled man with sandy hair and plenty of smiling charm. His handgrip could have been a crusher but never was, and behind the smile Rance sensed considerable intelligence.

"I'm not running for another term," Wallin began,

"and Bill's the man to take over. So I want you two working together. He won't inherit most of my committee assignments, of course, but I think we can swing the NASA liaison slot."

Not smiling for once, Flynn said, "If I can continue to further the senator's aims there, all the campaign hassle will be worth it."

Rance nodded. "You'll have my full cooperation." And now, with the air cleared, they got down to cases.

Back at GIT, next, Collier found Dr. Habegger in his cluttered office handling a lot of action by remote control. Entrance facilities for *Jovie* and for *Starfinder* had to be located for best convenience: fuel input from the production facilities, life support from the appropriate supply depots, and personnel—the relief cadres—from their briefing stations.

"The freight stuff, now . . ." Habegger shrugged. "Some on the moon; my terminal gear's under construction there. Some in high orbit, and that's on schedule, too. None of this I bother with, except to monitor how close to ready for activation; they have government people for the rest of it."

"And what will you be doing, sir?"

Habegger scratched the stubble that fringed his scalp. "Oh, the hard stuff, like always. Such as, once *Starfinder* goes past talk range, does time dilation do just what we expect, or maybe a little different? Somebody has to check those things." He grinned. "Somebody has to figure *how* to check."

"With two years' info lag each way, it may take some doing."

Habegger's answer made Rance feel foolish. "Actually, Collier, I'd already thought of that."

As *Jovie*'s launch time neared, the first relief crew cadre began its scheduled entrance into the Habegger terminal that would deliver its members two years later. Not all at once, but a week apart, they entered; the idea was to allow individual briefings, old crew to new replacements, without overcrowding.

Launch awaited linkage confirmation on the fuel and life support pipelines; even then, not until all supply tanks were filled could the ship raise. Who wanted to take chances?

Plenty of leeway, though, for the two persons added to the original eight; besides Irina Tetzl there was a Pakistani observer. Two things bothered Rance: would the man have time to absorb much useful training, prior to launch—and if he'd been brought in to restore the balance of the sexes, how would he and the colonel get along?

Collier shook his head. As Cassie put it: It was none. Of his damn. *Business.*

But still he wondered.

On sked, the pipelines delivered and *Jovian-II* left Earth. No systems problems, and if personnel gave any, Cleve Rozanski didn't report them.

Now Rance and Cassie could concentrate on the *Starfinder* project. Dr. Habegger's efforts were split between the two spaceward thrusts, but at this point Rance didn't need much input from him, anyway. Wallin had steered *Starfinder*'s funding through the traps of the Senate floor, so the star probe no longer had to mooch off *Jovie*'s leftovers. (With hardly a quibble, the president had signed the bill. These days, after his successful negotiation of the Antarctic crisis, the man was riding high.)

The important thing right now, Collier knew, was to sell the public and *keep* it sold. Mostly through Bill Flynn, emerging more and more in the role of Wallin's spokesman. So as Rance marshaled his facts, he tested his summaries first on Cassie and then on the congressman.

The hardest part was trying to water down the math. As he remarked to Cassie, "That's the heart of it. If they can't understand Earth time versus ship's time, how do we get support for something a lot of people won't live to see?"

She patted his hand. "You'll convince them. And if it takes Mickey Mouse or Huggly Hog cavorting on Tri-V, *do* it!"

So he tried to make starship logistics, simple enough to Rance himself, intelligible to Bill Flynn. The fact was that accelerating at one gee, from rest to $v = 0.995$ times the speed of light, would take nearly a year of ship's time "t" while Earth's "t_o" would rack up roughly fifteen months. After the specified 0.995c was reached, the ship and its crew would experience only one year for every ten that passed on Earth.

He'd made a lovely plot of t/t_o against arcsin v during acceleration: The integral of the cosine curve, descending from one to zero, gave the overall time ratio of $\pi/4$. But Flynn shook his head. "The year and the fifteen months are close enough." His smile looked strained. "Could you just tell me the things I need to know, not everything you'd *like* to tell?"

Rance blinked. "I'll try." He thought about it. "A major item is that when the ship levels off at the ten-to-one time dilation, that's the point at which the first relief cadre arrives, and Section A of the initial crew heads for home."

Because every six months, ship's time, beginning at the end of its first year, *half* the crew would be changed; the original Section B, only, would serve eighteen months aboard.

Flynn nodded. "The first relief section," he said, "enters Habegger's pipeline nine months before the mission begins? And all later cadres at five-year intervals, which are six months on *Starfinder*?"

"Right." Math or no math, Flynn did grasp the essentials. He had more questions, though, and Rance answered. Yes, sir; to maintain velocity against the drag of the interstellar gas, some drive force would be needed. How much? Indeterminate as yet. But until solid figures were forthcoming, fuel would be supplied on the high side of the guess; a little waste beat hell out of facing a shortage. And, with any luck, would be only a small percentage of the total.

Still, though, during its constant-speed phase the ship would be a zero-gee environment. So part of its hull—a midship belt—was designed to rotate, producing a centrifugal equivalent of weight in aid of the crew's physical condition. Both *Jovian* craft had made do with centrifuge chambers, but on *Starfinder* the entire living arrangements would be 'fuged.

Explaining time-distance relationships was trickier;

using rounded-off numbers, Rance tried to make them clear. At either end of any star trip, a ship's year (fifteen months, Earth time) spanned half a light year. In between, as nearly as made no difference, *Starfinder* rolled up one light-year per Earth year, ". . . but on the ship, only one tenth of that time elapses." Rance paused. "Okay so far?"

Flynn scowled. "Except for one thing."

"What's that?"

"Which rate governs Habegger's pipeline?"

Rance felt his jaw sag. Because he hadn't the faintest idea.

He did know that since distance didn't affect the time lag, neither should velocity or acceleration. But what about the respective input-output rates? Would ten years' supplies of fuel and food be appearing on the ship in only one year?

Quickly, Rance excused himself and called Habegger. As the doctor grasped the gist of the questions, his voice took on an edge. "Collier, don't you read *any* of our material except what's tagged for PR? You should know, anyway: these things are programmed into the logistical parameters, with deliberate small surplus as safety margin."

"Same as you do with the fuel, for holding at top vee?"

"The precise same. Now if you don't mind—"

"Of course; thank you, Doctor." Hanging up, Rance wiped away the sweat of embarrassment and went to reassure the congressman. Thinking, he'd damn well *better* find time to scan more of the project's data.

Pleased to learn that he (if not Rance) had asked a valid question and that it had a reassuring answer, Flynn wanted to get *Starfinder*'s crewing schedules straight in his mind. Rance's prepared diagram didn't help; he tried again. "Neither of us is going to be on *Starfinder*, so for now we can forget ship's time. Of the original crew, Section A gets home three-and-a-quarter years after launch, and each subsequent half crew at five-year intervals." Inhale! "As you know, first *relief* cadre goes in the pipeline nine months ahead of mission start." And before Flynn could interrupt, "Just keep in mind that except for the original Section B, everyone *experiences* one year aboard, but with two years in the pipeline each way, all after the first crew are off Earth for fourteen. That's really all there is to it."

Nonetheless the man's forehead wrinkled, and Rance asked, "You still have a problem, Bill?"

Decisive nod. "Yes. What if something goes *badly* wrong? Out there, with such a long communication delay—"

"Stop worrying. In a pinch, the crew evacuates and the ship plows ahead on automatic until someone goes out to fix the problem. Given the pipeline, there's no safety risk."

Flynn leaned forward. "What if *that* failed?"

"How? Power to the original receiver was accidentally cut; remember? But it kept right on working. Once established, the link can't be broken."

Two days later, Rance thought back to that confident remark and hoped with fervor that it was correct: on his return to GIT, Dr. Habegger called him in for a talk. The warehouse, cleared of all storage and devoted to construction of various types of experimental terminals, was now well lighted throughout. Well, President Elliott McCalder wouldn't be complaining about expense. Not these days . . .

Rance arrived to find Habegger throwing one of his rare, calm, quiet, utterly devastating tantrums. Someone, Rance gathered, had made one mistake too many. Looking at the six persons facing the doctor's ire, he couldn't guess which might be the culprit. None of them, it seemed, because dismissing the six and turning to Rance, Habegger said, "Job for you, Collier. We've lost our public relations man from cadre A, first relief crew. Medical problem: controllable here under treatment, but off Earth, too risky. You're qualified, or near enough. Five weeks to bone up, then into the pipeline. All right?"

His childhood head-over-heels infatuation with space had been long since abandoned and—he'd thought— forgotten. Now, out of the blue, *this*! Not thinking, yet, of what else the choice might entail, Rance found himself shaking hands on it.

With neither time nor need to unpack, he was hustled down to the Cape, then rode shuttle up to the old Bell Labs factory satellite. Object: to spend a week seeing how his body coped with varying gee, including none whatsoever.

After a few hours in zero gee, feelings of disorientation decreased and eventually vanished. Using Velcrosoled shoes, he learned to keep his footing on any bulkhead serving as "floor." And at week's end he was certified Approved for space duty.

Passing that test gave him mixed feelings; he'd had no chance to tell Cassie his news, and wasn't sure how to go about it. She'd been away on overseas liaison when Habegger sprung his surprise, and somehow Rance hadn't felt like broaching the subject over a phone circuit.

But when the shuttle brought him back to dirtside, Cassie was home. Furthermore, she would know where he'd been. So, he figured, he'd pretty much better get his act on straight.

The best situational lubricant he could think of was champagne. When he arrived bearing a chilled magnum, Cassie seemed a bit on the icy side herself, but at least she showed willing to talk and eat under truce.

After dinner, though, when he poured the last of the magnum and hinted toward bed, she pulled the chain. "Not so fast, Rancid," and he knew everything was going to hit the fan. "First tell me what you haven't yet. And *why* you haven't."

He no longer saw her face as harsh. The implacability, now, lay not in her features but in the remote look of her. "You do have to tell it, you know."

So he tried. ". . . out of a clear blue sky the old bastard sandbagged me. Before I could think, he was shaking my hand, making with the congratulations."

She jerked her own hand free. "My God, Rance! You really *are* a pudding. I'd thought you and I were important together—but Habegger punches the button and your bell rings. *Scheiste!*"

"Now look, Cassie. What do you *want* me to do?"

She looked, all right, but he couldn't hold her gaze. "Either Habegger can have your next fourteen years from this world, just for the asking, or he can't. I want you to make up your own mind; convince me you've done that and I'll accept it." She touched her glass, then pushed it away. "But don't shit me that because you purely can't stand up to the great man, you and I should go to bed and cry over each other, all the way to orgasm. Because, Rancid old buddy, I'm not having any."

Frowning, he shook his head. "You're right; I let him make up my mind for me. Now, though . . ." Part thrill and part shame, a shudder took him. Because there was more to this than just Habegger. "Cassie—given the chance to ride an honest-to-God interstellar ship, I *have* to do it. I'm sorry. . . ."

"Don't be; if you know what you really want, you have the right to choose it." She stood. "Would you like some coffee?"

"No, thanks. Cassie? Couldn't you come, too?"

She turned on him. "And what about my own work, right here? It does have some importance. Even if I *could* bump a crew member who's already selected . . ." A headshake. "I couldn't, though."

"I don't understand. Why not?"

She made a sour face. "You say the man you're replacing has a medical condition that's a risk in space. Well, so do I. A metabolic one. Unsafe, they tell me, at zero-gee."

Stumped, he said the first thing that came to mind. "The trip's not one-way, you know. I'll be back."

Her features went pale and taut; she spoke in a sing-song. "Hello, young lover, whoever you are . . ." Quite deliberately she raised her glass, and in one motion drenched him. "I am five years your senior. Going on *Starfinder* you will age one year while I add fourteen." As he wiped his face, her lips formed a snarl. "If you're still feeling horny, Rancid, I suggest you take a flying fuck at a rolling doughnut."

His thoughts plodded. "Age isn't all that important—"

Like a predator ready to spring, she crouched. "It is to *me*, you unutterable fungus! Get out of here, and take your things with you." All purpose spent, she sagged into her chair.

"All right, Cassie." His words sounded flat, lifeless. He began to gather the few clothes and accessories he'd let accumulate there; lacking a suitcase, he bundled everything into large plastic bags from the kitchen, filling one and almost a second. All the while he saw her, silent and immobile, watching every movement. As he reached the door, he turned.

"Cassie—is this any way to end it?"

Her blank expression didn't change: no anger, no scorn, nothing. She said, "I never could get it up for dead things."

So he left. When he called her, next day, he drew a blank; she'd changed to an unlisted number. And next he learned that she'd pulled up stakes and moved: no forwarding address given.

Checking in and registering for relief crew training occupied his next few days. When he returned he had another idea: what if he could transfer from relief cadre A to the original crew? B Section would help a little—probably not enough, though—but in A, living a year while fifteen months passed on Earth (plus the two pipeline years), he'd add only twenty-seven months to Cassie's seniority. Couldn't hurt to ask.

Getting in touch wasn't easy, but eventually Dr. Habegger's secretary divulged Cassie's new address and phone. The first time he called, she hung up. On his second try he said, "Five minutes; that's all. Fair?"

She sighed. "All right. Not in person, though. Start talking."

Hurriedly he made his pitch. "That wouldn't be so bad, would it? If I can get Habegger to agree?"

"You haven't asked him yet? Why not?"

Rance hesitated. "He's not an easy man to talk to. If it *would* make a difference with you, I'll have at him. But otherwise—I guess I don't really give much of a damn."

In the pause he heard her breathing faster than usual; then she said, "Two years added, a little more, I could live with. Another five, though—" Uneven breathing now. "No. I have to draw the line somewhere, Rance, and that's it."

"So it's cadre A, original crew, or nothing. Right?"
Her laugh carried no amusement. "Or stay home."
He couldn't. He said, "I'll do all I can; you know that."
"I *hope* that. We'll have to see, won't we?"

Anxious, Rance waited while Habegger tried to explain *Starfinder*'s mission to a reporter who had the mind of a raspberry. "Parsecs are—better you just say thirty-one light-years. Well, look it up! And thirty-two-point-five years to get there. Why? Because climbing up to speed and slowing down takes longer. Never mind, just say it. No, the star's got no name, just a number. That far away, F-types are too dim to name; just say it's out past Centaurus. And for the ship, takes only five years total. *Because Einstein says so!* And every five years, which is six months ship's time, half the crew we replace. Take my word!"

When the interview finally ended, Rance was as ready as he'd ever be; catching Habegger between preoccupations, he launched his plea. Halfway through, he heard his voice trail off when he should have been emphasizing; finally, looking into the silent face, he said, "Well, Doctor? Will you approve my reassignment?"

Habegger shook his head. "You want off the relief crew, tell me now. Time's short for getting replacements."

Unbelieving, Rance stared. "But why, Doctor? Why can't I go with the initial crew, when it's so important to me?"

"Not qualified."

"But I'd have much more time for training than I have now, going into the pipeline nine months early. I—"

"Different needs. Ship building up to c, first crew has to know all of it, check everything. After that . . ." Shrug. "Then we can afford supercargo, like you'll be. If you still want to, considering these personal problems you waste my time with."

The hell with it; Rance stood. "I'll let you know."

Like a stone sphinx, Habegger stared. *"Now* you let me know. Not later. Or it's now that you're out."

More than anything Rance wanted to break the man's stony look, make him show some human feeling. No chance, though; after a moment Rance knew he'd have to speak. After another, knowing his voice would waver, he merely nodded. Then he cleared his throat and could say it. "I'm in."

Turning, stalking away, he hoped his gait didn't reveal the way his legs trembled.

The phone wouldn't suffice; despite what Cassie had said, he went to her new apartment and waited outside the door until she came home from work.

She must have eaten elsewhere, he decided, because the hour was long past the tolerance of his own stomach; with hunger adding to his discomfort, he listened to his own words stumbling around the edges of the bad news, trying not to step in it and make the inevitable mess.

Until she interrupted. "You lost, didn't you?"

"Yes. I couldn't move him." He swallowed. "Rancid lost."

"But you tried?"

"Like all hell I did. A bulldozer wouldn't budge him."

"If you gave it your best, then Rancid doesn't apply." Her gaze was serious but not condemning. "Good-bye, Rance."

"Yes. Good-bye's all there is now, isn't it?"

He turned to leave but her hand caught his arm. "Wait. It needn't be quite so abrupt. You've had dinner, I expect, but I worked late, so come in and have some coffee while I eat. We could talk, maybe; it might help."

He waited until she'd led him inside before saying, "As a matter of fact, my last meal was breakfast."

They ate dolmathes, microwaved from the freezer, and an impromptu salad; it all tasted good when he managed to pay attention. The discussion, such as it was, stayed wholly impersonal, until over coffee she said, "It's nice to celebrate our farewell a little."

"Yes, it is. But—"

Cassie shook her head. "No buts, Rance. Once we're through talking, you kiss me good-bye and walk out. Fourteen years from now, when you come back only a year older, don't look me up. I won't want to see you. Or more accurately, the vice versa of it."

"I'm sorry."

"Don't be." Surprisingly, she reached and squeezed his hand. "I've thought about it. You belong on that relief crew. Habegger's a sonofabitch when it comes to people's feelings, but on the basis that he gets results, he probably knows what he's doing."

He stood. "I hope you're right." She rose to join in a good-bye kiss. As it ended he stood back, trying to think how to change what was happening—but it had been said now, all of it.

Except for good-bye. At the door he turned and spoke it; silently her lips mouthed the same word. For long seconds, then, he allowed himself the sudden need to look and memorize her.

Because he would never see her again. Not *this* Cassandra Monlux . . .

VI

THE CADRE

The other five members of relief cadre A had been training together for several months, so Rance was the new kid on the block and not at all comfortable in the role. It wasn't that the others rejected him, exactly, but it seemed to be his place to make the get-acquainted moves.

And he was simply no damned good at it. At lunch break the second day, chief-of-cadre Jimmy Hanchett announced, "This afternoon we begin skull sessions with lift-off cadre B. That's not a usual part of training. Do you know why, Collier?"

Rance looked at the tanned, darkhaired Canadian, shorter than himself but heavier-boned, and decided the man was trying to give him an opening. Ignoring the fact that since *Starfinder* was being constructed in high orbit, "lift-off" was merely a convenient misnomer, he said, "Well, we will be serving six months with them, on the ship. So it makes sense to—"

Fleurine Schadel, the heavy-featured blonde sitting beside Hanchett, cut in. "You're missing the point—which is that we're the only two overlapping groups that *can* have liaison ahead of time. Our own B cadre won't even be picked for another four years." Patting her wild, frizzy hair, she smiled as if she'd won some kind of argument, and Rance found nothing more to say.

Around the table to his right, the other three sat as a unit. In the middle Dink Hennessey, black hair curling over his pale forehead to shade startlingly blue eyes, more often than not had a hand on either Benita Torres or the taller, almost skeletal Su Teng. And sometimes both. As if staking territorial claims for all to see. Well, Rance had no designs on either.

Interrupting Collier's woolgathering, Hennessey asked a question, but Rance missed most of it. "Sorry, my thoughts drifted. All the way out of here. Come again, please?"

But shaking free of Dink's arm, Torres stood. "It wasn't important. Anyway, it's time we went to our conference."

So far, Rance decided, his efforts to fit in weren't having much success.

He knew the initial B cadre people by name and sight, but that was about all; as the session began, he looked them over. Maggie Sligo—chunky, gray-eyed, "black Irish"—was captain. Throughout the entire planned schedule, each B cadre provided the skipper and each A the exec—in this case Jimmy Hanchett, whose specialties were Instruments and Guidance.

Sligo was teamed with Art Cranston, similar to her in body type but somewhat taller: an average-looking fellow, losing much of his brown hair early, and generally quiet.

Now, though, he spoke up. "I've said all along, we're not putting enough emphasis on cross-specialty study, and as far as you reliefers are concerned, it's getting close to too late."

Unruffled, Hanchett asked, "What particular aspects bother you?"

Cranston cleared his throat. "Instrumentation and

Traction Drive make a good example. It's two different languages, and we need more crossing studies to know what the other party *means*."

One of the blacks spoke: the woman, Btar Mbente. Rance's first guess, that the two Kenyans were mates, had been wrong; Btar was paired with "Red" Macdougall, whose first name Rance didn't know, and her brother Jomo with Christy Frost, the small blond pilot-navigator from Belgium. Btar said, "Be easy, Arthur. In this new thing there *will* be mistakes in plan. But we adjust: Nine months, we and our own A section have." She gestured toward Hanchett's group. "Our friends here will be shorted in the matter, yes. But once aboard, they can make up for it."

Somewhat mollified, Cranston asked for a rundown of A cadre's specialties. Knowing the answers, Rance listened anyway: Hanchett had navigation, including outside sensors. As backup, so did Benita Torres—and to a slight extent Dink Hennessey, though along with Su Teng he was more concerned with in-ship workings, particularly maintenance. The latter was a sideline with Fleurine Schadel, whose main forte was Traction Drive.

Privately, Rance didn't feel the woman could match his own Drive savvy (actually his only real mission skill); for one thing, a sidelight of his Ph.D. thesis, before he'd drifted into PR and Liaison, implied possible refinements of the device. Now, of course, that work was rusty in his mind. But still . . .

The talk relaxed Cranston a bit. "I'd still prefer more time on these things. But I expect you're right, Btar; once we're all aboard *Starfinder*, we can caulk the cracks with OJT."

"So now," said Maggie Sligo, "let's quit talking about what we need to do and get started on doing it."

In Rance's view the afternoon session went well enough. He had to know only the bare bones of most jobs, himself, so that theoretically he could fill in if necessary; no one, it seemed, felt that contingency to be much of a risk. And in spite of Cranston's concern, somehow the cross-specialty talk had a ho-hum flavor to it. Not, Rance hoped, a sign of complacency.

Quartered at some distance, Sligo's cadre declined

the offer to dine with Hanchett's. Rance hoped the shop talk would continue, because it was something he could join in. But while discussion didn't revert to international politics, a subject that bored him to yawns, suddenly everyone was fired up about the imminent World Series—and the truth was that since his ninth-grade coach had given up on his fielding and named him equipment manager, Rance had largely ignored baseball.

Now, though, he wished he recognized the names of at least a few of the star players, or knew which "Sox" team was in contention and where it was located. The Yankees, he was fairly sure, still held forth in New York. . . .

"What kills me," Fleurine was saying, "is that I go into the pipeline the day of Game Four. So I won't know . . ." She pushed at her frizzy blond mop of hair. "Damn it all!"

Rance thought fast. Cadre members would enter the pipeline at three-day intervals: Hanchett first, then Schadel, Hennessey, Rance, Su Teng, and finally Benita Torres. Clearing his throat, he said, "It's sure to be over —the Series, I mean—before I leave. I'll make certain to get all the final results for you."

"It's not the same, dummy! Don't you understand *anything*?"

He felt his face go blank. *You try, and what does it get you?* As though Su Teng had read his mind, she touched her long fingers to his wrist and whispered, "You tried, Collier."

The fingers withdrew. Schadel and Hennessey began arguing the merits of various musical groups prominent on Tri-V. Rance thought he recognized the names of two of them.

The hell with it; he poured himself more coffee, sat back, and let his mind drift. When the others stood to leave, so did he—and was surprised to find Su Teng walking beside him instead of in the usual threesome. Automatically he adapted to her slower gait, lagging behind the rest as all headed for quarters.

He felt he should say something, but what was there? After a time, she spoke: "Do you really prefer being odd man out?"

"I—no—I don't know. . . ." Stopping, he turned to her, her eyes directly level with his own. "Some personal problems; I guess I've let them bother me too much."

A very delicate frown, her brows made then. "And aboard *Starfinder,* those will keep you busy?" Shaking his head, he found no words. "Then you'll be bored, won't you? And lonesome, perhaps? For in their year together, cadre B will form its own alliances; to them our group will always be outsiders." Her finely sculpted lips formed a brief smile. "Oh, no rudeness, I'm sure. But acceptance without absorption. Much the way—"

He knew what she meant—but how to say so? "The way I'm isolated from *this* group; is that it?"

She didn't speak; she didn't have to. As they stood, still facing where they had paused, Rance nodded. "I can't argue; you're right. But why spell it out?"

Her hand brushed his shoulder, then dropped away. "Because I wish to know, is this how you would have it?"

Later he couldn't remember just what they both said then. He began with "No, of course not," unsure of how much his denial implied, and at one point she was saying, ". . . Jim and Fleurine, of course, leaving the other four of us to our own choices."

Out of steam, he fell silent; her voice gained an edge. "Do you think I'd *choose* to be left, by default, to join Benita in a nice little harem for Dink Hennessey?"

"Are you—I mean, certainly you don't *have* to . . ."

The delicate features framed a cold expression. "Dink is an amiable person; I like him slightly but not to excess. I have not, should you be interested, sampled the pleasures of his person. Of the two, I like Benita better."

She didn't say whether she'd consummated *that* liking, and he didn't ask. She said, "If you wish to tender me an invitation, please do so now. Otherwise, once aboard *Starfinder,* our group dynamics will have me in triad with Dink and Benita."

His indrawn breath came too fast for comfort. "Invitation? Yes, of course. On *Starfinder* . . ." No. ". . . right now, I mean. *Will* you share quarters? Mine are a little small, but—"

Stately as always, she nodded. "Mine will be adequate. You may move your belongings either now or tomorrow."

"Tonight's fine; it's early yet." Wondering what to do now, he put his hand to her shoulder.

Gently, she removed it. "You don't understand. You are freeing me from an unwelcome attachment, and I'm grateful. But since we know each other only superficially as yet, for the time being we shall have, so to speak, a shack job in name only."

Surprising himself, Rance didn't find the setup hard to live with. He and Su, with all their gear and daily routines, fit into her quarters without strain. His concern about the modesty angle vanished the same night he moved in, when Su casually shucked her clothing and hung it up before taking a shower.

Along with her clothes went the illusion of skeletal thinness; the woman was simply very tall for her fine-boned structure, and small as her breasts were, they still flared out more than those of Cassie Monlux. Thoughts of Cassie, then, drowned the brief surge of desire Su's unexpected nudity had sparked; after Rance's own turn in the bathroom it was good night, lights out, and to sleep.

Although the shift of quarters didn't change Rance's own life much, the cadre's attitudes took a definite turn for the better. Suddenly Collier found himself treated like a real person; when he tried to join in off-work talk the others met him halfway. Whether Su had intervened on his behalf he neither knew nor asked; probably, he thought, they assumed he and she had become lovers, and accepted him for her sake. However it worked, he felt more at home in the group.

Hennessey, edgy for a brief time, soon reverted to lazy amiability. And Benita, one evening, actually flirted a little; it was, Rance decided, her way of offering friendship, so he played it back on the same low-keyed note and took Su Teng's half-smile as a stamp of approval.

Fleurine Schadel showed acceptance by explaining baseball in full detail, like it or not. He wished she wouldn't, but listened dutifully and tried to ask the right questions. Until once, watching a game on Tri-V with her and Jimmy, he actually found himself getting excited about it.

Only Hanchett's manner stayed the same, and belatedly Rance realized that the cadre chief had been ready to accept him all along, any time he put something on the line to *be* accepted.

It made Rance wonder: Was he more of a loner than he knew? One-on-one he could cope with a reasonable amount of closeness, but he'd seldom had to try it in larger gestalts. So: Could he handle this new thing *and* the strangeness of shipboard life in space, at the same time? Or would he go loner again?

Not, it seemed, if Su Teng had anything to say about it. In the evenings she kept him up talking, digging to find out what made him tick; more often than not, she ran them short on sleep. "We must know one another," she'd said, and matched his disclosures with revelations of her own. Until he began to see some of the fire and hurt behind the cool, contained exterior.

Getting her full height early, being tallest in her class and two years younger than most, had isolated her emotionally. At twenty she was virgin bride to a junior-college professor; two years later, "when I grew out of being his big windup doll and tried to become a person," he divorced her.

Hesitantly, Rance in turn spoke of hurts he'd never told to anyone, nor expected to. They found his cautious, arm's-length version of trust rooted in the sixth grade, when Toofie Schwartz, until then his best friend, spilled Rance's deepest secret and made him laughingstock of the class. Su laughed also, but *with* him: "So you read the *Survival Manual* and actually tried eating the fried slugs, but the *idea* of them made you throw up. Those who laughed: Did they have as much courage and initiative?"

Maybe so, maybe not. But, "I *limit* trust; that's all."

"And never, ever take a chance." She shook her head; at her waist, the ends of her black hair rippled. "Without taking chances, one seldom wins much."

"I've told *you* things! Changing isn't all that easy."

"Of course not. Or you'd have done it already. But you have to keep trying."

Inevitably the talk zeroed in on sex: what their attitudes were and how they got that way. And on one point Su was adamant.

"You first."

All right. In school he'd had all the standard instruction; the surprise was how good puberty could feel. Some kids, he knew, did stuff together. Not Rance; for him it was too private. And besides, those kids blabbed on each other. No thanks!

"How long, then, before you interacted with anyone?"

"Three years, about. Not until Shirl." When he was barely sixteen. Blond, a little pudgy but not too much, Shirl knew what to do and talked him into trying it. What she didn't know was that sponge-and-foam weren't a hundred percent.

At the peak of the fuss she miscarried; a few days later, her parents dropped the lawsuit. When she wanted to start again, not even his body agreed. She told stories about him at school, for spite, but soon graduation came and he was gone from there.

Through the summer, waiting for Gayle Tech's fall quarter to begin, he worked at a beach resort, managing athletic gear at the clubhouse. Sometimes, of an evening, he waited tables. A few of the younger women guests tried to flirt with him, but he didn't know how to respond so eventually they gave it up.

When the new redheaded lounge singer put moves on him, Rance was flattered but confused. Under the overblown costumes and heavy makeup, Jackie's age was a mystery. But late one night in Jackie's room, stoned out of his gourd on black hash, a nude Rance was introduced by fully clothed Jackie to the unsuspected delights of oral sex: passive.

He liked it well enough to go back a few times. He didn't understand why that was all Jackie wanted to do, or why his coworkers had begun to make snotty remarks: After all, how could *they* know what was going on? The next Saturday, though, Larry the lifeguard told him what everyone else seemed to have known all along.

Jackie was a transvestite, a female impersonator.

Though he stayed clear of Jackie from then on, there was no avoiding the jeers and snickers. "That," he told Su, "was one hell of a long summer."

At school that fall he tried living in one of GIT's dorms for the fall quarter, "bached it" with two other freshman for the winter term, and after spring vacation moved off campus and took a room by himself. "That worked best," he told Su, "so until late in my junior year, when I got mixed up with Charlyssa . . ."

Pausing, he shook his head. Su leaned closer. "That one, I think, still disturbs you. For how many years, now?"

"Twelve. But someone like her, you don't forget." Even now: green eyes; honey hair; slim voluptuous body; voice like a master cellist. And superbly persuasive. "What I could never figure," he said, "was why she wasted all that talent on *me*. Even when she skinned me clean, it wasn't very much money."

To please Charlyssa he'd practically turned himself inside out. Once she'd moved him in with her, she specified his clothing, haircuts, make of car, brands of booze, restaurants, and—of course—modes of sexual activity. In that line, anything she and her friends hadn't taught him (whether he liked it or not) probably wasn't possible anyway. Some of it, viewed in retrospect, was too humiliating to relate. But at the time, anything Charlyssa wanted had seemed the least he could do.

"Then when I was—thoroughly corrupted, I guess you could say—one night she left, and took everything that wasn't nailed down." He made a grimace. "If my scholarship had been a lump sum, rather than monthly payments, I'd have been out of school right there. As it was, the rest of the year I lived pretty much on the skinny side."

"In some ways, Rance, aren't you still doing so?"

Bowie and Cassandra were still painfully close to home. "From here on, no names. Okay?" She nodded. "Well, for several years a woman and I were good friends and should have been more than that, but I wasn't able to speak up."

"And she? It takes only one to ask a question."

"Not until she was leaving. And then it was too late." He paused, then said, "Only one more. The personal problem I mentioned earlier. It's having to leave a woman who can't come on *Starfinder* and who's been dear to me for quite a while now."

"This would be Monlux?" Before he could protest, she said, "You listed her address and phone as backups for your own; remember?"

His pulse eased off. "Oh, yeah." And then, "I guess I'm over it now. Or else never will be."

"So isn't it time to talk a little more about *you*?"

Being divorced so summarily had racked Su Teng. On the bounce, temporarily out of school, she'd picked up with a man called Dude. They lived on the move and on society's fringes; Dude's most respectable vocation, apparently, was gambling. "From things that were said, I think he may have pimped sometimes. But he never asked me to . . ." Her voice trailed off.

Dude's tolerance stopped at pregnancy. To the tune of "A Bicycle Built for Two" he sang an improvised verse. " 'It won't be a bad miscarriage, I can't afford a marriage'; that's all I remember of it. He paid for the abortion—which I wasn't sure I wanted—but while I was having it, he left. For keeps." She shrugged. "As I see it, he did me a favor."

Returning to college, Su bypassed her former school in favor of the state university. For two quarters a charismatic roommate had her convinced that her true orientation was basically Lesbian. "But that summer," she said now, "I found there was nothing total about it, after all."

She smiled. "I don't regret the interlude; it taught me some things I hadn't known."

Hesitantly, Rance asked, "Does that bring us pretty well up to date? Or is there more?"

"Much more—but not, I think, any that needs telling. I've made love in a variety of ways, some of which are important to me and some not. For instance, I—"

"Whoa!" Feeling nervous, Rance waved her to silence. "Let's don't start out with lists; okay? Can't we just take it slow and easy, and see what works for *us*?" Then he realized she hadn't agreed to anything at all. "If you want to, I mean."

"Of course. I don't—I don't need everything my own way!"

That's nice. Feeling a bit sulky, Rance was. But now when Su reached to him, and they finally got to the same bed together, he was enjoyably surprised. Acts he'd resented, retroactively, having done at Charlyssa's demand, were purely fun when prompted by Su's gentle hints. And unlike Charlyssa, Su Teng volunteered a number of tender services of her own devising.

When they were utterly, completely finished for that night, she said, "I think we'll do well together on *Starfinder*."

Rance could feel the silly grin on his face but he didn't care. "I've been getting the same impression."

"Eventually, I suppose, you will realize I'm not quite as fragile as you seem to think."

So he tickled her until she threatened to bite him.

As near as Rance could tell, his and Su's behavior next day was same-as-always. But no two ways about it, the cadre sensed a change, and approved. So *much* hinted approval, in fact—ranging from Fleurine Schadel's nudge in the ribs to a series of overdone winks by Benita Torres—made Rance uncomfortable. With no rational cause to feel embarrassed, he did, anyway.

He was glad when the hour came for their final meeting with liftoff cadre B. His efforts toward extroversion hadn't fruited soon enough for him to really get to know any of those people, but now, at least, he didn't feel quite so much the sore thumb.

He'd forgotten all about the group marriage thing, so when Sligo called for everyone to stand up together he was caught by surprise. A female JP rattled off the ceremony in minutes. Then as the two groups mingled he had a moment's worry that his cadre mates might throw hints, letting lift-off-b share their friendly voyeuristic interest in his love life. But no one did.

■   ■   ■

The time neared when Jimmy Hanchett would be first to enter the pipeline. And then—mentally, Rance went down the list—at three-day intervals would go Fleurine, Dink Hennessey, Rance himself, Su, and last of all, Benita.

The evening before Jimmy "left," the six partied together. There would be only the one farewell celebration to herald the leave-taking of them all; repeating, with diminishing numbers, seemed ludicrous. Training was finished also; the same attrition factor applied. And tonight wasn't exactly a going-away fling, either, for in sixteen days subjective (never mind the two years in the pipeline!) they'd all be together again, on *Starfinder.* So perhaps, Rance decided, they were celebrating the end of one stage and the start of another.

Normally they weren't much of a drinking crew, but tonight, while no one belted the booze to excess, everyone seemed to get a load on in a hurry. In the briefing room's corner the bar looked strange; so did the table laden with Chinese food from a nearby takeout. Judging by the way everyone heaped plates, Rance expected the meal to ease off the booze highs, but that easing didn't occur, even to him. After a while, talking up a storm like everyone else, he decided it was psychological. They *wanted* to be a little smashed, so they stayed that way.

Okay, the hell with it. Benita was hanging around his neck with her lips pouted, so he kissed her. And was surprised by her response; if they'd been alone he'd have been hard put to stop at that. Looking past her ear he saw Hanchett in a clinch with Su, and Fleurine with Dink Hennessey.

Somehow pairings shifted, and then again; Rance found Su's party-type smooching totally, unfamiliarly aggressive.

But then things began to wind down; sobriety, he supposed, could no longer be denied. "Okay, folks," said Jimmy. "It's been fine. Let's break it up now—and I'll see you on *Starfinder.*" In relative quiet, then, the group dispersed, and Rance walked with Su to their quarters.

After showers—the party *had* been a little sweaty—they lay on the bed, touching a little but not yet urgently. Rance said, "All that proto-swinging: It doesn't mean anything, does it?"

Su laughed. "No. It was just a way—*the* way, maybe—of affirming unity. Everyone kissing it up with each other. Well, between *teams*, at least. You men, with your inhibitions . . ." She didn't smile; she grinned. And then shrugged. "But it was all toward solidarity, not seduction." Now she did smile. "Speaking of which—"

"Yes." His hand moved. "Who, do you suppose, is on first?"

One by one, cadre A entered the pipeline. By some unspoken agreement, members did not go to see one another off, so Rance in his own turn was not surprised to find no colleagues attending; even Su had stayed behind. Habegger wasn't there, either, and Rance knew none of the tech crew operating the equipment.

After some thought he faxed a message to his parents, now living in Ireland; they'd been more or less estranged since the time of Shirl and then Charlyssa, but not until the fax went did he truly feel ready to leave. Having sent his luggage ahead, he carried only a kit containing a few personal items: last-minute choices for taking along. Including a printout, for Fleurine, of the World Series results (the Sox had taken it in five).

At the terminal itself, a gray-haired woman checked his ID. "Do you have your Velcro shoes on?" He nodded. "Then go right on up. The far end's zero gee, they tell me. But there's handholds; just grab on to one until you get your bearings."

So Rance walked up the stationary belt, into the coruscating field within the array of multicolored spikes. He looked back; beyond the shimmering mist of colors, nothing else was visible.

After a pause that seemed to take hours, for a moment everything *lurched.* Abruptly, gravity ceased; the colors died away. As he reached automatically for a handhold to steady himself, ahead Rance saw *Starfinder*'s receiving area, and people waiting. His vision cleared; he saw that first in line stood Jimmy Hanchett. Well, *that* was a big relief!

Something wasn't right, though. At first he couldn't figure out the wrongness, but then he knew. The silence.

Traction Drive was a relatively quiet piece of gear. But never silent.

VII

ENVIRON

Huge, huge—at many times pace of radiance, Liij Environ moves. Between its two mammoth ora—ingestor and re-creator—Environ's spacetime converters hum and crackle. Their familiar sounds give young Imon feeling of warmth and safety.

As befits apprentice navigationist, Imon crouches before its duty station. Its view—contrived picture, radiance shifted downspectrum to enable seeing at Environ's pace—is of spacetime ahead. Spackled with random matter it flows through ingestor into Environ's converter, then into plasma foursphere. There, as energy, it contributes to activity of Environ's plasma pool, maintaining level well above Ultimate Calm.

Small dribbet of pool's energy, for operational needs, Environ consumes. Greater part of intake, retransformed into new spacetime but now homogenous of all varied types of particles though still in overall proportion to intaken occurrence, outpours to form Environ's wake. If not for necessary operational drain, Environ could proceed through all of distance with no time measured. If such were possible, Imon considers, Environ would meet own earlier self, existing twice at once!

But Imon recalls what teacher Chorl has said: as re-creator builds spacetime from energy, extrusion of reformed product makes steady pushing, which reacts to move Environ.

If *only* re-creator were used, spacetime ahead, compressed and resisting, would limit Environ to pace of seen and unseen radiance. Thus—Chorl gestures with marking stick held in leftside palp—exists requirement for ingestor. At Environ's fore, that device absorbs spacetime, causes ever-advancing rim of void which pulls Environ to fill it. In need—to forestall or remedy plasma pool's depletion—ingestor can gape to encompass mass of entire world. And in time past, has sometimes done so.

Thus between push and pull, resistless both, Environ moves. From star to star, cluster to cluster—and once, early in long past, from one great wheeling spiral to next—Environ carries all of Liij life and spirit. For when home starwhorl collapsed into lightless maw its center had become, none but Environ escaped.

Under benign heed of Dutysetter Kahim, Imon and fellow juniors follow their ordered routines.

Liij are old species, among first to evolve when second-population stars coalesced from clouds containing elements beyond One and Two. Environ predates many stars that now exist. From long before its launching, Liij remain unchanged: large heads, smallish torsos, stubby mobile tail, forelimbs lengthy enough to hold torso at steep slant and let head ride high.

Growth patterns are unchanged since Environ left home whorl. Though grown to full length and height, young Imon is slighter and paler than it will be; only now, as belly node begins to swell and sensitize, does earliest breeding stage approach.

Softly scaled, Imon's pebbled skin peels and sheds at seeming random, mottling its slatish background in pleasing fashion with new patches: light blue, under-tinged by pink.

Its legs have grown their length but not yet their mature girth. Its longer, forward pair each carry five digits. Three splay out, side by side; remaining two, semi-fused, oppose for crude grasping. To accomplish finer work Imon uses its palps: extensibles at either side of long neck, less than a span below jaw hinge. Retracted, palps sit lumpish under either side of blunt muzzle, but may extend twice-headlength past its end; cluster of tendrils at each tip manipulates tiniest objects any Liij can see. Or, either separately or in attunement, palps may vibrate as meaning may demand, to augment and qualify communicative sounds made by mouth. While forelimbs manage well in larger usage, or to hold and steady.

At each stocky rear leg, digits are less dextrous: forward three largely bound to curl or straighten together, while rearward two, stunted and wholly fused, support leg's lowest joint clear of any surface Imon may walk.

Imon's two far eyes sit wide-set near head's top, forward of oval ear shells which Imon can lower to shade or cover them. Near eyes, one at either side of muzzle's base to workteam with corresponding palps, lie hidden by surrounding skin until needed, then extrude past irislike dilation to expose their forward arcs.

Imon's mouth serves both food and breath. Lipline bisects muzzle horizontally, back to within digit's width of near eyes. As moods alter, muscles changing lips' curves or tensions expose one's feelings to any watcher; older Liij learn, as routine, to control or suppress such displays.

In taking food, not only does jaw move; so also does great muscle that floors mouth. Both it and mouth's horny roof bear modified scales: fields of small, hard pyramids that grind even hardest food to pulp. These, like dermal scales, shed frequently and are continually replaced.

Imon loses focus on its position's instruments; as its age nears eight *dre* and official maturity, sometimes growth to breeding concerns it more than navigation, its assigned study. Environ's healthwatchers say all Imon's functions balance well, that with full optimality it approaches time to first breeding. Surely its belly node, twice quiescent size and growing ever more rapidly, is become sensitive enough already, its new delights intense to verge of discomfort. Yet Imon knows that over next few hands of cycles both aspects will increase, until swollen node drips pheromonic juices and even light touch may rouse toward frenzy. Then nothing less than welcome pressure of another, similarly excited node can bring relief—and with it, longlong ecstasy of juncture, bringing bodies' choices to decision.

Time of joy. May it come soon!

From its own nesting space, Overwatcher Seit also views forward. After only three *dre* of experience, Environ responsibility of Overwatch still weighs heavily; Seit feels anxiety that must not be sensed by any other. Of naturally open temperament, Seit finds concealment distressing.

Spacetime ahead, now, seems normally hazard-free. At various distances and angles—all quite safe to Environ's route—stars exist; nearer, but not perilously so, nondescript materials edge in slowness along individual paths. And between visible objects, particles and energies seethe and boil in eternal wash, to dot and wrinkle that pristine smoothness that exists only ideally, never in true observation.

Yet here, well outward from this whorl's core, which Environ skirted in passage for so many, many *dre*, spacetime begins to hold again that smoother, less turbulent character familiar to earlier Liij history held in ancient memory bones. It is, thinks Seit, almost as if Environ had never left home whorl.

With final cautionary glance at foreview, Seit turns screen and attention to duty areas: nutriment proliferation, life gas quality maintenance, spacetime/energy equivalence, fluid reserve availability, and all Environ's lesser yet needful workings.

Discovering, as usual, naught but trivial corrections to advise, at its final checkpoint it pauses. Watching on screen as Dutysetter Kahim supervises both adepts and apprentices—navigationists and spacetime instrumentators, intake analysts and foursphere pool-level monitors, all such major and minor functionaries who comprise Environ's sensory and motor activators—Seit finds attention dwelling on one young, fidgeting navigationist. Spawn of first of Seit's three breedings, only Imon has Seit birthed rather than seeded. Now, as Imon itself nears breeding stage, all too well Seit understands its fears and urges.

But like all Liij, Imon faces change and its uncertainties alone. Of entire vast body of data Environ has to offer, thinks Seit, none gives youngthon any real view of what must come.

Duty period ends; Imon and its dutymates disperse, some to nesting spaces of selves or groupings, others to feeding or diversion areas. Seeing Tev turn toward feeding space, Imon follows.

Breeding choices depend on availability of partners, on number of Liij nearing breeding stage at simultaneity, and can sometimes be quite limited. At now, only few other Liij bear nodes at development matching Imon's. Those further along will breed together before Imon readies fully; those less ripened cannot match completion in time. Tev, though, if appearance tells truly, is as near to breeding as Imon itself.

Making little sound, Imon overtakes Tev; playfully it hums with palp-tip behind Tev's ear. At first startled, Tev turns and makes twin-palped chirr of pleasure; then, with tendrils of Tev's right palp entwining those of Imon's left, sharing buzz of comfort their contact brings, both go forward to take food.

As well as various kinds of root and stalk and leaf and seedbearer, at this point of cycle, feeding includes grown flesh. From nutriment proliferator, this; only at rare times, such as Harkenings, are any of Environ's discognizant living creatures taken for food, and in Imon's life to now—not yet eight *dre*—only five such have occurred. Having so little experience of comparison, Imon finds grown flesh hearty enough for its taste.

With ritual courtesy of mouthsounds—and humcounterpart of palps, though without touching any other—Imon and Tev accept food service and proceed to eating platform sized for two. As they eat, Imon considers its node, and Tev's. Which, it wonders, is most ripe? Which, when pressed against other's with breeding force, will be softer, spreading and accepting as less-ripened node contracts radially to form their joining's core?

With shyness, palps qualifying mouthsound bluntness, it asks Tev <Which (when time comes) would you (for yourself) wish? To seed (divesting) or birth (retaining until nodes detach)?>

<No matter> Tev responds. <Bodies (as always) make choice.>

As impossibility happens, Seit sits at Overwatcher's station—viewing summary-depictions of Environ's instrument arrays, conferring with Dutysetter Kahim.

No sensor warns. One instant: spacetime, only minimally turbulent, streams into ingestor, while Environ outpaces radiance by manyfold. At next: Seit's viewer display, of radiance downspectrumed to Liij visual range, explodes into hurtful actinic bursts.

Environ shrieks and shudders; nausea wrings Seit as weight undulates with struggle of Environ's straining generators; lighting flickers, dies, glares, and stabilizes at weaker level; air rushes in hot and cold blasts.

With great, jarring lunge, Environ throws Seit from duty seat to strike painfully on deck surface where it lies trembling, hearing sounds of Environ being wrenched and battered.

Slowly, gradually, tumult dies away, lesser stressings heard now as greater ones abate. Wincing, Seit rises and seats itself at viewer. But no view appears, only random dots and streaks of radiance. Experimentally, Seit makes trivial reduction of spectrum's downshift. Then more, and then yet further, to end of normal range scale. With annoyed hum Seit changes scales; still no view appears, nor by access to next adjacent scale or two more past it.

Seit pauses; *it cannot be*! But if worst is true, better to know now than later. Seit cuts spectrum shift to zero. And on viewer, image appears, of spacetime ahead. Image formed of radiance unshifted, radiance striking Environ uncompressed.

Somehow—*somehow*—Environ is riven from stride

of vast pace, almost to crawl of drifting matter. This much, Seit must believe, for so say all instruments.

What it cannot believe, though true, is that instruments found no danger of which to warn. Viewer showed no thing, no sign of deadly obstacle in Environ's path. But what, shown or not, could do to Environ what is now done?

Leaving Dutysetter Kahim to bring this central station back to order and summarize results afterward, Seit from Overwatcher's seat demands and receives reports from Environ's more important outlying activities.

At end of questionings Seit knows its situation. Damage to Environ is widespread but minor; although time-consuming, repair is neither urgent nor technically difficult.

Damage to Environ's *situation* is crippling. Instead of moving at accustomed pace, with plasma pool's reserve energies more than adequate to maintain pace and operation, Environ lazes near drift. At which, intake cannot so much as maintain energy level, let alone build pace.

For Environ, then, condition is that of earliest departure, from original world orbit. To build pace, to move again, Environ must ingest vast amounts of spacetime, greatly heavy in matter.

Perhaps, even, as at first outset, consume worlds.

Lesser worlds, these must be. Worldlets. For with plasma level so lowered, ingestor field has only narrowed scope.

But from Environ now, at crawl pace, *all* worlds are far.

Operations tube, forward half divided into three decks: working area, crew-supporting supplies, equipment deck

Habgate terminal

Rotating section

Transfer ring

Access ramp area

Water storage (8.4 megaliters, 2.2 megagallons)

DV control room

MacroGate components

Control

Drive, fuel tanks, life support, ship's supplies

Drive, fuel, life support, crew supplies, landing cargo space

Deployment Vehicle (DV)

Tunnel, with side hatches

Major cargo space ("destination" cargo)

Length, 120 meters (394 feet); diameter, 50 meters (164 feet). Volume = slightly over 6,000,000 cubic feet. Overall weight, approx 187,500 tons. DV: Length, 60 meters (197 feet); diameter, 20 meters (66 feet). Volume = 517,740 cubic feet, weight approx 16,150 tons, plus cargo.

(Lower half same as upper)

VIII

STARFINDER

From a distance it doesn't look like much, but our first starship's a B-I-G souper. The shuttle I rode, up to assembly orbit, wouldn't make a decent-sized puppy to it. Of course, the shuttle isn't going any twenty parsecs, either. (Ten. Editor.)

The numbers don't sound all that big, because the science mahouts think Metric. Basically there's a cylinder, seventy meters long and fifty across, with a fifty-meter cone at the front. In English that's about 394 feet long, overall, and 164 feet thick. Rather stumpy and frumpy looking, for a starship.

As my sketch indicates, running up the long axis is a central core, twenty meters across. Its rear half is cargo space; its front portion is the DV, the deployment vehicle that is the only part of Starfinder *that can ever land anywhere.*

Next outside that core comes the Operations tube, forty meters outside diameter which means ten meters thick, also tapered at the front. It contains the drive, fuel tanks, ship's supplies, controls, life support, interim living quarters—actually, nearly all the ship's workings.

That leaves one more outer tube, this one five meters thick, giving us the overall fifty-meter width. The rear fifty meters is more cargo space, because at the end of Starfinder's trip they're going to put together a Habegger receiving terminal big enough to handle ships, and the parts for that device use a lot of room. What surprised me was that if it weren't for the radiation shielding, that skinny-walled tube would hold nearly twice as much space as the twenty-meter core cylinder—and it's shorter, too! But math was never this reporter's strong point.

Now it gets interesting. The forward part of that outer tube, twenty meters plus the front ten where the cone starts, covers a big ring that's supposed to rotate, to give an area with a substitute for gravity when the ship gets up to speed and isn't on accel anymore. Remember, I said "interim quarters"? Well, for nearly the first year, speeding up under drive, the ship's rear is "down." But for the main part of the trip it's strictly zero-gee country, all but the rotating belt, so that's where everyone will live except when they're on duty.

The machinery for spinning this belt, keeping it balanced, and so forth, is quite complicated, but the important facts are that it will simulate one-third gee and that at the "floor" level it's moving about twenty miles an hour. So you don't just jump on and off; there's a transfer ring that can speed up or slow down to match either the belt or the ship.

The Habegger input and output terminals are in the middle ring, one on each side. I could have returned to Earth through the Habegger pipeline—but I'd have missed my deadline by two years!

[Item in People magazine by Arlene Hofer; photographs by Reggie Aikens.]

As Hanchett came toward him, moving almost in slow motion, Rance made an effort to orient himself. All right; he knew he was in the arbitrary "port" side of the Operations tube, shaped like a sharpened pencil with the lead missing. The drive, fuel tanks, and supply storage filled the rearward forty meters; the other forty, up to the tapered end that stored eight-point-four megaliters of water, comprised all the working space. Considerably more, that, than the mere numbers gave one to think. And here, at the rear of the Ops sector, this rounded, three-meter Habgate cube.

So much for space—but also, time had to be considered. And for Rance it was two years later than it had been five seconds ago; already he'd added that much to the age difference between him and Cassie. As if it mattered now . . .

Stepping forward until one Velcro sole engaged the unmoving exit belt, Rance let go his supporting hold and reached to shake hands. "Hi, Jimmy; I see we made it. But what's wrong with the drive?"

The new executive officer's grip was sweaty; in higher pitch than normal, he said, "Jeez, am I glad to see *you*! The drive—I don't know; nobody does. You'll have to hear Sligo's chip—"

"Message capsule? Why can't I just ask her?" Inside Rance, something sank like a lead Frisbee. "Is she—?"

Quick words. "Not dead; doped up. In traction harness; smashed vertebra." Quick, nervous laugh. "Don't dare take the fixed hardware loose, so we can't get her to the pipeline to send her home. And too much pain to handle without dope."

Working his hand loose from the exec's spasmodic clutch, Rance said, "So—a chip, you mentioned?" Marveling that his own voice sounded so calm and detached . . .

"Yeah. Right after the accident, she must have made it. Because, before anyone got to her, she'd passed out." He shook his head. "Collier, I hope to hell what she said makes some kind of sense to *you*. "

"Yes. Me too." Looking past Jimmy, Rance saw fewer people than he'd expected. Standing back a little was Fleurine, and well to one side, the deck's upward curvature making him seem taller, Dink Hennessey. But no

one else. None from either cadre of the launch crew—
and at this point, only three of the A group should have
gone into the pipeline. Rance frowned. "Where is everybody?"

Hanchett shrugged. "Having a meeting; I'll explain
later. But before we join them, they thought I ought to
tell you how things stand."

"So tell it."

"Not here." And heading forward, Hanchett led the
way.

The surface they trod was the Operations tube's outer
wall, their longitudinal route now protected by two meters' width of Velcro carpet. Stepping gingerly, taking
care that shoe soles gripped properly while at the same
time making use of handlines along the walkway's sides,
the four passed through openings in bulkheads that had
until quite recently been working decks. *Starfinder*'s
accel phase, when "up" was toward the ship's nose,
could have ended only two to three weeks earlier; since
then, the Habegger units themselves would have had to
be reoriented.

At each deck, Rance noted, the trim on the basic
offwhite surfaces was a different color, coded to indicate
the level at a glance. Looking aside into various working
spaces as he passed them, Rance saw that some rear-
rangements had been made while others were still to be
done, or in progress. The Control space was a good
example: For psychological reasons, duty stations now
faced forward.

What bothered him was that those stations were unattended.

All the way forward, past Control to the final bulkhead
that marked the beginning of conical taper, Hanchett
led them. Here the corridor ended in openness; to either side, unobstructed space extended, curving upward to form a circumferential ring, ten meters wide
and ten deep also, around *Starfinder*'s central core.

Following the exec, the party turned left. Not far
ahead, the surface underfoot divided; the rear half continued its circular path, but the other sloped and tipped
to merge into a wide ramp that dropped away, rear-

ward, into the ship's outer tube. Hesitant at first, Rance found he didn't need to make allowances for the slope; if he forgot to flex his ankles, his body simply stood out perpendicular to the ramp. *In zero gee*, everything's *level.* . . .

Reaching the "lower elevation," Rance was struck by the realization that only *Starfinder*'s outer hull lay between his feet and the chill of interstellar void. Momentarily he shivered, then said, "Next, the transfer ring?"

"Yes." Hanchett stopped before a large pair of elevator-type doors, curved at top and bottom, in the rear bulkhead, and pushed the single button. In less than twenty seconds the doors slid aside to reveal a slightly curved, brick-shaped space, about four meters by four by eight.

The transfer ring had three such compartments, matching the entrances in the ship proper and the rotating "weight" belt; when the ring was free of its latest user, any call button brought the nearest cage. Over the long haul, that redundancy could save a lot of time. . . .

Three buttons here; "Station Two," said Hanchett, and pressed the middle one. "Hang on." The doors closed and Rance grabbed a hanging loop of strap; as the box accelerated, a feeling of weight grew.

The ring, Rance knew, was not powered. Its controls merely braked it to rest with respect to the rotating belt or to the ship itself: a solution, he felt, of truly classic elegance.

Soon the lateral accel ceased, but the weight stayed. Only one-third gee, he'd been told, and that felt about right.

At the cage's rear, another pair of doors opened—onto a corridor much like the one they'd recently left, but colored a light green, and along its rearward side a series of doors. No Velcro on this floor, he noted. Over his shoulder the Exec said, "Rec lounge; that's where we can play the chip. Not far."

Well—with entrances to the belt only a little over fifty meters apart, it *couldn't* be . . .

Among other amenities, the brightly colored lounge had three smallish tables, a dozen chairs, a Tri-V screen, coffeemaker, and a minibar. Legs tensed from unfamiliar exertion, Rance was glad to sit alongside Fleurine, as Hennessey poured coffee all around. To his own, Dink added a little brandy; the others declined.

Setting up to play the capsule, Hanchett said, "This happened about ten days before I got here, just after the Habegger terminals were swung for zero-gee operation. The ship *hit* something, or something hit the ship. Nothing material—apparently some kind of shock wave in space itself. Well, here's what Sligo said about it. She had the watch solo at the time."

He sat, and the voice began. "—hell, anyway! Should be up here by now. All right—Margaret Sligo, captain, recording. Ugh—God *damn*, that hurts." A deep, shuddering breath, then, "What it was, going by the computer-corrected view of outside, looked like a huge ripple coming at us. Stars bouncing up and down like corks behind a powerboat—only they couldn't, of course; *space* moved, between us and them." Another pause. "The thing came so damn *fast;* then it hit and all hell popped loose."

Her voice caught in a ragged sigh. "Drive's dead; nothing on the board makes it flicker, even. Have to get somebody on that. What else, now? Oh, yes—there were two big hits, about a second apart, then lesser ones, dwindling down, probably the same interval. But the big thing—what it might have *been*—well, every time we took a hit, the chronometer ran numbers *backward*. So that means—"

She broke down into coughing before she could say, "Jeez, Art! About time you got here. No—don't try to move me! My legs are dead, and there's something grating, in my back. What you do—" Then there were several voices; Rance couldn't make out what was said, only the tones.

Hanchett switched the machine off. "Collier? Do you have any idea what she was talking about?"

After a moment Rance said, "I might. Do you?"

"Several of us have a guess—but it's impossible!"

"Not if it happened. Jimmy—if Sligo saw what she thought she saw, about the chronometer, then *Starfinder* may have hit the wake of something that was going faster than light."

At one corner, the exec's mouth twitched upward. "I was *afraid* you were going to agree with us."

Pouring himself more coffee, Rance said, "Dink? I could use some of that brandy after all. If the offer's still good." It was; Collier thanked the man, then said, "I'm still asking, where *is* everybody? From the launch crew, I mean. Except for the three who've probably left already."

Jimmy Hanchett looked uneasy. "Well, the ship's had some problems, personal things nobody expected. Pretty bad, Rance."

"Too bad to tell straight out?"

"Not sure where to begin, is all. Look—did you know any of the original A cadre?" Rance shook his head; he'd met those people a couple of times, but that wasn't "knowing." So Jimmy rattled off a capsule listing:

Hans Niebuhr from Germany, the exec. Nadine Potter, African-American. By departure time those two were paired. So were Ali Saud from Egypt with Swedish Steffi Holm, and Liz Pendergast, another U.S. citizen, with Takeo Yamata from Japan.

"Things were stable among them, and the other cadre, too, for about six months. Then some of the folks started playing around a little. Art Cranston . . ." He shook his head. "No, that doesn't matter. He—"

Impatience itching at him, Rance cut in. "What does?"

Hanchett frowned. "At first nobody got too worked up about it; they were all friends, after all, and the group marriage thing more or less sanctioned a little fooling around. But then Red Macdougall walked out on Btar and set himself up with Steffi Holm in a vacant compartment. Ali Saud put up with it for about a week, before he came apart and killed them both."

"Killed?" The exec nodded. "Then what happened?"

"Niebuhr took Ali's knife away—got cut doing it, but not seriously. Ali, tied hand and foot, went into the pipeline, along with his two victims and a sworn statement signed by all the survivors. What they'll do to him on Earth, nobody knows or cares. But he left *Starfinder* shorthanded, by three. That's why, even though four of our relief cadre are here already, nobody's gone back into the pipeline yet. Not since Ali Saud and the two corpses, nearly four months ago."

He gestured futilely. "What they're trying to decide in meeting right now is who stays and who goes—without regard to the original plans, and keeping in mind that Captain Sligo may be out of action for keeps."

Mentally, Rance made a quick count. "Besides her, we have twelve aboard; Su and Benita will make it fourteen. So if the T.O. stays at twelve, two would leave." Hesitantly he asked, "Any idea how the launch crew plans to choose which ones?"

For the first time in a while, Dink Hennessey spoke. "That gang hangs together so tight, they don't tell us *anything*. But ask Jimmy what's really chewing on him."

Rance let his raised brows do the asking; Hanchett said, "Is Hans Niebuhr going or staying? With Sligo down he's acting captain; if he stays, he keeps the job. Otherwise it's mine."

"And?" Because Rance had never figured Jimmy Hanchett to be power-hungry.

"And that's the prospect, scares me the worst. Because with the drive dead, what do we think we're *doing* here? But I'd hate to have to be the one to say, hit the pipeline and abort."

Rance reached to clasp the other's shoulder. "Maybe no one will have to. The drive's been out how long?"

"Twenty days, a little more."

"Then there must be things that haven't been tried yet."

"Maybe." The Exec stood. "Well, let's go see if the meeting's done with."

It wasn't; Hanchett's knocks at the Conf Room door brought no answer. He shrugged. "Well, Dink told you they're funny that way. Anything else special you'd like to do now?"

What should he say? He needed to know more, so, "Yes. Could we go have a look around Control?"

Jimmy nodded. "Sure. But if we're going inship again, let's all take a leak first."

It made sense; the zero-gee facilities required very careful attention.

* * *

To use the transfer ring now, Belt Station Three was nearest. Once inside, Hanchett punched for Inship One, and the ring took them to the ramp leading most directly to Control.

Entering that space Rance paused, eyeing the forward viewscreen. He knew in theory what a direct view of space would look like, the ship just short of light speed; for one thing, it wouldn't be much use to a navigator. But the view wasn't direct. The nav-computer processed data from outside sensors; what the screen showed was where the surrounding stars "really" were —if "really" meant anything under the circumstances. Even so, the panorama impressed Rance mightily.

Hanchett's voice broke his reverie. "The drive controls are frozen; that is, manipulating them has no apparent effect. We don't know why; we're hoping you might be able to tell us. So take a look?"

Moving forward, Rance said, "None of the original crew has any ideas? After nearly three weeks? How about you, Fleurine?" *Somebody* had to know something. . . .

Looking, he saw her stifle rising temper. "Six *days* I've been here, and just started getting sorted out." Smiling, trying to take some of the heat off, he nodded as she said, "The launch crew's drive specialists were Holm and Macdougall. And that maniac Saud, who was sent home tied up for basting and putting in the oven, was their best understudy." Still speaking loudly, she'd stopped glaring. "So get to it, will you?"

"Yes, of course." Seating himself at the primary Control console, Rance studied the slow random flashings of indicator lights. He was sure others had tried everything in the way of control-activating combinations, but he went through the motions anyway. As expected, results were zilch; from the exciter stages all the way through to final output, drive activity indicators stayed at zero. He frowned; telemetry, assuming it was still trustworthy, showed the vital energizing plasma to be intact—but he couldn't get it to *do* anything.

Largely for the benefit of his three watchers he fiddled some more, then sighed, shook his head, and stood to face them. "Nothing?" said Hanchett, looking ready to break down and cry.

"Not *nothing*, exactly. I do have sort of an idea in the back of my head. But it's really more Su's field than mine; I'd want to check it out with her first."

"Su?" Hennessey scowled. "Ship's maintenance is her line."

"Including circuits," said Rance. "Including telemetry and activators. I think that may be where the problem is."

Hanchett, then: "The launch crew has people—"

But the launch crew *hadn't* fixed it. And could they be trusted? "I know Su's capabilities. These other people, screwing around and killing one another—no, let's wait for Su."

To make his position palatable to the original crew members, Rance proposed to put it that Su had the benefit of special advanced training. So a bit later, when the entire ship's complement finally met in the galley, there weren't too many rough edges. And through dinner—lunch, for some—the talk was mostly introductory.

They had *aged*, the launch crew had. Rance figured back: After he himself had gone into Habegger's grabber, this bunch had spent nine months on Earth plus a year on *Starfinder*. They looked older. But murder and drumhead-sentence and catastrophic drive failure weren't the best kinds of things to preserve the bloom of youth. . . .

Hans Niebuhr, now acting captain, looked particularly haggard. Leaning forward, slate-blue eyes fixed on Rance with fierce intensity, he said, "You do think you have a solution? But you want to confirm with your colleague who arrives in three days?"

"A *possible* solution. Please, let's not raise false hopes."

Almost as one, the Kenyan siblings shrugged. With their clipped haircuts the two looked much like identical twins. Beside Jomo, it was Christy Frost who spoke. Rance recalled her as a pretty, vivacious young woman; now she seemed plain and ageless. "What you mean," she said, "is that you can't promise anything."

Surprised, he said, "No, of course not. Whatever hit the ship is totally new in our experience. So how could I—?"

"Come down to *real*, Christy!" The harsh voice came from the large, heavy woman, Liz Pendergast. She rubbed fingers through her short, dark hair; in it, gray sparkles caught the light. "Collier's in the same boat with the rest of us. So naturally he'll do his damnedest to fix things. All right?"

With a wincing, shrinking movement, Frost nodded. It was Yamata, the Japanese man seated beside Pendergast, who said, "We can wait, surely. For what else is there for us to do?"

Shocked, Collier realized they expected *him* to tell them. He looked around at those who hadn't spoken. Nadine Potter, the small, slimly built American black, sat holding Niebuhr's hand; when Rance's gaze caught hers, her headshake was almost too slight to notice. And both Mbentes faced him eye-to-eye but gave no sign with voice or face or gesture.

Art Cranston's face had sagged into wrinkled lines. "Collier—you're thinking we haven't done too well here, so far. Maybe we didn't know ourselves well enough. But if anyone can start the drive again, *we'll do better.*"

There had to be something he could say to help. "Don't tie the two problems together: the personal difficulties I've heard about, and this unprecedented phenomenon from outside the ship." Cranston nodded, but Rance felt that more reassurance was needed. After a moment he said, "Even if it means replacing the whole thing, a dead drive can be repaired. We'd lose a lot of *time* on the mission, sure, with all the back-and-forth in the pipeline. But the ship's still moving, up near light speed and only slowing a little from interstellar gas friction. So you see . . ." Hearing himself give the pep talk, he felt he was remembering it instead. Then he realized: It wasn't all that different from the one he'd given Congressman Bill Flynn, back when Senator Wallin was still pushing for authorization to *build* this ship.

So now he wrapped his pitch up the same way. "Because this mission's backed with the pipeline, it *can't* fail." Then, as he'd hoped, he saw them beginning to relax. Some more than others, of course . . .

In a soft, throaty voice with a trace of Boston accent, Nadine Potter spoke. "Do you agree with the consensus —that if Maggie was right about the chronometer reversing when the shock waves hit, it means something was moving faster than light?"

"It does fit theory. Except of course that theory says it couldn't really happen, and apparently it did."

She was waiting for something more, so he said, "By our books, FTL is impossible. It looks as if somebody hasn't been reading our books."

IX

TESTINGS

He didn't think he was done with Potter's questions, though. And sure enough, after the meal when he headed back inship and to Control, she and Niebuhr tagged along. They weren't saying much, and Rance liked it that way.

Strapping in at one of the aux stations, he booted up that position's readout terminal and scanned the ship's log, starting a few hours before the shock waves hit. Sligo's recording was there, of course, and from that point on, he checked at least the first line or two of each entry, so as not to miss anything that might be important. He found little he hadn't known already, but still he had to look.

After about an hour, caught up to date, he paused. With Niebuhr and Potter watching, he didn't really want to put his own guesses onscreen. On the other hand, he'd be rude to cut the monitor and enter his data "in the blind"—and anyway, as soon as he left they could play it all back. For that matter, log entries also printed out on a terminal at the Habegger input, to be fed into the pipeline at regular intervals. (Daily? After each watch? He couldn't remember.)

Monitor or no, he punched for entry of the date-time numbers by ship's reckoning and began recording— first his name, and then:

> *Situation summary. I agree with previous evaluations surmising that* Starfinder *crossed paths with something moving at FTL speeds. My guess is that the resulting brief time reversals jammed telemetry and activation code patterns into a fixed configuration—something on the order of standing waves— that's blocking transmission of signal impulses. My only idea for correcting the malfunction is so tentative that I shall not discuss it, here or otherwise, until I've had the opportunity to confer with Su Teng. At that point we will announce our conclusions, and of course acting Captain Niebuhr will make final decision as to what measures are to be attempted. Collier out.*

Closing down the terminal, he swung the seat around and grinned at the two standing behind him. "Talking that official jargon—it's work. One thing, though. Niebuhr, do you approve, so far?"

The blond German frowned. "More or less. But why the secrecy?"

"Because I'm guessing about matters I don't know, that I'm not sure anyone aboard can evaluate, but that Su Teng *does* know."

"And you're afraid," Potter said, "that we might go off halfcocked, without waiting for your expert's opinion. Because we're unstable, all of us on the launch crew, and can't be trusted."

Cautiously, Rance countered, "You said that, I didn't."

Niebuhr shrugged. "Let it rest, Nadine. If he thinks that way, maybe he's right. And since we've marked time for twenty days already, I expect we can manage three more."

∎ ∎ ∎

For a moment, Potter still scowled. But she didn't seem to be one to hold a grudge; her brow smoothed and she said, "I'd still like to hear more about those time reversals. If only for my own curiosity. Are you willing to discuss that part?"

He nodded; she said, "Well, then. I thought I knew the math, about velocity and mass and time. But I don't see how any of it could make time go *backward*."

Turning back to the terminal he brought it up again. He didn't really want to clutter the log with this stuff, but unfortunately he didn't know the codes to disconnect that function. Typing up the standard equations, he plugged in a few values, running velocity through the familiar time-dilation curve from zero to c. "Now, then. If we make v *greater* than c—" Onscreen he did so. "—we get imaginary numbers in our solution." Potter's eyes narrowed but she didn't protest, so he cleared the screen and began again. "Now, then . . ."

This part, he knew from his student days, wasn't easy to follow. He hoped he wasn't losing her; the terminal couldn't handle some of the transformations, so a few times he had to wipe the screen and make the transitions by mental calculation; near as he could tell, he was getting them down correctly.

Potter didn't seem convinced, exactly; Niebuhr, showing no reaction, simply watched. Suddenly impatient, Rance said, "If the math doesn't sell you, consider this: Do you know how Three-fingered Annie got her nickname?" They didn't, so he told them. "The breadboard prototype of our Traction Drive threw a warp into time; it aged one of Anne Portaris's fingers past the point of death, and did much the same to some tools and a wristwatch. To do so, the equipment had to be flanged badly out of phase; I'm sure our own drive has safeguards against that grade of maladjustment. But what the incident proves is: Monkeying with spacetime can bring some strange results."

Potter smiled. "And moving faster than light qualifies as rather extensive monkeying. Is that what you're saying?"

"Close enough." Inwardly he gave a relieved sigh. And then they all left Control and went back to the spinning belt, where there was enough weight to help Rance relax a little better.

As he knew, *Starfinder*'s normal crew of twelve had the option of spreading out into quarters designed for up to twenty. The margin was partly for flexibility, but also so that if/when a habitable planet were spotted—or even a "possible"—additional specialists from Earth could be accommodated. To Rance the timing sounded awkward, but since that end of the trip was out of his field, he tended to accept what he was told.

At any rate, spare rooms were available; with Su in mind he requested a double. The first one shown to him —by Christy Frost—showed signs of previous occupancy. Rance asked, and Frost seemed embarrassed as she said, "Yes; this was Ali's and Steffi's, first."

Rance shook his head. "I don't have to be superstitious to pass this one. Why don't you use it for storage?"

Christy looked at him. "That's what we're doing with the one he did the killings in." So, changing his mind in a hurry, Rance accepted the first offer.

She left, and he began to unpack. The mindless activity left his thoughts free to roam, but he didn't much like where they took him. The situation here: all the problems seemed to be running loose; no one was really in charge. So his question was, what could he do? And then, how much should he *try* to do? Feeling more helpless than not, he found himself speculating on a few things that had *not* been said. But before he came close to reaching anything that smelled like a conclusion, the door opened and Jimmy Hanchett came in.

Grateful for the distraction, Rance smiled welcome.

"Sligo's awake," the exec began. "By her own orders, every few days she stays all the way off sedation several hours, to be clearheaded for briefing. You want to come along?" Closing a drawer, Rance nodded. Hanchett said, "Niebuhr wants to talk to you a minute first. Should we go?"

"Right." They left the room. Just outside stood Btar Mbente. Momentarily Rance thought he saw disappointment in her expression; then she gave greeting and followed the pair to the lounge, where Hans Niebuhr waited.

The man stood. "Just wanted to say, Collier, try not to excite Maggie. It's all right to ask questions, but if she seems to be getting bothered, ease off. And what you *tell* her—well, stick to the line that even after all your group gets here the investigation may take a while. Understand?"

"Sure. But—" Niebuhr was turning away; Rance gestured to get his attention. "One thing, first. Your group met, all but the captain, to decide who stays aboard and who doesn't. How about letting the rest of us know, too?"

For a moment the man looked blank; then he nodded. "All right. Until we find out, one way or another, about the drive, nobody's leaving. If we get it going again, the choices will take some thinking—another meeting, including your people also."

Hanchett cleared his throat. "And if we fail?"

"That's the tough one." Shrugging, Niebuhr said, "I think we set the jettison controls to start dumping the excess from the pipeline—fuel, food, all of it—when the tanks and bins fill up. And we *all* go home."

"That's stupid!" Rance and Jimmy both fired protests: Didn't it make sense to keep the ship crewed? To keep working on removal of dud components so the replacement job would be easier when new parts arrived, and new people to help with the assembly work? "Why slow things down any more than we have to?"

Niebuhr looked stubborn. "The way I see it is, why not turn the job over to a group that knows what it's doing?"

Clearly the man felt defeated on a level that logic couldn't touch. Rance tried to think of an angle; Hanchett said, "One moment, Mr. Niebuhr. While you're aboard, you're in command. But once you leave, *I* am."

"Not if I send you back first. I—"

"Wait a minute," Rance protested. "We just got here; our assignment is a year's stay. The ship's perfectly safe to *live* on. I think you'd find it hard, back on Earth, to justify aborting our mission against our own best judgment of the situation." Another idea was floating at the back of his mind, and suddenly he caught it. "Besides, how about Maggie Sligo? I'm told she can't be moved. Do you plan to leave her here and let her starve to death?"

"That's not a problem." It was the Kenyan woman. "At least, it doesn't have to be. Jomo's plan—"

"Your brother," said Niebuhr, "knows nothing of medicine."

"But he knows how to build things." In a rush, now speaking mainly to Collier and Hanchett, she told it. A light, strong framework, just large enough to clear all of Sligo's extremities. Transfer the traction lines to that framework. "No adjustments possible, that way, but for a short time . . ." First slide a sheet of strong, flexible plastic under the captain; fasten that to the peripheral structure as the framework is built. Rance nodded; yes, if it worked, Sligo could be moved safely.

Thinking quickly, he said, "Send someone else—or the information, at least—into the pipeline well ahead of her, to give the receiving end time to round up all the necessary gear." Btar smiled; Rance knew he'd just helped deal a blow to his own greater cause, his and Hanchett's, but this was a woman's life they were talking about. He looked to Jimmy and guessed the man was thinking the same way.

Niebuhr seemed to relax a little, but not much. He said, "Maybe it'd work, at that. But I'll make the decisions." He turned away. "Let's go see the captain. And remember what I told you."

"Don't worry," Rance said. "We realize she doesn't need any hassles." Then they followed Hans Niebuhr to Captain's quarters, where Maggie Sligo lay in traction harness.

Awake, she looked alert enough to be coherent. At first meeting Rance had thought her a bit chunky, with face to match. Now the face, at least, was gaunt and pale below a severely clipped shipboard haircut; the gray eyes looked bigger. Under a sheet, maybe the torso was thinner or maybe not. To one arm was taped an IV tube. Leaning toward Btar Mbente, Rance whispered, "Is that all the nutriment she's had for twenty days?"

Btar's voice was also hushed. "No. Every day, before she gets her next shot, she's out of sedation enough to swallow a little something. And the times like today, when she comes all the way awake, she eats more. But—" They were too close now, to the injured woman, to talk more.

Sligo tried to say something, coughed instead, then tried again. "Well. Got here, did you? How many? Hell of a mess you've arrived at. Any ideas?" Out of breath she lay gasping; Rance decided she'd asked all her questions at once, while she was sure she could.

Jimmy didn't speak so Rance tried to sort things out. "Four of us here so far, out of our six—at three-day intervals, as you know. I'm the latest. And you'll remember Mr. Hanchett here, in charge of our cadre."

Sligo's grin wasn't much, but Rance gave her points for effort. "My new exec, eh? Welcome aboard."

Hans Niebuhr cleared his throat. "Now, Maggie—there'll be time to consider these matters. Don't worry; we'll—"

The gray eyes narrowed; Maggie Sligo's voice went flat. "I'm not worrying, Hans. Not now. You're relieved of duty, this minute, and directed to—" She broke into coughing again, but quickly recovered. "—directed to pack your gear and report to the pipeline terminal. You have two hours. I'll dictate my commendation for you and have it ready so you can take it along, because for a solid year, you earned it."

Niebuhr's shock showed. "You can't do this! I—"

"I can and I am. Past few days, since I got hurt—I've heard you talking, when you thought I was too doped to hear. Saying, abort this mission! Well, you won't do it. Now you—"

"Maggie! Why are you turning against me?"

Her right hand twitched, raised slightly from the sheet, then fell back. "It's you who's turned, Hans. Since the accident you're not the same man. I don't know why, but—"

Suddenly Niebuhr went to a half-crouch; stunned, Rance saw he held a pistol. Btar Mbente was nearest to him; from behind. Niebuhr grabbed her and held the gun to her head. "And *now*—" he began. But his movements and Mbente's, together with the Belt's Coriolis force, were swinging the two slowly around, both pairs of feet shuffling to keep from falling.

Without benefit of light speed, Rance's adrenalin slowed time for him. Just as though he'd planned it, he noted with approval that he'd moved to clutch Niebuhr's neck just below the ears and braced himself to stop the grotesque pirouette; his other hand reached around the face to dig its middle finger into an eye.

Niebuhr gasped; Rance's voice came high and shaky. "If you hurt her I'll take the eye; you can't stop me!" Against his leg and chest he felt the other man stiffen, and said, "Please lower the gun now; let Jimmy take it, or—" He pushed harder against the eyelid and heard Niebuhr gasp. Then Hanchett came closer, and in a moment backed away, holding the gun pointed downward.

In Rance's grasp, Niebuhr went limp and began to shake. Btar pulled loose, took a step and turned to face him. "Hans—" Shaking her head, she put both hands to her face.

Rance turned to Sligo. She was breathing fast; had the excitement harmed her? She blinked twice, seeming to have difficulty reopening her eyes, but when she spoke her voice was almost steady. "I'm sorry, Hans. But go do exactly as I said. And you gentlemen—please see that he does." She paused. "The commendation still holds; I won't count this exhibition against a year of fine work. But I'm recommending a total checkup, Hans, and a good rest." A sigh broke into more coughing; when she mastered it, she said, "Everybody please get the hell out. Send Art with my shot; I'm starting to need it. But wake me again tomorrow; don't wait the usual interval." Her eyes closed; maybe she wasn't asleep, Rance thought, but she was done talking.

He turned to Niebuhr. "Let's go pack your things, eh?"

Rance's trouble was that never in his life had he been any kind of fighter. Walking in one-third gee as he followed the others to Niebuhr's quarters, he felt his knees going wobbly with delayed shock—and any time his course deviated from the tangential, found himself struggling against Coriolis force he hadn't previously noticed. Trying not to let the effects show, he was glad when they reached destination and he could lean against the doorframe.

Inside, Nadine Potter reclined, scanning a capsule in her hand-held viewer. At sight of the group, she sat up. "What's the celebration?"

Niebuhr's face contorted. "I'm *sorry*!" He ran and threw himself down, his head in the woman's lap, sobbing like a hurt child. "They don't understand! Those *things*—whatever they were, that wrecked our drive—we don't belong out here. We belong back on Earth, where it's safe!" He pushed himself up, enough to look at her. "You see that, don't you?"

He collapsed again, and it was up to the others to explain what had happened. At the end of it Nadine nodded, looking as though she'd never smiled in her life. "I should go with him; he'll need someone. But I'm not going to. Not until I'm sure this *ship* doesn't need me."

She helped the man assemble his belongings, and aided the rest in carrying them to the transfer ring and then to the Habegger input terminal; standing before it, she kissed him good-bye. "I may be along in a few days, Hans, or I may not. It depends on what's necessary, here. If I stay the distance for B cadre, though . . ."

"I know," he said. "For me, that will be five years." He looked past her, to the others watching. "I'm not like this. Not like what you saw today. Ask anyone; I'm no coward. Something, though—that kills a ship and cripples its captain, and turns *time* back—I'm sorry." A headshake. "I suppose it crippled me also, in a different way." His expression caricatured a smile. "Well, maybe you all can handle it, where I couldn't. Or perhaps not."

His luggage was already gone into the pipeline. Following it, Niebuhr didn't look back.

What Rance wanted was to get away by himself, and let the churning inside him ease down to a state nearer calm. To the others he mumbled something, hoping it came out polite, and strode away.

When the transfer ring came to his call and he entered it, he couldn't recall which Belt station was nearest his own digs, and arrived almost opposite them.

Coriolis shifted his first stride; he waved his arms for balance and used more caution, then, until he reached "home." Inside he shucked shirt and shoes, and lay down. A little deep breathing couldn't hurt; soon he was half-dozing.

A knock brought him awake. He'd left the intercom and door chime turned off, so the knock was anyone's only recourse. Shrugging, he got up and opened the door, to face a bottle held up for his inspection. Close up, at eye level.

"I thought we might use a drink, you and I," said Btar Mbente.

A drink, as it turned out, wasn't all she thought they might share. Confused, Rance let his surprise show, and she said, "Well, you don't have to, of course. But you did save my life, I think, and I can't imagine a more pleasant way to repay you."

There had to be more to it, Rance felt, so he asked questions. The answers depressed him. After Btar's pairmate Red Macdougall left her and was killed by Ali Saud, she'd been the only unpaired person on the ship. Her problem was not merely the sexual lack, but more importantly, aloneness. "Everyone else had a partner, you see. Oh, I had friendly charitable interludes now and then—not too often, so as to avoid seeming intrusive—with Art or Hans or Takeo. Jomo being my brother, of course . . ." She shrugged. Somewhere along the line she had shed her blouse; her pointed, grape-nippled breasts shifted with the movement.

Rance forced his gaze back to her strong features, the smooth curves of jaw and cheekbones. Feeling the wine's impact, he wished the conversation hadn't gone quite so serious. He said, "But mostly, here, you've had a pretty thin time."

Her mouth twitched. "Very thin. After the accident, Art Cranston aged and shrank; he had no energy left, to be a man. And Hans—well, you saw. He was hiding from ghosts, more than not. Takeo? Well, Liz never wanted him out of her sight very often, at any time. Lately, now, it's been out of the question."

How had his fingers gotten to her breast? Hoping she hadn't noticed, he withdrew them. "Poor kid. Being hard up isn't any fun at all, is it?" *Change the subject, for Pete's sake!*

Abruptly she moved back a little, away from him. "No! You miss the point entirely. Well, not quite, perhaps, but—"

He tried to shake his head into sobriety. "Then what—?"

Her hand turned his chin up so that their gazes met. "Rance Collier, I'm trying to decide whether to stay on *Starfinder* or take the option—which seems damned attractive right now—to go home. Since I *am* alone, Maggie Sligo would give me my choice, either way. And what I want to find out, assuming we could cut all this talk and get to it, is whether I'd be choosing Earth simply because I'm fed up with being unrequitedly horny."

Well. Uncomfortable, Rance said, "Uh—you know I have a pairmate of my own, arriving here in two-three days."

"Yes, of course. And is she jealous, possessive? Enough to begrudge me one occasion?"

Probably not. But "I know someone who isn't: Benita Torres, who'll be joining Dink Hennessey. Back on Earth, Dink was setting it up for a while with her and— uh, another lady; Benita didn't seem to mind."

Btar shook her head. "No, thanks. Mr. Hennessey's already offered to be my port in a storm."

"You don't like Dink? First impressions—"

"I don't dislike him, really. It's just that he lets it be so obvious, what a big favor he'd be doing me." She grinned. "Oh, I'd take *that* out of him in a hurry. In the village where Jomo and I grew up, girls are trained, from a very early age, by the old women."

"Trained?" His voice came out thinner than he liked.

Along the side of his neck, her fingers trailed. "I think I'll show you." Other things began to happen. Since he couldn't protest very well with his mouth full of tongue, they kept on happening. Finally he put both hands to her face and, as gently as possible, disengaged it from his own. Short of breath he said, panting, "Excuse me? Please let go for a minute?"

Briefly her hands gripped tighter; then she released

him and sat back. Expressionless, she said, "I'm ugly to you. Is it because I'm black?"

"Of course not. I mean, you're *not* ugly. You—"

"Then in spite of the group marriage sanction, you and your pairmate have sworn monogamy?"

"Not exactly." Actually, he and Su hadn't discussed the matter—yet now as he stopped to consider, it struck him that their unspoken understandings did lean that way. "But—"

Hands on hips, chest thrusting forward, and head high, Btar could hardly have looked more provocative. "Why *else* would you push me away?"

Stalling for time, Rance stood. "You ever hear of a full bladder?" And suddenly realized he wasn't lying.

Well, not by much. In his minibathroom he took longer than was strictly necessary; he needed to think. What came to mind, though, was *This wouldn't be important to Su, not really. In a sense, it's not important to me. But to Btar it is.* . . .

So when he emerged, prepared to respond in whatever way Btar indicated, he was surprised to find her buttoning her blouse.

"What—?"

She grinned at him. "I've thought about it: how I'd feel here if I had a good solid share of you, and if I didn't. The odd part is that *it doesn't make any difference.*"

"How—?"

"Either way, you see, it's not what I signed up for, and I know it's right for me to go." Somehow clownish, her eyes widened. "To return, perhaps, to the place of my growing up. Plains, trees, mountains, dust—maybe relive, for a time, my childhood of herding cows, with clay plastered on my body to ward off insects." She smiled. "I don't imagine you'd like me that way, but you never know."

Gulp. "When do you intend to leave?"

Btar laughed. "Not until your entire group is here, and I've done my bit to help train the newcomers. Also, I'm sure your pairmate is worthy of you, but I want to meet her and see for myself. Do you mind?"

Mutely he sat. *There's just no figuring people!* Finally

he said, "You sure know how to sober a man up. Join me in another drink—to toast your homecoming?"

Five minutes earlier, he'd never have thought Btar Mbente could look prim. "Yes, thank you. That would be nice."

X

SHAKEDOWNS

When Btar departed a bit later, Rance was ready for his first real sleep shipside. During his brief course of testing and acclimatization on the satellite he'd slept in zero gee, so he didn't expect one-third to be a problem.

Somehow, despite the recent sexual tensions, he wasn't wound up in the slightest. So after a brief, water-conserving shower, Rance lay awake hardly at all.

The intercom woke him: Jimmy Hanchett's voice. "Calling council. All hands in the galley. Twenty minutes." Rance's chrono showed he'd had over seven hours' sleep; certainly he felt refreshed. The stated deadline cut things close, but by at least two minutes, Rance wasn't the last to report.

The entire mobile complement was present, thirteen in all. Since shortly after the accident, no continuous watch had been kept; Control "duty" consisted of checking the instruments every four hours and at the same time making a fruitless run, just in case, through the drive activation procedures.

As the last arrivals found seats, Rance leaned to hand Fleurine Schadel a few sheets of paper. "The World Series readouts. I forgot, earlier. Sorry. The—"

"Don't tell me! I want to read it in order, the way it happened." Then, as if in apology for her barking tone, she smiled. "Thanks, Collier."

"Anytime."

Hanchett began the meeting. As first order of business he explained, in case anyone hadn't heard already, that Maggie Sligo had sent Hans Niebuhr back to Earth and named Jimmy himself as acting captain. "Naturally, I'll check with her every time she's fully awake. So unless an emergency arises, it's her policies I'll be carrying out."

Christy Frost raised a hand. "I haven't seen her for more than a week; she wasn't tracking too well then. Are you sure she's competent to *set* policy?"

Overriding angry protest from a suddenly red-faced Art Cranston, Hanchett said, "You people know her better than I do, but near as I could tell, she's making perfect sense."

Amid a flurry of comment Rance said, "I'll second that," and things quieted. Next, Jimmy began to describe Jomo Mbente's plan for moving the captain safely, but bogged down in construction details and needed to have the Kenyan finish explaining.

Then he said, "She doesn't want to be moved, though, until we know one way or the other about the drive. And unless her condition changes for the worse, I see no reason why she should be. Pendergast says the captain's been improving, slowly but steadily, so maybe that's a problem we can put on hold for now."

Some of Hanchett's talk was new to Rance; certainly the man hadn't been sitting idle. But waiting for the question he knew needed raising, Collier fidgeted with impatience. Until finally Jimmy held up the handgun he'd taken from Hans Niebuhr.

"I want to know where this came from, and if we can expect any other weapons to turn up aboard. We can't have that. And if I need to pull a surprise inspection right now, to see to it, I'll do so."

Blinking, looking surprised, Art Cranston gestured. "I don't follow you. Hans would have brought the gun aboard in his personal luggage, of course."

"Of course?" Jimmy said. "You mean it was allowed?"

"Nobody searched our things. For weapons, drugs, or anything else. Did they paw through yours?"

"Well, no. But—"

Cranston was going strong now. "Right. Same as we have all the booze we want. NASA knows we're not going to binge out and neglect duty. They chose us as responsible persons, and—"

"Responsible," Fleurine put in. "Like Ali Saud, you mean?"

"That was different." But now Cranston looked subdued. "Anyway—Hanchett, if Hans gave his gun to you, I don't see—"

Looking both baffled and embarrassed, Jimmy said, "He did, but not voluntarily. We will not discuss that incident, if you don't mind." Stalling, or so it appeared, he cleared his throat. "Nonetheless this handgun, and any others aboard, get locked up; but we don't need such things lying around loose. But Ali Saud used a knife. So my question is whether any other weapons are aboard this ship. Guns, knives, whatever. I'm still asking it, and still prepared to do a shakedown to confirm the answers."

Art made a tentative smile. "Well, I have a multipurpose knife—you know the kind, practically a tool kit in itself. The large blade could certainly be a weapon, though I confess I'd never thought of it that way. But if you think—"

Frustrated with all the fiddle-faddle, Rance cut in. "We can't get rid of *everything* dangerous; we'd put the galley out of business. Let's stay with things designed to be lethal."

Jimmy seemed ready to agree; before he could, Nadine Potter said, "I have a pistol, a very small one. It's my good luck piece; I won it for target shooting when I was fourteen." She shook her head. "It's in the bottom of my duffel; frankly, I'd forgotten all about it. But feel free to lock up my ammo—all six or eight rounds of it!"

Laughter, then, eased tension. But not for long. Jomo Mbente stood, waited for quiet, then said, "My knife is assuredly a weapon, but with it I have drawn only the blood of animals." He grimaced. "Had we been on Earth when Red Macdougall shamed my sister, I might have drawn his. But on this ship his useful knowledge was of more importance than my outrage. So—"

"You'll have to turn it in, though," Hanchett said. "For real weapons we can't make exceptions; you can see that."

The Kenyan gestured. "No. It is the knife that cut me for manhood. It is mine forever, or I am not a man. No one takes it from me." His sister put a hand on his arm and whispered to him. Rance sensed urgency, but then Jomo smiled. "If you wish to shut my knife into a box, Mr. Hanchett, and keep the key until I leave *Starfinder,* I will agree. But the box stays in *my* custody. And for any other such compromise, that condition holds, also."

The man sat; for moments Hanchett seemed to have trouble finding an answer. Then, "I expect we can work something out."

He still insisted on the shakedown. The only way to keep the operation secure, while giving no appearance of favoritism, was for the entire crew to stay together, going from one room to the next until all areas had been covered. So as soon as everyone was fed and otherwise ready for an extended search, Hanchett led the way.

At first the group atmosphere was suspicious, even grim, but as time passed and each room was pronounced "clean," the mood lightened.

Only the previously noted weapons turned up. Jomo's "knife" was actually an ornate bolo; carved, polished handle and engraved blade, it hung from a ring welded to the bulkhead. For a moment Jimmy squinted at it, then said, "Why not seal it there with a band-lock? I mean, it'd be a shame to hide a work of art like that." Immediately Jomo looked more cheerful. Nadine brought and applied the band-lock, and Btar draped a ribbon of green cloth to hide the unesthetic device.

Cranston offered to "disarm" his tool-knife by squirting epoxy into the large blade's slot. "Then I could use it anytime. Just as soon as I soaked it loose with solvent!"

After a moment, Jimmy said that wouldn't be necessary.

Eventually the inspection ended, the assembly broke

up and Rance returned to his quarters. As he reached his door, Btar came past, heading toward her own. He gestured, and she stopped. Hesitantly he asked, "Did you tell Jomo what he should say?"

"No. Only that it was his responsibility to find an answer that would suit both Hanchett and himself."

"He's quite a guy, that brother of yours." A thought came. "If we had—uh, when you were here before— would he have thought I was shaming you?"

She shook her head. "No; he would think that of someone who rejected me." Rance must have looked alarmed then, for Btar laughed. "You didn't really, you know. You simply didn't bring yourself to accept my offer until after I'd changed my mind."

They were still standing; Rance motioned toward the door. "Would you like a drink or anything?"

"No, thank you. Well, I have some belongings to sort." She smiled. "I'll see you again now and then, before I leave."

"Sure." Thinking, too bad she was going; she was a strong person, the kind the ship could use more of. . . .

Over the next day and a half Jomo built his framework to surround Maggie Sligo, attached to the plastic "floor" under her and fitted with clamps to seize and hold the traction links, the outer ends of which could then be freed. He didn't tighten those clamps yet; until the time came to move the captain, Liz Pendergast wanted to retain capability to adjust traction. But when everything was ready, Maggie could be lifted, frame and all, and taken to the pipeline's input without danger.

When the arrangements were complete, Sligo had a big smile for Jomo Mbente. "You're a good 'un, Jomo; all year, you have been. If I haven't told you before, that's my error." The man barely smiled back, gesturing as if to brush away the compliment. If his skin hadn't been so dark, Rance thought, it might have shown a blush.

Jomo left; Sligo looked up at Rance and Jimmy. Standing behind her, Art Cranston put a hand to her shoulder as she said, "Nothing new on the drive yet?" Headshakes. "Your expert's due in today, isn't she? The Chinese woman?"

"Su Teng," Rance said. "You remember her? Tall—

well, my height, anyway. Quite slim. Yes, she should arrive—" He checked his wrist chrono. "—in about two hours, if Earth and time dilation have both kept schedules. I'll go to the terminal early, just for luck."

Maggie's head made the slight nod she could still give. "Oh yes—you two—well, once she's settled in, what are your plans for the drive?"

All of them were watching Rance—and at this point he had only one answer. "When Su has looked it over, I'll ask what she thinks and then tell her what I think. If we can agree on a way to tackle the problem, we'll put it to you for decision." Carefully, he made sure his gaze moved to include both men also.

Sligo cleared her throat; lately she wasn't coughing so much. "I'm due for shots again; my next wake-up's not until tomorrow. If your plan turns out to be a hurry-up thing, don't wait for me. Hanchett, you make the decision."

Jimmy's relief, not unleavened by apprehension, showed all over his face.

Pendergast came with the sedative; Rance nodded to her and left before the others. Back in quarters he looked around, wondering how Su would take to the place. Beige ceiling and light green bulkheads looked clean enough, but he suspected those colors wouldn't survive long once Su had time to consider the matter.

Now, though, was a good time for a nap. Rance took one.

A knock woke him. Full awareness came slowly; feeling a bit fuzzy-minded he went to open the door. Btar entered; without speech she gave him a firm hug, then released him and stepped past, inside, before she said, "I thought we could say goodbye privately, before your Su arrives."

"Uh—look, Btar. I—"

She laughed. "You don't know why, do you? What you mean to me, or anything about it."

"No, I guess I don't." Because they hadn't . . .

As she sat, she made a pouring gesture. Rance blinked. "Wine all right?" She nodded, so he brought out a cold carafe of Chablis and filled a glass for her. Seeing her brows raised, he did the same for himself.

"Cheers?" They touched glasses; each took a sip. Then Rance sat also, and waited.

"Who you are, Rance, is the only person I was able to *talk* with, to tell how I've felt, these past four months, and how bad it was."

"But you don't even know me."

A nod. "True. Which meant, I didn't have to break through the image I'd built, not meaning to, with all the others: the stoic African, the woman nothing can hurt. I could let my hair down." Grinning, between thumb and forefinger she pinched the clipped growth at one temple. "Well, figuratively. So—"

Confused, Rance said, "Your brother? Couldn't—?"

"No, I couldn't. Because when Red left me for Steffi, I took no action against either, nor did I ask Jomo to do so. To his way of thought, I consented to my shaming and had no further right to complain of it. Jomo does love me, but our culture's strictures are stronger in him than they are in me."

"And so?"

"And so, when you new ones came I studied each of you: Jimmy, Fleurine, Dink, and then yourself. You were the one I decided I could trust—and I was right. You heard me out, and let me make up my own mind." She raised her glass. "Bottoms up, don't they say?" And drained her glass. Rance followed suit, then stood when she did and accepted her kiss.

As if on cue they released each other. "Btar, I'm glad you came."

"So am I. And regardless of when I leave, this is our *real* good-bye." Her tone lightened. "When you get back to Earth, send word: how things have gone here on the ship, and all. I'll probably be in Kenya and settled down for years, by then, but I'll keep my address current with NASA. All right?"

"Sure. Maybe I'll come and report personally."

"Better not. I won't be the same person—though I'll still be interested, of course, in the mission's good." Smiling, she touched fingers to his cheek and left. Standing alone now, Rance wondered what it was he hadn't said that bothered him now.

He shook his head, and began sprucing up to meet Su Teng.

* * *

Even in these open-ended Habegger terminals, no one ever saw a thing or person appear or disappear; the change was hidden by a burst of colors from the field-producing elements. The effect wasn't a mere dazzling of the human eye; it also balked any attempt to record the phenomenon by the most sophisticated of cameras, electronic or otherwise. About twenty minutes before his best guess for Su's arrival, Rance went to the terminal area. That deadline came and went; he spent the next endless minutes telling himself he refused to get jittery about the delay. Then colors flared; he blinked, relieved, then saw that only a few cartons and two suitcases had arrived. But as he activated the belt momentarily, to move the luggage, he recognized it and could relax. Jimmy Hanchett, who had been chatting rapidly in apparent effort to calm Rance's nerves, shut up—allowing Rance to do his own calming.

Then colors flickered again—brighter this time—and faded to show Su Teng standing poised, one hand straphanging and the other moving, evidently completing a gesture Rance couldn't interpret. She let go the strap and walked down the belt, then stepped off it and came to Rance. For a skinny woman, he thought, she had a hug like a grizzly.

"I've missed you!" Both said it together, kissed hard, and pulled back for a close face-to-face look. In wonder Rance said, "Only three days, conscious time, since I saw you. But by God, I *feel* those two years we didn't experience."

"I know. I feel the same. . . ." She stopped in mid-phrase; slowly, like a radar antenna on scan, her head moved. "What—? Rance, something's wrong. What is it?"

With Hanchett filling in parts of the situation, Rance told her. Ending with, "So the personnel thing—who's staying on as launch cadre B, is up for grabs some, officially." Actually, Btar's decision pretty well settled the matter, but apparently she hadn't told anyone else yet, so neither did he. "And the drive problem—well, let's get you settled in a little, have a chance to meet everybody. Then you and I can have a look."

* * *

With Jimmy helping, the three of them got Su's things to the compartment with only minor awkwardness. Once everything was set down, more or less out of the way, Hanchett stood as if he weren't sure what to do. Rance waited, and then the man nodded and said, "Okay. See you in the galley in—oh, about an hour?"

Gravely, Rance said, "Or possibly two," and the acting captain left.

The door closed; Su Teng said, "The drive, and all the other difficulties—Rance, you've had three days to consider these things, and Jimmy's had nine more. So before I have to tackle them, too—a little time for *us* first?"

"That's what I had in mind." So twice they went to bed; between times, while getting Su's gear unpacked and stowed, they talked. Afterward, on the way to the galley, they put suitcases and cartons in the room now used for extra storage. Meeting Hanchett, who had everyone present except Sligo, they missed the two-hour guess by only a few minutes.

Jimmy gave everyone, in turn, a chance to talk. Some passed it, on grounds that nothing remained to be said. Finally Su nodded. "I think I understand our situation," she said, "if not, as yet, what may be done about it. But you'll have to pardon me on one count: The deaths are old news to you, but I'm still working through the shock of them."

"Don't apologize," Art Cranston said. "Most of us are, too." He and Takeo Yamata had begun preparing the next meal and were nearly done with the task. Conversation switched to asking Su about the most "recent" events on Earth. Rance grinned; he'd been through that quizzing, and supposed the earlier arrivals had had the course also. Well, nothing like checking all available sources against each other. . . .

Dinner, when they got to it, wasn't the best Rance had tasted aboard ship. Cranston, or maybe Yamata, had an imaginative way with spices: imaginative, yes; restrained, no. Rance ate his full helping anyway, resigning himself to a fairly burpy "evening."

After helping clear the table he led Su back to the transfer and then to Control. At the main console he said, "Look it over first and try any changes you like.

Then, unless you do get the drive active, we may as well brainstorm the problem and see if anything rings a bell."

No one had come with them; Rance had done his best to put thumbs down on that idea the day before. He wanted Su able to concentrate without distractions. Now he watched while she studied the instruments and experimented with operations sequences—including a few that he himself hadn't derived or tried. No luck, though; finally she stepped back and shook her head. He said, quietly, "How's it look to you?"

About the same, it turned out, as it did to him. Nothing wrong with the core plasma: its oscillations were well within normal range; output, though, was zilch. Instrument readings, apparently dependable, showed a quasi-static condition—and from the console no impulses at all seemed to reach or affect the drive's workings.

That was as far as Su carried her analysis. So now Rance told her of his idea, that the FTL shock wave with its time reversals had thrown something analogous to standing waves onto the telemetry systems, locking it into stasis. When he was done, she nodded. "And you have an idea what to do about it?"

"Yes. Do you?"

"I think so. But let's hear yours first."

Fair enough. "Cut power to the telemetry/control network, let the mutually blocking impulses attenuate by the circuits' time constants, then crank up and start over."

"Yes. That's how I see it, too. But why haven't you done this already?"

"Because I don't know that part of the hardware well enough. I'm not sure what else might be affected."

Her hand grabbed his arm and squeezed it. She said, "It's a good thing you're cautious. You'd have killed the drive plasma, too."

To Maggie Sligo next day, Su explained in more detail. The immobilized captain was hurting less now, needing less sedation, and spending more time awake and alert. Also, Rance noted, she had regained considerably better movement of arms and hands. Now the woman said,

"So your problem is how to isolate the power feeds of control circuitry from those of the plasma box itself?"

"Not exactly," said Teng. "It's that the switching functions are *part* of the 'frozen' circuits; there's no way to accomplish such a separation." Rance knew what she meant; it wasn't a matter of wires or cables that could be cut physically. The functions they wanted were located somewhere inside a rather large mass of solid-state microcircuitry; the problem simply could not be attacked in any direct fashion.

"Then what can you do?" Sligo's voice stayed calm.

Su didn't hesitate. "Take advantage of differentials—the differences between the time constants of the drive plasma and those of the control circuits." She paused. "I *think* it will do the trick."

Maggie sighed. "I'm sure it makes sense, what you're saying, but lately my brain works like cold mush. Too much residual glop in the old bloodstream." Sedatives, Rance guessed she meant. Now she blinked, saying, "Collier? You agree with her plan?" He nodded. "Then go try it. You can explain it again later, when you let me know how it comes out. Right now, I'm afraid I'm too tired to care much." Her eyes closed; she may have been asleep before they left the room.

Jimmy Hanchett insisted he should be on hand when Su made her try. As usual he spoke quietly, but Rance detected an intensity behind the words. So, first looking to see if Su intended to make any objection, he decided she didn't, and said, "Okay. But just you, nobody else. And *you don't talk*. Not until Su says we can." Then, sensing the man's feeling of rebuff, he added, "Hell, that goes for me, too." So with the tension eased the three went, via the transfer ring, to Control.

Su took the main console's seat; Rance sat at her right. At first Jimmy stood hovering behind the woman, but Rance looked up and gestured toward the other flanking position; Hanchett gave an apologetic shrug and sat also.

Glancing first to Rance and then to Jimmy, Su smiled. "If we're all settled in comfy, I think I'm ready to take a crack at this obstinate bastard of a ship."

Nobody laughed.

XI

PREDICAMENTS

Slowed to crawl pace, Environ proceeds. Forced away, by impact with unthinkable manifestation Environ must have struck, to angle from former path. Overwatcher Seit makes no correction; so slow is progress that error of diversion is not significant. Otherwise, repairs continue well.

Analysis of damage shows unbelievable result: along slanted plane bisecting Environ and barely missing plasma foursphere itself, lies *seam,* hardly more than molecule's thickness but as if Environ had been sliced apart and rejoined. Careful examination of Liij who were in those parts of Environ shows similar, barely discernible marks. Yet except for shock of disrupted motion accompanying Environ's disaster and shared by all, no harm appears. Only in such finely structured devices as fibered radiance tubes are interfering anomalies found; for most part, functions continue to operate, near-totally unimpaired.

Among all known happenings and results, what could cause such strangeness? Seit's own knowledge contains nothing of help. Rising from its Overwatcher station, Seit proceeds to Environ's repositorum of forebearal observation.

Past due time, it may be, to seek enlightment from vast overall store of Liij experience. From memory bones.

Not that Imon disregards disaster, or importance of remedy as quickly as may be done, but body's growth imperatives struggle to override outside occurrence. Even as Imon works, its efforts guided first by Dutysetter Kahim and at later time by others, ache and throb of belly node command much of its attention. Tev, Imon is certain, must also experience difficulty in keeping mind to tasks.

When duty period ends, Imon seeks out Tev and is pleased that Tev is of same purpose. Time *must* be proper, now, to breed. With hum and chirr of tendrils adding shades of meaning to blunt declaratives that limit mouth-sound ideation, Imon seeks to persuade. < We are (healthwatcher will surely say) ripe. We must (for necessary approval) go. And (also, then) ingest (to sustain for time of juncture) (and joined-node growth) much nutriment. >

Tev responds < Only then can go (Imon, Tev, none others) to nestspace. >

Unison then, mouthsounds alone as palps clasp: < There to breed! >

At base of throat and behind ears, as well as area surrounding belly node, thrill crinkles Imon's skin.

So far past that no record exists, perhaps originally inspired by process that replaces tissue with minerals to form solid, enduring image of life form when life is ended, Liij treated newly dead nervous systems with successive, varying concentrations of semiconductor salts. Whether soon, or after long period of varied trial, nevertheless at some point—long before Liij broke free of home world—memory bones were achieved; these hold direct and derived experience which, even now far after, may be consulted.

Though Liij annals hold incalculable store of observation and conclusions, some are no longer in original form. Memory bones have very long duration of utility but still finite; at certain deteriorative point, best information comes at second hand from later ones who had consulted originals.

Eldest original still of function is Haef, cosmological ideationist who, holding Overwatcher post, built Environ's pace to escape implosive, radiant destruction of home whorl.

Perhaps, thinks Seit, something in Haef's experience of that building may succor Environ now.

Occupied with examination of slightly injured youngthon, healthwatcher first approached by Tev and Imon shuffs them away. < Go (for approval you ask) to another. This moment I cannot (needing more time for youngthon's care) help you. >

Taking leave, they ascend one level, to other healthstation. Healthwatcher there, newly returned from feeding, willingly gives attention and fulfills their expectations of overall fitness. Then by touch and taste and chemical comparisons it judges states of belly nodes and their secretions. < You are each (one neither more nor less, discernibly, than other) breeding-ready. Go now (without need to inform your dutysetter) to chosen nestplace and (having joy of your act) complete this development. >

Expressing grateful satisfaction, they depart station.

In safeplace of records, memory bones occupy special area. For wellbeing, molecular activity must be kept within strict limits, and at all times each requires carefully regulated trickle of power, individually set, to keep it safely quiescent yet available for consultation. Too much, and memories may evolve and develop, losing accuracy; too little, and subtler definitions can be lost. Fine balance is requisite.

Seit is here after long absence; with disuse, its skills have lessened. Rather than first addressing Haef memories, then, Seit chooses to begin by consulting Dron, immediate predecessor under whom it had studied.

Dron, it knows, had often consulted Haef, and may give
Seit help in choosing where, with Haef, to begin.

Entering cubicle in which Dron and four others are
esconsed, Seit adjusts room's single seat to face Dron at
convenient height. Its palp-tips moistened with electrosolute, it inserts both tendril-groups into affixed semiorganic connectors—one for Dron's sensory input,
other for its response—which enable consultation.

Near eyes self-cinctured, ears muffling both far eyes
and themselves, all distraction damped as well as may
be, Seit offers Dron greeting.

Almost as though memory bone yet lived, its acknowledgment has flavor of gladness, of cheer at being
greeted.

Inside nestplace and closing it, Imon sets lighting dim
and weight dwindling to naught. Slowly, they two face
and grasp: hindlimbs twisting to lock and hold, forelimbs clasping to strain bodies together—and between,
belly nodes crushing flat in exquisite, fearful blend of
pain transmuting to joy.

Secretions, pressed forth, spread and mingle; separate beats of throbbing, Imon's and Tev's, slowly change
to match each other until soon their very meeting of
surfaces pulses back and forth in single rhythm.

Long and long this endures, until Imon fears they are
too closely paired, in development, for either to yield
opening for other, radially contracting, to implant.
Stalemate should not be possible; always some slight
difference, given time, allows body choice to occur.

Sensory storm now overfloods; willingly Imon sinks
from active thought to sheer acceptance of body's rag-
ings.

Until, time-uncounted later: choice *IS*.

Strange, to consult memory bone and be *recognized;*
not certain how to proceed, Seit greets Dron as though
alive, then quickly shifts to telling of Environ's mishap
and current plight, asking for pertinent facts Dron may
have. But Dron, responses sensed as if made by mouth
and palps, only compounds questions.

Environ slowed, in catastrophic haste, from many

times pace of radiance to crawl of lazing matter? < How came this? Why? >

Marks detected, showing Environ cut clean through, along uniform plane, yet rejoined with almost no harm? < How possible? When (in experience of any) (throughout all Liij history) has such thing ever happened? >

Here in zone of matter rarity, how to rebuild pace? < Never (since Liij migration [endless] began) has such been needed. And then from (matter-rich) place of origin. So, how indeed? >

Has Dron ever consulted with one who might know? Finally, now, comes answer. < Haef (Overwatcher at leaving of home whorl) has experienced great building of pace. >

Uncomfortable with memory bone which gives feeling of living Liij, self-consciously Seit transmits thanks before disconnecting.

Yet feels glow of progress. Skills now are of better ease, and Dron confirms Seit's choice of Haef as source of aid.

Pulsing back and forth, of area where nodes press together, heightens in vigor, until at each change Imon expects movement to surge resistlessly and not reverse. Until at one push toward Imon, its node trembles and almost gives way—but then from inside that node comes *thrust*, which carries through, not stopping. Tev's node softens and expands radially, leaving thinness at center that Imon's node, contracting, penetrates.

In ecstasy and relief, Tev and Imon both feel onslaught of rapid change. From porous tips of both nodes, secretions spread back to coat node surfaces—Tev's now inverted to receive and contain Imon's—distributing complementary genetic templates, which then over entire near-spherical intersurface unite into complete cells.

Not quite forming closed sphere, the new growing organism: to begin, necessary opening exists at base of Imon's node where lip edge of Tev's new concavity now constricts, and another at Tev's center depth which had been tip. But as hollow proto-Liij grows, thickening as it feeds both from Imon's central node and Tev's now-outer one, two things must occur.

First, over next several sleep-cycles constriction will narrow connection of Imon's node until in final ecstasy it separates and drops away; with climactic release, then, role of seeder completes.

Next, later by a *dre*'s quarter part, the growing Liijling, having absorbed all nutriment from both parental nodes, comes free of its birther and rids itself of nodal husks, inner being ejected as outer sloughs away. So it occurs that Tev's part, also, comes to end.

But now, and for long joyous time to come, Tev and Imon clasp in pleasure. Strain is past; present is only sweetness.

Not until two *dre* after parenting do breeding nodes regrow to function. Next breeding stage, Imon's ripeness will appear well ahead of Tev's. From this cause, seldom does any Liij share same two genitors with another.

Converse with Haef differs from that with Dron. So old now, leached of living personality, this memory bone provides only impersonal data. Relating situation in detail, Seit solicits evaluation. But Haef responds with little or nothing not already known to Seit. One suggestion may be of aid: to link ship's farsensors with electrologic integrators in fashion to route Environ through regions of overall maximum matter density during any next immediate period of at least one *dre*.

No great advantage, this, but better than none. With touch of slight amusement, since memory bone no longer holds any trace of personhood, Seit closes consultation with thanks.

Preparing to leave recordsplace, Seit receives summons from Chorl, who teaches. Bare meaning, limit of signal device capability, is < Seit come Chorl> plus place of origin.

In accordance, Seit goes to meet Chorl at upper studyspace. Chorl is older—still with many *dre* left for learning and teaching, but long past expectation of again-ripening belly node. Reaching destination and entering, Seit finds Chorl peering at and palping studyversion of navigational farsensor. Curious, Seit asks < Why do you (for what especial reason) summon me? And what (which of many possibilities) do you seek with that (specialized, non-utile in routine starplacing) instrument? >

< To tell you (as Overwatcher) > says Chorl < what I find (that may explain much) by this individual (detecting not mere radiance but much else) sensing array. >

< What (of importance I would realize also) is found? >

< Origin and terminus, perhaps (barring unlikely yet still ever-present possibility of coincidence) of that which Environ struck. >

< First, what (in terms known to both of us) *did* Environ come (with such devastating effect) upon? >

Chorl pauses. < You know (among phenomena we have each here studied) of thin (molecule's width) yet massive (as world compressed to thinness) strands. >

Seit does know: "mattergy" from primal moment, spun out to threadlike form, drifting through spacetime in silent menace. Not to be seen or sensed, those strands, by normal means. Only by *effects,* to be detected—and Environ's sensors found no such.

No, but—< Pseudostrand > says Chorl. < Not from Birth of All (raw stuff of emerging universe in violent collapse) but some type of (strange, not understood) *constructed* thing. >

< How (what proof?) know you this? >

Eagerly Chorl shows instrument records: views lateral from Environ's path, before and during and after catastrophe. And if *not* coincidence, then plane of Environ's bisection is determined by line between two things observed.

< To one end (note direction) is star with worlds. To other (directly opposite) is object, departing Environ's nearness at pace approximate to radiance. >

< Object (evident only by emissions not found in nature) in motion not from natural force but (conclusion derived from character of emissions) by use of (high-level) energy. >

Observing recorded data, Seit cannot but agree. One point puzzles: < It is correct (understood, generally accepted) that strands naturally occurring (drifting as vectors dictate) pose no danger (may be detected, thus avoided) to Environ? >

< That conclusion is, to our knowledge (in past occasions, limited in scope and number), true. >

< This one, then (why different?), Chorl? >

< Verdict (only partially clarified) of instruments is that given Environ's proceeding (as Environ did not) at pace less than radiance, detection and avoidance (of this, as yet still hypothetical, fabricated strand) ensues. Also, at such pace (all prior Liij ideation predicates) no damage befalls Environ. >

Standing back from close observation, Seit touches palps with Chorl. < My (warmth and pleasure) gratitude, Chorl. I will consider (strive for understanding and useful mastery) these ideations further. >

Leaving, carrying recordmark plates for study, Seit visits briefly at central aggregate of duty stations, seeing that among navigationists, instrumentators, and the like, all proceeds normally. Imon and Tev, it knows, have finally sequestered to breed; to their joy Seit gives fleeting wellwish. At goal, in nestspace, feeding from nutriment stores Overwatcher is privileged to maintain, Seit ponders; without volition, movement of mouth and palps accompanies thought.

< This object, moved (in what fashion?) by energy: Liij (since all Liij are on Environ) did not build.

< Who, then? >

XII

ADJUSTMENTS

Su didn't play around; with one abrupt move she pulled the main switch. Instrument lights dimmed, glowing only from residual current in the "wave-clogged" circuits. Digital indicators flipped through meaningless figures, then some began to steady. Plasma activity showed decline, but slowly; when it approached the redline warning of shutdown, Su threw power back on. Briefly *Starfinder* bucked, but the drive had only hiccupped.

She nodded. "See? Blockage action is down. It's slower; you can tell by the blinking on the outage lamps. And putting the power on didn't start it building back again. But the plasma, you'll notice, *is* rebuilding."

She looked at neither man, but both nodded—and stayed silent. Again she cut power, and as before, just short of plasma shutdown, restored it. If she had her theory right, she'd made further progress. "Some more, then." She hit the cycle another time, and another, and—

On the sixth restart a hum grew; the ship surged, and Rance felt his chair back pressing gently. He scanned indicators, and whooped. "You did it! The drive's working!"

Coping with hugs from Rance and Jimmy at the same time, she said, "Well, you *said* it would, if I could clear those damned circuits."

Su pleaded hunger; Rance accompanied her to the galley. Hanchett, after posting Christy Frost and Jomo Mbente to the reinstituted Control watch, went to give Maggie Sligo a full report. When he returned to join Su and Rance, he said, "A little punchy, Maggie is, but she got the gist of it." To Su, "She wants a full writeup of the phenomenon and how you handled it. To take with her, back to Earth." He filled a cup with coffee, and sat.

"Rance," Su said, "I need your help with that report. You diagnosed the problem; all I did was figure what to do about it."

He squeezed her hand. "That's what teamwork's about." To Jimmy, "You're in charge now?" The man nodded. "What particular plans do you have in mind?"

Hanchett cleared his throat. "Reinstating the watch schedule as much as I can before we know for sure who's leaving."

Puzzled, Rance decided Btar still hadn't told anyone else her decision. *Oh, well* . . . "Not much of a problem, is it?"

"Yes and no. *Starfinder* splits the standard twenty-four-hour day into three watch periods. At any time, out of a four-person watch group, two will be on duty. That gives each person eight hours' duty every two days. On the average, that is. I want to rotate personnel—teams within a group, short-term, and pairs *between* groups every so often—so that everyone's skills have a chance to rub off on everybody else." He grinned. "And that does take some juggling."

Nadine Potter, bringing a cup of coffee to the table, chuckled. "Sounds like a nice lazy sked, doesn't it?"

"If standing watch were all, it would be," Hanchett cut in. "But there's a lot more, remember, to keeping a ship running. As is, mind you, we'll not be overworked. Though after the Ali Saud mess, running shorthanded, I guess things did get sticky sometimes. Now, however . . ." He shrugged. "Once I get the setup figured, it should run on tracks pretty well."

"Yes," said Rance. "And right now, what else needs doing?"

A frown creased Hanchett's forehead. "We've lost ground—both speed and distance—from what Earth expects. Rough-guessing from computer simulations, I've tried to figure how to get us back on sked." He shook his head. "Not sure I have it dead cert, of course. But if we set drive to buck us up to dot-nine-nine-six of lightspeed for a spell—time dilation of eleven rather than ten—we should catch up before too long."

"You'll check progress by matching our own chrono time against the outside view?" said Rance. Jimmy nodded. *Yes, that should work.*

"But why bother?" Nadine asked. "On a trip covering light-decades, what does it matter if we slip behind a little?"

Jimmy didn't answer immediately, so Rance said, "Distance isn't that important, actually. But velocity is, because that's what determines our time ratio. And if *that's* off by much, so's our supply rate: fuel, food, the whole lot."

Nadine wasn't satisfied. "They could change the rate, couldn't they?"

"You're forgetting," Su Teng said. "Earth's always two years—and two light-years—behind whatever we know aboard here. That makes four years turnaround communication time." Then, correcting herself: "Of course that's only about five months, ship's time, but still—"

Hanchett nodded. "Right. For everybody's benefit, it behooves us to meet schedule."

Going by Nadine's expression she still wasn't sure it made all that much difference; but why argue?

Benita Torres, when the time came, arrived safely and not too far behind expectation. To start with, she was briefed on ship's problems including such solutions as had been reached, and quizzed on any late-breaking Earthside news. When, eventually relenting, Hanchett excused Torres from further grilling, she and Dink Hennessey left posthaste. Well, Dink had been aboard, solo, for all of nine days now. . . .

Two days later, after reading Su and Rance's report concerning drive repairs, asking additional questions and making note of the answers, Maggie Sligo decided it was time to wrap up. She had Jimmy Hanchett send word ahead through the pipeline, to Earth, and call council in the galley; intercom viewscreens allowed "attendance" by Art Cranston and Nadine Potter on watch and by Sligo herself, along with Btar who had sickbay duty.

Once the group assembled, Hanchett gave Maggie the floor. The screen was off-color, but Rance thought she looked more alert than he'd yet seen her. She began, "Hello. I *hate* to leave this way, but I'm no damn good to this ship and I know it. Back on Earth they can get me working a lot faster—if anyone can, at all. And Btar here—" Weakly she gestured toward the Kenyan woman, who stood at bedside. "She's going with me." *Well, about* time *that decision was announced!* "It might as well be today. So to the rest of you, all the best luck I can wish. Now I'll shut up and let *Captain* Jimmy Hanchett carry on from here."

There wasn't much Jimmy could say, Rance felt, that Rance hadn't already heard—but he listened anyway. Because he might have missed some points, or the skipper might surprise him with something new. But all he said was, "One thing you can tell 'em, Maggie. That if anything like this happens again, the FTL backlash or whatever, we'll be ready for it."

To Rance and Su, where they sat together, he gave a wink.

At meeting's end, Sligo directed that her hardware be rearranged so she could be carted, frame and all, to the pipeline terminal. No point, she said, in drawn-out farewells. So except for Art and Nadine on watch, the entire crew trooped to help with her duffel, and Btar's. "Make sure everything goes safely into Habegger's Mouth," said Maggie; Rance decided not to ask what she called the output terminal.

Liz Pendergast made final adjustments to Sligo's traction links, then clamped them to the frame and disconnected the outer, now-superfluous ends. With four persons to lift and carry, Maggie rode her framework to the terminal area and was lowered onto the entrance belt. Then, one by one, each crew member said goodbye to her and to Btar. Jomo and Christy first, to relieve Cranston and Potter from watch for their own farewells.

Rance had never really known Maggie. Now he saw that by those who had, she was not only liked and respected; she was loved. In his own turn he said only, "Best of luck on Earth. We'll take good care of *Starfinder*."

And along with a hug, said much the same to Btar.

Cranston, at the last, couldn't hide his tears. "I wish you could come, too," said Maggie. "But you know as well as I do, you're *needed* here." Then, all good-byes said, she told Jimmy Hanchett, "All right. May as well move it."

"Right." He put the belt into motion. When it stopped, the two women more or less centered in the Mouth, Btar waved a hand and Sligo tried to. Then the colors flared; when they faded, both were gone.

More than three weeks the ship had coasted, dead and slowing. Now Hanchett needed to recoup: first velocity and then distance. For his first move he cranked the drive up to twenty percent above normal "holding" thrust, and over the next few days, monitored velocity change. "The way we do that," he explained, "is by the distortion factor: how much 'English' the computer has to put on its sensor data from outside to give us a 'real' picture onscreen." All this was something Rance hadn't studied, but he assumed it made sense.

When vee crept up to .996 of c (time ratio roughly eleven, Rance remembered) Jimmy cut drive to normal. "We'll hold this until my best guess says we've made up distance, then drop drive level enough to ease vee back to nine-nine-five."

Figuring distance was something else again. There were two clues. One was relative position of "marker" stars on the outside view as corrected; for that method, no one claimed any great accuracy. Nor for the other:

rear sensors' measurement, corrected for velocity, of old Sol's brightness. Each set of data carried a fair-to-hefty error margin, but both together, showing reasonable overlap, gave a good horseback estimate.

And one day Jimmy said, "We're as close to sked, I think, as makes no difference," then set all controls back to normal.

On the initial watch roster, Su and Rance drew shift with Art Cranston and Nadine Potter. Under Jimmy's six-day partner rotation scheme, each person worked three of the six but in varying order. Rance, for instance, began his six-day "week" with a day off, stood watch with Su and then with Cranston, had two more days off and ended with Nadine.

Jimmy, Fleurine, Jomo, and Christy formed the team that followed them on duty; the third was Takeo Yamata, Pendergast, Dink, and Benita. Jimmy planned to rotate, monthly, one pair of each team, forming new ones "to spread the expertise around better." Maggie had done much the same, and until the troubles hit, it worked pretty well. So why mess with a good thing?

Ali Saud had messed with it plenty; so had the FTL wake. By plan, Takeo and Liz and Nadine would be enroute to Earth now, along with Ali and Steffi Holm and Hans Niebuhr. The B cadre intended for this six-month hitch consisted of Maggie with Art Cranston, Btar with Red Macdougall, and Jomo with Christy. As it was, though, three from each section were still aboard.

Except for Cranston and Potter, everyone was paired and sharing quarters. How it went with those two, Rance wondered but didn't feel like asking. It wouldn't have bothered him, except that on duty with Nadine every sixth day, he felt tension he couldn't ignore. Sitting on the unasked question, eight hours at a stretch waiting for that tension to pop, gave him no comfort.

Then one day, after instrument readings and log entries passed routine check, Nadine said, "I had no idea how thin it was for Btar, left alone, until now when I'm in the same boat."

"Well, not exactly." Rance tried to sound both cheerful and impersonal. "At least now we have even numbers."

"Do you really think that helps?" Flat-voiced, "In bed, Art and I don't get along." She didn't say why, and no reason she should.

Still, the exchange left Rance even less at ease than before. He had the distinct feeling that Potter was leading up to something; more to the point, he wasn't at all ready for it.

What he had to do, Rance decided, was talk to Su and get some fresh input. Back in quarters after his shift ended, he tried to open the subject but found himself saying nothing much at considerable length. Until Su broke in: "So you feel that Nadine is smitten with you?"

"Well, not exactly, but—"

The glint of her eye told him he was in for it. "And why, do you suppose, are *you* so irresistible?"

He felt his face warming. "It's not—well, Liz never lets Takeo out of her sight, and whatever it is that's bothering Christy, she needs all the support Jomo can manage."

Su nodded. "And being on different watch teams, Nadine hasn't actually gotten to know Dink or Jimmy."

"I guess that's right."

"So it is by default that you become her prince on the white horse." Feeling sheepish, he nodded. "But surely you don't think Nadine intends to take you all for herself?"

"Well, no, but—"

"Of course not. What she would propose, I imagine, is a sharing. And in this, would she have your agreement?"

The hell of it was, he partly liked the idea and partly didn't, and maybe that was what itched him. More truthfully than not he answered, "Only if she had yours. Because—"

Headshake. "Oh, stop it! Don't come asking mommie if you can stay overnight with the little girl next door. It's your decision; make it."

"Without knowing how you feel, I can't."

"Then don't." But her expression softened. "Give it a little time; see how you really feel. All right?"

Relieved, he agreed. The next five days, before his and Nadine's next shift, he stayed out of her way. When they did report for duty, taking over for Dink and Liz, she headed straight to Hennessey, and the two moved off for a private chat.

Off the hook! Oddly, Rance wasn't sure whether he felt gratified or disappointed.

So much had happened so fast, aboard ship, that Rance simply gave no thought to Earth. Routinely the pipeline's various outlets fed *Starfinder* fuel and all life-support needs, along with other supplies. But in the way of communications, nothing whatsoever.

Over his first few weeks, Rance came to take that situation for granted. Until one day, near the end of the first month, Hanchett called assembly in the lounge—with Art and Su, on duty in Control, watching by intercom.

With the others gathered and seated, Jimmy turned on the lounge's playback screen and inserted a dataview capsule. "I don't know what this is," he said, "but the label says to play it immediately, to the entire crew. So here goes."

He thumbed a switch; the screen lit, to show Senator Wallin with Bill Flynn alongside him. Behind them sat various other dignitaries; Rance recognized perhaps three.

Wallin spoke. "Greetings to *Starfinder*. Here, it's the same day you left orbit. To you it's—let's see—two years of Earth time gives you a year for our next fifteen months, plus a tenth of the following nine, so you're nearly a month since your first relief cadre arrived." He turned aside. "Do I have that right?" Apparently reassured, he nodded. "So I greet Captain Sligo's section, still with five months to go aboard your ship. And Executive Officer Jimmy Hanchett's group will be settled by now, with most of your ship duty year still to come."

And, thought Rance, *don't we wish you had all* that *right!*

"I realize," the senator said, "that shipboard life may get monotonous. You stand your watches, log instrument readings, and cope with the perpetual round of maintenance. You may come to feel like mere caretakers, trading fourteen years' absence from Earth for seeing *Starfinder* ten light-years closer to its goal. You may wonder if it's all worth it."

What's he trying to do? Kill morale completely?

"If ever you do—then remember our *goals*. Getting *Starfinder* to its F-type star is only the first phase. There may be a habitable planet with all its glories, even intelligent life: neighbors. Gates could move colonists and equipment to their new homes as easily as you receive fuel and food.

"But even if that star disappoints us, a big step will have been taken. Because then the great 'shipshooter' Gate *Starfinder* carries can be assembled in orbit. So that other ships can come through, in two years' Earth time but subjectively none at all, to *begin* exploration with a thirty-light-year head start."

Thirty-one, actually, but close enough . . .

"We envision a vast web of Habegger Gatepaths, from Earth to the ones placed by your ship and others soon to follow, and from those to second-stage outposts. There is," he emphasized, "no foreseen, finite end to our ongoing effort."

Now Rance got the point. This speech was aimed every bit as much to the American public as it was to *Starfinder*!

"So congratulations," Wallin continued, "to each of you. That's really all we have to say, just now. Wanted to let you know we won't be forgetting you. Now that you're on track again, timewise, you'll be getting news from here as it happens. So the best of luck, and I know you'll keep up the good work."

In a way, Rance supposed, Wallin's message was pure PR fluff. But somehow it made him feel good—and looking around the group, he saw that feeling reflected.

The second month, Hanchett's shift realignments put Su and Rance with Jomo and Christy. Whatever had worn Frost down, earlier, now her looks and animation were recovering. Rance could hardly say so to her face, but was glad to see the change.

Actually he had enough other, unrelated worries to keep him occupied. For one, the fuel situation. The initial constant flow, needed during the months of acceleration, had been cut drastically when *Starfinder*, strictly on sked, leveled off to merely holding speed against the slight drag of interstellar gas. Due to the four-year lag, by Earth timing, in round-trip communication—as Rance had told Congressman Bill Flynn—the constant-vee quota was set to give an estimated ten percent leeway, any surplus to be vented if need be.

The way Hanchett heard it was that until the accident, the system had worked fine. Then, with the drive down and tanks full, for three weeks all input went straight out the spout.

"The catch was," Jimmy said, he and Rance having a brandy off-duty, "the business of catching up to schedule. We were slowed, near as I could guess, almost to nine-nine-zero."

"Ummm." Then Rance nodded. "Time-ratio seven. So—"

"So when we started up again, pouring on extra power to rebuild vee, we were getting seven tons of fuel for every ten we were supposed to get. Counting in the intentional surplus, about three-quarters. Of mere vee-maintenance quota, at that. So getting up to nine-nine-six, we ran the tanks from full to nearly empty."

"But now we're leveled off, aren't we? So the ten percent surplus factor—"

"Ten percent crack-ass!"

"I don't understand. What—?"

"What we've run into, Rance, not even a bloody light-year out, is higher density. Greater resistance."

"The interstellar gas?"

Hanchett nodded, and Rance thought, *Yes. Oh, hell, yes.* With full tanks, as planned, it wouldn't matter. But nobody anticipated the drive being down for three weeks, and the ship slowing. Now, with tanks low, any extra drag was trouble. Rance thought, and said, "Restarting the drive when the fault was in the control circuits, that was one thing. If it goes dead from running out of fuel—well, we're cooked. I wouldn't have the slightest idea where to begin."

Hanchett nodded. "I thought so." His face twitched. "We needn't tell the others, just yet. Right?"

"No. Of course not." Racing, his thoughts wouldn't settle down. "We have to keep speed; slowing, letting the time ratio drop again, would only lose us more fuel."

"I don't know how long—"

"Put the computer on it. Set it to hold vee—just that, nothing more—taking advantage of any less-dense belts to save fuel." He shrugged. "After that, Jimmy, I just don't know."

He left; from then on he made it a point to monitor gains and losses in fuel levels. Seldom did the readings cheer him.

The third month's watch roster put Rance and Su with Yamata and Pendergast. Each seemed impenetrable to close acquaintance, and for different reasons. Reserved and quiet, the man spoke only with respect to the needs of watch duty. Liz, seemingly open in her volubility, never gave a hint of her own thoughts or feelings.

It wasn't as though their remotenesses could really matter. But on other teams he'd more or less liked Cranston, felt considerable empathy toward Nadine, and become moderately fond of Jomo and Christy. But with Pendergast and Yamata, Rance had the nagging feeling that the thermostat in Control needed turning up.

Well, the hell with it. He had work to do; his life and Su's were meshing well; Jimmy for the time being had *Starfinder* on the thin edge of operational status, and the rest of it could go jump. That's how Rance Collier saw it.

After a period of increased outside drag brought fuel supplies perilously low, the ship had respite; a few days of lesser gas-density allowed the tanks to build a moderate reserve. But coming so close, the dodged bullet gave Rance a real scare. So that no part of his mind could leave it alone.

They had undressed, he and Su—were sprawled on the bed to play the slow, teasing game of rising passion, bare seconds from one or other giving way to tension and moving in earnest—when a sudden thought froze Rance to immobility. Feeling his face go blank he sat up and waved away Su's questions. "I have to go. Go see Jimmy."

"Jimmy?"

"Yes. Tell you later."

Hanchett was no more pleased than Su. By no means *en flagrante*, obviously he and Fleurine had in mind the same idea Rance and Su had been pursuing.

Not bothering to mask annoyance, Jimmy asked Rance what the hell *he* wanted. Determinedly courteous, Fleurine offered coffee. Rance ignored both. "Why can't we slow the ship down?"

Hanchett sputtered. "Is that what—? Hell, you know as well as I do."

"Tell me."

"Are you popping alkaloids? We can't slow down because the time ratio would give us even less fuel than we're getting now."

"Precisely." Now Rance did accept the cup Fleurine was holding, and sat. *"So why don't we speed up?"*

"You *are* nuts, aren't you?"

"First, hear me out. . . ."

According to the computer, *Starfinder's* tanks held fuel to get vee back up to dot-nine-nine-six, or nearly. The move was risky but they tried anyway—and with very little margin, made it. At that point, by virtue of a time ratio that had climbed to eleven-dot-two, and no significant stretches of higher-D gas, fuel tank levels had actually risen.

So *when you're on a roll:* Jimmy Hanchett cranked up his drive activity until it pushed to a vee of nine-nine-seven, then -seven-five, and finally to nine-nine-eight. With time ratio approaching sixteen and fuel intake roughly seventy-five percent above the standard vee-maintenance quota, while usage exceeded that level by a mere thirty percent, the tanks kept on gaining.

When they reached half-full, Rance reported: "Jimmy, you can slow down now, get back to sked."

Any vast waves of overwhelming gratitude that Hanchett may have felt, he hid nicely. "And lose all the advantage we've just accumulated?"

"You won't." Jimmy's sour mood didn't bother Rance a bit. "If you cut drive to minimum, to make the decel, then until we level off we keep practically *all* the fuel input."

"If you say so. But after all this superhigh vee we've

been running, how in hell do I program to match sked again?"

"Su can do it." Rance turned to leave; then another, more personal thought turned him back. "In an hour or so, that is."

Whistling, he made his exit.

XIII

VISITORS

Free of his preoccupation with the fuel crisis, Rance began to notice other happenings. Despite the unfortunate results of previous liaisons aboard ship, they definitely seemed to be making a comeback.

Except for his inconclusive episode with Btar, and the time of unvoiced pressure from Nadine, Rance himself had received no offers. Nor had Su mentioned any. Nadine, he knew, had a share of Dink Hennessey's attentions. Benita at one point moved her belongings and roomed alone—but the estrangement, if that's what it was, lasted only a few days.

Starting his third shipboard month, he and Su sharing watch with Jimmy and Fleurine, Rance noticed that off duty those two were seen singly more often than together. What it meant, if anything, he didn't know and didn't ask.

Also, Art Cranston seemed to be around Liz Pender-

gast a lot, giving Takeo Yamata opportunity to attend
Nadine. Remembering the Ali Saud calamity, Rance
worried more than a little about this new round of musical beds, but except for occasional outbreaks of hot-
house politeness, nothing untoward occurred.

Fervently he hoped that nothing would.

The first samplings of Earth news, events happening
after the ship's departure, had everyone interested. But
once the novelty was gone, the reports appearing in
Starfinder's compressed time seemed like a speeded-up
cartoon sequence; Rance, for one, ceased to take them
seriously. A "war scare," obviously more of a media
event than genuine threat, might well have been fright-
ening and suspenseful in real time. But with a month of
it arriving in three days, the herky-jerky sensationaliz-
ing was far too evident. And much other headline material came out looking equally contrived.

The new U.S. president, no friend to the space program, caused a certain amount of anxiety—until two
months into session, five days by ship's time, Congress
made it clear the new man had little clout on Capitol
Hill.

After a time, all news from Earth took on an air of
unreality. Not only was it running on Fast Forward; it
was also two years out of date.

Near the end of Rance's third shipboard month came
time for the ship's one scheduled course change. A direct shot to its destination star (a slightly dimmer version of Sol—somehow Rance wished it had a name, not
merely a catalog number) would pass through fringes of
a visible dust cloud. To avoid the cloud's frictional drag,
Starfinder's route took a jog around those fringes.

Turning the ship was no great piloting chore. Ordi-
narily its three drive nodes produced equal thrust, but
to change course, the "outside" had to push harder than
the "inside."

Given time, the math for assigning thrust values to
each node wasn't all that formidable, but it was hardly
something a pilot could do on the spot. Luckily, the
computer could: just crank in magnitude and direction
of the desired swing, and regardless of the nodes' posi-

tions with respect to the turn's axis, *Starfinder* obediently made a smooth, controlled arc.

All this stuff was totally outside Rance's fields of study, and Jimmy Hanchett was obviously getting a big kick out of quizzing him about it and watching him squirm. "So," Jimmy went on, "what's the energy requirement?"

"Energy? But you're not changing speed. . . ."

Wrong answer; velocity is speed *and* direction; change either, and it costs you. *Yes, all right.* Amount of decel along the original course, related to cosine of the turn angle. Accel perpendicular to that course, sine function. "And either you add enough thrust to make up for those, or lose a lot of speed."

"Is this going to put us back in a fuel bind, or not?"

"Not." Rance's relief was tempered; Jimmy hadn't finished explaining. "If we didn't have some mass around to help us, we'd be in tough. But we do. So we can make a kind of sling turn."

"Around what?"

"The dust cloud. The way it's coalesced, so far, it has to have enough mass to form a star eventually. Right now, hidden in the middle, there's probably all kinds of aggregated matter."

"If you say so." And Jimmy did make the turn okay. . . .

But on the eighth day after the turn was made, *Starfinder* hit another FTL wake. Or so it seemed. This time the impact effect was minor: for only seconds, chronometers bucked back; Traction Drive hesitated momentarily, then resumed operation.

Helping Jimmy word the report for Earth, Rance speculated: "Those things can't be all that big. What are the odds against our hitting two of them?"

"What difference does it make? We did, didn't we?"

"Or maybe the same one twice. If it paralleled our *average* course, in reverse, but cut straight through the dust cloud, we could have crossed it again. And this time it was a lot weaker—which could mean spread out, attenuated. *Older.*"

Hanchett shrugged. "I'll include the suggestion if you like. Though what they'll make of it, I can't imagine."

Rance felt one eyebrow lift. "Well, they might decide

to keep an eye on things out this way. In case something's homing in on them."

His and Su's watch-month with Dink and Benita brought no special problems. The sixth month, then, put them back with Cranston and Potter. When that tour ended, give or take a bit if *Starfinder* weren't precisely back on sked, relief cadre B would begin arriving —and all original crew members still aboard could go home. To arrive six and a quarter years after "launch"— seven, since Rance had entered the pipeline. And *Starfinder* five and a half light-years on its way.

Well, with luck, closing in on five any week now.

Three weeks early, Habegger's Tush gave signal. Among those gathered to see what was happening, Rance blinked away aftermath of the color-glare, stared, and wondered who was going nuts around here! For hobbling off the exit belt, with the aid of a woman in nurse's whites and carrying hand crutches, came Senator Wallin.

He seemed no older than before, but at Wallin's age a person didn't change much. Looking around, the senator caught Rance's gaze and nodded in recognition; probably, Rance thought, his was the only familiar face in the crowd. He stepped forward, waited while the old man freed his hand for shaking, and did the honors.

"Senator! You're looking well. But why—?" Which was to say, except that he couldn't bring himself to do so, what in the living hell did an octogenarian think he was doing, saddling a starship with responsibility for his health and well-being?

"Hello, Rance. I'll brief the whole crew at once, later; saves time." He grinned. "Right now, take me to your coffee. And by the way—" He nodded toward the nurse. "This is Maxine Durand, my keeper. Maxine—Rance Collier."

He paused to let her register on him: thin; fortyish; medium height; triangular face; brown, curly hair. Briefly the two shook hands. Then, one on either side of Wallin as others carried the newcomers' luggage, they set off for the transfer ring.

Surprising Rance, the senator seemed no stranger to

zero gee; his economical movements showed familiarity with Velcro soles. Just in case, though, Rance kept a guiding hold on the near arm.

In the transfer ring Wallin had little trouble bracing himself at the right times and in proper direction. When ring and Belt matched speed, they all trooped along to the galley.

Except for Art and Nadine on watch, the entire crew assembled. Jomo and Christy, who hadn't joined the group at the terminal, had coffee waiting, and a snack tray. Rance made introductions all around, including Cranston and Potter via intercom. Then, turning to the senator, "You're up to bat."

"Hmmph, yes." Wallin looked around the room. "First off, this is an inspection tour, of sorts. A short one —three days, maybe a week. Well, that's the official excuse. Unofficially I simply wanted to set foot on this ship, in deep space, before I die—and I had the clout to swing it." He faced around to Rance. "I did about a month on *Jovian-Two,* by the way. Left Earth shortly after we did the launch day transmission to you." He smiled. "Good timing; I caught the ship just starting back from its farthest out, and was aboard long enough to watch the Neptune fly-by on the way in. Something to see, that was."

Leaning forward, the senator continued. "As you know, our major, long-term goal is a *network* of terminals; in fact, my first order of business is to warn you that in a day or so you'll start receiving components for assembling another pair."

"Connecting to where?" Hanchett asked.

"To *Roamer,* our second star probe. Due to leave four months after I did. You've heard about it." Well, yes, Rance thought; it had been on the news. But not quite real, somehow.

"So, Rance." Wallin jarred him loose from reverie. "How far out would it be, by now?"

Thinking fast: *twenty months by Earth time; that's fifteen in accel and five more cruising,* Collier came up with an answer. "About eleven light-months. Which puts them roughly four light-years behind *us.*"

Wallin chuckled. "Not behind, exactly. Their course points more than ninety degrees away from this ship's."

"Destination?" Jimmy asked.

"I don't recall the star's number. A little brighter than Sol, and almost forty light-years out."

"But once our new terminals are working," Su said, "we could go directly to that ship, and vice versa."

Then she frowned. "Why?"

"Flexibility," the senator replied. "In case you or *Roamer*, or some other ship in future, runs into unexpected trouble the way you did, there'll be more options."

"Trouble," said Hanchett. "Sir, I'm not sure I have the timing straight. When you left Earth, what was the latest word you had from this ship?"

"You'd solved your fuel problem, was the last big item. But maybe you mean the other kind of trouble. I was on my *Jovie-II* jaunt when Saud and his two victims were returned; didn't learn of that fiasco until later, because NASA put a lid on it. Then of course when Niebuhr and Sligo and Mbente got home, school was out." He glared. "What I want to know is: in the framework of the group-marriage formality, have you had any further problems of that sort? Even incipient?"

Red-faced, Hanchett shook his head but said nothing. Rance spoke. "According to Btar Mbente, Saud had hidden insecurities he couldn't handle, isolated out like this in time and space both. Now I wouldn't say we've all been disgustingly straitlaced aboard here—"

From the intercom, Nadine's voice: "*You* sure as hell have! I hinted like crazy, and all you did was polish your halo."

Feeling his own face warm as Wallin suppressed a grin, Rance tried to pass the remark lightly. "Maybe— but what's a party without a party pooper?" He heard Nadine chuckle, probably despite herself, and continued. "My point was that this present gang seems to handle a little hanky-panky without too much stress. Near as I can tell, I mean."

Waiting for reaction, Wallin stared around the room. When his look met Benita's, the woman shrugged. "It came up antsy for a while, but I got over it." Hennessey squeezed her shoulder; she looked to him and smiled.

The old man nodded. "Any comments?" None came; he said, "Then for the moment that's all I have here.

Captain Hanchett, I'd like to confer with you privately." Then, as though in afterthought: "You come along too, Collier."

With Maxine Durand at Wallin's elbow the four left the galley. First, Rance and Jimmy deposited the visitors' luggage in the compartment, newly cleared of miscellaneous storage, assigned to them; then, on to captain's digs. Once inside and everyone seated, Hanchett said, "All right, sir. What's up?"

Wallin said, "Give me a minute. I'm still getting used to the idea of where I am. And when."

Collier realized, then, why Wallin hadn't aged. Their last meeting—how long ago? By Earth time it had to be six years and a bit. But relativity or no, what with three jumps through Habegger pipelines, the bit was all the senator had actually *lived.* Preoccupied, Rance spoke his conclusion aloud, and Wallin nodded. "That's right. Since we last saw each other you've aged—oh, call it six months. For me it's been roughly five."

But on Earth, more than six years. Yes, there was more than one way to trick time. Now Wallin said, "At my age, healthy or not, I could go like *that.* " Snapped fingers. "So, can you think of a better way for a curious man to follow a project past his normal Earthbound life span, and see how it all comes out? Matter of fact, when I go back again I'll debrief for a week or so and then hit the pipeline for *Roamer.* Unless you get your new Gate installed soon enough for me to route *by way of* that ship."

Fascinated, Hanchett and Collier asked questions. How could a *senator* go gallivanting through spacetime this way? Easy. With his state's governor pledged to appoint Congressman Bill Flynn to the Senate seat, Wallin had resigned. Whereupon, also by prior agreement, Flynn appointed him a special roving consultant to NASA. (Bill had done well in the Senate, winning election to the next full term. And at the time Wallin was back from *Jovian-II,* before pipelining to *Starfinder,* seemed a cinch to repeat.) "He got the Space Committee too, Collier, if you weren't noticing. Didn't I tell you he's the man I needed to take over for me?"

As Rance nodded, Wallin said, "And I was right. Well,

enough of that." He turned to Durand. "Let's have the double-timer now."

From a briefcase she handed him a small oblong device; on its upper face Rance saw two digital time displays, one stopped, the other progressing. Holding it out to Hanchett, the senator said, "On Earth they're wondering how nearly you've come to restoring schedule. Here's how we can find out."

He explained: the fixed display read Earth time as of the moment Wallin entered the pipeline; the moving one showed ship's time elapsed since his emergence. "You say your velocity's level now at dot-nine-nine-five c?" The captain nodded. "Then go take one of your computer-corrected star sightings, and check the distance it gives you against what you get from the sum of these two readings—translating the current one to Earth time—plus the Habegger delay." A bit sheepishly the old man grinned. "Well, that's what they told me to say. Does it make sense?"

"It surely does." Jimmy stood. "I'll get right on it."

Rance didn't offer to go along; navigation was by no means his best specialty. Feeling somehow anxious, he drank more coffee than his nerves really needed, and didn't help the conversation much. Then, without thinking, he heard himself blurt out, "How's Cassie? Still doing NASA liaison?"

The senator shook his head. "Not two weeks after you left, she quit. Dropped out of sight; when I got curious, my staff couldn't locate her."

"She just . . . vanished?"

"Seemed as if. But a funny thing. Not long after I got back from *Jovian-Two*, she turned up again. Caught me just finishing lunch, sat down, and had coffee; we talked a while."

Rance found himself leaning forward. "How—how was she?"

"Oh, fine, I guess. Hadn't changed a whole lot, though of course I'm not the world's greatest observer. Never did say what's she's doing now—*then*, I mean. Wanted to know *my* plans. And when I told her I was coming here, asked me to give you a message. 'Tell him I changed my mind,' is what she said."

About what? Rance asked the question aloud, and the

old man answered, "Didn't say. And then she got me telling her about my time on *Jovie.* "

Before Rance could think of anything else to ask, Jimmy Hanchett came in smiling. "Within limits of error we're right where we're supposed to be." He turned to Rance. "Our other tests indicated we were, but it's nice to know for sure."

Once the surprise was over, Rance found himself truly enjoying the senator's visit. He hadn't expected, he realized now, ever to see the old boy again.

And Wallin, with the aid of Durand or whoever else was handy to help, prowled the ship fully and with gusto. After a time Rance decided that having acquired the knack of zero gee, the man found those areas easier to cope with than the low-weight Belt.

On the third day of the visit, helping Durand escort the senator to the cabin they shared, he was surprised to find the bed segments formed into a double, not two singles. He hadn't thought his reaction showed, but when he left the room, the nurse followed him. Outside, she caught his arm. "You look like a man full of questions. Ask them."

What—? He shook his head. "No. None of my business."

But she moved to block his way, and he knew the issue wasn't his curiosity, but her need to speak. So the hell with it: "What's your trouble? Does his snoring keep you awake?"

Her eyes narrowed; Rance decided he'd allow her one free hit, but no more. Instead she spoke quietly. "He didn't hire me to sleep with him. He'd had the stroke, though—" Rance blinked; he hadn't known about that. "—wasn't taking much *interest* in life. So one night—"

She halfway shrugged. "It's made a world of difference." Rance didn't speak; after a moment she said, "So first it *was* pity, his need, whatever. Then I came to value him for himself." She grinned. "And he's good, Collier. Not often, but good."

Rance smiled. "Relax, Durand. I think we're friends."

Briefly she clasped his hand. "Fine. Can't have too many."

∎ ∎ ∎

It took Rance another day to realize something was niggling him. What it was: he had a nose for people hiding things from him, and right now the senator was twitching it. He tried sneaky questions and got bland answers; well, on the Senate floor Wallin could always skate rings around anyone trying probe tactics. But in this case, what did he know that needed covering?

On watch with Su, Rance went through his portion of the routine checkups and collaborated on the log report for Earth. Then he sat back, and thought out loud. What, he asked, was Wallin sitting on? After shaking her head and then making a couple of half-hearted suggestions, too far off the wall for either of them to take seriously, Su shrugged. "If it's trouble at the Earth end, we have no clues at all. And no way of knowing what to ask. Not that we could *do* anything . . ."

Rance caught himself frowning; he knew it made him look peevish, so tried to relax those muscles. "All right; so it's the ship. But what could he know that we don't?"

Then it hit him. "The relief cadre, it's due in about two weeks." He felt his grin stretch, and knew it had to look more mean than nice. "The roster. That's what he's not telling."

Su nodded. "I suspect you're right. But why?"

"Once this watch is over, let's find out."

It took longer, because Rance wanted a private talk and couldn't find a way to cut Wallin out of the group. Eventually, at a moment when only Su and Maxine Durand could overhear, he said, "Senator, I need to talk with you alone." As the white, bushy brows raised, Rance added, "Just the four of us, I mean. And Jimmy, I guess. But not this mob scene."

Wallin nodded. "In a bit. Maxine, please escort me to our cabin. Collier—I'll expect you in thirty minutes."

Right on sked, Rance knocked at their door; opening it, Durand admitted him and Su. "We'll have to do without Hanchett," Rance said. "He's not the greatest at catching signals; I couldn't pry him loose from the card game."

"Yes." The senator gave a sort of haroopmh. "All right, Collier. You've been sniffing questions all around

Robin Hood's barn. Are you ready now, to ask whatever it is you really want to know?"

"Sure. What the hell is it you're sitting on that affects this ship?"

The old man's laugh verged on coughing, but he controlled it. "What doesn't? You'll have to do better than that."

Go with the hunch. "Who's our relief B cadre?" And as Wallin gave a narrow-eyed look, "I've tried, and can't think of any other info you'd have reason to be close-mouthed about. Unless NASA's shutting down the whole mission and we just haven't heard yet—"

"No." A headshake. *"Starfinder's* fully Go; you should have deduced that when you got the news about *Roamer.*" He paused. "You always did show signs, Rance, of being a pretty good bird dog when you put your mind to it. It's the cadre, yes."

Again silence. *The old warhorse wants me to guess some more.* All right. "Political problems, or individual?"

"Both." Wallin leaned forward. "Remember Cleve Rozanski, who commanded *Jovian-Two?* And Colonel Irina Tetzl, who rode with him as Exec?" Feeling tautness grow, Rance nodded. "Well, they'll both be coming. But due to some finagling at the UN, this time she'll be in charge. Your new captain. And two of the others are her people."

"Old Iron Tits." Before he thought, Rance said it. And decided not to speak of his one encounter with the woman. "Well, she has to be competent, right? Or she wouldn't get the job."

With a snort, Wallin said, "Competent, sure. But on *Jovie* she made waves. They all tried to show a cool front, but I wasn't behind the door when the brains were handed out. The tension showed, couldn't be hidden."

Su Teng spoke. "What sort of tension?"

"I was never quite sure. But it smelled a lot like the same kind that sent Ali Saud home with two corpses."

Further query brought no more detail; if Wallin knew specifics, he wasn't telling. He did show a copy of relief-B's roster, with names, ages, national origins, and specialties, in proposed order of arrival. Rance looked it over and read it aloud: "Cleve Rozanski, thirty-six, USA, pilot-navigator. Sergei 'Sarge' Dimitrov, twenty-eight, USSR, Traction Drive. Zsana Ionescu, twenty-six, Romania, inship maint, instrumentation. Ramon Juan Rodriguez, thirty, Colombia (naturalized USA), navigation/telemetry. Margrete Van Der Veer, thirty-two, Holland, inship systems maint. And finally, folks, we have Colonel Irina Tetzl, forty, USSR, captain. That's all it says for her, just captain." Looking up from the list, Rance said, "I thought you said *two* more were hers."

"The Romanian," said Wallin, "trained east of the Urals."

Rance shrugged. "Well, it's not the Cold War years. Except for national pride—and the New Soviets *are* touchy about that—we only have to worry about Tetzl herself, not her country of origin."

His grin came wry. "Politics is the least of our worries."

XIV

CHANGES

At first opportunity, Rance and Su told Jimmy Hanchett what they'd learned. But new developments left no time for stewing over the situation; next day the Habegger Gate components began appearing.

Surprising everyone, since Wallin had made no mention, a three-person installation crew arrived. "We're just here for the job itself," reported Shirley Tate, the team's chief. "And we brought our own sleeping gear, so we can cork out in the lounge, or wherever."

Her coworkers, Fred Hawley and Pete LeMieux, seemed equally cheerful. As Pete said, "For a week's work we're drawing two years' pay. That's hard to beat." Recall came to Rance: yes, according to the Astronauts Protective Association's original agreement, pipeline time did draw half pay. . . .

Tall and rangy, with a thin face and short, sun-streaked blond hair, Tate wasted no time getting the job under way. Curious, Rance tagged along with Hawley and LeMieux as they began assembling the transmit terminal.

The existing Gates sat at the outer rim of the Operations tube, input terminal directly forward of Number One drive node and output diametrically opposed. Now Rance discovered that *Starfinder*'s design allowed for two more sets of Gates, similarly placed with respect to the other two drive nodes.

What for? "Well," Tate explained, "besides contact with Earth, the idea is that every ship should have a link to two others. Right now, of course, two is all there *are.*"

The new Mouth was to be installed forward of node Two; that's where Fred Hawley, stocky in a worn jumpsuit, began removing bulkhead plates and opening the nearest junction box for power, while the slimmer, more dapper LeMieux checked carton numbers against an inventory sheet.

Jimmy Hanchett and Jomo Mbente brought another batch of equipment. Massive objects, though weightless here, still had inertia; Rance, who found himself terminally awkward at carrying such things in zero gee, admired both men's skill.

Checking job-spec drawings on her hand viewer, Shirley Tate marked locations for the mounting bolts, making sure they went into structural members, not mere bulkhead plating. As Rance left for a quick lunch before his watch trick, Pete began drilling at the marked positions and inserting studs, as Fred unpacked parts that would form the baseplate.

Leaving the area, Rance met the senator and Maxine. "Ready to give it the once-over, sir?"

Wallin nodded. "Yes. I want to see how everything's going, whether it's best to wait for completion and go straight to *Roamer*, or head for Earth earlier."

"Well," Rance commented, "they certainly know what they're doing. The estimate for this job is a week; at this rate, they'll meet schedule with time to spare."

Three days later he wasn't so sure. "If Murphy's Law can't get you any other way," Shirley said, fuming but trying not to let it show, "Murphy himself checks off the shipping invoice!"

"And on *this* job," Fred Hawley added, "we can't exactly call the supplier to highgrade what's missing and get it here yesterday."

What was missing was one of the power-separation units. Mentally shaking the rust off his knowledge of Habegger Gate technology, Rance recalled the sensitivity of these terminals to feedback between the various polyhedron-outlining patterns of metal spikes that generated the operating fields. The way Habegger had beaten the problem was by isolating the respective power supplies. Totally: in each fully shielded branch the current was first rectified to DC, then choppered back to AC, but now at a new frequency.

Here, though, with the Mouth complete and gear unpacked for the Tush, one AC-DC-AC conversion module was just plain out to lunch—and back on Earth, at that.

Fleurine Schadel had the best familiarity with ship's stores' inventory. First she ran a computer search for any piece of gear resembling the missing component; it showed nothing of any real promise, but she and Takeo went rummaging on an eyeball check for items of even the remotest likelihood. Back from that attempt, she and Yamata equally sweaty and dust-smeared, in the lounge she opened a beer and sat. "We don't have one damn thing aboard, that anyone could even haywire from."

Sitting next to her, Hanchett sighed. "Then the whole thing's dead?"

Carefully, it seemed, Shirley Tate chose words. "Not exactly. At any given time, one terminal or the other could be operated. But not both—and there'd be at least a day's downtime, both ways, while you made the switch." She sipped coffee. "Coordinating your skeds with *Roamer*'s, what with the Habegger Lag, might take some doing."

Wallin looked glum, but made no comment.

It was strictly no damned good: Rance could see that, but he couldn't accept it. There *had* to be a way.

And finally, Murphy to the contrary, an idea came to him. As had been the case the last time inspiration flowered, he and Su were in bed. This time, though, inspiration awaited a more seemly instant. And lucky it did, was Rance's thought; leaving Su in the lurch a second time, at such a moment, could have been hazardous to his—well, hazardous, anyway.

As it was, he lay there happy in their mutual satisfaction, letting the idea add to his pleasure until Su's stirrings gave him leave to disengage.

Rolling over, in one move he swung off the bed and stood. "I've got it!"

Sitting up, Su shook her hair back. "Got what? Besides a bad case of the jumpups?"

He told her. Then he went to tell the others.

The explanation took several tries, but eventually Shirley Tate unpursed her lips and nodded. All right; a very faint feedback linkage between related elements of *separate* Gates shouldn't raise difficulties. And because standardized components were cheaper to procure, power isolation modules for the various branches were built all to the same specs. But some units needed a lot less juice; in fact, one major function of each Gate used less than a third the capacity of its supply.

"So at the Tush," Rance said, trying a fourth paraphrase of his idea, "we power that area from the corresponding feed for the Mouth." And this time Tate agreed.

"Does this mean you can get both Gates operational in a reasonable time?" the senator asked.

"Soon if at all, yes," she answered. So again Wallin decided to stretch his stay. Just in case.

When it came down to actually making the idea work, the usual unforeseen problems arose. For one thing, between the two locations no shielded circuit existed, nor any nonstop conduit through which such a cable could be snaked. Rather than opening numerous junction boxes on a circuitous route, running short cable sections between them, and stuffing a shielded splice into each cramped space, Tate routed her cable along a lateral bulkhead across the Operations Tube as directly as possible, skirting the inner cylinder and punching through all surfaces that got in her way. "Quicker," she noted. "And who said we had to be neat?"

· · ·

So, late in the visiting crew's Day Six, Shirley fired up both new Gates. Meters read correctly, and the glows looked right. Yet no one moved to test further. Rance wondered why, but it was Hanchett who asked. Shirley Tate looked to him. "A matter of timing. Making sure both ends of the pipeline are ready. And leaving plenty of safety margin." She checked her chrono. "As near as I can figure, converting from the Earthtime departure point they gave us, you hold off sending your first test subject until eighteen hundred hours tomorrow."

She shrugged. "We're supposed to be gone by then. But the hell with that." She looked over to Pete and Fred. "I think we'll stick around and see what happens. Any objections?"

Both men grinned.

At the appointed time most of *Starfinder*'s people, plus the senator and Maxine, gathered at the Mouth. As instructed by Shirley Tate, for his first test Hanchett used a compact-dataform copy of the ship's log, beginning at restoral of Traction Drive. "Up to that point," she'd told him, "they already have copy, from before they left Earth. A few days further, possibly, but a bit of overlap can't hurt."

So he set the packet inside the terminal, stepped back, and actuated the Gate. Colors flared and died; the thing was gone, its departure celebrated by a certain amount of whooping.

The new receive terminal couldn't show them anything yet, of course, except indicator lights glowing their signs of proper function. It would be—Rance considered the numbers—two Earth years before anything came through from *Roamer*. Or roughly seventy-three days by ship's time.

Which was really too long for Rance to hold his breath.

That same day, the Earthgate Tush brought Rance a surprise: personal greetings from Anne Portaris. Like Senator Wallin, she had managed clearance to ride a starship. "The senator gave me the idea," she wrote, "junketing around the way he's done. And after Haal died suddenly—I don't suppose you've heard—I needed something to do, something different. So I've wangled me a spot on *Roamer* for about a month. I'll be running tests on the Drive under acceleration, checking out some thoughts Haal and I had come up with, possible improvements. We'd done a brief hitch of our own on *Jovie* earlier, just the shakedown run before mission departure, and it gave us a few ideas. So I'll be busy. I guess that's all, Rance—except, I wish you the best of luck. Perhaps we'll see each other back on Earth, whatever year . . ."

Feeling his eyes moisten, Rance blinked. "Good old Three-fingered Annie. She never quits, does she?"

In accordance with further instructions passed along by Shirley Tate, other items were sent: starfield viewprints corrected to determine position with respect to time, density cross sections of the interstellar gas as correlated with those sightings to confirm velocity estimates. And so forth: The inevitable comments on merits (or lack thereof) of various aspects of ship design would probably draw some laughs.

For some while, in fact, the sending seemed almost like conversation in real time. Only when Jimmy Hanchett found himself asking two questions in a row did he pause and say, "Oh, hell! I'll be five months waiting for answers!"

Feeling a little depressed, Rance saw the group settle back, more or less, to reality.

A day late, Shirley and Fred and Pete went singly into Habegger's Mouth, the original one. Jokingly, Jimmy asked Tate if they'd rather go home via *Roamer*. "Not so you'd notice," she answered. "Nobody's paying us for side trips." It struck Rance, then, that such a "side trip" would add two more years to the team's absence from Earth. And what would such an addition do to their various personal plans, whatever those might be?

Personal plans, huh? After *Starfinder*, Rance didn't seem to have any. . . .

Jimmy broke the mood. "Well, I hope she turns in a good report on us."

Startled, Rance said, "What do you mean, 'report'?"

Hanchett shrugged. "Tate's used to supervising more than just two other people; it shows all over her. And so does that unmistakable Evaluator way of looking at things."

Rance hadn't noticed, and said so. Su touched his shoulder. "Jimmy's right, most likely. But I don't see why that should disturb us. Surely she found nothing here to complain of."

"Hmm. I suppose not."

"Of course not," said Wallin. "*I* certainly haven't. But I think I'll stick around and see how the new cadre shapes up."

All else aside, Rance rather looked forward to seeing Cleve Rozanski again. How long had it been? Let's see —*Jovie*'s lift, about six months before Rance hit the pipeline, was roughly seven years ago, Earthtime. Of those years, Rance had actually lived only one. Cleve, pipelining back from *Jovie* and then out here to *Starfinder*, but otherwise living at Earth's pace, would have experienced three.

When he appeared at the Tush, within minutes of sked and early at that, Cleve hadn't changed much: still medium-tall, husky, darkhaired, and wearing the same confident grin. "Hi, Rance. Long time," and he stepped off the Belt to shake hands.

"Yes. It has been. Glad to see you aboard." And although the corollary, imminent arrival of Irina Tetzl gave Rance no joy, his greeting was sincere.

Cleve and Dink and Benita, it turned out, knew each other from early training days; the other greetings went quickly, and with Cleve's luggage picked up, the group proceeded forward by way of Control (for introductions to Nadine and Su, on watch), then via transfer ring to the rotating Belt.

Cleve, Rance supposed, would be sharing captain's quarters with Colonel Tetzl. But Jimmy and Fleurine still had those digs, so for now the luggage went into Art Cranston's compartment.

Then onward to the lounge, for ritual drinks in the way of further welcome. Sitting, Cleve looked around. "Must say, this makes *Jovian-Two* look like somebody's woodshed. Not that it wasn't a great little ship. Short on elbow room, though."

"What was it like—?" Jimmy asked the first question, more followed, and for the next hour Rozanski told of exploring the Solar System. When the watch changed— Su and Nadine joining the group after being relieved by Liz and Takeo—Rance caught Su's gaze and moved to meet her.

He was ready to leave, but Su wanted to share in the party for a time, so beside her he sat again, and listened. Noting, when his attention sharpened, that with regard to personal interactions on *Jovie,* Cleve was saying not Word One.

What he did say next, that interested everyone, concerned a third starship, barely under construction when Cleve left Earth, and named *Arrow.* "Totally different approach to crewing," he said, and Rance paid attention.

The plan was different, all right. Acceleration at five gees? "Beefed-up drive," said Cleve, "and a heavier feed to bigger fuel tanks." Then the kicker. "During the accel stage," he said, "nobody's aboard."

Five gees would get *Arrow* up near c ("Dot three nines and a two," Cleve said. "Time ratio twenty-five.") in about ninety days' Earth time, seventy actual ship days. "So the crew—" He grinned. "—the crew, the whole crew, and nothing but the crew, hits the pipeline *twenty-one months* early. And with no replacements, rides it all the way in."

"All the way?" Jimmy Hanchett scowled. "Even at twenty-five to one—and then a year of one-gee decel . . ."

Cleve laughed. "Here's the real payoff. Decel's at five gees, too—but the crew doesn't feel it."

How so? Before he'd tell, Cleve made everyone guess. When no one had any luck, he sprung the McGuffin: "The ship's on automatic again. And the crew—they go into Habegger Lag between two Gates, there on *Arrow* for just that purpose."

Rance's mental calculator clicked in. Twenty-one months ahead of decel, the crew would have to go into their Gate. But at t_o/t at twenty-five—hell, they'd hit the local Habegger Loop a mere twenty-six or so of *their* days before the crunch began. Or a bit less, to be *sure* and miss those five gees. . . .

"So you see," said Rozanski, "maybe it didn't really pay off, catching the first boat out."

Getting lively then, for a time the discussion diverted Rance from his forebodings. And back in quarters with Su, later, he didn't mention any of the ideas he wished he weren't getting.

What Art Cranston had in mind next day was that his staying on, while the relief crew arrived and undertook OJT "—makes no sense at all. This Rozanski *skippered* a ship; he doesn't need me to hold his hand. That stayover time the rule specifies—look, Jimmy, three days here is a *month* on Earth. And Maggie's waited too long already."

Taking Art's place on the watch roster, teamed with Rance, Cleve displayed immediate competence. Never inflexible, Hanchett agreed Cranston could leave; with his gear packed, Art submitted to a brief, sedate farewell party, and said his good-byes with more feeling than Rance expected.

Then, quiet and unassuming as always, he led the way to Habegger's Mouth. As he vanished, the Gate's colors flaring, Dink Hennessey said, "Yeah. Nothing like going out in a blaze of glory."

Next to report was Sergei ("Call me Sarge") Dimitrov, a short, muscular young man with dark blond hair, pale eyes, and broad Slavic cheekbones hollowing down to a blunt, stubby chin. Not especially voluble, he had a friendly smile and seemed easy-going. His arrival cleared Nadine Potter to depart; after his OJT runthrough came a gathering in the lounge: sendoff gettogethers, it seemed, were the new tradition.

One drink, it seemed, affected Nadine enough to make it plain she had strong feelings about leaving. But not to express them out loud. On the way to the Mouth, though, walking beside Rance and holding his arm, she said, "Collier, you party pooper—I think we missed something good together, you and I."

"I wouldn't be surprised. But it just didn't seem—" They were there now, at the Mouth, the point where he stayed and she moved on. As her luggage vanished and colors faded, he gave the good-bye kiss. "Good luck, Nadine." Then, "You'll do fine."

"You do the same." Turning away she stepped forward, up the Belt, and the Mouth did its trick.

Zsana Ionescu arrived next. The slim, olive-skinned, classically Mediterranean brunette matched height with Sarge—who was, it turned out, her roommate. Currently he was filling Nadine's watch slot, working with Su, but when all turnover was complete, no doubt the shifts would be reshuffled.

The next leavetaking, two days later, featured Christy Frost. Rance had never felt he'd known the woman, and he still didn't. But as with the others, he wished her luck.

All too rapidly, it seemed to Rance, people came and went. Ramon Juan Rodriguez in, Jomo Mbente out ("Send word how it goes with Btar. At ten-to-one ratio, it'll reach me." "Yes. All right . . ."). Margrete Van Der Veer appeared, Liz Pendergast vanished.

Only one more to go, then, and Takeo Yamata had his things packed. For it was hardly likely he'd be needed to help train Captain Irina Tetzl.

Puzzled, Rance sat alone next day in quarters and tried to analyze how, exactly, Old Iron Tits had spooked him so much. By inviting him to join her and Cleve in bed, to cheat on Cassie?

Except that even leaving Cassie out of it, the idea still gave him the cold twitches.

Why? Well, as a spectator sport, copulation didn't impress him much. Having someone watch *him* rated even lower.

Still, if that were all—but of course it wasn't. Not by half. The real bogey was the other male just being in the same bed. That thought brought back Jackie the lounge singer, and the shame he'd felt.

Shame, not guilt. Guilt was from knowing you'd done wrong, shame from the contempt—real or potential— of others. Rance had never been one to load up on guilt.

Regrets, sure; mostly for things *not* done. Jackie, though, was strictly a shame trip.

Whatever, he wanted no more part of *that* bag.

Aside from Rance himself, the one who seemed most perturbed about Tetzl's coming was Jimmy Hanchett. And he'd never even *met* the woman! Snacking together in the galley, Rance asked: "What's eating you, ol' buddy? Dreading the new broom?"

Looking anxious, Hanchett said, "Something like that. Or maybe just—well, I came on here expecting to serve as exec; that's the way things were set up. But now, having run this show for six months, I don't think I'm going to enjoy stepping back down." He shrugged. "I know it's right and proper that I do; I just don't feel good about it."

"Sure. That's natural. It couldn't have been easy, picking up on the job without notice, and now that you've got the hang of it . . ." Oh, well; done eating, Rance stood, gave Hanchett's shoulder a brief clasp, and left.

He'd never told Su Teng of his run-in with Irina Tetzl; now, he decided, he should. But not until they were preparing for bed did he work up the steam for it. "Su? There's something, maybe you ought to know." Then, all in a rush, he spilled the works.

She didn't seem terribly surprised. "You and Rozanski, she wanted? And he stayed, but you didn't."

"That's right."

"Why now?"

"Beg your pardon?"

"If it wasn't important enough to mention before, why tell me now?"

"Because she'll *be* here now, and except for Cleve and me, nobody knows about her. I thought someone else should."

Her brows lifted. "No one? What of the other eight on *Jovian-Two*? If the senator's guessed right, they'd be fully aware." She paused. "Besides her and Rozanski, are any more from that ship in the new cadre?"

"I don't think so." He made half a grin. "But they've all trained together long enough."

"Then either they know, or else she's changed and

there is no difficulty. So you can stop trying to spread your wings like a mother hen, to shield everyone."

"There's still Jimmy and Fleurine, and Dink and Benita. I should—"

Su smiled. "Let me. I'll put little bugs in the ears of Benita and Fleurine—not all the lively details, surely, but enough hint that they know what to watch for."

Relieved, Rance let out a sigh. "Yes. That should do it."

"Thank you. May we sleep now?"

They had made love already that day, not a great deal earlier, so her suggestion seemed as good as any.

When Irina Tetzl did step from the Belt, Rance felt let down. He wasn't sure why; maybe his mind had built her into a larger-than-life menace. What he saw, now, was the same trim, sturdy, medium-height figure, still spring steel and whipcord. And the same striking face he'd seen at the Cape—cheeks slightly fuller, perhaps, but basically unchanged. Different, only, was the head; no more gray soup bowl. Now her hair shone copper-blond: short curls on top, with sides and back sheared to sleekness.

More makeup, maybe? Except for vivid color on the wide mouth, he saw none. And no matter how he sliced it, the colonel was still a knockout.

Cleve Rozanski moved forward and gave first greeting, then proceeded with introductions. At Rance's turn the woman offered a fingertip handshake. The corners of her eyes crinkled as if in amusement, but she kept her expression grave. "Mr. Collier. A pleasure we meet again."

"Yes. Pleasure. Uh—charmed." Feeling somehow chastened, Rance made way for whoever stood next in line.

When the group headed outship toward the lounge, Rance and Su trailed. "I'm not sure," he told her, "what kind of hex that witch has on me. But I keep waiting for the other shoe to drop."

Su squeezed his hand. "Why don't you just relax?"

Entering late, the two waited their turn at the bar, where eventually Rance fixed a couple of bourbons-on-ice. While nearly everyone stood around making small talk, Irina Tetzl sat with Rozanski at one side and Hanchett at the other. Moving closer, Rance listened as Jimmy said, "All right; Dink and Benita with you two, Sarge and Zsana with Fleurine and me. That leaves Ramon and Margrete with Su and Rance, and all pairs together. I'll get everyone shifted for you as soon as I can. Not all at once, though; we don't need anyone working two tricks straight, do we?"

"I have done so," Tetzl answered, "and more. But very well; everyone shall have proper rest. These assignments, however: they are temporary. Later I shall plan schedules to better utilize skills of all."

Having heard enough, Rance drifted away, to find himself facing the senator. Wallin gave him a wink. "They always have to put their stamp on early, these new skippers. I see she's not wasting time at it. Well, if it makes her feel better . . ."

"Yes." But Rance doubted that a mere juggling of watch tricks was the other shoe.

A bit later, when she had everyone troop down to Control and Senator Wallin complied with her request to read a brief, perfunctory group marriage ceremony to both cadres, Rance decided she was still working up to it.

XV

PROGRESSIONS

Several cycles now, Tev and Imon clasp in breeding rapture. Except once each cycle, young Liij bringing fluid and nutriment to maintain health, joyous isolation is not breached. Sleep with its dreams comes and goes; waking begins with communing of palps and mouth-sounds. But always, greatest part is lying clasped, sharing feel of what occurs.

For long, feeling is near to stasis, with only slight stir of melded nodes. But then, well into fifth cycle, change begins: In joined mass pressed between them, new throbbings. Now comes clenching stricture, fully around lip of Tev's nodeshell, answered by resisting surge at stem of Imon's node. A new stage, precipitating Imon toward final climax of node's separation.

What came before, sense-shaking almost to limit, is nothing to what comes now. Tremors from encircled stem throw shudders throughout Imon, from central source to each extremity. For nearly whole cycle, spasms' strength grows and grows; other senses blur, until to Imon no other thing exists.

Dimly, thought comes: *End must be near.*

Star nearest Environ, outviewers show, sits at unfortunate angle to Environ's path. Yet no other choice; others much too far, given current pace and plasma level, for any chance of reaching. Palps vibrating in unthought grumble, Overwatcher Seit accepts situation. Ceasing unmeant protest sound, Seit informs teacher Chorl, then instructs Dutywatcher Kahim in change of aim.

Kahim assents. <This star (to be our goal) is (constitutes) one end of (catastrophe causing) pseudostrand?>

<True.> For this, no qualification needed. Then <Hope is (instruments consulting) we learn (understand) nature of (in future to avoid) pseudostrand.>

Under Kahim's guidance, navigationists and instrumentators begin Environ's great, wheeling movement, to aim toward star.

At upper studyspace, Chorl pauses in scrutiny of outview farsensor, considers instrument's configuration, and makes delicate change. Then views again. Scanning area surrounding star and its worlds, path to which Seit has chosen for Environ, Chorl among much data of little import discovers here and there various manifestations worth recording.

Soonest to Environ's reaching, not two *dres'* travel distant, drifts conglomerate of accreted material, clumped into swarms all roughly following similar age-slow path around yet-far star.

Not star's major outhalo, these straggles. Far behind Environ, and so of no use to it, lies that greater, cloud-like ring. But what lies ahead is sufficient in mass to aid Environ significantly, in gaining pace.

Outview shifts, changing, as Environ alters path. Major clumping of matter fragments moves, slowly, from edge of viewscreen toward center.

Senses drowned, mind of Imon dims. Bare remnant of consciousness fills with total joy as node-root gives way; separation sends euphoric floodings throughout each nerve, large or small, in Imon's body. Upper and lower limbs, long cramped in taut embrace, straighten almost as explosion, flinging Imon free of Tev's loosened grasp to drift in lowered weight, then come to rest, panting, on weight-directed surface.

In dim light it looks to Tev, who by recoil drifts to farther wall, then down to sit across from Imon. Back against wall, feet almost together—while lower-limb joints, spread wide apart, cradle melded nodes against belly where still attached. Digits of upper limbs touch nodes' outer extreme, site of separation. Imon notes fluid exudation there, not undue in amount and already diminishing. <It is (to my knowledge) as should be, Tev.> Imon pauses; it would say much but has difficulty forming thought to sound. <Tev—joy (shared) ends. But thought of joy (now, ever) does not. Tev, we (through all life) have this (same for each of us) thought.>

<Will always (not regarding what may come), yes, Imon.> But already Tev's attention drops away, inward toward growing, developing Liijling now attached to Tev alone. For all of next quarter *dre*, Tev's thought is bound thus.

Knowing so, Imon touches palps with Tev, then goes to inform healthwatcher of Tev's progress and undergo inspection of own condition. Before proceeding to feeding space: there, as with any Liij newly node-shed, to eat enough for six normal feedings.

Environ ingests matter swarm, energy of foursphere rises, ingestor field expands. By little, yet noticeably, pace grows. Meeting with Chorl, Overwatcher Seit seeks knowledge. Using Chorl's specialized outviewer, Seit examines star ahead, and its surround.

To Chorl, Seit says <This is (not unusual) lifebearer we go (at such slow pace) toward.>

Answer comes. <Not unlike (though discernibly less bright) that which (so long, long past) bears Liij.>

Chorl shows recorded views, by instruments' artifice much neared, of star, its worlds, even largest of secondary worldlets. With, also, detected indications of scattered smaller fragments, lacking sufficient mass to appear directly. Without surprise Seit notes that major

objects include four small, dense worlds near to star
while larger, less dense objects take wider paths; of latter type, five are noted in range of star's major gravitic
clasp. At reaches more outward still, only loosely held
by starmass, drift aggregations clumped by own collec-
tive mass. Star's outhalo, its this-side now behind Environ, marks limit—if such may truly be assigned—of
starmass's warp in spacetime.

Not without interest, these worlds. Among larger,
one lies brightly girdled by striated disc of shining sub-
stance; two more carry similar formations, much lesser
in display.

Two of four smaller worlds are gas-enveloped: one
heavily, and therefore greatly heated, but other—accompanied by large worldlet, itself near worldsize—
most possibly lifebearing.

< This (indicated) world, then, > Seit informs Chorl
< is (of great likelihood) origin of (deadly obstacle)
pseudostrand. >

Time comes—Liijling shedding husks, core and shell, of
seeder's and birther's nodes—for Tev to birth it. Prior to
expected moment, Imon comes. Even did custom not
specify, Imon would be with Tev at birthing.

Together they wait, as soon-to-live youngthon, now
with pulse all its own and shudders presaging indepen-
dent breath, strains against constricting outer husk.

Until husk splits, all its length one place and then
another. Youngthon writhing causes segments to creak,
flake away, until one breaks and limb protrudes.

This much, youngthon must achieve alone. But now
its strength is proved; by tradition, birther and seeder
help to tear away remaining shell while youngthon itself convulses, expelling shards of inner husk.

Now, aided by palps and forelimbs of Tev and Imon,
youngthon stands. Helping clear last husk-shards from
Tev, then leaving Tev to hold youngthon from falling
and to soothe it, Imon goes to bring its first nutriment.

Crossing predominant route of matter aggregates at
long, slanting angle, Environ encounters and ingests
many. Larger now, and growing with each increment
taken, mouth of ingestor field accepts all that comes.

Except one object, size anomalously great for this milieu. Field cannot encompass it; to attempt would mean cutting *hole* through mass, leaving outer portion as hollow shell. In past, Environ has done so—even to actual stars—but with pace that took it free and far before collapse ensued. At current crawl, gutted object would fall inward upon Environ, causing damage if not destruction.

With reluctance—for this mass would aid pace mightily—Seit orders ingestor field contracted to nullity and Environ's path kept safely clear of tumbling aggregate. Only when it is passed can field again be spread.

Yet Seit's regret is meager. For it has learned that even at this range from star, large masses exist. And at some such encounter, ingestor field will have size enough.

As with all newbirthed Liijlings, youngthon of Tev and Imon at first sleeps much. Healthwatchers' pronouncement of its fitness confirms seeder's and birther's observations; it feeds with vigor, takes sufficient fluids, and excretes punctually. Though too young to understand discrete meanings of specific mouthsounds or palp vibrations, such general tones as urgings, encouragements, or determents can even now be learned. When Imon has been returned to duties only a few cycles, Tev with pride announces it has taught youngthon how and where to excrete, properly and with neatness.

During this period Imon spends maximum of time with Tev and youngthon. For now it is not many more cycles until Tev is also returned to duties, youngthon is given name, and joins agemate herd to share learning.

Toward that time, Imon and Tev labor to teach it meanings, that it begin herdlearning with good basis.

When both their duties permit, it sleeps between them and is warmed.

Still and again Seit visits memory bones, not only to seek experience but also to add its own to data store. Yet neither Dron nor Haef nor others give data to aid present difficulties.

Once more to Chorl, to upper studyspace with outviewer where solutions may be found, goes Seit, and offers greeting. <Does viewer (your study now) tell more of Crippler (world producing pseudostrand) to Liij advantage?>

<Facts (deduced from observation) come in slow order. One such (of possible interest) is now made clearer. Time of circuit (around star) appears (assuming short period of observations valid) like to one half *dre.*>

Seit chirrs palps in assent; such estimate accords with Seit's understanding of interactivity between mass and distance. Though without recourse to electrologics, Seit would not presume to specify accuracy closer than, perhaps, fourfold limits.

Another question it finds more cogent: <When Environ nears path (projected by viewer analysis) of Crippler world, at what margin (given median estimate of ingestion and thus of pace growth) does Environ pass that object?>

Chorl's palps convey only lack of detail; without qualification it mouthsounds <Not yet knowable.>

Feeling empty of gain or gratification but nonetheless sounding thanks, Seit descends to place of major duty stations. There approving diligence of navigationists and instrumentators, along with those Liij of lesser function, Seit commends current Dutysetter and retires to own nesting space.

Before Environ's path nears Crippler world, actions for that time must be decided. For Environ's assured continuance, for certainty of best choosings, Seit must know more.

Crippler has damaged and endangered Environ once; how can Seit think it may not again? And how to know all ways of threat this world yet holds?

Of itself, nearness to Crippler is, in some coming time, inevitable condition. But of projected events, to be sought or avoided at that time, variations and their separate possibilities already exist.

It is only that Seit cannot yet know what they may be, or of their scope or limits.

At time of naming for youngthon of Tev and Imon, more than few attend. As birther of Imon, Overwatcher Seit leads all throughout procedures. Others present, of importance, bear no node-relation to either birther or seeder but also have direct interest: Dutysetters Kahim and Persa, Teacher Chorl, and Pnet who oversees herd-learning of this youngthon's agemates. Others here assembled include a number who share one or other genitor with either Imon or Tev.

With all grouped and quieted, from memory Seit tells nodelines of Tev and Imon many steps into past, to degree that reaches inevitable stage of ancestral convergence. < Further extent (if desired) is found in memory bone Hilin. > In courtesy; others palp agreement.

Naming, then. Imon and Tev, agreed, have informed Seit; now it tells group: < By right (of node-giving) I say this youngthon (Imon's and Tev's) is Alev. > And repeats name, until Alev, comprehending, sounds and chirrs it back.

All feed then, and afterward Pnet takes Alev to living place of agemate herd. Where Tev or Imon may visit, but by custom limit selves to three times per quarter-*dre.*

Left to itself after proceeding ends, Chorl ascends to upper studyplace and considers further. Crippler at moment moves to same side of star Environ's path now aims. Before Environ reaches nearness, though, Crippler will circle star some several times. And at time Environ passes, where will Crippler lie?

Of themselves, Chorl not willing it, mouth and palps sound uncertainty, to echo in studyplace. For pace determines location, foursphere's plasma level governs pace, level of mass ingestion controls plasma level.

But distribution of mass along Environ's path is only as it *is.* Not as Liij wish or need would have it. And not yet known.

Troubled, Chorl unpowers specialized outviewer, closes its exposed operational surfaces against particulate contamination, and descends to feeding area.

XVI

MAKING WAVES

Two days more, Wallin stayed and observed before announcing his and Durand's departure—via *Roamer,* he had decided. First, though, at a terminal in Control he dictated to her a report of his inspection tour. Of this no copy went to *Starfinder*'s log; Durand's skills, it seemed, were not confined to nursing.

Referring to his twin-display timepiece, the senator dated his report by Earth time, then hand-carried the sealed readout and personally saw it dispatched to Earth. "Now, except for the luggage, we're ready to go."

Not without a farewell gathering. Irina Tetzl, on watch with Dink Hennessey, had Rozanski and Benita relieve them long enough for a look-in at the party, but stayed for only minutes: observing the formality, nothing more.

When she left, so did a certain amount of tension.

. . .

Walking the two toward their departure point, the group saw that for the first time anyone could remember, Control's sliding doors were closed. Nudging Rance's elbow, Wallin grinned. "Making it clear, the woman is, that I'm not obligated to any more leavetaking."

He shrugged. "Suits me fine." And stepped on past.

At the new Gate, first the baggage went; then came final handshakes. At Rance's turn, Wallin said, "You did good work for us, Collier. If you ever . . ." Stepping back inside the Gate, he shook his head. "*I* may see you again, or I may not. But Bill Flynn, now: Any help you need, ask him. I'll pass the word."

Before Rance could answer, Wallin gestured for action; the Gate's corona masked his going.

No one had to wait long, to learn how Irina Tetzl meant to do her job. As Rozanski led the way forward and past Control, she slid the doors open. "Cleve. You have now the watch. Everyone else to the lounge, where you will hear me."

As Rance sneaked a sidelong look to Su Teng, he caught her in the same move. Sensing the captain's pale gaze like tangible pressure, he stifled a reflex urge to grin. In the transfer ring compartment he avoided looking at her, and entering the lounge he led Su to a pair of chairs at the room's far corner.

The captain wasted no time. Pointing to a small stack of paper on the table beside her, she said, "Now the nosy old man has gone, you will see how a ship is commanded. I have made a new watch schedule, to take effect immediately this present shift ends." Thin-lipped, she smiled. "Any questions may be brought to me at my quarters. One person at a time, only."

She stared around the room. "If there is nothing further to consider . . . ?" No one spoke; she stood and made her exit.

Getting copies of the new sked became almost a scramble. Rance picked up two, backed out of the crowd, and handed one to Su. After a moment she said, "This thing is a farce. Deliberately inconvenient. Rance, we must go and protest."

With a quick glance at his own sheet, he said, "No. Not right away. Let's wait a while, until we have some idea what her rationale's going to be."

"But she is—"

He took her hand. "Come on; we need to take a good look at this thing. Maybe have a drink over it."

Su looked mutinous; he tugged at her. "One thing I learned a long time ago: it doesn't always pay to be first in line."

Back to quarters, Rance gave the list a closer scan. It didn't get any better. "Watch chiefs: Captain Irina Tetzl, Executive Officer Cleveland Rozanski—what in hell is the woman trying to do? Jimmy's our exec and she knows it!" But James Hanchett, no title, was listed only as the third trick chief. Then: "For her own shift she's taken Dink, Sarge, and Fleurine. Cleve has Margrete and Benita and me. And you're on Jimmy's trick, with Zsana and Ramon. I don't see—"

Handing him a dark-complexioned drink, Su touched her glass to his. "I think I do. Look—including the chiefs, each group has one male and one female from either cadre. And all—I do mean *all*—pairings are split between watches." Frowning, "I fail to understand her purpose."

Rance knocked back a slug of bourbon not much threatened by water. "That part's easy. Plain old boot camp chickenshit. I'm surprised she's being so obvious about it, though; maybe there's something more here, at that. But get this now: at the bottom." He pointed. "Says here, no more shorthanded watches. Each officer's group shall stand duty in its entirety. Doesn't say anything about the chiefs' own august selves, mind you; just the Indians."

The paper contained one more sentence: *Except as may be directed by the captain, these assignments are permanent.*

Three hours later, at watch change, Irina and her chosen team began the new order of business. A few minutes later, primed to scout the situation, Rance went to the lounge—and found Jimmy Hanchett in process of repainting its walls a rather poisonous mustard yellow.

Standing silent with raised brows, Rance waited for Jimmy to notice him and say something.

Eventually the man did look around. "What she said was, I must not have enough to keep me busy, or I wouldn't be wasting time on silly complaints. So here I am."

"And you're taking it? Not just stepping down to exec, but losing that, too? *And* being put to scutwork?"

Hanchett shrugged. "What're my choices? She's captain, and it's her bunkie she's making exec. The two of them together, I'm outvoted."

"But—"

"I should gripe to Earth—that what you want? Round-trip communication five months, nearly. And hollering for my rights here on the ship would just split everybody down the middle—if I didn't get charged with mutiny."

Damn. Why was Jimmy taking this crap sitting down; what kind of handle did Old Iron Tits hold on him, anyway? And did she have the silly idea that One Size Fits All? It went against the grain; he didn't want to do it, but *somebody* had to take a stand, and it looked mighty much as if no one else would.

Rance turned to leave; Jimmy said, "Where you going? There's no point *your* getting in trouble."

"What trouble? Maybe you could use some help."

In Control, Tetzl surprised him. He began, "We'll pass the watch sked, for now, and putting Jimmy Hanchett to dusting erasers. But Jimmy's our exec on this ship. NASA gave him the job and they've never said any different. So where do *you* come off, lifting his command status?"

More than not he expected a reaction on the order of lightnings, but apparently unruffled, the woman said, "Qualifications. Cleve commanded *Jovian-Two* for a year, during which I had ample opportunity to assess his performance."

Performance? Yeah, I'll bet! But Rance stuck to cases. "And Jimmy took command of this *starship*. New aboard here, in the middle of an emergency, and under other difficulties. You weren't around to evaluate *that* performance, but on Earth they think pretty highly of it."

Pursed lips, then a nod. "This is true, what you say. Very well, I will modify my initial assignments."

"And Jimmy's our exec again?"

"Co-executive. He and Cleve will share that rank and its responsibilities." Her eyes narrowed. "Will this change be satisfactory to you, Mr. Collier?"

It wasn't, really—but reluctantly he nodded. Before he could add anything, Tetzl said, "Your business is over, and you are not on duty here. You will leave the area—and do not return until it is your time to report."

With the others watching, Rance found nothing to add. Heading outship, the most he could say for himself was that he could have done worse.

Since he didn't expect to like the new setup much, Rance wasn't especially disappointed. He had nothing against any of his watchmates: he'd worked alongside Benita, Cleve was easy to get along with (though keeping in mind that Rozanski was captain's bedmate, Rance made sure to edit his thoughts before speaking in the man's presence).

And Margrete Van Der Veer, once she got acquainted a little, seemed amiable enough; her initial sober face, square-chinned, became more attractive when she smiled. A tallish woman, with straight, dark gold hair past her shoulders, she struck Rance as an odd match for the shy, mustachioed Ramon Rodriguez; on the other hand, maybe some thought the same about himself and Su.

The schedule, though. Instead of three shifts in six days, now it was duty *every* day; all other chores were to be performed in each person's much-reduced offshift time. And instead of Rance and Su having sixteen mostly-free hours in common daily, now they had eight or less. Just like everybody else.

Except the chiefs, of course: while Tetzl and Hanchett and Rozanski reported punctually to log their teams in and out, during the rest of any given watch trick its officer might or might not be on hand. At first, Su said, Jimmy was the exception, staying dutifully for his whole shift. But then the captain, or sometimes Jim-

my's co-exec, took to calling him away from Control.
There seemed to be no rationale to it—and more than
once, intercom calls to captain's digs went unanswered.

Rance asked no questions; all he did was get more and
more pissed. Quietly, though.

The next straw was Tetzl's announcement, at a meeting
she called to order in the galley, of a number of new
projects she had in mind. A complete inspection and
maintenance check of the Deployment Vehicle. "This
team I shall supervise personally." Co-executive Rozanski drew the inventory-update group, while an all-
around instrument-recalibration program would be co-
executive Hanchett's. Well, Jimmy did know outside
sensors. . . .

Rance spoke up. "We do this as part of our watch
time, right? I mean, two people have been handling
Control for the past eighteen months, so—"

Old Iron Tits cut him off. "I have said, all watches will
be fully crewed. This I have not changed. These other
tasks you will do, four hours per day, as I assign them."

Rance was out on a limb and knew it. If not for Su
Teng's surprisingly fierce grip holding him back, he
might have gone right ahead and sawed that limb off.
Instead, giving not so much as a nod of acknowledgment, he turned away and left.

Keeping her hold, Su perforce went with him. When
they reached quarters he waved away her offer of a
drink, drew breath to launch a denunciation of Irina
Tetzl, then stopped cold. When he spoke, the calmness
of his tone surprised him.

"If she were stupid enough to pull this crap out of
sheer meanness, the psych tests would have disqualified
her. No—" He shook his head. "—there has to be something more."

If there were, none of it came clear. In the project
assignments, Rance drew a spot on Tetzl's own team to
inspect the Deployment Vehicle, four hours each day
following his own watch. Whereas on Cleve Rozanski's
inventory-update group, Su's extra half-shift came before her watch trick.

The good part was that since Su's watch followed

Rance's, neither had to work during their joint spare
time.

    . . . so since we're coming past the Personnel
Staging Center on our way back, I can put this in for
immediate Habgate transfer and you'll get it in a
mere two years.
    I enjoyed myself, those years living out on the
Coast. I'm married now, you know (or maybe you
didn't), and I have twins just walking. Sam and
Davy: lookalikes. But I missed good old GIT, so
Charles and I both put in for jobs here, and . . .

It was hardcopy printout, not a disk or capsule, that
Bowie Fleming had sent him, so Rance could pause and
reflect without missing anything. Married, huh? All
right . . .
    Then it was Habegger she talked about:

    . . . hopes you're doing well on *Starfinder*, be-
cause he says he feels a little guilty about shanghai-
ing you into the first relief cadre. Guilty? Him? Fat
chance. He only wants to sound noble and contrite,
does our good Dr. H., to distract everyone's attention while he weaves his next web.
    He did suggest I tell you his latest thoughts as to
how the Gates really work. So I will, and if they
make sense to you, please explain to me. No—that
would take four years, wouldn't it? So never mind.
    The main thing is that you don't simply flip from
one Gate to the other end. You go, the man says,
into and through and then back out of another universe, congruent to ours throughout. But in which
—and I quote—every point is equidistant from every other.
    I won't blame you if you stop for a drink here.

No need; Rance already had one and had barely begun it. He did have a sip, though.

    That impossible-sounding condition, the man
says, is the only way transit time could be constant
without regard to distance *here*. And that any ques-

tion of size is meaningless: The distance between any two points is however far an object moves in two years. Cue Eee Dee.

I think he really believes the point-to-point distance *and* transit time there are each single quanta. But he's too cagey to go that far out on a limb.

One curious corollary: He claims that if anything in our universe *could* go faster than light it would necessarily create an extension of itself in this other one he's hypothesizing. And that anything we send through it must also leave some kind of trace here. One that might have some weird properties.

So in the accident, just before you reached the ship, maybe *Starfinder* didn't hit a faster-than-light wake. Maybe an FTL ship hit yours. At least that's what Dr. Habegger seems to be saying.

Well, good luck, Rance. Take care of yourself.

She signed it simply "Bowie."

"You want to read it, Su?"

"Yes, I'd like to," so he passed the sheet over. When she finished, she said, "This is the one you felt attracted to for quite some time but didn't speak up?" Rance nodded. "Do you still regret not doing so?"

Headshake. "If I had, I wouldn't be here with you. I like it better this way." *Iron Tits or no Iron Tits!*

"Good." Then she frowned. "Habegger's speculation makes no sense. An entire universe can't possibly have *all* its points equidistant."

"Sure it can." So he was ahead of her on this one. . . . "All you need is enough dimensions."

It took more than just a few moments; then her expression cleared. "Oh yes; n dimensions can hold n-plus-one such points."

Grinning: "See? I knew you'd catch up."

Coming off his next watch, Rance found his way along an inward-spiraling ramp and reported to Irina Tetzl, waiting at a major entrance to the ship's inner cylinder. With him came Margrete Van Der Veer; alongside the captain, Dink Hennessey also waited. After brief greetings, Tetzl led the way, clambering "up" through a cargo hatch into *Starfinder*'s center.

Practically all Rance's duties had been on the Control "level," the outer boundary of *Starfinder*'s operations tube with its twenty-meter radius. Here, a mere ten meters from the ship's axis, the curvature looked wrong and felt wrong. To the rear he saw access ramps and entrances to the three major cargo holds; between those and the forward bulkhead, this entire central cylinder was essentially clear space.

Not for long, though. At a control panel mounted on that bulkhead Tetzl punched in a command, and a strip of the cylinder's curved surface, three meters wide and extending roughly sixty degrees around that curve, pivoted from a point at one side of the hatch; slowly the far end moved, rising from its rest position, to latch into place beside the forward bulkhead's central entrance.

Hennessey whistled. "Instant ramp! How about that?"

Tetzl's brows raised. "This you have not known before? Or you, Collier?"

They hadn't. Rance said, "With all the other problems we had here, I guess the DV didn't seem like much of a priority item. Earth didn't say to do anything about it, so we didn't."

"But maintenance and inspection procedures are specified. So now you shall." Not surprisingly, the ramp was surfaced for zero-gee walking; as they proceeded along it, the captain recited data in a disapproving tone. Twenty meters across and sixty long, the forward twenty forming a conical nose, the Deployment Vehicle was in some ways a miniature of *Starfinder* itself and formed roughly eight-point-six percent of the overall volume.

Like its parent ship the DV sported three nodes of Traction Drive: smaller versions, though, and fueled from ordinary tanks. Lacking Habegger facilities for refueling and resupply, the vessel began its career fully stocked; when operational it would depend directly on *Starfinder* for replenishment. So as Rance *did* already know, its range and capabilities had fixed limits.

". . . in free space, its overall delta-vee." Pausing before the DV section's entrance doors, Tetzl continued. "But to enter a gravity well and ground safely, then again to rise, perhaps half so much is left for spatial maneuver."

As she droned on, spouting facts and figures, Rance abstracted his own summary. All right then: in the Solar System, say, landing on Earth and lifting again, where could this gocart start from and return to? Figuring with shortcuts and approximations, after a while he nodded. Well past Mars, maybe close to the asteroid belt. *If they got lucky.*

Talked out for the time being, Tetzl activated the door controls. For moments nothing happened. Inwardly, Rance groaned. Those doors were *hull* when the DV was out; they had to be heavy muthas, and the idea of cranking them open manually didn't thrill him a bit. But then came clicks and whir of mechanism, and the portal opened.

Dim lights came on; ahead, a ramp swung down to reach the DV's own entrance a few meters away, while around the cylinder's periphery lay the Vehicle's landing legs, all three now folded inward against its stern. And between those, near the perimeter and protruding only slightly, the drive nodes.

Entering the lander was a two-stage process: first into an airlock chamber and then, when that door closed and an inner one opened, all the way inside. Immediately Rance saw that this smaller craft followed different design criteria. No Velcro walkways here: the three-meter central tunnel was lined with handholds. Well, of course; like *Starfinder* in its first year, acceleration substituting for gravity, "down" would be rearward.

And decel? For slowing in space and for landing, the pilot would swap ends and proceed, as Jimmy Hanchett put it, "bassackwards." In between, though, hitting atmosphere, the needlenose heat shield had to go first. For swinging the vessel, side thrusters were provided. Thinking about it, Rance felt glad he wasn't a pilot!

Tetzl still leading, they propelled themselves along the dim-lit tunnel. Better lighting was no doubt available, but Rance didn't know where the switches were; if the captain knew, she didn't bother.

By the time they reached the far end, Rance saw forward as "up." Here, below the nosecone, the tunnel ended as a hole in a larger deck surface, circled by a safety railing. With zero gee, they ignored the railing's gate, swinging past and planting feet on the only Velcro surface they'd seen aboard.

Standing with one hand on the rail, Tetzl used the other for pointing. "Control, there; consoles with acceleration couches for two pilots and communicator, only. They share major viewscreen for forward view, five auxiliaries available to see behind or laterally." She turned. "To this side, food preparation and consumption. At far side, two latrine cubicles, one for zero-gee usage. From peripheral bulkhead, ten more couches will fold out." Nodding, she added, "Three gravities, this vehicle can produce. Though not for extended periods. One gee is standard thrust." *Yes, teacher.*

Now the woman sat in the left-hand pilot's seat and began to finger the controls. "These are the test procedures. You will observe." The other three gathered behind her. "Before warming up Traction Drive, ascertain that Virtual Thrust switch is operated and locked. Drive components may now be activated and adjusted without danger of ejecting Vehicle from the ship."

Right; the drive's respective components would go through all the motions; it just wouldn't *push.*

On and on she went. Rance lost interest; his attention wandered, then returned. ". . . thermocouples. Going into atmosphere, temperature differential of heat shield feeds current into warm superconductors for magnetic deceleration coupling." Irina Tetzl laughed. "It has not been tested, this. First time should be interesting."

Eventually she finished. Rance knew he hadn't picked up on more than half the procedures she'd demonstrated. But what the hell; that's what manuals were for.

Powering down the equipment, Old Iron Tits concluded by returning lights to their original dimness. Why? There'd be a switch in the airlock, surely, with which to turn all lighting off when they left the DV. "By the book," though. Right . . .

As they clambered back through the tunnel, rearward became "up." Into the airlock, then out of it, the curved ramp forced still another reorientation. They walked its length to the curved deck. Waiting, then, as the ramp pivoted to its original position as a deck section, Rance said, "Captain?"

"Yes, Collier?"

"What I can't figure—how can you be so fired up over all the DV's ins and outs? I mean, by the time that thing's used, we'll all be back on Earth more than twenty years."

Over one pale eye an eyebrow lifted. "By the plan, yes. But no plan is certain."

XVII

SPLASHING

Between the early crises, getting to know his way around *Starfinder,* and the surprises of Wallin's visit and the new Habegger Gates, Rance's first six months had gone fast.

This second half year, though, dragged along interminably. Earlier he had looked forward each day to what might happen next, what he could discover; now all he awaited was "getting out of this chicken outfit." He didn't like feeling this way, but neither did he seem to have much choice.

Despite himself, though, Rance Collier still enjoyed learning new things. And although it wasn't exactly his own idea, like it or not he was coming to know a lot about the DV, about the means of transshipping fuel and cargo—not to mention personnel—when the Vehicle was separated from *Starfinder,* and about portions of the larger ship he had previously ignored.

Such as, for instance, its outer shell.

■   ■   ■

It was at the end of Irina Tetzl's watch, one day early in the third month of her command, that one of the forward sensors blew and a quadrant of that viewscreen turned to senseless, writhing blotches. When Rance reported for his own watch trick, coming from a small celebration of the approximate date the starship *Arrow* was due to "launch," he found everyone in Control just standing there, looking at the malfunctioning unit.

Called in to troubleshoot, Jimmy Hanchett went through the routines of readjustment, replacement of modules, and patching across between circuits at different points to pin down the fault. Finally he shook his head. "It's the sensor itself," he said, "out on the hull's surface. Everything else checks okay."

The captain nodded. "Schadel?" Fleurine, starting to leave Control, paused and looked around. "You are well acquainted with ship's stores. Draw a new sensor unit from inventory and take it to—" She hesitated, then said, "—to transfer ring entrance A. Hull access nearest defective sensor is adjacent."

As Fleurine left, Tetzl continued. "Hanchett, you are best qualified to make the replacement. And to carry and hold tools for you—uh, Collier, you will do that. For the time necessary, Sergei will fill your place here." Sarge didn't look especially happy, but he didn't protest, either. "You may leave now."

Jimmy cleared his throat. "You ever check out in a suit, Rance?"

Collier shook his head as Tetzl said, "Suits? I see no need."

Hanchett's air of patience, Rance thought, was somewhat overdone. "We don't know what killed the eye. It's *supposed* to disengage and pull inside easily, with the flex cuff cinching down to hold air. But what if a pebble got it, and warped the holding collar? We'd have to pull the mounting plate, too, and that'd leave a hole—about eight inches by six, if I remember. I don't know about Rance, but I'd sort of like to keep breathing."

The nomenclature part was Greek to Rance, but he figured Jimmy knew his business, so he stayed clammed. The captain frowned, then said, "Yes. Of course. Leaving the access tunnel you will seal the hatch and isolate the maintenance cubby. Very well. Hennessey—if you hurry, you can reach Schadel before she leaves stores. Have her draw also two light vacuum suits. Of the medium size."

"And a new mounting plate for the sensor," Jimmy added, "in case the old one is damaged. With a fresh gasket, of course."

"Yes, that too," Irina confirmed. Then, "Hanchett—meet her by ring entrance A; there you can help Collier with the suit and instruct him in its use."

That quickly, Rance was dismissed, off to what might turn out to be his first encounter with vacuum.

Gathered near the transfer entrance, Dink Hennessey and Fleurine waited while Rance and Jimmy stripped down to briefs, then assisted them into vacuum suits. Never having used one before, Rance needed more than a little help.

The suit was insulex fabric, only a few millimeters thick, an elastic total-body stocking with but one semi-rigid component: the collar that pulled up and forward to circle from below his chin to the crown of his head, and formed a seal with the transparent facemask. Riding high on his back like a flattened, flexible rucksack, the built-in air tank made no great inertial burden and balanced well.

Just now the mask hung, slightly ajar, from its top-mounted hinge. Closing it, Hanchett had told him, automatically started a flow of air from the tank and activated the short range talkset. "Move around a little," Jimmy said now. "See if you've got it all on smooth, not binding anywhere."

Following instructions, Rance said, "It feels okay. What else do I need to know?"

"Heat control." Yes; the small knob low at his right hip. "It adjusts your thermostat setting. Don't ever move it very much at a time, and wait about ten-fifteen seconds after you do make a change, to see where it stabilizes."

"Like the hot water in a shower."

They both grinned. Hanchett handed Rance the sensor unit and a shoulder-bag tool kit. "All right. Time to go."

. . .

Across the corridor from the transfer entrance and a few meters along, Jimmy undogged the hatch and climbed into a narrow tunnel, leading into the start of *Starfinder*'s forward taper. From his stints on the DV, Rance found the dim lighting familiar. Since this outer tube tapered down to nothing in a mere ten meters, he knew they couldn't have far to go, and in fact the tunnel dead-ended after about five. At its hullward side, here, was another hatch; Jimmy opened that one also, and once the two were inside the smallish compartment it led to, dogged it down again and turned to Rance. "Temperature all right?"

Since Rance hadn't noticed one way or the other, he guessed it was and nodded. "Okay then. Let's close faceplates and get started."

Done, and done. The compartment was equipped with mooring lines; to counter the problems of zero gee each man chose one to attach to belt-level loops on their suits, giving them anchors to brace against. Then at Hanchett's request Rance handed him tools, held them for him, or returned them to the kit.

After a time Jimmy shook his head. "Sonofabitch; the mounting's jammed, all right. Dogging wrench?"

As Rance found the desired tool he hesitated; Hanchett's stance put him *behind* the hole he intended to open. "Jimmy?"

"Yeah? What is it?"

"Look where you're standing. When you open that thing—"

"So the air goes out. What—?"

"And you've got your head in a particle accelerator beam. The interstellar gas—protons, dust motes, whatever—it's going to be coming in here at relativistic speeds."

"Oh Jesus! You're right." Quickly he unhooked his mooring line, switched to another, and positioned himself out of the line of fire. "Got to watch where I keep my hands, too. And another thing . . ."

"Yes?"

"Once the hole's open I have to do this job fast and get it right the first time. Because that stuff's going to bombard the rear bulkhead. And you know what happens to beam targets; they get radioactive as all hell."

Rance thought about it. "Finish the work quickly, yes; the secondary emission's not for basking in, even with the suits. But this won't be a *focused* beam; once the plate's back in place, I doubt there'll be enough residual activity to notice."

Through the faceplate Jimmy's grin looked skeptical. "You sure about that?"

Challenged, Rance had to hedge. "Well, *almost.*"

"That's what I thought. Gimme the wrench."

It hadn't been exactly peaches and cream, Rance reflected, but the new sensor assembly was in place. When the plate pulled free, escaping air howled like a banshee until the sound slowly diminished and then died. In vacuum the suit felt *looser;* otherwise Rance noticed no difference. During their exposure time, certainly, temperature gradient hadn't penetrated.

Acting on second thoughts, Jimmy had put his sensor-plate-gasket combination together *before* pulling the old one, so the hull hadn't been open more than three or four minutes at most before air could be restored. Now, back to the corridor and stripping off his suit, Rance was pleased that it drew only scattered clicks from Fleurine's counter.

Also, it felt good to get his own clothes on again.

With Dink and Fleurine carrying the suits, Rance the toolkit, and Jimmy Hanchett the damaged components, the four walked together as far as Control; there Rance followed Jimmy inside.

Tetzl was gone; on duty were Rozanski, Margrete, and Benita, with Sergei Dimitrov still filling in for Rance.

Holding out the plate with its sensor, Hanchett showed it to Cleve. "See? A gouge, melted right across the eye and one side of the collar. Couldn't possibly have separated them."

"You were right, yes." Rozanski gestured to the forward screen. "You'll notice we have picture again. A little out of whack, though; needs adjustment."

Sure enough, that quadrant's view was a bit off focus, and flickered unnervingly. "Half a mo," and after a little fiddling, Hanchett brought it back in sync. "That does it." He looked around. "Well, guess I'm done here, for now."

As the man turned away, Rance said, "Okay, Sarge, I relieve you. Sorry about the overtime."

The Russian shrugged. "It is all right. But I am just as glad to have rest of shift free, before Zsana goes on duty."

Cleve shook his head. "Afraid not. And you hold up a minute, Jimmy. Irina wants your report in person. And Rance's. She said to tell you both, she'd be in quarters."

Rance might have been the only one close enough to hear; what Jimmy Hanchett said was, "Oh, *shit!*"

Outside Control and moving forward toward the transfer ring, Rance said, "Getting a little tired of her using up your free time, are you? Same here."

Hanchett's glare surprised him. "If *that's* all . . ."

Puzzled, Rance waited, until they reached the nearest ring entrance. Punching the button, Jimmy said, "She likes to play games; hadn't you known that?"

Rance didn't need to ask what kind. He hoped he was wrong.

Even after standing the last half of his watch, Rance when he got back to quarters was still churning in the gut. "Su, you're not going to believe this! Old Iron Tits—"

And he told her. How the woman had interrupted Jimmy's report by shucking her robe, wearing her uniform trousers and nothing more. "The tits may not be iron, but just by looking, the nipples could be." How she'd told them exactly what she wanted. Well, told *him*, mostly; Jimmy already seemed to know. "Said we could draw straws or something, for work stations." He made a face. "That's my term, not hers."

"And which did you draw?"

Of all things, Su was grinning. "It's not funny, dammit! I told you she's trouble. I walked out, was what."

Not, though, before Irina Tetzl had the last word—to the effect that while she wouldn't push the matter at this moment, eventually Rance could either cooperate or the captain could change his and Su's off-watch duty schedules ". . . not, perhaps, so convenient for you."

And then, shaking her head, "If Teng is bad influence on you, something more may be needed. Perhaps she should return to Earth."

He had Su's attention now; she said, "This isn't play, is it? Or nymphomania, either, in the classic sense. What it's about is power."

Glumly, Rance agreed. "She's had Jimmy under her thumb, or whatever, for some time now. He and Cleve —the three of them, that's one reason they're gone a lot, from their watch tricks. And how many more do you suppose she's put her mark on?"

Su's brows drew together. "Fleurine doesn't talk much these days. I couldn't think why—but having Jimmy at that woman's beck and call? It's no wonder she's touchy."

Having aired his upset, Rance felt some relief. He said, "Right. And I don't want *you* getting that way."

"But I wouldn't." Rance must have looked dubious; she added, "I'm quite serious. If it means getting into a battle of rank and authority—Rance, go ahead and prong the silly slut. In any orifice she offers, up to and including her left ear!"

Almost but not quite, he had to laugh. "Nice thought. But it might not be possible. Today, for instance, I couldn't have.

"It's a peculiarity of mine. Anger and arousal are mutually and totally incompatible."

Her eyes widened; he waited for the barb. But all she said was, "Then I do hope you're calmed down by now."

Waiting for the trap to spring kept Rance wound up like a three-dollar watch, but for several days Old Iron Tits ignored him. Sometimes he told himself she'd only been throwing a scare into him for a joke, but he couldn't really believe it. Still, days passed and she made no move. Unless you counted the way she stared, eyes narrowed, any time she had occasion to speak to him.

Preoccupied as he was, even the first reception of objects at the *Roamer* Gate failed to interest him much. But Su wouldn't let him vegetate; she took him with her to the lounge, where the new development was under discussion. Since Tetzl wasn't there, he was able to relax and pay attention.

Roamer's log brought no major surprises. The ship had come up to nine-nine-five on sked, in time for the first relief cadre to replace its original counterpart. Otherwise the first info packets contained mostly the same kind of things *Starfinder* had sent in the other direction.

Including, of course, full rosters. Of the names listed, Rance recognized only Anne Portaris, in visitor status for a month or so as supernumerary observer.

He rather hoped, then, for a good meaty report from Anne. All he got, though, was a brief note:

Rance:
     We have our gates up and running, so hello! I do love being out here, will hate to have to leave.
                    More later, if I find time.   Anne P.

All in all, the occasion felt like a letdown. *Roamer* had communicated; big deal. Here on *Starfinder,* Rance felt like a beginning dog paddler trying to evade a barracuda.

So at first he almost welcomed the distraction of the unexpected dust cloud, taking the captain's mind off personal considerations.

But not for long; the way Dink Hennessey explained it, in meeting at the lounge, *Starfinder* could be in deep. "We had no way of knowing this was here," he said. "Earth didn't spot it because you can't see one cloud hidden behind another. The one we detoured to miss," he added. "And our own sensors don't notice anything so tenuous, up close."

It boiled down to a density, in average particles per stere, which didn't seem like much, between two and three times what they'd been passing through. And no way to tell how far the cloud extended ahead of them, or if it might get denser still. "All we know is what we're hitting, and that we're seeing no signs of the stuff thinning out."

"The effect so far," said Cleve Rozanski, "is that we're slowed down, using extra fuel just to hold current speed, and what with increased particle friction, we may have to ease off further to keep hull temperatures down."

Superficially the numbers didn't sound so bad: Vee

down from dot-nine-nine-five to nine-nine-four, and
fuel drain up maybe ten percent. But the delta-vee
changed t_o/t from ten to roughly nine-point-one-four,
". . . so we're getting eight-point-six percent less fuel
and using ten percent more. That's not a deficit we can
live with indefinitely."

Same bind as before, thought Rance. Except that then
we speeded up to help the time ratio and this time we
can't; that trick won't work. He tried to think what
would happen if they simply cut drive and coasted,
letting the tanks fill and then powering up again. But
too many other things had hooks in his mind; he
couldn't concentrate.

One thing he did know: coasting long enough to slow
very far would screw up the Habegger Gate schedules
something fierce.

The problem gnawed at him until he found it hard to
think of much else. So that when Old Iron Tits finally
made her play, she caught him with his pants down.

Figuratively and literally, both. Finishing four hours
of after-watch inspection duties, he returned to quarters. Su was on watch shift; Rance steamed in the
shower for a time and came out to find Irina Tetzl,
unclad, waiting for him.

"What is this?" As if he didn't know.

On the small table beside her sat a tray of small,
steaming pastries; they smelled of cheese and herbs. "A
gift. For you and Teng. You may have one now."

Anything to gain time; he took two and nibbled
slowly. They tasted as good as they smelled, so he
reached for another.

"That is enough." She flicked his towel free and
tossed it aside; she touched herself, then stroked her
finger along his lip. He'd never thought himself especially susceptible to womanscent, but suddenly he felt
hazy; before he could tell her about anger incapacitat-
ing him, his body's reaction made that claim moot. Still
unspeaking she drew him with her to the floor.

Somehow, resisting was just too damn much trouble.
Fatigue and confusion slowed the pace of his responses.
He felt surges of intense physical pleasure—but some-
how they didn't connect to *him*. Like some kind of

puppet he went through the motions and waited for it all to finish. But before his climax ended matters she put him through nearly all the paces he knew, and herself cried triumph more times than he would have thought possible.

Finally releasing him she sat up, and spoke. "Now you see, Collier. We shall have good times. But not alone in this fashion. All these things *together*, I prefer."

Standing, she clothed herself. As Rance pulled on his slacks, not bothering with anything more, she turned to leave, then paused. "I had forgot. A celebration, this has been."

His voice came out flat. "Of what?"

"The dust cloud. It thins. Soon we shall again build speed." She laughed. "That is why we had no others here. Hanchett is making the calculations, to regain schedule with Earth's gates. And Cleve—he sits alongside, learning, so that he can do such things when Jimmy is gone."

Rance poured himself a drink. Just the one, and the hell with being a good host. "You happy now?"

"I have been less so. And you?"

He thought, then shook his head. "You don't want to know."

Oddly, her smile looked sincerely warm, no hint of gloating. "Submission does not come easy to you; I am sorry. But take heart. You have already begun to learn."

Before he could find any answer, she was out the door.

Though he was sensitized and on the lookout, Su when he told her showed no hint of hidden amusement. "These acts," she said, "they humiliate you? As in earlier times, perhaps?"

He still felt a little offtrack, but finally the association connected. "Yeah. Performing to order. This is probably what Charlyssa wanted to be when she grew up."

"Perhaps." Absently she sampled one of the pastries. After a moment: "Rance? did you eat any of these?"

"Yeah. Why?"

Now she laughed. "The oregano disguises it rather well. But has it been *that* long since you had hash brownies? Or—" She sniffed more closely. "—something rather similar. . . ."

Doped? Bedammt! Inside him, mirth stirred feebly but did not surface. Su frowned. "But you, Rance. Are you going to let this—this silly *charade*—truly affect your emotional level?"

"*Let* it?"

"Precisely. Consider her a machine, like—like the drive exciters. And also like them, in need of maintenance."

"So you're saying I'm just part of the service crew? That's all you see in this?"

"Of course not. But I find it a good, calming way to view the matter. And you?"

Rance shrugged. "No, but I'll give it a try."

Belatedly he stood and made her a welcoming drink. At her first sip she nodded thanks. "Rance? It could be important, to have her pleased with you and thinking you feel the same way."

Remembering, he gulped. "Oh hell yes. Her threat; I'd forgotten. To bump you back to Earth."

Su shook her head. "Not that. I doubt she could get enough people to agree. Though I'd as soon not test the matter."

"What, then?"

Leaning forward, she said, "We decided, didn't we, that she's up to something? Insinuating into her good graces might be the best way to learn what it is."

"I suppose so." But he didn't have to like it.

He didn't like living with suspense, either. A week passed with no summons; was Old Iron Tits trying to soften him up?

Then one day, at change of watch when his group relieved hers, she beckoned. "After your shift, Collier—"

But then the Earth Gate buzzer sounded; when its cycle was done, an indicator light stayed on, blinking. Irina Tetzl turned toward Cleve Rozanski. "Your team has the watch. Sergei, Dink—come with me to the Gate. If more help is needed, Cleve, I will call from there and you will arrange for it." Leaving Fleurine standing alone, looking as though she wanted to go along but couldn't think how to arrange it, Tetzl led her assigned helpers away.

Rance walked over to Fleurine. "Don't worry about it. She doesn't seem to like women much, is all." Grinning despite himself, he added, "Maybe you're lucky."

The watch shift passed without further incident, and afterward he received no summons to captain's digs. Instead, the entire shift reported to Habegger's original Tush.

Because incoming from Earth were the components for *Starfinder*'s third pair of Gates, the ones that would link the ship to *Arrow*.

And with them, taped to one of the larger crates, notice that help on the installation would be along shortly.

Out of Tetzl's earshot Rance heard somebody say, "Well, this ought to keep her busy for a while."

XVIII

SPILL

Without delay, Irina Tetzl put off-watch personnel on schedules to move the incoming equipment crates around the peripheral corridor to both installation sites: transmitter directly forward of Drive Node Three and receiver diametrically opposite. Knowing how poor he was at handling massive objects in zero gee, Rance hoped with fervor that most of those would be managed before he got off his watch.

But when Jimmy's team came on duty and Rance followed Cleve and Benita and Margrete to take over this new chore, a formidable pile still awaited—and at intervals, more kept coming.

Returning from a haul, Dink Hennessey grinned. "Take a look," he said. "Whoever packed this stuff must have been talking with Maggie Sligo."

After a moment, Rance saw what he meant. To each crate was fastened an envelope containing its detailed shipping document, which listed all contents. Also, these papers specified whether the gear was part of the transmit or receive Gate. But now Rance saw that opening the envelopes wasn't a first necessity. On the front of each was marked a single large letter.

M for Mouth, or T for Tush.

Dink grinned. "Beats hell out of having to read those flimsies, and keep track of them, *before* we move the stuff."

After four hours of jockeying mass and securing it at its new location, Rance was glad when Tetzl excused him, along with the rest of Cleve's watch crew, from further stevedoring. Back in quarters he showered, put on clean clothes, made a light drink, and sat back to watch a disk. It was an old film in new form, this version synthesized from its flat-screen original by the holo process, so he knew the added, auxiliary view angles came not from nature but by calculation. Still he was surprised at how good a job someone had done. As the eighteenth-century sailing ship *Bounty* (in replica, of course) crashed and shuddered its way through a tropical storm, a quick close-up sent Rance shying back from driven spray.

Chuckling at himself, he sat back to see what new cruelty William Bligh would visit, under the guise of discipline, upon his hapless crewmen. But fatigue sent him into a half doze, filled with confusion. The next relief cadre wasn't due for another three months, so what was Bligh doing here? And there was Su Teng, embracing the new captain's second-in-command!

What—? Blinking daze away, he sat up. The woman in the holo had hair like Su's, long and black; that was what had fooled him, created this sleight-of-mind illusion. That and exhaustion, nothing more.

Or was there?

After a watch trick on top of four hours moving cargo, Su came in bushed, content to nurse a glass of wine while Rance readied their meal: salmon "fresh" from Earth, with a side of miscellaneous vegetation—including several kinds that must have become popular since *Starfinder* left that planet. Rance wasn't sure whether he liked them or not. But Su didn't complain, so he kept silence on the subject.

As he poured coffee she said, "How much more bale-toting do you think we have left to do?"

"Not sure. When our crew finished up, the pile at the Mouth site looked about the size of what I remember from before." He shrugged. "Just have to wait and see. But I think we'll be into uncrating, next round. That, and disposing of the crates and other debris." Back to Earth, that stuff went; with Habgates, starships had no significant garbage disposal problems.

Reminiscing, Rance grinned; Elliott McCalder had had the right idea at the wrong time.

Another thought came: "The installation crew. Do you suppose Shirley Tate's coming again?"

Then his mind clicked into gear; before Su answered, he knew what she'd say: "But it's been less than four months, here, since she and her crew went home. So—"

"Yeah. And round trip to Earth—that's nearly five. Sorry; my head's only running on about two nodes." Now the numbers came to him; these new installers would have entered the pipeline roughly a year, Earth time, before Shirley and Fred and Pete could have made it home.

He said as much. And "Keeping track of us and Earth and *Roamer* isn't going to be the half of it."

"Oh?"

"*Arrow.* What with cranking up to speed in three months Earth time, and then running at a time ratio of twenty-five, it's going to take a computer program to figure relative time scales."

But after another three months by *Starfinder's* clocks, that certainly wouldn't be *his* worry.

The installation help turned out to be not a team as before, but only one technical supervisor. Blackbearded and burly, Rafe Purdue looked more like a blacksmith than a skilled tech, but as Margrete Van Der Veer put it, aside to Rance, "Brains and muscles aren't necessarily incompatible." Unless Rance misread the signs, muscles and Margrete weren't, either. He didn't look to see how Ramon, standing beside Margrete, felt about it.

With only one knowledgeable person straw-bossing a

bunch of part-time grunts, Rance expected the installation job would take at least a month and be screwed up more often than not.

But the way Rafe handled things was to give two or more people a specific, limited piece of work to do, explain it carefully, and leave the scene. When he came back, either the task was done, or else—also by instruction—if a snag had come up, the team had stopped and *waited* for him. "If you're not sure what you're doing," he'd told them all, "don't bull ahead. Delay is better than having to do it over again."

It sounded fine to Rance. He wasn't in all that much hurry to see this job finished, anyway.

Because aside from the other two watch officers, Old Iron Tits never pulled anyone from duty for her private games. And since the installation began, she'd left even them alone.

One step followed another. Soon the base mountings were in place, the power leads run, and both Gates well into assembly. Not until Rance finished his third day's stint of helping in that process did Tetzl request his presence.

And then for a totally unexpected reason.

Reporting to captain's digs, he found both occupants there and was relieved to see they had their clothes on. Well, Cleve was shirtless, but in quarters that was standard for him.

The man offered a drink; Rance said, "A little bourbon would be nice," and Rozanski poured a healthy slug over ice. Taking a seat, Rance waited.

Setting down her own pale drink, Irina said, "This ship *Arrow*. Tell me what you know."

Where to start? As he considered, she said, "Not the five gees, cutting accel and decel to three months each where this ship requires a year, almost. Or the time ratio of twenty-five, which covers fifty light-years in two years of ship's time."

What, then? He asked it; she leaned forward. "Tell me how its time scale relates to our own."

Hmmm. "Let's see—we need a baseline. If *Arrow* left Earth eight years after we did, and accelerated and then leveled off to constant speed, all of it right on sked, then they'd start their constant vee and their twenty-five time ratio when *our* chronos read one-point-seven years out from Earth. And since that time, which is only a few days ago—I'm not sure just how many—they're living two days for every five of ours."

"Or fifty on Earth," Cleve said.

"So they will reach their goal," said Tetzl, "in only two years. How splendid!"

"Two of *theirs*," Rance corrected her. "This ship still gets where it's going nearly twenty years before *Arrow* does."

The captain shrugged. "These things tax my understanding. Which is, needless to say it, the reason I ask questions."

"Right. All clear now, though?" Rance took the last gurgle of melt-watered bourbon and stood. "Then I'll be going."

"Oh. You are tired, Collier?"

"After twelve hours' duty? Tired and sweat-stinking and hungry. So if I may—"

"Yes, of course. And thank you."

As he opened the door and left, Rance expected her to add a parting shot about there being other times.

But she didn't.

Remembering the *Roamer* Gates, Rance had his fingers figuratively crossed. But while these equipment inventories did show some discrepancies, they were minor and caused no crises. So that during the tenth day after Purdue's arrival, the man announced that the Gates were ready for activation. "Let's break for dinner," he told his current crew, "and then we'll fire up."

Good enough. Rance and the rest of Cleve's gang had about two hours left on their installation shift; they'd be in at the finale, not just standing by. Now, instead of separating to their own various quarters and eating alone, all four trooped along with Rafe to the galley and broke out frozen rations. Rance chose a spicy curry dish; at Cleve's doubtful look he said, "Hey, why not live dangerously?"

"It's your stomach."

"And it's hungry." With his packet zapped and steaming, Rance sat and opened it. Hmmm—not too spicy, after all!

For a time, eating, no one had much to say. Benita finished first; after a sip of coffee she said, "Someone else is on *Arrow* now, getting their Gates set up?"

Rafe shook his head. "No. Theirs were installed as part of the initial construction."

"All three sets?" Margrete asked it.

"Yes. But only two in action." Using his fingers, Purdue made a diagram in air; Rance found it hard to follow. "This is you, this is *Roamer,* this is *Arrow.* And this—" his coffee cup—"is Earth. Now you, here—you can gate to all three other points. But if *Roamer* and *Arrow* were hooked up the same way, that'd make a closed net. See?" Rance nodded, but Rafe wasn't looking at him. "That's not what they want. So *Roamer* and *Arrow* don't connect to each other; *Roamer* will gate to the Number Four ship when it goes out, *Arrow* to the one after, and so on."

After a moment Rance saw the pattern. "Making a connected *string* of ships, adding to either end, but each with a direct link to Earth?"

Purdue's finger aimed like Bang-you're-dead. "Got it."

"How do they know," Cleve put in, "when to turn their end on? *Arrow,* I mean—their Gate to *us.* "

That was something Rance had puzzled over, too. Rafe said, "They don't. They fired up, I expect, as part of getting the whole ship tuned, soon as they came through their Earth Gate. So at their end it's been operational for some time, likely."

"All right, so I asked the wrong question." But Cleve wasn't done. "How do they know when to start sending?"

"They still don't. They put their test object in and hit Transmit. When your end's ready, it goes."

"But—" Four people tried to ask what sounded like four different questions; when they subsided, Rance was first to try again. "You're saying that Habegger's Mouth swallows when it knows that *two years later* its Tush is going to be ready to function. Do I have that right?"

"Reckon you do, Collier."

"But that's"— Rance had the momentum; the others'

protests died as he continued—"faster-than-light communication. It's passing information from future to past. And that's impossible."

"If you say so." Purdue didn't seem at all bothered. "But that's what happens. In tests on Earth, plenty of them." No one spoke; he stood. "What say we get back to it?"

On the way, Rance tried to assimilate this idea he didn't really understand. Then he gave it up—in favor of trying to think how to use the effect for *practical* communication.

"Power on!" The new Gate, somewhat different from the others in physical layout, showed all the proper indications; inside its chamber glowed the familiar ionization. Along with a half dozen others on hand, Rance waited for Rafe—or possibly Cleve—to lead off by placing the obligatory ritual copy of *Starfinder*'s log in position for sending.

But nobody did. Rafe and Cleve stood looking along the peripheral corridor. Oh, sure—the queen bee! And yes, finally, there came Old Iron Tits, absent from her watch trick and gussied up in her best uniform.

Smiling, she approached. "Thank you for waiting." She held up a packet. "I have brought the log totally up to date." And most likely, Rance thought, edited it more than a little. "Shall we now forward it to *Arrow*?"

Purdue gestured; she stepped up and set the object at the platform's center, then moved aside as Rafe punched for activation. Rance shaded his eyes against the flare of colors; when it died, he saw without surprise that the space was empty.

"So it functions!" The process might have become routine to most of the group, but Tetzl, shaking Purdue's hand, still seemed enthusiastic. Still holding that hand, she said, "Come. We will celebrate the occasion." And looked to Cleve Rozanski, who followed the two away at a fairly rapid pace. And even in this farcical situation, Rance noticed, Irina's whipcord movement carried the inward certainty of command.

So. Purdue would be leaving shortly, but meanwhile, Old Iron Tits had no intention of letting him go to waste!

. . .

Su, when she came in from watch, was pleased that the Gate was working and amused at Rance's comments. "Won't she be a trifle cautious? After all, the man *is* going straight back to Earth, so wouldn't she be concerned as to what he might report?"

"Beats me. I don't know how she thinks. *If* she thinks." He shrugged. "Let's eat, shall we?"

With no further mention of *Starfinder*'s captain, he and Su enjoyed a pleasant evening and retired early.

Next day after watch Rance and Margrete drew DV inspection. By now, this was routine: getting to and then into the Vehicle, running the tests, and logging them. As they prepared to power down and leave the craft, Margrete said, "Rance? Do you like Captain Tetzl?"

Thinking fast: "She's competent."

"Yes. But *personally*?"

"Hey, we all have our rough edges. Sometimes she and I get along better than at other times." There; no lies, yet nothing incriminating. "Why?"

"But in bed. With her and—and other people."

"I wouldn't know." *And I'd like to keep it that way.* But didn't say so, out loud.

"But how do you—? I mean, Ramon . . . ?" No way was Rance going to answer that one. Margrete said, "I hate her. She takes and takes and takes. And he says he has to; there's no choice. How do you—?" Tears streaming, she waited for his answer.

Her hands reached out; unthinking, he drew her to him. But only in a hug, for comfort. "We go back a way, Old Iron Tits and I." Mistake? Too late now . . . "We win some, we lose some—she and I both." Oh, all right; spill it. "But so far—I repeat —*so* far, she's only caught me once, and solo." Moving back, so they could look at each other, he grinned. "No bets on keeping ahead of the game, though."

Wiping her eyes, Margrete made a shaky smile of her own. "Thank you, Rance. There's nothing anyone can do, I suppose, but it's so good to *talk* with someone."

"Any old time." So they buttoned up the Deployment Vehicle and took their report back to Control.

. . .

Whatever Rafe Purdue may or may not have experienced, he hadn't yet left *Starfinder*. Entering Control, Rance saw on the forward screen, low and to the left, a dim, flattened disc. And watching it, along with the watch crew, was Rafe.

Turning to Rance, Su Teng said, "It's about half a light-year out; the view's hi-mag. A solar system, we think, in process of formation—just another dust cloud clumping together." And a cloud of that density, of course, was easily detectable. Especially at a distance that put all of it into the sensors' field of view, showing dim gray against star-pierced black.

The first thing Rance noticed was that the central mass, barely seen, wasn't luminous. "Not much of a star, is it?"

"What they call a gray dwarf, I think," said Jimmy Hanchett. "Of course, it's not finished yet."

Su said, "A little over a hundred times Jupiter's mass, the computer reads it. And it does radiate, in the low infra-red."

Speaking in a soft voice, Zsana Ionescu added, "Some radio emission, also. And now I think the apparent bulge, to the side we will be passing, is actually another large planetary mass, emerging from behind the greater object."

Rafe nodded. "Three of the big ones, then. Plus a lot of other lumps, probably, too small to make out from here."

"Such objects may show on the cube," Su said. "We're recording at higher mag than the screen circuits are set for."

"And this thing's floating out here all by itself," Rance mused. "Funny." Then he leaned forward. "Even funnier. Why's the whole thing *tipped* so much? I mean, our navigational baseline incorporates the solar ecliptic and an approximation of the galactic. But look at that!" He waved a hand. "Must be twenty degrees of tilt. How come?"

Su shrugged. "Why not? Or you might also ask, why Pluto? Seventeen degrees, isn't it? Rance, the ecliptic is just the average, the condition from which specific instances deviate."

"Some more than others, yeah. And out here by itself,

this batch of stuff might have peeled off with a little extra spin some way. Is that what you mean?"

"More or less. You see—"

But he wasn't listening. In the dust cloud, well out from its center, a speck of light appeared. Rance pointed. "Look at that! What's a star doing *there*?" Because if the central body gave no light, how could a lesser object?

As everyone watched, mostly without speaking, gradually the speck grew brighter. Abruptly, Jimmy Hanchett reached out and made an adjustment; on the screen the cloud showed greater contrast against surrounding blackness. Within the outline of the cloud appeared a small black oval, and at its edge sat the glowing point. "Hell's bells!" Jimmy blurted. "That's a star. Shining through a *hole*. "

No doubt about it. They were looking at the hole from a slight angle—any more and they couldn't have seen it at all—which to their view flattened what was probably a circle. Su shook her head, hair rippling at her waist. "Dust's eddying in, fuzzing the edges a little, but something swept a circular path straight through that cloud. And not too long ago, either, or diffusion would be filling it in more, by now."

"What?" Rance said. "Comet? Rogue planet? Something we should be on the lookout for?"

Another headshake. "No ordinary object, passing, could produce what we're seeing. The dust would just swirl in behind it, even before it got all the way through. No. Whatever did this had to be *fast*. And not merely displace the dust—but take it along."

Rance cleared his throat. "Would something going faster than light fill the bill?"

At *Starfinder*'s course angle, another two hours saw the hole's image flatten and disappear. Su's tapes, though, were there for everyone to view and comment on. With the entire group gathered, Control was crowded and most had nowhere to sit.

One after another, those who had opinions gave them. At the end of it the captain said, "What we *know* is that the dust cloud has a hole through it. All else that has been said is only speculation. But, of course, any

conjecture may be a lucky guess." She nodded toward
Rafe Purdue. "You have recorded all this, to take to
Earth along with the direct viewing data. Is there any
way I might assist you further?"

Purdue stood. "No, I think that does it. With this stuff
I can give 'em everything we know and let *them* do
some figuring."

By now, Tetzl's team had the watch. Nonetheless, she
went with the off-duty personnel to the rec lounge for a
brief farewell gathering before Rafe entered the pipeline.

Throughout, she stayed close to the man. Rance
couldn't help wondering whether she'd managed to
hook him into her triad game, but even given the opportunity, he could never have brought himself to ask.

Fairly soon Rafe finished his single drink, shook hands
all around, and allowed the captain to escort him to the
original, Earth-linked Habegger's Mouth.

Rance had been running scared so long that when Old
Iron Tits finally trapped him in her quarters with Cleve
Rozanski, he was almost relieved. It seemed to him that
part of his mind simply moved aside, watched, evalu-
ated, and took mental notes.

He knew better than to refuse the cheese puffs; he
took two. But unobtrusively, a bit at a time he crumbled
them and wastebasketed the fragments.

Again she used scent as stimulus. This time he
thought he understood: Her own was augmented by
some other essence, blending to heighten the effect.
Pheromones?

Whatever: Without the cheese goodie's hash-equiva-
lent, the stuff didn't bowl him over. *If I wanted to, I
could walk right out of here.*

But that wouldn't be too smart. Instead, when the
other two stripped, so did Rance. Moments later, all
three enmeshed into a soon-sweaty tangle. Immediately he found his dread-filled anticipation of homosex-
ual overtones groundless. Not that he could always tell
who was hugging whom, but between himself and
Cleve absolutely nothing sexual took place. Irina Tetzl
was the focus; no need or even allowance for peripher-
als to interact.

And at the pitch she was enjoying various simultaneous activities, she didn't seem to notice what Rance was doing—or rather, not doing: All his kissing was above the waist; below that line, it was all strictly hand action.

Even so, he found he'd never known how loud, at climax, a woman could get.

Or how long she could keep repeating.

When he first woke, Rance took a moment to figure out where he was. Then it came to him: He hadn't exactly been encouraged to go back to his own quarters. He looked around; surprisingly, he was alone in the big bed. *Get out of here!* But as he pushed the cover back, Irina Tetzl entered the room.

"Stay. We must talk." Dropping her robe, she sat down and slid to lie beside him, close enough to feel body warmth.

"About what?"

Not aggressively, she laid an arm over his shoulders. "You need to understand, Collier. I am not an ordinary woman; for good or bad, I am cursed with greatness. And greatness, you must comprehend, carries with it the burden of great needs." She caressed his shoulder, then the side of his neck. "You have been slow to accept and understand, but now it is all right."

"Sure." Yeah, *sure.* What the hell to say? "You've been —uh, carrying this burden all along?"

Eyes wide, she looked to him and nodded. "Oh, yes. I have known since I was very young, when I had an experience . . ."

She shook her head. "No, never mind; you would not grasp its meaning."

Maybe not, but I bet a shrink would! All he said, though, was, "Does the agency understand? About your greatness?"

"Of course not. They would not approve, would they? They want to control their captains—but I will not be controlled."

Against his better judgment he said, "But how about the tests? All that psych stuff. Wouldn't they show it?" If she wanted to think "it" meant greatness, let her.

She laughed. "Those tests showed a disciplined, obedient little woman, just the kind they like. Oh, somewhat headstrong; I needed to stand out in the field of candidates. But in general I gave them the characteristics they sought."

His eyes narrowed. "But the tests. How—?"

"Self-hypnosis. I outlined a personality profile to fit their template; I memorized it, and keyed it to a code word. In the test situation I triggered the code, passed the tests, thanked my masters nicely, and became myself again only when it was safe to do so."

"What'd happen if they found out?"

Another laugh, deeper this time. "And you think they would believe anyone could fool *them*? Why, you don't really accept it yourself. Do you?"

He shrugged. "Does it matter?" Now he sat up, looking down to her. "I'm curious. What's it all for?"

The lines of her face firmed with purpose. "So that when *Starfinder's* world is reached, *I* will set foot on it. As you can see, this will require some changes from the agency's planning."

Lady, you ain't just whistling "Dixie"! He pursed his own lips. "Yes, that's true." And then, "But why tell *me*?"

Her brows arched. "That is obvious, I would think. Now that you know, and understand, and are sealed to me, you will be another to help me."

Her fingers dug into his shoulder muscles. "I shall need the help of *all* I choose for my new world."

XIX

APPROACH

All too slowly, Environ adds pace. Yet Seit warms with hope, for *rate* of adding, itself grows. As Crippler's star, still distant, nears, unseen matter increases in concentration, even where viewer sees spacetime barren. *Dre* follows *dre*. Resistless, Environ proceeds.

Reaching breeding stage for second time, Imon finds itself ripening in consonance with Tith and again breeds, becoming birther to resultant Liijling.

As with Tev, earlier, totality of breeding experience overwhelms. When youngthon grows to join ageherd, Imon and Tith find its parting dolorous, yet somehow warming of internals.

No longer new adult, now established over several *dre*, Imon foresees toward third occasion of breeding stage with no anxiety, only pleasing thoughts.

Not soon to be: At least one *dre* must pass before that

happening. Yet already Imon finds comfort in its envisioning. As it pays mind to navigationist instrumentation, duty to Environ at mind's forefront, joy to come makes constant underflow.

After long proceeding through spacetime sparse in matter, outer worlds of Crippler's star come slowly nearer to reach: some too wide of Environ's path, but not all. In especial, world of striated surrounding disk lies within Environ's capability.

World itself masses far too large for ingestor field, but in world's sway of spacetime warp, worldlets are many. Seit and Chorl, with usage of electrologic, choose two of useful volume that may be taken: one easily, another in movement toward eclipse behind parent world so as to be possibility only if unprecedented risk is dared. One other, though less difficult to intersect, has yet itself too much bulk for encompassment.

< We (of necessity) forgo greater one > Seit affirms.

< And thus (on present path) take lesser? >

< Of (as before) agreement > Seit considers. < Still (not to curtail following gains) we study (to utmost limit of accuracy) how path of meeting with first worldlet best leads (by our changing) to taking of one beyond. >

< Study (as considered earlier) > states Chorl < proceeds. >

Life of Dutysetter Kahim ebbs toward completion. It displays no failure of mind, reports no distress of body; only onset of weakness, growing ever more quickly, signals coming end.

As do all Liij, Imon knows this fashion of ending is rare and to be envied, most suitable for one such as Kahim, from whose life Environ has great benefit.

Truly, some consider such ending may be *achieved* by so giving value. This belief Imon holds questionable; it offers comfort, but to Imon's thinking lacks notable support of fact.

Concept of such reward does not occupy thinking of Overwatcher Seit. Of importance now are dedication and consent of Dutysetter Kahim before weakness becomes too great, so that preparation may begin: semiconductor salts and other solutes ready, Healthwatchers at hand to commence infusions—all so that conversion to memory bone, of Kahim's brain and nervous system, be not delayed.

By good happening, mind of Kahim approaches ending in all proper function, of capability to produce exceptional memory bone.

But once life's last tremor begins, each instant is vital.

At Kahim's nesting place Seit greets it. < How passes (your experience of) time? >

Resting, Kahim raises and turns head, lifting ears to bare far eyes for seeing. Only faintly, at first, do palps add detail to mouthsounds as Kahim replies. < It moves (even at this time, so near ending) with (not expected) ease. You come (for which purpose) here? >

< To ask (needed formality) that you consent (dedicate) to join forebearal (memory bone) records of Environ. >

With vigorous assenting chirr, Kahim says, < I would (failing your request) send (of my own wish) even such word. >

Seit shows pleasure. < Most gratifying (though not, in slightest, unexpected), this decision. Might I (by your consent) summon Healthwatchers to (helpful in advance) prepare for ending? >

< With (your) permission, even more. > Kahim tilts head. < As Haef (if records truly state) chose, I would end (by means of) infusing conversion (to memory bone state) solutions. >

Seit is overcome. Palps entwined with Kahim's, it conveys, < Dutysetter, you are (always, but now in even greater portion) among Liij of highest (throughout Environ, for all *dre* to come) regard. >

Lacking ability further to express thought or feeling, Seit takes leave.

As Environ, ingestor field spread to limit of plasma energy support, sweeps on toward nearer worldlet, Imon fears. Being now primary navigationist, Imon must fit aim to pace, changing either or both as viewseer shows need for more curve, or less, to path.

To take and absorb first wordlet by direct approach is

not of difficulty. But resulting path then would intersect striated disk surrounding world, penetrating from below at narrow angle and emerging above—as ingestor, sweeping, created diagonal, cylindrical hole devoid of matter.

Of this result, disadvantage exists: At slow pace, hurtling matter *not* ingested can make impact on Environ's unprotected flank. To avoid such risk, Seit's decision is for Environ to veer, skirting outer edge of disk before pursuing second worldlet Seit hopes may be ingested. And veering slows pace, lowers probability of reaching second worldlet's path before it passes and escapes.

Surer procedure, Imon reasons, should be possible.

Having not yet status enabling it to consult memory bones directly, nor instruction in that process, Imon has sought knowledge from Liij who have done so. In particular, Imon regrets necessary leave-taking of Dutysetter Kahim, who answered well those questions Imon asked.

But now Imon knows more and could ask more, and there is none at hand to give answers. Learning-dutysetter Tith, Imon's second and most recent cobreeder, is helpful-minded and willing but has little more knowledge of advanced navigationist skill than Imon itself.

One who may, thinks Imon, is Chorl. The teacher's learning, Imon knows, spans many unrelated aspects of Environ's functions. While Chorl has not formal training as navigationist, it may well comprehend and disclose some point vital to present need.

And if not, what harm is caused by asking?

Preparing to leave nesting place and meet with Seit and others to share in final honor to Dutysetter Kahim, Chorl is met and delayed by navigationist Imon, saying < Here (soon to come) is need of Environ to encounter (for ingestion) worldlet on path that is (as determined) at limit of probability for reaching. How (in knowledge you possess) can probability improve? >

Thoughts held firmly on meeting to come do not easily disengage. Chorl chirrs hesitancy, tilts head in consideration, then slowly iterates memory long unheeded. When it is done, Imon with palps and mouthsounds utters gratitude—and easing demand on Chorl's attention, takes leave.

In Kahim's nesting place, six gather for age-old deed of homage to ended one becoming memory bone. Unusual is that Kahim, not yet ended, aids in sayings of ancient ritual. Joined by palps touching each to each in circle with Kahim, all crouch as Seit speaks sounds and Kahim responds.

As saying proceeds, Healthwatchers enter, quietly and with slow movement so as not to disturb what occurs. One moves beside Kahim, gently inserts channelings at neck and spine for infusion of conversion solutions and concurrent draining of superfluous fluid from vein. Other two Healthwatchers place solution containers and blood receptacle for firstranked of Healthwatchers to affix to channelings. These acts effected, all three withdraw to await.

As movements of fluids begin, Seit accompanies mouthsounds with strong, rhythmic patterns of palp vibration. Liij at either side of Seit sense patterns, add to them, repeat altered combination to next Liij, until at circle's far side each relayed grouping reaches Kahim itself. Dutysetter strains forward, muzzle agape, as palps sense augmented patterns. Kahim's mind unites these, changes them still more—to be sent out again, each way around the circle, back to Seit. Who melds them into its original transmissions, still echoing, and begins new cycle.

At sixth rendition, Kahim upon receiving vibration writhes and stiffens, returning brief response to circle, then nothing.

Dutysetter has ended, conversion to memory bone begun.

As five depart, only Seit remaining, Healthwatchers return to oversee conversion until it reaches fullness. Nearly all one duty cycle Seit remains away from Overwatcher's station, sitting vigil as Kahim's old, faded skin yellows and then browns with absorption of solutes.

Point of no further change is reached. Most advanced Healthwatcher, using instruments from time before Environ departed original home of Liij, separates memory

bone portions of Kahim from remainder of ended
Dutysetter, places these in encasement equipped with
molecular activity controls and other maintaining
needs, affixes semiorganic connectors for sensory input
and response.

Seit follows Healthwatchers taking Kahim to
safeplace of records, designates consultation cubicle,
sees Kahim properly installed. With Seit's expression of
appreciation and gratitude, Healthwatchers depart.

Seit with electrosolute moistens palp-tips, inserts
them into Kahim's connectors. < Kahim (honored
Dutysetter), Seit would (be first to) consult. >

From Kahim, initially confusion. Then < This (new,
strange) way of sensing—yet, Seit (recognized), useful. I
remember (but am not now, in total) myself as Dutysetter Kahim. Have you (Overwatcher) questions? >

< Yes. Do you (from observation) wholly endorse Tith
(now in study while occupying station) to succeed you as
Dutysetter? >

< This (well before ending) I have done. Is there
cause (some error or uncertainty) for reconsidera-
tion? >

< No, Kahim. Merely (of my interest) to confirm. >

More truly, to confirm that Kahim as memory bone
functions well, retains skills and knowledge. Testing
done, Seit makes end to consultation, extricates palps
from connectors, and leaves place of records—overdue,
by much time, to return to responsibilities of own duty
station.

Approach of Environ toward first to-be-ingested worldlet proceeds. Attending continually to electrologic integrator, Imon sees that Seit's assigned path gives scant
hope of success in following and meeting second desired worldlet. Path must bend around outer edge of
disk, slowing to curve more sharply, losing pace that
cannot be regained quickly. What uncertainty exists,
vanishes under integrator recalculation: Second worldlet will with inevitability escape.

Other path, though, which teacher Chorl has described: With apprehension, Imon puts it to electrologic
test. And finds it suitable!

Overwatcher Seit is not present to grant approval,

may not return until too late for path change to have
desired effect. Balancing haste against care, Imon replaces assigned path with Chorl's suggested one.

<Now> Imon says to no one <we (all Liij) will see
that Imon is true (effective in accomplishment) navigationist.>

Arriving at duty station, Overwatcher Seit puts attention to Environ's operational indicators and confirms all
internals to be within (or near and approaching) proper
limits. Last to be noted are pace and direction. Here,
Seit finds surprise: Pace is greater than planned for
bend of path; path itself is too wide from great, disced
world. Worldlet will not be taken!

With far eyes Seit peers down to major stations and
sees that navigationist is Imon, birthed by Seit itself.
Distance is too great for full direct speaking. But as Seit
reaches for fartalking signal device, raising it for activation, objects shown on large foreviewer begin vast, slow
wheeling motion, until target worldlet moves fully to
view center.

In itself, this satisfies. But when worldlet is ingested,
Environ's path will *not* pass outside world's surrounding
disc.

Danger! Environ must not be risked! Again Seit
grasps and raises signal device, ready to call Imon to
account. But then views instruments again—and sees
that if Imon at this moment made change again toward
assigned path, Environ could not turn shortly enough to
miss disc of hurtling matter.

Whatever causes Imon to peril Environ so desperately, path is chosen; by it, all Liij will live or die.

According, Seit puts signal device aside. None but
Imon, now, is positioned to act for Environ's safety in
coming danger, nor can be. Unwise, Seit feels it, to
divide navigationist's attention.

Until after, if after is to be. Then sayings will be made
to Imon. To itself, Seit formulates some few of these.

Excitement and anticipation aroused, Imon monitors
Environ's stately turn to meet worldlet. By swinging
wide of world until this point, then sharply (for Environ)
inward, path strikes first worldlet squarely, then cuts

plane of disc *inside* its inner edge, between disc and world itself. Without loss of pace. Even *gaining* pace, for Environ points itself deeply into warp of spacetime surrounding world's mass, and pull of warp draws Environ forward. Not downward fully, to impact and destruction, for pace and motion already achieved are too great for world's pull. Should Chorl's recalled formulation be correct, Environ will emerge having added considerable fraction to existing pace.

And with no expenditure of mattery from plasma foursphere.

If Imon is in future honored for this choosing, it thinks, teacher Chorl must receive great portion of acknowledgment.

Dread-numbed, Seit scans auxiliary instrumentation as Environ meets and ingests first worldlet, then slantward approaches great world to pass between it and disc's inner edge. Expecting Environ's capture and destruction, Seit watches uncomprehendingly as pace builds—and Environ, rather than crashing to be destroyed on world, draws away.

With second worldlet almost directly in line of movement, and Environ overtaking, to ingest!

Seit recoups postponed breath. Before next ingestion, it muses, will pass sufficient time for achievement of calm, and for rethinking, at great extent, what need be said to navigationist Imon.

In meanwhile, Seit gives thought to further path. Present aim holds some few sizable objects to be ingested, but then Environ faces again long distance, barren of all but minor specks of matter. Closer in toward star, largest world of all bears within its warpspace many worldlets, several of rewarding size, and path diversion to pass near these creates little difficulty.

Reading electrologic integrator's time and distance forecastings, based on current unexpected pace, Seit allows itself more feeling of content than for many *dre*.

Perhaps, it muses, when largest world is reached and worldlets pursued, Imon by bending path around it may contrive to add even greater leap of pace. Such would indeed be well.

Yet at greater thought depth lies forbidding question: when Crippler world is neared, will *any* pace give safeness?

INTERLUDE: INTIMATIONS

With two days' vacation left and his wife sequestered on
jury duty, Arnold Blaize was spending a quiet evening
at his telescope. His job with the National Security
Agency seldom gave him much time for this hobby;
now, blessed by clear weather, he welcomed the chance
to indulge it.

Tonight he wasn't looking for anything special,
merely revisiting some favorite celestial views. One of
these was the Saturn system; adjusting aim and focus,
Blaize scanned once again the well-remembered display.

And then sat up, blinking. Because just as he put his
attention to Dione, the fourth nontrivial satellite, currently riding a bit aside of the rings' left limb, Dione
vanished.

It couldn't, of course; squinting, Arnold rechecked
the area. No Dione. Well, maybe he hadn't really seen it
the first time; maybe some errant reflection misled him.

Dione could be passing behind its primary; how long would that take? He couldn't remember, so he tried to look it up. But eventually he had to calculate passage time from basic scratch: masses and distances. A little over sixteen hours, if he hadn't made any mistakes.

Just for kicks he went back to the 'scope and checked on the other named moonlets. All there, he noted, except for Rhea. And how long could *that* one hide? Back to figuring: nearly nineteen hours, it looked like. So shut down now and come back tomorrow.

The next night, neither missing satellite had shown up. As a veteran NSA man, Arnold Blaize knew exactly what to do.

He called his chief.

Duvall Crane tended to do most of the talking, but after a while he let Arnold get his two cents in. "Yes, all right, you can blanket the Astronomical Society's membership with a husheroo memo: This apparent anomaly is part of a Top Secret project, so clam it; we don't want the shit scared out of the voters when there's no reason to do so." Arnold's voice rose. "But at the same time . . ." Meaning, as he'd tried to say earlier, that muzzling the press wasn't putting any moons back in the sky. But he'd been around long enough to know that you go with what you've got.

So while he had the chance, Blaize said, "And you can't shut *everybody* up, so where you have to clamp the lid is at the media level." He paused. "Of course, the supermarket tabloids will ignore us, print it anyway, and stretch out the legal proceedings until nobody cares."

Crane laughed. "Any blubs who believe *that* stuff, who worries what they think?" With a chuckle, the chief hung up.

Arnold Blaize wasn't laughing.

XX

CRUNCH

Su Teng never failed to surprise Rance. When she came off watch and woke him, he told her what Tetzl had said, skimping past the orgy aspect to get to the blockbuster part. What he expected was for Su to assert flat-out that the woman was stark, raving mad. Instead, frowning delicately, Su said, "We *thought* there was something more behind her strange edicts and"— a smile flickered —"remarkably acquisitive lusts. And we were right. But the logistics of her plan must be rather daunting."

"Huh?"

"The timing." Counting on her fingers, Su looked into distance. "By the time this ship reaches destination, six additional half-crew relief cadres are scheduled to arrive on board. Two of these will leave Earth before she is expected to return there. Once she fails to appear, however, there is a considerable period—let me see—" She paused. "—twelve Earth-time years, a bit more,

216

that anyone could Habjump to board *Starfinder* before it arrives and goes into orbit."

Rance wasn't following too well. "And so?"

"NASA may very well take exception to this self-styled great woman's changes to their own plans. How does she expect to keep Earth deceived all that time? So that NASA doesn't send a few large men in white coats, perhaps armed, to remove her forcibly?"

Rance didn't answer. Because the truth of the matter was, he hadn't thought things out that far. What he did say, after a bit, was, "This is off our main subject, but I just may have figured something out." Su's expression showed inquiry; he said, "The way she moves. You know, all spring steel and whipcord. I think I see what makes her that way."

He sat up straight. "Command. Inside her, what she *is*. Look, Su—admittedly, her tent's not pegged down properly all the way around. But whatever it is she's got, by now it's totally built into her; it works."

Su nodded. "Well, why not? The German dictator, some decades ago. Hitler. I understand that in public appearances he, too, was very convincing."

Plaintively, Rance asked, "Do you have to go out of your way to make me feel so good?"

Inevitably, then, Su did ask about the sex part. Rance grinned. "For starters, I skipped the doped munchies. Then I sort of faked it." He explained.

"And she didn't notice? Not even that you were left, um, unsatisfied?"

"I think *she* was high. And afterward I just curled up and lay there. Went to sleep, in fact. A good thing, too; it wasn't until I woke up that she told me all this stuff."

"So you fooled her."

"Yes. But I doubt it would work another time. And dammit, I do wish I could avoid there *being* another time."

Was there any leverage that could give him the choice? What they needed, Su said, was to nose around (discreetly, by all means!), sound people out, and see how many were involved in Tetzl's plans. And how deeply: convinced, or only passively going along? Was anyone else ignorant, as Rance and Su had been, of the whole scheme? Either way, how many might be willing to stand up and *do* something?

"Well," he said, "we'll just have to play it by ear and see what happens." He checked his chrono. "Not quite halfway into the queen bee's own watch. Whether she's actually there or not." He stood. "While you get some sleep, I think I'll mosey around a little."

On a hunch he checked the snack galley and found Zsana Ionescu reading over coffee. Pouring some for himself, he sat near her but not directly across the long table. "How's it going? Sarge has the duty, right?"

She looked up; from her expression, maybe she'd been brooding more than reading. "Of one sort or another, much of the time."

He slid over to face her more directly. "Tell me about it."

On watch, later, Rance couldn't say anything until Cleve Rozanski was, as usual, called away by the captain. On first entering Control, Rance was afraid the other man would make some kind of smirking reference to their experience in triad. For some reason he didn't quite understand, the idea made him cringe.

But no; Rozanski simply gave him the same cheery hello everyone else was getting. And Tetzl herself, on hand as usual for the actual watch change, also treated him and everyone else with impersonal aplomb, then left.

The business of relieving her shift one-on-one was hardly finished before her voice on the intercom summoned Cleve. For some minutes, then, Rance stayed busy bringing himself up to date on routine log entries and anything new from the sensor records. Except for the dust cloud with the hole in it—and now with the angle changed, that hole wasn't visible—all data were routine.

Then he was caught up: nothing more to do except watch for new developments and log their presence— or, more likely, lack. Plenty of time to get info from Margrete and Benita.

Except—where was he supposed to start? *Well, dig in. . . .*

"We already knew she has Ramon on a string," he told Su later, "and that Margrete hates her guts for it. Benita, now—she's used to tolerating Dink in his harem mode; I don't think that part bothers her as much as we might expect. Except that Old Iron Tits may be getting a bit too greedy; I got the impression, Benita may actually be feeling deprived. So—"

"So after discussing everyone's hormones, Rance, did you learn anything about the *political* aspects? Such as, are any of the other men involved against their will?"

"Sarge Dimitrov, for one. Zsana says the situation really has him stressed—feeling guilty, that he's betraying Zsana and not able to help himself. Frankly, Su, she's scared. Thinks he's apt to crack wide open." He cleared his throat. "Should one of us talk with him? Maybe help him off the hook?"

"That, too," said Su Teng. "But primarily, Rance, we should have a try at recruiting him."

Next day, after less sleep than he really wanted, Rance hung around hoping to catch Sarge before the latter went on duty. On that he had no luck, but found Fleurine Schadel having a quick snack. He'd eaten already, but coffee wouldn't hurt.

His first question opened floodgates of resentment. "Jimmy? He's sold on the bitch and all her trimmings; he'll go along with anything she wants." Almost snarling, she said, "Pussy-whipped, I think they call it. Except, that's not all. She'll do other things with him— that I *won't.* "

Fleurine reached for his hands. "Rance—I can't compete with her and still be who I am. What *can* I do?"

He gave her hand a quick squeeze. "I wish I knew. But Su and I—hey, talk to us, any time. If it helps."

"Sure." She stood. "I'd better not be late for watch."

Back at quarters, when Su woke up he ate lunch while she had breakfast. "The count," he said, "looks to be about even. If we assume the sex thing is part of her power play, and I assume we can. Old Iron Tits has most of the men in her back pocket but doesn't rate well with the women. Sarge's vote would give us seven to five." He grimaced. "For what good numbers might do."

"Yes. She's still captain."

"And plans to keep it that way. *All* the way."

He thought. "Not that it would help things right now, but maybe to throw a monkey wrench into her long-term machinery, how about sneaking off a report to Earth? Alert them a little bit to just what the hell's going on?"

Su made a sour face. "Have you tried sending anything lately? Or been at a Gate when it was being used?"

"No. Why?"

"Nothing goes in, now, without inspection and approval by the captain. And to ensure this, she's had Rozanski install locks on the Transmit switches."

He didn't say what came to mind then. Su didn't like strong language, and when he remembered, he tried to accommodate her. So after a few deep breaths he said, "Give us a kiss."

She did, and only then asked, "Why?"

"Because love laughs at locksmiths. And before I go on watch, let's get in shape to do some laughing."

With more than one purpose in mind, a little later Rance called Control to say he'd be a few minutes late reporting to duty. "Sudden digestive upset, and the pills haven't taken hold yet." To shut off the protest, "Yicchh! Oops—" and he killed the intercom circuit.

To Su's unspoken question he answered, "I want the few minutes so I can ambush Sarge and find out where he stands. Also I think I'm about due to be tabbed for another of the Iron Maiden's happy little clambakes."

"And—"

"An unreliable gut should be the perfect excuse for a rain check." In parody, he leered. "Think about it."

"Look, Sarge, it's not your *fault*. " Six minutes overdue and standing in a corridor out in plain sight if anyone came along, Rance wanted to wrap this up fast. "Zsana knows that; she doesn't blame you. Old—uh, the captain —swings so much clout you haven't been able to turn her down. She's pulled that on every man on this ship. Some of 'em like it, I guess. But you don't, and I don't. Now here's the thing"—hearing sounds up forward, he grabbed Sergei's shoulder and leaned close—"if some of us come up with any idea to try to change things, are you willing to help? Or would you cave in to her?"

Dimitrov looked lost; for certain, he wasn't going to come up with any fast answer. Rance shook the shoulder gently. "All right, think on it. Talk to Zsana. And for God's sake don't say anything to anybody else."

Someone *was* coming. Rance gave Sergei a final, supportive pat, turned, and walked with the best simulated fatigue he could manage, into Control.

"Hi, Cleve. Margrete. Benita. Sorry I'm late, but the ol' gut's been kicking up, and I'm not sure it's tamed yet."

Whether or not Cleve passed the word, Rance got through his watch trick and later chore tour with no summons from Irina.

Coming forward after vetting all three sets of fuel-flow sensors, the final items on his checklist, he came near the Earthgate Mouth in time to see Captain Tetzl, carrying a small armload of sealed packets, approaching from the opposite direction. At the Gate he stopped; this could be a good chance to watch her operate the locked-up terminal. "Hi, Cap'n. That's quite a stack there, you have for Earth."

She gave him a brief, precise smile. "Collier. I trust your digestives improve?" Not waiting for an answer, she said, "Here. Take these. See that they are in order, by date and time, earliest on top." As she wrestled a key with its attached thong from the holder at her waist, she added, "With one and another thing, my log reports lag behind schedule. This group of notations will correct the matter."

Judging by the number of containers, she had to be one *hell* of a way behind sked, and Rance had no difficulty guessing why. He made no comment; as directed, he rearranged the packets. But mainly he watched Tetzl set up the Gate for operation.

*   *   *

"It's a standard tumbler lock, Su: the kind they use on security files. I suppose Cleve found a few spares someplace. Except in minor ways, the design hasn't changed for decades." Ruefully, he grinned. "No need to; it's efficient."

He'd napped after his chore hitch, through the latter half of Su's watch trick. Now, wide awake as they ate, he described the setup. "Really a crude job, Cleve's welding. As they say, though: Not much fer purty, but hell fer strong."

And strong was all Tetzl needed here. A heavy, hinged flap to cover the Activate controls—and the lock, welded into the panel itself, its integral flanges turning with the key to hold or release the flap. "Which is a snug fit; there's no getting a pry bar under it."

Delicately, Su dabbed away a dollop of cream sauce from the corner of her mouth. "So that without the key there is no way to operate the Habgate?"

Absorbed in a new thought, Rance missed her question. When she repeated it, he said, "There's always a way. But whether it's one we can find materials for, or use fast enough that we could get away with it before the balloon went up . . . that's something else."

The problem would be solved, of course, if they could lay hands on a key. Rance had no illusions about trying to snaffle Irina Tetzl's own; what he wondered was, who else had one? Rozanski, probably; maybe Jimmy Hanchett. "But," he said, "I don't see myself finagling one from either of those guys."

"Nor I," said Su, "seducing it away from one of them."

"Somewhere," Rance said, "there has to be a backup. But where?"

Su shrugged. "Under the doormat. In the mailbox. Near any Gate, what would be the equivalents?"

"Damifino. But any time we're around a Gate, let's give the area a good hard look."

After several tries over the next two days, eyeballing the vicinities as best they could, both he and Su had to admit total failure. If Old Iron Tits had a key stashed anywhere near one of the three outgoing Gates, she'd hidden it well indeed.

So he needed a different answer. Okay, what possibilities existed? The covering flaps themselves, crudely formed steel plates, were too springy to shatter and too thick to bend—even if a pry bar could have found purchase. The meager clearance quite effectively blocked movement of the Activate switch handle. As for the hinges, their heavy, rivet-type pins had been so battered at each end as to make removal impossible.

Oh, they'd done a job of it, Cleve and Tetzl had. And the welding gear Cleve had used, the cutting torches and all that, were secured behind a lock much stronger than the ones on the Activate controls.

But somehow Rance couldn't bring himself to give up, to admit that Irina Tetzl and Cleve Rozanski with a few pieces of crude hardware could control anything so marvelous as the Habegger Gates.

With all his scheming, plus the routine of watch duty and added half shift of assigned chores, Rance had put Tetzl's other demands to the back of his mind. So much so that her summons, relayed over the intercom by Sarge Dimitrov, who didn't wait for an answer, caught him totally by surprise.

"Which makes me feel silly as hell," he told Su.

The time was more than halfway through their eight-hour stint of free time together, after her watch shift and before his, while the captain herself had nominal watch duty. It didn't strike Rance as ideal from Tetzl's point of view, but apparently she thought different.

His own reaction was basically resentment, and his response followed logically. "Su? Honey? Why don't you and I wring me out like a dishrag? I'll tell her we already had."

For a moment Su Teng frowned, then she laughed. "Why not?"

Arriving at the captain's digs in "dishrag mode," Rance had himself braced for Tetzl's anger. But he found her and Cleve and Jimmy, all three clothed though looking somewhat mussed, seated around her table with drinks in their hands and a bottle sitting centerpiece. "You are too late this time, Collier," she said. To Rance's view she looked and sounded a little blasted. "A pity. Next time

more advance notice, I promise." She gestured toward
the sideboard where he saw, alongside an ice bucket, an
empty glass. When he'd filled it to his satisfaction she
said, "Join us." Pulling a chair over to the table, he did
so.

"We discuss," Irina began, "how to maintain control
of *Starfinder* through arrival and reconnaisance of destination world. Your thought is welcome."

"If you have any," Cleve said, grinning.

All right. Play it their way. Rance nodded. "Happens
I do, that." He leaned forward. "You're looking at one
hell of a problem, Captain. Aboard here we're the *first*
relief crew, you in B cadre and me in A." Counting on
his fingers but not aloud, he came up with, "You know
what group arrives here when decel starts? Relief Four-
A, is what. And B, as I remember, gets here about the
time the ship settles into orbit."

"These facts," she said, "I know." Gaze and voice
both level. "Your point?"

"All right." Rance thought. "Earth has you scheduled
to return home at t-sub-zero—counting from departure
—a little past eighteen years. By that time Relief Two, A
and B both, will have entered the pipeline, with Three-
A due to start in another year."

Her expression, or lack of it, didn't change. He said,
"When you don't show, just what do you think's going to
happen? And how do you plan to cope with it?"

Cleve snorted. "You dummy, Collier! That's what
we're here trying to figure out."

"Well then," Rance said, "if you send the relief crews
back, you've shown your hand. If you don't, figure how
to take care of thirty-six extra people you'll be getting
over the next three years or so, courtesy of Habegger's
Tush.

"And while you're at it, how to keep Earth happy."

He didn't see any cookies, but Tetzl might have eaten
some. Her answers, inconsistent to the point of contra-
diction, alarmed Rance Collier more than a little. For
starters: "Suppose we return no one to Earth. At some
point we may have to claim that the Gate refused to
transmit anything large, such as humans." Who'd believe it? "But what choice would they have?"

And all the extra *people*? "One of ours, not the same one twice, takes a cadre through to *Roamer*, or perhaps *Arrow*, and immediately back again."

Simpler yet, thought Rance: *Arrow*'s pair of "closed-circuit" Gates could keep any number of people circulating indefinitely. Of course, in that case, Tetzl would have to control *Arrow*. Not to mention, how one shepherd was supposed to handle six sheep.

None of this he said aloud. In fact, when he noticed Tetzl acting nervous and harassed, he backed off his objections and quit pushing. Because the closer his arguments came to boxing her into a corner, the more she spoke, with raised voice, in ominous generalities.

So. About forty minutes before he was due on watch, Rance excused himself on the plea of needing a shower first.

"The scary part, Su, is what she didn't ever say. In the back of her mind, I think her ace in the hole is killing."

"With what? Rance, weren't Niebuhr's gun, and Nadine's, sent back to Earth eventually?"

"Right. But I *have* heard there's a store of firearms aboard, locked up—for contingencies such as a landing party meeting up with large, predatory animals. So who would have access to the weapons? The captain, that's who."

"And you think she's capable of using them?"

"That's the hell of it. I don't know *what* the woman's capable of."

Bedwise, he found at his next summons, she was capable of quite a lot. The presence of both Cleve and Sarge inhibited normal arousal on his part, but Tetzl said, "Be easy, Collier. I am also a fellatrice of some skill." And when she had everyone correctly arranged, surrounding her, she proceeded with considerable enthusiasm to service all three men at once.

When every bit of action finally wound down, the sweating Irina toweled herself to moderate dampness and sat back, one hand resting her ice-chilled drink against flushed bare cleavage. Abruptly she nodded. "Sergei, I wish to know your place in my plans. For this ship, I am meaning. Do you pledge to stay and uphold me as captain, to the end of this ship's mission?"

Poor Sarge! He stalled, tried to weasel; he wriggled on the hook, but nothing got him free. After a time Tetzl said, "Then I cannot rely on you. Is that correct?"

"Well, but you see, Captain, I—"

"Enough. Cleve!" At one side Rance heard a tiny pop and hiss. Sarge clapped a hand to his neck; his head fell back and his mouth opened. Tetzl moved to him. "Sergei! You are not truly with me in this endeavor, are you? You may speak frankly."

"Uuuuh—I—no, I could not be part . . ." For nearly a minute more he babbled; any chance he might have had of playing along with the captain's schemes while secretly opposing her aims was up the flue. Then, slowly, he began to keel over to one side. Bracing him up, Tetzl motioned to Rozanski.

"The drink, Cleve." As Rance goggled, wondering what he should be doing, from a short, square bottle the man poured a shot glass full of milky liquid and tilted it into Sarge's mouth.

The Russian swallowed; Irina Tetzl gave a relieved sigh. "Good. We shall have no trouble with *him.*"

What the hell? Rance fumbled for words. "Is he dead?"

The captain turned on him. "Dead? Of course not." She plucked something from Dimitrov's neck, a dart of some kind. "Drugged, yes. By this. Tipped with a fast-acting sedative, and one of its effects is that for the moments before sleep he could not lie. Shortly, you two may take him to his own quarters and let him sleep it off."

Time to say something. "Sarge won't talk, won't tell anybody. He's not the type." Blowing smoke, that was, out of fear she might do something more drastic.

But she let out an explosive "Hah!" Then said, "He will not, no. Because the drug erodes memory of roughly twenty minutes before its use. Simply, he will not remember."

"But—then what's supposed to have made him pass out?"

Holding up the shot glass, Rozanski chuckled. "An ounce of this stuff gives a very convincing hangover."

"So he'll think he just got pissy-ass drunk?" The man and woman both nodded. "Where'd you *get* all this fancy stuff? How did you even know about it?"

Amazing, Rance thought, how regally Irina Tetzl could draw herself up, sitting bare-ass with sweat drying on her skin. "At age twenty-six," she said, "I was major of police. Some years ago I left that work. But when preparing for this voyage, obtaining necessary materials, I made use of old connections."

Feeling like a tightrope walker in a cyclone, Rance said, "I have to hand it to you. You really do think of everything. I guess you have to be one in a million."

The smug way she smiled, then, gratified him a lot. For one thing, it verified that a big enough ego could swallow *any*-sized compliment without choking on it.

For another, it got him out of there without a hassle.

"Su, you won't believe—"

Entering quarters, she waved him to momentary silence. "You'd be surprised what I wouldn't believe. But over a lime soda—tall, with ice—if you would, please."

"Sure." Drink served and both of them seated, he told it. "Now what do you think?"

Sipping, she looked thoughtful. "Of her actions, that I am beyond surprise. Of her plans, that we still don't know enough."

"We know enough to warn Earth. We have to get a message out, or maybe even get away, ourselves."

"I agree. But with the Gates locked up, our question is *how*. And I don't believe we're even close to an answer."

Frustrated, all he could find to say was, "Just give me time. I'll think of something."

He wished he could believe his own words.

XXI

POPPING THE CORK

The main trouble, Rance felt, was that he simply wasn't the right man for the job. Not the only trouble, of course. To begin with, he needed tools or materials or gadgets he didn't have; in fact he wasn't even sure what they should be. He needed a plan, a way to use whatever gear he might decide on.

But even if he had those things, he'd still be in too deep. Because he wasn't, and except for that one self-surprising moment with Hans Niebuhr and the pistol, never had been, any kind of action person. A talker, not a fighter: that was Rance Collier all the way, his whole life long.

Well, maybe something had to change.

Not wanting to sound any sillier than he had to, he didn't tell Su what he was thinking. For that matter, much of the time he tried to ignore it himself.

So when the first items came through the new Hab-gate from *Arrow,* he almost welcomed the distraction.

• • •

Irina Tetzl, putting the other ship's log onscreen in Control, also relayed it up to the rec lounge. "So that all may view, who so wish."

Nice of her, Rance guessed, but he found it rather dull. No reason he should expect to recognize any of the names on the official roster, and sure enough he didn't.

Part of the log was text, but some was talk-and-picture. Ellery Dawson, *Arrow*'s captain, seemed far too much the goshwowboyoboy type to be running a starship; any time a person was too thrilled for words, Rance felt, he should quit saying so. But then, Rance wasn't on the personnel selection board.

The poop concerning the ship itself, its similarities to and differences from *Starfinder*, was interesting enough. Bulking considerably smaller than its predecessors, *Arrow*'s longer needlenose swelled to the same twenty-five-meter radius, but only briefly; behind the rotating point-three-gee "living space" belt its girth shrank, the remaining seventy meters of length tapering down to a diameter of only twenty at the rear.

A cross-sectional diagram showed the layout of drive equipment, fuel and water and food reserve storages, control area, Habgate locations, and Deployment Vehicle, which wasn't much altered from the earlier model. From what little info was shown, instrumentation hadn't advanced greatly, either.

When the whole thing seemed to be wrapping up, Rance got a surprise. The scene cut jarringly, and there, in what was most likely *Arrow*'s own rec lounge (its walls painted a delicate pale blue), stood Anne Portaris.

She hadn't really changed: no new lines to speak of, slender and energetic as ever. Hair a little shorter? She said, "Hello, *Starfinder*. Rance Collier, you still there? Should be, if I have my numbers right. It's tricky; my week aboard here will be almost six months on Earth. Well, I'm sending you a letter on datacap, not to take a great lot of recording time here. But while I'm at it, good wishes to everyone else on *Starfinder*. I'd like to visit you, take the full tour—but this side trip, from *Roamer* on my way to Earth, used up all my political credit." Then Captain Dawson appeared again briefly, and the log ended.

On intercom, Tetzl said, "The cap is here for you, Collier. You may fetch it now, or wait until your watch."

"I'll be right down."

Whether or not Irina had read his mail, her expression didn't indicate and Rance didn't ask. He took the capsule up to quarters; while he was readying it on his terminal, Su came in from her chore stint, so first they shared a snack. Then he keyed the cap for onscreen viewing. After the datetime group (Earth reckoning) and salutation, they read:

> I don't know a soul aboard here but they're all friendly, and the ship itself has some interesting features. For one thing, at the rear of the point-three-gee living-space belt there's another, separate ring, which can be accelerated to give a full gee spin for exercising purposes. It's felt that without such a facility, two years at reduced gee may be too long for best health considerations.

Hitting the Pause key, Rance said, "That's another thing. Old Iron Tits figures to stay aboard here, all the way through to destination. After that much time at point-three, what kind of shape does she expect to be in? Let alone everyone else."

Su shrugged. "After our scheduled *one* year, what proportion of stamina will we have lost?" She gestured; he hit Pause again. It toggled, and play resumed.

> . . . two meters wide, and of light construction, with only a small part of the circumference actually used. But at the increased spin rate, which comes to roughly thirty-five miles per hour—as compared to twenty in our living quarters, or yours—even the weight of a few persons could make a nasty imbalance. So on the far side, water is pumped automatically between tanks to restore mass symmetry, while the ring revs up.

Well, *Starfinder* had similar mechanisms to balance its own, heavier rotating belt, so presumably *Arrow* did also. But since those corrections were comparatively minor, they took place unnoticed. Everyone took them for granted, forgot about them.

.. . tell you a funny thing that happened the day after I arrived here. Number Two watch team was ready to leave the rotating belt and go on duty, but when they punched for the transfer ring, it didn't come. I was down in Control, and with all the talk going on, it was a while before anyone noticed the intercom beeping. Then three of us trooped forward to *our* nearest set of doors and couldn't get any action there, either.

So we went around the peripheral corridor to the next doors; no luck. But at the third set—well, there's a child aboard here, a girl around ten or eleven. A nice kid; the exec's daughter. I *think* he spirited her away from his ex-wife just before departure, but no one's saying much about it.

Anyway, she has a little tote bag, keeps her zero-gee shoes in it when she's on the Belt, and an ordinary pair when she isn't. Coming down to Control to visit her daddy, a little before watch change, she didn't notice one shoe falling out of her bag. Yes, you guessed it: when the ring came to rest, the shoe slid over and blocked the doors from closing. Just like an elevator; if the door won't shut all the way, the ring doesn't move.

Well, no harm done, but now everyone's alerted to make sure nothing of the sort happens again.

Portaris told a couple more anecdotes before signing out, but Rance was fairly well preoccupied with her first one.

He reported for watch hoping that his after-watch chores would involve the Deployment Vehicle; somewhere in the back of his mind lived a dim hunch that the DV held some kind of key to what he needed. As he began the routine checks, part of his thinking continued to worry at the problem of escape.

Still, he did pay close attention to the instrument readings and his logging of them. Nearly two days now, for instance, lowered density outside had been saving the ship some fuel. While the velocity-to-distance integration figures showed *Starfinder*'s position slightly ahead of sked by Earth time, which meant that scheduled shipments from Earth would arrive late by *ship's* time.

So it all evened out. Or did it?

As Rance expected, after about half an hour Cleve Rozanski's intercom station buzzed. But instead of excusing himself and leaving, Cleve came over to where Rance sat. "You're wanted. Captain's digs."

"Me?" The co-exec nodded. Well. Never before had Rance been called away from watch, let alone leaving Cleve behind, but apparently there was a first time for everything. Looking closely, Rance wondered if the other man resented this turn of events, and decided he wouldn't ask. "All right." He made sure his portion of the log was ready to be signed out, and then, under Rozanski's scrutiny, did so.

He stood. "I'll get back when I can." As he walked out, Cleve didn't answer.

Hail, hail, in Tetzl's quarters the gang was certainly all there: Irina herself plus Jimmy, Ramon, Dink, and Sarge. Whether or not this was her premiere with a five-man coterie, she gave orders as if she knew exactly what she was doing.

Embarrassingly, yet not without a certain spiteful satisfaction, Rance found himself totally incapable. The intrinsic grotesquerie of the situation, all those people groping around: *hell!* Sexual response wasn't even remotely possible.

When Tetzl noticed, she glared at him and motioned him nearer to her, but her would-be helpful efforts had no effect at all. To his relief, after a time she gave up; as he watched, close to disbelieving, she went ahead with the rest of the circus. When it ended and she disengaged, she spoke coldly.

"Collier, return to your watch; we will speak later."

Not waiting for permission, he was already clothing himself and merely nodded assent.

She wasn't done. "Rodriguez, you also leave."

Rance stalled until he and Ramon could walk out together. Outside he said, "You couldn't come to attention either?"

Mumbled, "Didn't *want* to."

"Yes; I know. Ramon—I asked you before if you'd stand up to her, trying to change things." Before the other could answer, "I think it's too late for that. Now I want to know, if there's a chance to escape from this ship, are you with me?"

Rodriguez shrugged. "What chance could there be?"

Goddamn; maybe it was just too complicated, trying to bring other people into it. "Never mind. Forget I said it."

The man grinned. "Forget what?"

So at least maybe he hadn't worsened the odds.

Returning to watch duty, Rance avoided any inquiring looks from Cleve Rozanski and busied himself with some slightly overdue calibration schedules. As usual, none of the equipment needed more than nominal re-adjustments.

At shift's end he wasn't assigned to the hoped-for DV inspection. Instead, he and Benita drew the job of checking equipment and materials storage. Not ship's stores, where sheer variety of items might spark thought of some unorthodox application, but simply a checkup on miscellaneous gear kept stashed out of the way. In various cabinets along his assigned corridor— Benita had the one next clockwise—he found paint, cleansers, air filters in crates brought from stores but not yet emptied. Leftovers from the Habgate installations. Circuit components pulled for possible malfunction, yet to be tested—quite a backlog of those, and whose job was it, anyway?

A little farther back, the vacuum suits, spare gloves, and faceplates. Air tanks, some red-tagged for recharging. Alongside those, a cabinet door reading Cryogenic Storage. Well, sure. For *outside,* possibly extended work in vacsuits—not at these relativistic speeds where interstellar gas would shred suit and flesh alike, but in or near an orbital situation—air was carried in liquid phase.

Those tanks had to be kept at VLT—very low temperature—until shortly before connection to a suit via the converter couplings that brought the gas to breathable temperature. And even though they were sheathed in insulex, you wouldn't want to handle one very long without gloves of the same material.

It struck Rance that liquid air under pressure, not checked by the coupling, could be a rather nasty thing to squirt at somebody. Of course, he had no idea how long a tank would keep squirting. Maybe he could hang a couple on a belt for spares.

Or maybe the whole thing was a stupid idea.

One thing he found, not properly put away but standing in a corner, was one of the wrenches used to cinch down the base mountings of the Habegger Gates; the heavy box-end fit a three-centimeter hex nut. His checklist was finished; for no particular reason except that he felt like it, he picked up the wrench and took it along forward. At the rear side of the Earth Habgate, between its mounting feet, the bottom of its casing cleared the deck by a couple of inches.

Into that space, just out of sight, seemed a good place to slide his wrench.

The pieces weren't coming together yet, not by any means. But he did have some pieces.

For the next few days, entering the latter half of his twelfth and final scheduled month aboard *Starfinder*, nothing much seemed to be happening. The apparent calm didn't feel right; with relief cadre Two-A coming in soon, Old Iron Tits had to be near to making her move.

A thing that bothered Rance—and Su also, it turned out—was the prospect of jumping ship by themselves, leaving the others to face Irina Tetzl's reaction. The least they could do, both agreed, was to feel out possible confederates a little more.

They talked it over. Who were the possibles? Not Cleve, of course, and it had been months since Rance felt able to speak any major truth to Jimmy Hanchett. Fleurine was bitter as hell but counting on herself and

Jimmy going back to Earth soon; the revelation that maybe Tetzl wasn't going to let that happen was something neither Su nor Rance intended to share with anyone who didn't already know it. Not at this critical stage.

Dink Hennessey seemed complacent; if he did let himself get disturbed, all too likely his reaction would be to go talk it over with the captain. Scratch Dink. And Benita? Hard to tell; maybe she had let the man think for her too long to change.

To Rance's earlier feelers, Sarge and Ramon had been —well, call it sympathetic apathy at best. Margrete simply froze up and didn't respond, and Su found Zsana overly fearful of authority, so took the hinting no further.

"All we can do, I guess," Rance summed it up, "is give somebody a last chance if it's handy when the moment comes."

Meanwhile, watching for signs of that moment and finding none, he stewed and fretted.

Until the day Su came in from watch flourishing a data capsule. "This is it, Rance! Her plans, practically all spelled out." Pausing as he broke a rack of ice cubes loose into a bowl, he tried to ask a question; she shook her head. "I've skimmed only a few parts, but I think it's all here."

"How in the world—?"

Well, Tetzl had come into Control, looking very purposeful. She'd sat down at the command terminal and punched to copy something onto a capsule, which she took with her when she shut down. "It looked as though she was consulting coded files, and I had a hunch it might be what we need. So I checked the time, figured back to when she'd started, and after a while, when no one was paying attention, I went over and simply told the terminal to go back and repeat all operations from that point on. I wasn't sure it would work, but it was worth a try. With this cap plugged in to take the data, of course."

Surprising Rance, Su giggled. "In the mode I used, all the commands appeared onscreen. You know what her secret code was, to hide this material?"

"Couldn't guess. What was it?"

"Old Iron Tits."

Once the text began rolling, laugh time was over. Tetzl's plans went farther than either Rance or Su had guessed. The more they read, the worse it got.

For starters: On arrival, relief cadre personnel would be questioned rigorously under drugs; before then, existing crew was slated for the same treatment. The "most suitable," preferably twelve but not necessarily so, would remain as crew. With the caveat that crew size could be allowed to increase toward the end of the trip, the same culling procedure also applied to future relief cadres.

What about the rejects? Obviously they couldn't be allowed to go tattling to Earth. Tetzl's first choice was the conducted Habgate tour to *Roamer* or *Arrow*, and back. With the sheep doped to the gills, they'd be docile enough. And if one or more on the other ship happened to see anything? Zap—the memory-blanking sedative darts (to be retrieved, of course, not left as clues).

More elegant, but obviously touchy on the timing, was the idea of taking people to *Arrow*, putting them into that ship's back-to-back gates, and returning later to recycle them.

But how to square it with Earth, if people didn't come back on sked? Why, tell Earth that people left *Starfinder* okay "and you say they haven't arrived?" "Unsuitable" relief people could be zapped and sent to another ship; Earth would be told that the gate lit up but no one arrived. So they showed up on the wrong ship: perhaps some feedback between gates . . . ?

"But that's impossible," Su protested.

"Sure. Still, as Tetzl says here, who can *prove* it? And what with the transmission lag, by the time the folks on Earth get an answer, they'll have forgotten what the question was."

Still, Su wanted to know: given the story that gates were malfunctioning, wouldn't Earth take *some* action? "Send a troubleshooting team? Or perhaps simply hold off and send no one at all? They might even cut off *all* support."

"Old Iron Tits doesn't seem to think so. And she may be right. Well, let's see here . . ."

There had to be a bottom line, and sure enough, there was. Rance's guess had been right; the plan noted that "loyal" personnel would be armed. "I'd assume that's Queen Irina herself, Cleve, and Jimmy. At the least." Rance snorted. "Dink? Possibly. No one else, I'd imagine."

"But would they—?"

"Who knows? Look right there, what she says: In event of unfortunate accident occurrence, bodies to be placed in hull sensor compartment and air evacuated." Momentarily he grasped Su's arm. "So we know what she's thinking, don't we?"

He stepped over to the table and lifted the bowl of ice. "Hell. They've all melted together. One big lump."

And that did it. Suddenly, like the ice cubes, all the pieces came together in his mind.

"Su?" She looked across to him. "First chance we get, we go. Tomorrow, even. When I'm on watch. I'll call you, so be ready.

"And here's how we're going to do it."

It had to be during the first half of his watch. The last half was Su's time for chores, but through his first four hours no watch group had that duty. Possibly for that reason, this was also the preferred time for Old Iron Tits to hold her sybaritic soirees. And if the other five men were gathered with her, they wouldn't be around anywhere else, to interfere.

So that part was settled.

Reporting for watch next day, Rance had difficulty keeping his mind on the necessary routines. He forced himself to give Irina Tetzl and the others what he hoped would sound like normal greetings, and waited impatiently until she left, along with Dink and Sarge and Fleurine.

The question was, who would she summon? Cleve, or himself? When Rozanski got the call and took his leave, the relief Rance felt was flawed by tension; now he *had* to move.

He figured to give it another half hour; by then the

captain should be fully involved in her fun and games. Then he thought, Su would need a few minutes to prepare and join him, so call it twenty. But right now, maybe he'd better make some small talk.

Except that he couldn't think of any. So, looking around, abruptly he made his decision and opened the intercom. He spoke softly, and when Su answered, said, "It's time. Meet me here."

"Yes. Ten minutes at most."

All right. Margrete and Benita were talking together; in their general direction he said "Back in a few minutes" and left Control to head aft, past the locked, unattended Earthgate to the miscellaneous storage space. On his return he set part of his booty behind the gate—no point in lugging the whole of it back and forth—and went on forward to meet Su, carrying a load of her own, just before she reached Control.

His grin felt tight. "Leave the stuff outside here for now. Any problems?" Headshake. "Everybody else still on the Belt? For the next hour or two?"

Her own smile looked more relaxed; he wished he knew how she did it! "At a rough estimate. What next?"

He motioned toward Control. "We take a vote."

When he told Margrete and Benita a very abbreviated version of *Starfinder*'s situation and offered the chance to come along, it seemed that neither could decide. So while they were trying, Rance cut lengths of flex cord and began tying them, hands behind backs, to their duty station chairs. For that job he had to set down the liquid air container and peel off his insulex gloves.

Margrete took the whole thing passively, but Benita flared. "Just because we won't leave with you, do you have to tie us up?"

"Yep." How it worked he wasn't sure, but even this much action helped take the tension off. "When Tetzl starts yelling on the intercom, maybe you'd hold out or maybe you'd go let her off the Belt too soon."

"I wouldn't—!"

"Then if you *weren't* tied up, you'd be in deep shit with Old Iron Tits; see what I mean?"

Scowling, Benita said, "Well, maybe. How long are we going to be here? Before somebody comes to untie us?"

Rance shrugged. "How long does it take four pounds of ice to melt, so the transfer ring doors can close?"

Consternation. *"What?* But—but I have to take a *leak.* "

There wasn't time for this. "If you have to, you have to." First, mistaking his meaning, she smiled. Then as he and Su turned to leave, she let loose some fairly inventive cussing.

Nonetheless, he took time to copy the data cap with Tetzl's plans on it and stuff the new capsule into Benita's pocket. "Read this at your leisure. It'll give you a better idea of why we're skipping out and what *you* might want to do. Don't show it to anyone you can't trust—and for God's sake don't let the captain know you have it."

Then, feeling more than a little sheepish, he bade them both courteous good-byes, anyway. After all, it wasn't their fault they happened to get stuck with the dirty end of the stick.

Su could hardly have gone traipsing around the point-three Belt with all their belongings, so they had pared their travel gear to a minimum: strictly personal items plus one change of clothing each. Two bags, then, sat in the corridor; picking these up, they went back to the Gate.

Rance took a deep breath. "Now it happens." *Or doesn't,* but he couldn't give headspace to that thought. He pulled the big wrench from under the Gate housing and brought it, along with the satchel containing two more air tanks, around to the locked activating console.

"Cross your fingers." Opening the first tank's valve a little, he played the chill jet along the crude, hinged locking flap. The hell of it was, he had no idea how long it should take. After what seemed hours, he closed the valve and put the tank down. Lifting his wrench, he gave the steel flap the best bash he could muster.

Like glass, the steel shattered. With a whoop he reached for the Transmit enabling switch.

It broke off in his gloved hand.

Su groaned. "Rance! What—?"

"Roamer. Come on." Scooping up his gear, he led off around the peripheral corridor. At the Gate to the other

ship he stopped; breathing equally hard, Su caught up with him.

"A little more delicate touch," he said. "That's what we need." This time he aimed the hissing stream only at the immediate area of the lock itself. When he smashed the wrench down, taking a sidewise swipe, only the lock and its near end of the flap flew into fragments.

"More *like* it!" His gloved finger flipped the hinge back, out of the way. The enabling switch, when he touched it, moved smoothly. "Come on, let's put all our stuff in." Once they'd done it, "Are we ready?" She nodded. "Set the timing for ten seconds and get in." Because for fine work the gloves were prohibitively clumsy, and it would take too long to pull one off.

As she took her stance inside the gate and grasped a handhold, Rance had one last look around. Good-bye, *Starfinder*.

He threw the Transmit switch, scrambled into the gate, and closed his eyes against the flare of colors.

When he opened them, he saw a large, disgruntled-looking man approaching. "All right, just stay where you are. Captain Tetzl warned us there might be subversives deserting her ship."

"But that's not—" Su began.

Rance grabbed her hand and squeezed it. "No time for this crap. We pick up our stuff." Doing his part of it, slinging the satchel of air tanks from his shoulder, Rance held up the one he'd been using and pointed it at their challenger. "This thing can freeze your face. Unless you want to chip your eyelids open, walk us quietly to your Earthgate and don't give me any trouble at all." As the man's shoulders slumped and he turned obediently, Rance found time to think: *This is* me *doing all this stuff,* and to feel a dazed wonder at himself.

On the way they met a stern-faced woman who barred their path and tried to ask questions. Before Rance could speak, Su said, "We carry urgent news to Earth. If you truly need to know it immediately, come with us and hear it there. Otherwise I suggest you stand aside." It worked; the woman stepped back and shut up.

At the gate another man stood. To the big one Rance

said, "Tell him to pass us through." Sensing hesitation, *"Tell* him."

And in less than a minute, colors flared again.

After nearly a year at point-three gee in quarters and zero on watch, Rance expected Earth gravity to hit him like a hammer.

What he didn't expect was to find himself still in zero gee. And looking out to black, star-specked space.

INTERLUDE: EXPLOITATION

Like all lawyers, Constanza Aguilar was cautious. But if
Roddy kept working on her long enough, he knew he
could talk her into taking a chance. And with ten years
on the *Enquirer* under his belt before he got his shot as
editor on this new rag, Roddy Baines knew just what to
say.

"Sure they'll sue us. Or take out an injunction. Back
on the *'quirer* we got that crap all the time. So you know
what?"

The set of Constanza's lips showed aggravated patience. "I suppose you're going to tell me. But I still
think—".

Roddy didn't wait. "So I put my next editorial, protesting the injunction itself, right on the front page of
U.S. Wrap's next issue. So naturally I have to discuss
what the injunction's about, don't I?" He gestured.
"Piece 'a cake."

WHO'S STEALING SATURN'S MOONS?

That was the first headline. The next week's editorial, under the guise of defending freedom of the press, amplified the original write-up. The government's official cover story, dutifully carried by all national dailies, weekly newszines, and Tri-V networks, got short shrift from readers and viewers. They'd been conned too often before by appeals to national security; the excuse of some Top Secret project, which they were supposed to take on faith with no details to back it up, simply didn't make it against facts obvious to anyone with access to a mail-order telescope and a high-school astronomy book.

Emboldened by the public nature of the controversy, soon the respected pundits of the straight media began dabbling their own genteel toes into the roiled waters. But the *Wrap* was wet all over, and the color of its wetting was a healthy monetary green.

"What really gets me," Roddy told Constanza over dinner, "is that for once *we're* the ones leading with the truth."

Later, when Europa vanished, the *Wrap*'s cash register wasn't the only thing that rang a lot of bells. Events as far away as Saturn had been freaky enough to draw faddish interest but not to cause alarm. Jupiter, though, was nearer home—plus, whatever *was* happening was coming closer.

Not yet to the edge of panic, still the public at large was incubating one huge case of flaming jitters. Arnold Blaize, for one, worried that his chronic heartburn was working up to be a full-fledged ulcer. He felt much better after he managed to convince his chief *not* to recommend to the president that martial law be declared.

He needn't have worried. As the Chief Executive told Duvall Crane, "I'm concentrating all resources toward understanding and countering this threat. *You* keep issuing placebo releases. And stay out of my hair for a while."

XXII

ARRIVAL

Reflecting thought and feeling, Overwatcher Seit's palps make hum of contentment. Ingestion of two worldlets brings foursphere plasma well above median energy. Ingestor and re-creator now process spacetime near to full capacity, adding pace at rate essentially limited by matter content encountered.

As result of its venture at disced world, Imon—though still young—is given precedence of navigationists; when Environ nears star's greatest world, its course is to be of Imon's choice and execution. To this end, Chorl now instructs Imon in art of consulting memory bones. In particular, that of Haef is certain to yield useful thought; no doubt Dron as well.

So taken by learning and study is Imon that as Environ becomes nearer to great world ahead than to lesser, girdled one left behind, onset of breeding-stage brings less of joy than of distraction. Consulting with memory bones, exercising instrumentation results by use of electrologic integration to determine Environ's best path—when Imon is not at duty cycle these activenesses fill its thought to exclusion of other matters.

So strong is inward compelling that Imon wholly forgets to visit its Liijlings at their herdlearning: for nearly one quarter-*dre* it sees neither Alev, seeded to Tev, nor Fahar, birthed for Tith.

Only when Tith, least precedent of three Dutysetters, reminds Imon, does Imon chirr rue of obligation failure and hasten to perform redress. First going to place of older Liijlings it greets Pnet, foremost in herdteaching. <I come (past due time) to say with Alev.>

<Alev (long waiting) bides in study place.> Yet Pnet's saying does not accuse.

Imon proceeds and finds Alev. Near to finishment of herdlearning, youngthon with mouth and palps grasps saying well. It hopes, Imon now learns, to apply self to instrumentation studies. Imon approves. <This is honored (yet difficult of performance) duty task.> Further thought: <At later time (when much is learned) teacher Chorl is (if help needed) amenable to question.>

Alev sounds and chirrs pleasure, gratitude, as Imon takes leave to see Fahar also. Knowing much of mouthsounding and also some part of palp vibrations, not yet does Fahar combine them well. Often as not, chirrs contradict or misstate rather than adding clarity.

Yet Fahar has marked degree of skill for its brief age; feeling pleasure, Imon for some time exchanges saying with its birthed Liijling before returning to nesting place.

There it notes, with concern overriding normal anticipation, increasing size and sensitivity of belly node. Breeding stage grows near—and so does great, banded world bearing many worldlets. With all heed and concentration needed to choose Environ's path and follow it precisely, ecstasy of breeding looms more as danger than as joy.

Environ's path meets and crosses that of straggling group of objects now falling inward from path's far point. None is large, Overwatcher Seit notes—but total aggregate masses well, and ingestor captures goodly portion.

Forward at considerable distance but only slight angle proceeds more massive thing: conglomerate of frozen gases packed around enclumpment of heavier materials. This, Seit determines, is wanderer from far reaches of star's warp, inbound to pass near star itself before again retreating to long, slow movement beyond paths of larger worlds.

Electrologic integration shows object reachable by Environ with only minute path change and minimal disturbance of route toward largest world. To Dutysetter Persa, now in duty cycle with navigationists and instrumentators, Seit directs that change to be performed.

In brief time while its directive is given implementation, Seit notes curious aspect. Were wanderer not ingested by Environ, its path meets that of Crippler world.

Of interest, perhaps, to see that meeting. But pace of object is too slow. Before it could reach Crippler, Environ must long since confront and hope to pass what may lie there.

At place of records Imon consults memory bone of Keht, great Healthwatcher of time long past, when Environ moved between starwhorls. < With duties (most urgent) soon to come, my breeding stage (imminent) is danger to Environ. How (possible, from your knowing) to avoid difficulty? >

Answer comes slow, thought not embellished. < Attempt to force breeding early. Ask living Healthwatchers' instruction. >

< And if (my knowledge is small) not possible? >

< Extirpate node. >

Disengaging from memory bone, feeling continued throb of belly node, Imon suffers threat of loss to many hopes.

Overtaking hurtling wanderer, Environ ingests, then by Seit's direction turns again toward star's greatest world. Not long, now, until path must bend around that world, using its warp's pull to produce leap in pace, while in same arc ingesting worldlets. Of these, two large can be taken, and several smaller.

This much is gratifying. Not so, uncertain status of navigationist Imon, which Seit blames self for not heeding until too late to attempt training another in same skills. Now, if Imon comes fully into breeding stage and cannot perform duties, Environ must forgo maneuver Imon made at girdled world.

Consulting Healthwatcher, Seit receives little comfort. Breeding disables from other efforts. Yet if Liij, node ripened, does *not* breed, disablement may be even worse, and longer of duration. Alternatives that will allow Imon to choose and execute Environ's best path are these: Imon must seek to breed before belly node is wholly ripened, or Healthwatcher must sever node from Imon.

Seit thanks Healthwatcher, then asks for names of other Liij at proper ripened condition for breeding. Not many, these, and most have already chosen pairings.

It may be, thinks Seit, that for Environ's good, one such choosing must be overridden.

Studying through many cycles, Chorl to electrologic integrator proposes imaginings: *If* pseudostrand, deduced from Environ's catastrophe, holds actuality, then what physical virtues must it also hold? And by what types of farsensor could it be foreseen?

Answers, long and slow in coming, surprise Chorl. They do not, because they cannot, carry proofs of any sort. Yet if headway is to be made in avoiding other such disastrous contact, unproven data constitute sole beginning places.

Therefore Chorl redesigns and recalibrates one entire group of farsensors. By all that has been known, resulting devices can avail nothing. Yet Chorl perseveres, unsleeping through three cycles as observations are noted, entered for integration, and extracted for comparison.

At third cycle's end, Chorl knows satisfaction and prepares for sleep. First, though, instructs communicator at central aggregate of duty stations: Overwatcher

Seit now sleeps, but before cycle's end, teacher and Overwatcher have need to meet.

Before heeding summons of Chorl, Seit again confers with Healthwatcher. Decision is, Imon to be given opportunity of early breeding. No time for breeders' own choosings—saying together, growing in appreciation, propinquity leading to congruent ripening. In attempt to override Imon's lack of readiness, Healthwatcher designates Liij with node of greatest ripeness. That one, and Imon, are summoned.

Seit does not remain to attend their meeting; Chorl awaits.

As Seit arrives, Chorl feels Overwatcher is not at best calm. And understandably; much concern exists. With only minimal display of greeting courtesies, Chorl describes what it has deduced from observation. < These farsensors> With palp and forelimb, it gestures. < Their sensings (qualities changed by my reconfigurings) show pseudostrands (previously known only to our imaginings) indeed emanate from (or converge upon) vicinity of Crippler world. >

Seit makes no dispute; sharing view of electrologic depictions with Chorl, it accedes to Chorl's determinations. From near Crippler world three pseudostrands lead out toward different farnesses—one being origin of Environ's more recent path. Thus that construct must be cause of disaster.

Also from near to Crippler world extend several shorter bits of pseudostrand: one from world to its worldlet, others which show Liij no purpose but have each, at farther end as well as nearer, objects of constructed nature.

Appearing to puzzle, Seit asks < Crossing of such strand (should Environ's path so militate): What would it do? >

< By all Liij knowledge (though never can *all* be known), at less than pace of radiance (many, many times our own, at now) no peril should occur. >

Seit chirrs amusement. < Yet unless of need (circumstance not foreseen by me), no such crossing is of intention. >

. . .

Tesel's duties lie in attending foursphere instrumentation, noting plasma energy levels, and constraining outlays where necessitated. Liij in such categories quarter largely near their duty stations and take nutriment at auxiliary place of feeding.

So it is that Imon itself and Tesel, presented each to other by Healthwatcher, have only slightest familiarity. But, when informed by Healthwatcher that they shall breed together, much unease. Tesel more than itself, Imon thinks, because Imon has for longer known itself committed to unusual course.

Greeting Tesel, Imon feels it should seek pardon for disruption of whatever choosing Tesel has likely made. Yet nothing in Imon's knowing contains saying for such condition. Imon recites greeting of pleasure in remeeting someone met only rarely and long past, and waits while Tesel makes similar saying.

As best could, Healthwatcher has prepared Imon. Other Liij at or near breeding stage have been summoned; following Healthwatcher's direction each rubs secretions from own node onto Imon's, with especial heed to sensitive tip. Pleasure of senses warring with growth of tensions, Imon shudders. Further, as has been done previously over past few cycles, Imon is fed extracts from node husk freshly shed by birther.

Tesel, crouched slightly as it sits to room's side, seems disaffected by strange procedure. Though it is not, thinks Imon, that any of this is Imon's preference. Circumstance of Imon's node cycle, of Environ's path, of Chorl's instructing Imon in means of using masswarp to aid Environ's pace—all together these bring Imon to loss of dignity, and both itself and Tesel to lack of choosing.

Can Tesel not understand these things, the less for Tesel.

Still, in deference to Tesel's feelings, once Healthwatcher finishes with observation and instructions, it is to Tesel's nesting place that both repair. There Imon waits while Tesel adjusts weight and illumination to its liking. Then, as Imon has experienced twice before but now without expressions of affection or regard, they face and engage: hindlimbs locked, forelimbs clasping, nodes flattened between bodies' pulsings.

Possessing greater ripeness, Tesel's node at center softens, allowing penetration, while outer part expands, rolling forward to circle and encase Imon's. But Imon's, yet unripe, does not contract at stem; girding ring at lip of Tesel's growing concavity strains against unyielding protrusion.

In both previous breedings Imon at this stage has felt pleasure made almost unbearable by growing tension, yet still wholly pleasure. This time, though, tension turns to pain that Imon cannot silence, and pleasure declines to fitful bursts; Tesel also makes sounds of hurt.

Guilt, complex yet only half understood, worsens Imon's pain. < Tesel, we must (of our own helplessness) seek aid. >

< We (of your unripeness forced upon me) must indeed. >

Disengaging one forelimb, Tesel reaches for calling device and summons Healthwatcher.

Seit grieves. Need for Imon's navigationist skills necessitate premature breeding, which has not gone well. To aid process, Healthwatcher first puts binding around stem of Imon's node, drawing it tight to allow lip of Tesel's to contract and engulf. Experimental measure eases Tesel's pain but heightens Imon's to agony.

Administration of nerve specifics avails little unless carried to point where Imon lacks consciousness and cannot maintain breeding stance, placing such great stress on Tesel that others must help support the two. After three cycles thus, Healthwatcher reports to Seit < Now must (to release Imon with time to recover) separate (with risk to Tesel and youngthon) Imon from joined nodes. >

< So (if no alternative) be it. >

Binding on stem is further tightened, in hope process of seeding accelerates, but no improvement occurs. Healthwatcher then resorts to measure of finality, severs stem—while sealing, as best possible, fluid loss from each wounded surface.

Result benefits none. At interface of joined nodes on Tesel's belly, Liijling ceases development and diminishes in vital process until waste poisons of dying endanger Tesel's own life; entire necrotic mass must be cut away.

Bitterness of Tesel, pointing out that none of this terrible misadventure comes by own free choice, is tempered but not lessened by fact that Imon fares even worse: Stump and very matrix of its node partakes of tissue death. To save life of Imon, entire breeding structure is extirpated.

Failure to foresee possible need of substitute navigationist has cost both Liij much. Seit grieves.

Slowly Imon loses pain and gains strength. In thought and feeling it has numbness. Breeding, always fearful joy, has become horror—but one that now cannot come again. Ever before marked by cheer and vigor, now Imon goes about its life's doings joyless but determined, with dedication to duty its only respite from grief and remembered pain.

Sympathy and pity of Seit and others help little. Oddly, saying and touch from Tesel, at first infrequent but then more often, gives greatest comfort. <When (not soon) I next breed> Tesel informs <you (if so choosing) help youngthon's nurture.>

Overcome, almost with sensation of healing, Imon mouthsounds and palps signs of gratitude.

Passage near great world goes much, if not all, as planned. On approach one worldlet meets ingestion, then world's pull swings Environ's path properly toward Crippler world and adds pace at better than predicted rate. But influence of other large worldlet, by error omitted from electrologic integration, alters path. Worldlet intended for ingestion during departure from world lies apart from changed, unintended path and escapes.

But for this, not Seit nor any other reproaches Imon.

In all, path gives Seit satisfaction more than not. Ahead lie courses of minor objects between largest world and next inner, which is small; many of these can ingestor field intercept and take. Next world itself, fourth from star, follows sequence of positions not susceptible to pursuit from Environ's present vantage—but to this world Seit has never given thought of serious effort.

Aside from maximizing, as may be possible, ingestion of scattered masses, Environ now has only one next challenge.

Crippler world itself.

Past and through Environ, spacetime flows. Path of fourth world is neared; crossing is to be at much distance from where that world now moves. Now sensed, from Crippler and from sources near it, are emissions each of singular energy content and formed into seeming patterns. Instrumentators study these patterns but discover no purpose or meaning therein.

Also from Crippler region come constructs at vastly growing pace. First such, notes Seit, meets and is absorbed by ingestor web, to benefit of foursphere. Second, barely short of striking web, does in crude fashion convert part of matter to energy; again, web pours resultant into foursphere. Third construct unfortunately veers away, its valued content unutilized.

Furtherward nearer star, then, forward yet aside Environ's path, larger construct is discerned: First ring-seeming, its turning discloses tubular form, length and bore roughly equal.

Visible rim, notes Overwatcher Seit, projects rounded forms emitting varied radiances parallel to axis; glimpse of further rim indicates it similarly equipped though not now active. Seit and Chorl confer; both agree that in greatest likelihood, these circles of studdings serve purpose of propelling construct.

Gauging size, instrumentation shows girth of object greater than that of ingestor's maw. Not of ingestor *field*, of course; only of forward hull opening from which field issues. Yet for non-Liij construct, great of size.

Puzzlement remains. At now construct moves to meet Environ's path—at point Environ reaches in same timespan.

But why? Though construct terminates no pseudo-strands, still must it derive from Crippler world. What new threat may it hold? Seit apprehends unknown danger.

Implacable, path of Crippler construct brings it squarely into Environ's and now moving in same direction. But more slowly; Environ cannot avoid overtaking. After number of cycles, yet still before Seit can find itself prepared in thought or act, event becomes imminent.

< What > Chorl asks < is your (unable to ignore) concern? This construct (admittedly puzzling) is grist for ingestor, nothing more. >

< I would wish (extreme stress) to know (with certainty) that you are (as should ordinarily be assumed) correct. >

Distance dwindles; object is near to ingestion. But then, only instants from touching field, its appearance changes. Emitted radiances vary chromatic property *along own length.*

< What—? >

INTERLUDE: PERTURBATION

Even from where he stood, Arnold Blaize could see that the president didn't like turning the press crew's attention over to Senator Flynn. But if you don't have any answers, make way for someone who does. Or can fake it, anyway. . . .

Flynn was good; Arnold gave him that much. ". . . not at all clear *why* the Intruder came here, or what it wants.

"What we do know—" made a very short list: The Intruder was a *big* mutha, was speeding up as it came, had accounted for two moons of Saturn and one of Jupiter's, and—

"Well, we're not sure," the senator equivocated, "why Rhea and Dione were taken, and others spared. One hypothesis is that Titan may have been too big to handle. And Japetus—another largish moon—was off the Intruder's apparent course. A circumstance shared by the planet Mars, to the relief of investors in that world's resources." No further mention, Arnold noticed, was made of the missing Jovian satellite Europa.

The media certainly weren't being easy: What in the bleeding hell about *Earth*? Are we just going to sit here and be swallowed? Is anybody *doing* something?

Flynn's face went grave. "Under tight security, so tight that the senior deliberative body was not notified, a trio of high-boost Traction Drive missiles was launched to intercept the Intruder inside the orbit of Mars. Warhead megatonnage exceeded the combined total of all fusion tests ever conducted."

So what happened?

Flynn gave a shrug of defeat. "The first one tracked well; then, just short of impact, it simply vanished. The second warhead assembly detonated quite near the alien vessel, but no damage to it could be detected."

And the third? Flynn grimaced. "Oh, come on, guys. When you go with the lowest bidder, two out of three isn't so bad." Then, impatiently, "It missed, dammit."

"So, Senator, what will happen now?" The woman who asked the question looked as if she knew the answer already—that it would be on the order of "Your guess is as good as mine."

But Flynn said, "Ask me tomorrow. We're working on it." Abruptly, asking not even the president's permission, Senator Flynn turned and walked away.

Late-night news pundits debated the effect of his actions on the ambient hysteria level. Consensus agreed pretty well with Arnold Blaize, who assured his boss, "It couldn't hurt."

He'd have felt better, though, if Flynn himself hadn't looked quite so worried.

XXIII

RENDEZVOUS

"What—?" Braced for gravity and finding none, Rance felt as though he'd hit a top step that wasn't there. Only his Velcro soles saved him from taking an awkward header.

If Su were affected the same way, she didn't show it. "What is this place? Why are we here?"

The woman stationed at this Tush rose from her chair and pushed longish, tawny bangs aside from her forehead. "If you're Collier and Teng, you have a lot of questions to answer."

Rance snorted. "I think you'll find we have answers you're not even looking for."

The woman's name was Jeannie Hurd. Medium height, slim, maybe thirty-five, she was senior Habgate attendant on the second "shipshooter," an orbital macroGate designed for eventual transport of entire ships through

Habspace but currently enroute to the asteroid belt for an experiment in "pipeline mining."

"Second macroGate?" Well, yes. After speaking briefly into an intercom, the woman explained. The first was well on its way to intercept Niflheim. That huge low-albedo iceball, discovered by a probe not too many years previously and believed to be anomalously plagued with vulcanism, lumbered along in an orbit with more than twice the semidiameter of Pluto's. Scientific, investigation was one objective, pipeline-style mining a contingent possibility; for Niflheim, the tenth planet, outscaled Jupiter by a bundle. *And* had no detectable magnetic field—thus no radiation belts to make reconnaisance dangerous.

As long as Hurd would answer questions, Rance was willing to keep asking. "How come the Tush is up here?" Bewildered look; he said, "The receiving Habgate, from *Roamer*. We expected Earth."

The answer came, but Jeannie Hurd's expression hardened. "A decision was made to move all extrasolar pipeline terminals into space. Security precaution. Now *if* you please—I believe Captain Cohaign is waiting for you."

The thing was *big*. Not world-class, maybe, but compared to your average starship this shipshooting Habtube was like having a barn to put your car in. The idea, Jeannie told them (duty or no, disapproval or not, she couldn't seem to suppress a naturally helpful nature), was to give arriving and departing ships plenty of clearance and allow the Gates' own fields to center any ship that came in sloppy.

She escorted Rance and Su along a roomy longitudinal corridor, then some distance around a peripheral crossway to the nearest set of transfer ring doors. Doors and ring compartment alike were outsized by *Starfinder* standards, and when the ring came up to belt speed, Rance had all the gravity he could handle. If it wasn't a full gee, *he* couldn't tell the difference; after nearly a year with never more than point-three, it felt like a six-hundred-pound gorilla.

"This way," said Jeannie, and off they plodded.

■   ■   ■

Austen Cohaign was a tall, lean-jawed man with brown hair showing gray and ebbing at the temples. After greeting Rance and Su curtly, he ordered—not invited —them to sit. "Two years ago, Captain Tetzl alerted us about you two. She thought you'd arrived here already, and wanted to short-circuit any subversive stories you might be telling. Going by way of *Roamer,* you seem to have fooled her." He leaned back in his chair. "All right. Whatever you have to say, let's hear it. Including how you managed to sabotage *Starfinder*'s Gates. Before we send you back to Earth, under arrest, you're going to tell us a few things."

Trying to think fast, Rance noticed the date on the captain's desk chrono: fifteen years and nearly three months since *Starfinder*'s departure. Which meant— "Relief cadre Two-A left here about six years ago, didn't it? And Two-B last year?" Cohaign nodded. "What do you hear from Two-A? And did the rest of our own cadre get home okay?"

"You know they didn't! Whatever it was you did, somehow they went into the Gate there but never came out. Four good crew members, *lost.* And only two of their relief cadre arrived safely on *Starfinder;* the others simply vanished. Captain Tetzl reported—"

Unable to stop himself, Rance laughed. At Cohaign's appalled look, he said, "Sorry. But you see, we *know* what the captain said. Or rather, what she planned to say. Su?"

He didn't think he had to ask the specific question, and he was right. "Yes, Rance, I have it. Just a moment." She rummaged in her duffel and brought out the data capsule. At Rance's nod she offered it to Cohaign. "This holds a copy of the plans Irina Tetzl made, something over four years ago, for the future of *Starfinder*'s mission. Learning about them is what decided us to jump ship. Perhaps you would like to view it."

"It's access-coded," Rance added. "For the file you want, the entry key is Old Iron Tits."

Finished, Cohaign popped the capsule free. "I'll keep this; all right?" He sighed. "Well. It's a whole new pail of mackerel, isn't it? The question is, what to do about it." He looked to Rance. "What's the timing?"

Rance knew what the captain meant. "Shipside, not quite five months since we left. Two-B due to arrive on board in five weeks, roughly, and no telling what they'll run into. Nothing we can do about that part; if you send a takeover team of some sort, this minute, it'll be a further five weeks getting there." Ship's time, of course; he hoped Cohaign was keeping the difference straight.

The man scowled. "I'll have to confer with the brass, call Earthside. Policy matter; I'm not authorized to act."

Surprising Rance, Su said, "Neither were we. But we did." Then, "Are you still going to arrest us for it?"

Don't push so hard! But Cohaign answered mildly. "No, of course not. It's a damned good thing, though, that you brought hard evidence: this planning brief, unmistakably using Irina Tetzl's own characteristic turns of phrase. Otherwise you'd still be in hot soup up to your ears."

He stood. "I'll have you assigned quarters and issued some extra gear." Gesturing, "You can't have brought a whole lot in just those two bags. Now then; I have other, extremely urgent matters to deal with. Is there anything else you need?"

There was. Rance said, "Something to eat would be nice. We had our last meal more than ten light-years from here."

A chunky, fair-complexioned young man named Hugh Branson, some sort of junior officer in this quasi-military setup, first took the new arrivals to a smallish dining space and had coffee while they ate, then to a supply area where they drew standard dress kits in their respective sizes, and finally to quarters: a room that would have held three of their shipside compartment.

"Make yourselves at home. The captain'll want you again at eleven hundred hours tomorrow." He displayed his chrono so that Rance and Su could set their own "Local" ranges to match it. Then he left.

After showering, Rance and Su went to bed. They hadn't made love in over ten light-years, either.

Next day they learned that Irina Tetzl was among the lesser of Cohaign's worries. Sitting near Branson's desk at one side of the executive room, waiting the chance to ask the captain when and how—unless there was something more they could do here—they might expect to leave for Earth, they listened with growing bewilderment to the captain's end of a succession of Earthside calls, to intercom exchanges, and to reports made in person. After a time, with a fill-in by Branson when they joined that young man down the corridor on his coffee break, they began to understand what was scaring everyone.

Or maybe they did; Rance wasn't sure. "Let's see if I have this right. . . ." Alien artifact, a *big* son, coming through the Solar System and picking up speed as it came. *Swallowed* two of Saturn's moons and one of Jupiter's. ". . . plus, you said, a hefty-sized comet?"

"Yes, and that's the confusing part. Mostly this thing's seemed like a threat, and still does. But that comet, near as anyone could figure, was headed to bash right into Earth."

Su spoke. "So the aliens did us a huge favor?"

Branson nodded. "That's how it worked out. Whether they *meant* to, though—"

"We can't know," said Rance, "so no point in assuming anything. Especially since—if I've been hearing right, all morning—the alien ship itself is moving toward Earth?"

"Not exactly; the Intruder's course keeps curving. But near enough."

Done with coffee, the three trudged back to Cohaign's working office, where Rance asked and received permission to use Branson's desk terminal. "How do I punch up data on the Intruder?" When Branson showed him, he brought up a graphic of the artifact plus dimensional and other data, some exact but much of it estimated.

What it looked like, more than not, was a football— except that instead of a rounded point, the forward end extruded into a short stem, squared off flatly. "Presumably," Branson said, "the rear would be much the same." The blunt stem appeared to be hollow, its opening tiny compared to the Intruder's bulk yet only slightly smaller than the macroGate's own bore. Still, nothing that could swallow a whole *moon*.

Saying as much, Rance drew a snort from Branson. "Turn up the Bright control."

He did; now the screen showed, flaring from the Intruder's nose, a shimmering, immaterial-looking trumpet bell. The object itself was huge enough to be a minor satellite in its own right, but this—this inverted lampshade it wore like a hat—"Hell, it must stretch nearly as wide as the moon!"

"Wider," said Branson. "You see why we're worried?"

"You mean—"

"Yes. That's what it gobbles with."

Subdued, Rance fiddled access to more data, scanning more or less at random in search of something useful. For instance, where did the thing come from? The coordinates didn't mean much to him, but the reference star listing seemed familiar. Then it hit him; involuntarily he slapped his hand down onto the desk, and spoke louder than he intended. "You know what? This sonofabitch came sneaking down *Starfinder*'s backtrack!"

At first Cohaign looked irritated by the disturbance; then he called Rance over to his desk. Before following, Su Teng punched for a readout to bring along. When she handed it to him and sat down, the captain said, "I know your ship had some sort of catastrophic encounter in space, but not the details. In your opinion, do they connect to the Intruder?"

Deep breath. "I think so." Briefly, Rance told it: the starship apparently hitting *something* that turned chronos backward and put Traction Drive on hold. "The wake of an object moving faster than light, we thought at first. But by a theory Dr. Habegger came up with, which we got at secondhand, maybe such an object hit *our* wake. Not the Drive's, but a trail Habegger thinks the Gates themselves may leave, some kind of link between them. Either way, though—"

"Either way," Cohaign cut in, "the Intruder's not running at FTL. Or anywhere near it."

"Not now, it isn't; I can't argue with that. But it's coming from where *Starfinder* had the anomalous incident, so maybe it followed our trail, straight back to the source."

The trouble was, what *use* was that information?

Apparently deciding that Rance and Su might be of some help, and having a little free time for a change, the captain began to discuss the options he and his superiors on Earth were trying to pursue. "Saturating all wavebands with signals, for one thing. Ever since the object passed Big Jupe, we've been doing that. Math combinations, progressions, and so forth—along with various linguistic experiments sent up by API, the psychologists' institute. Plus, of course, straightforward pleas for communication, in several major languages, just in case."

But no response, right? So what else? Damned little, it seemed. MacroGate Two had been diverted from its assigned mission, to intercept the Intruder's course and try to run *ahead* of the alien for as long as possible, while still attempting communication and hoping someone—*anyone*—would come up with a workable course of action.

"Why not let it go past," said Su, "and come up behind it?"

"Delta-vee," Cohaign said. "It was all we could do to turn and get in ahead of it; if we'd waited until it went by, we'd never have caught up. As things are, it's closing fast; sooner or later we have to turn aside and run for it. If we wait too long, we'll have to abandon the macroGate altogether. Let the Intruder eat it, and make our own escapes jammed into whatever supply ships we can manage to get here in time."

Flat-voiced, Rance asked, "Just how long before you couldn't save the Gate?"

"Oh, four days, I'd guess. Maybe five."

Four or *five*? Shocked, Rance began rethinking his own options.

For dinner he and Su were placed at the second of four officers' tables, this one presided over by Arnie Rike, the exec. Towheaded, with skin that most likely would sunburn badly in five minutes, the tall man sat and spoke with a languid air Rance didn't fully believe. As one indication, his eyes never stayed still for long.

Discussion at table, naturally enough, centered on the Intruder. While a middle-aged woman who looked like a Gypsy fortune teller in uniform told everyone *her* ideas of how to handle the situation (more of what was already being done, near as Rance could tell), Rike's eyelids sagged to half mast. When she paused, he said, "Sound thinking, Milla. But what next?"

She didn't answer. He said, "Well, maybe we'll get some fresh input here, later this afternoon when Portaris arrives."

Rance sat up straight. "Three-fingered Annie?"

Rike looked around to him. "Why, yes. You know her?"

"From way back. Before she got the nickname no one uses to her face."

The exec nodded. "You know her, all right. Anyway, she's been back from *Arrow* for—I'm not sure just how long—and for the past two-three weeks, briefing back and forth with Senator Flynn and the NASA brass. None of us has any idea what she may be holding up her sleeve, but we sure to hell hope she has *something*." He checked his chrono. "A little over an hour from now, the ship docks."

"I hope no one minds," Su interposed, "if Rance and I are there to help greet her."

"I'm in charge of that detail," said Arnie Rike. "Be my guest."

How old, by now, would Anne Portaris be? Waiting near the docking portal with Rike and Su and a half-dozen others, Rance tried to figure it. To begin with, she'd been—how much older than himself? Four years, he thought; five at the outside.

That difference, though, no longer applied. Einstein and Habegger each had made some changes. Rance, now: what with three Habgate passages he'd skipped six years entirely. And on *Starfinder* had lived one year, roughly speaking, while Earth experienced ten. So his body was fifteen years younger than its calendar age. Or near enough for government work. . . .

Now how about Portaris? She, too, had made three gate jumps: Earth to *Roamer* to *Arrow* and home. She . . .

The jar and vibration of a ship docking, probably quite gentle as such things went but with seismic overtones at such close quarters, disrupted his concentration. When he recovered, finding himself grinning (probably sheepishly, he thought) for no particular reason, he continued his thought. A month on *Roamer* would be close to an Earth year, an *Arrow* week nearly half a year. Okay, call it seven and a half years' absolute age slippage for Annie? Then about the same for the difference between her and himself. Shouldn't be too embarrassing. . . .

When the lock hatch opened, though, and Portaris was the third to walk through it, she looked younger than he'd expected. But the intensity of her expression and movements drove all such irrelevancies from his mind.

Straight off, she spotted him. "Rance! Rance Collier! Where the hell have you been?"

In the face of Arnie Rike's obvious impatience, Anne having fobbed the man off with a perfunctory greeting, Rance tried to explain quickly. Portaris cut in: "Down at NASA HQ they'd written you off. One of those inexplicable Habgate malfunctions Tetzl kept having. She'd sent warning that you were a subversive and not to trust you, but you *hadn't* shown up, so—"

Rance laughed. "There weren't any gate malfunctions; that was just Old Iron Tits covering up some dipsy-doo maneuvers of her own. She . . ." He told it fast, skipping a lot. "I don't know if anyone's deciding how to get back on top of that situation, or not. But meanwhile, this Intruder—what do *you* think can be done to stop it?" Her brows went up. He said, "Stop it from eating Earth for dessert, I mean."

Smiling to include Rike in the conversation, she said, "Well, first, there's no question of that. Its web, or whatever it may be—the trumpet-shaped iridescent net that precedes the object—spreads to just about one third Earth's diameter. The Intruder only swallows objects the net can encompass. And while it's grown some, since first observed, it grows only *after* swallowing something. So you see—"

"The Moon," said Arnie Rike. "It could eat the Moon."

And aside from the colonists and Moon-based ships and industrial installations and capital investments, what might the Moon's disappearance do to *Earth*? Orbital dynamics, Rance mused, were touchy things. Not to mention psychological impacts.

He touched Anne's arm. "As I was saying . . ."

The hell of it was, as came clear when Portaris spoke with the group assembled by Austen Cohaign, that she didn't really *have* any good ideas. MacroGate Two's basic function, the gate itself, was of no use at all in this. If a whopping big asteroid had been put into its pipeline about seven hundred twenty-eight days ago and were due to come popping out soon—but the sender for Two's primary receiver matrix was as yet unassembled, its components riding *Starfinder* as cargo.

"I've thought of one possibility," she said. "If this macroGate were butted up against the Intruder's flank —very near the nose or tail, either one—and max drive applied, the side thrust just might divert its course from whatever target it picks next. *Might,* I said. Because we have no decent estimate of its mass. But—"

"I can get you a good horseback guess," said Arnie Rike. "Half an order of magnitude, if that's good enough."

Cohaign shook his head. "It would be, probably. But the trouble with that idea is, we'd have to be coming in from the side, to match courses and make contact gently. Instead we're right in the bugger's path, running at top accel just to stay ahead of it a little longer. No room for maneuvering."

Anne Portaris shrugged. "So we can't get there from here."

More talk came, and other suggestions, but none even approaching practicality. Eventually Cohaign adjourned the meeting; Rance and Su wound up with him and Anne and Rike, sitting around a table in the officers' lounge—a room that dwarfed *Starfinder*'s rec lounge— talking desultorily over drinks that seemed to be quite durable.

Portaris said little. Her right thumb, Rance noticed, rubbed the stub of the missing index finger in a gesture that looked to be unconscious habit. Somewhere in his own mind a thought rose, wavered on the edge of awareness, but vanished when he tried to bring it into focus. Much like a dream, he thought—the way one fades with awakening. And no more help . . .

Arnie Rike, now drumming fingers on the table, looked up. "A bomb. Let 'em swallow a damned *bomb*."

"What's to explode?" Rance hadn't noticed young Branson coming to stand behind him and to one side; the man's question seemed reasonable enough.

Cohaign shook his head. "Not much, I'm afraid. Here, sit down."

Under Rike's glowering scrutiny, Branson pulled up a chair. "I was coming to that," the exec said. "That part we need to improvise. Bring up a shipload of stuff, really high-ex, the best we can get—and fast. Stuff the tail end full of it. Set a proximity fuse, minimum feasible distance." He spread his arms. "Then we evacuate, get the hell away, and watch the fun."

For what seemed a very long time, no one spoke. Then the captain said, "Get HQ on the circuit and put the orders in. My authorization, Priority One."

He shrugged. "I don't like it. Don't like it at all. But just offhand, people, it might just be the best we can do."

Captain and exec left; moodily the remaining four sat, saying little, until Anne Portaris yawned and stretched. "I've lost track of time, totally," she said, "but I do know I'm overdue for sleep."

Rance stood. "I'll take a carton of that, myself." Branson moved to join another group across the lounge; Su and Rance walked Anne to her room, not far from theirs and on the same corridor. "See you tomorrow."

In quarters, too stressed for anything but sleep, nonetheless Rance lay a long time while his mind chased answers that wouldn't hold still.

At breakfast next morning, Arnie Rike approached the table. "Join you?" Rance nodded. "I expect you think I'm some kind of bang-bang crazy." Pause; carefully,

Rance held his best deadpan expression. "Well, I'm not. If anybody comes up with a better idea . . ." Rike gestured. "But these doobies in that overgrown darning egg—assuming there *is* somebody in there, not just a big cosmic robot vacuum cleaner—they have to realize we're out here, trying to talk. But they don't respond, don't show any indication they know we're here at all. Or give a damn.

"So we have to do what we *can* do to protect ourselves. And so far, Collier, giving them some high-explosive indigestion is the only thing that even looks like it might work."

"I suppose so. But—but couldn't you pull this macro-Gate off sideways out of danger and just lob in some small explosive charges as warnings? Then, if they don't respond in some way—"

Rike sighed. "Maybe. I don't know. It's all such a damn rush, ever since we got the word to scrub our mission and go for intercept. No time to do any real brainstorming."

Su Teng said, "And yet there are possibilities that no one seems to have considered. This ensnaring web, for instance, that the aliens use to engulf matter. What is it? Does anyone know?" When no answer came, she continued. "Obviously it's not material. Some kind of generated field phenomenon, visible only by photons emitted when it is struck by spaceborne particles."

The exec stared at her. "You sure about that? Because it's more than anyone else seems to know about it."

"Sure about what? That the web is not matter as we know it? I would say so. What it truly is, though, is not so certain."

Rance sat up straight. "Hey. That thing swallows objects that strike its *surface*. What if we could come at its edge, at its perimeter? With the input of this Habgate, maybe, to take a bite out of *it*?"

For a moment, he thought he had something; then Rike shook his head. "There's no receive terminal in operation yet for our send matrix, so it wouldn't accept anything for pipeline transmission." Then the exec grinned. "Even so, Collier, for sheer inventiveness that's the best idea I've heard in a while."

He stood. "When you two finish your coffee, I think

the skipper wants a confab. With our other plans set up, now he has time to discuss the problem you came to warn us about."

Offered more coffee in the captain's office, Rance and Su both declined. With that formality done, Cohaign turned to a tall, thin-faced woman whose dark hair was cut very short. "Rance Collier, Su Teng, I'd like you to meet Dana Ferrell, my Security chief. She's been roughing out schemes to tackle this Tetzl mess, and could use some on-the-spot input."

After greetings, Ferrell said, "HQ considered the overall situation. While there's really no reason Irina Tetzl couldn't have had command at the end of *Starfinder*'s journey, if she'd applied for it in proper form, it's not acceptable for her to take over the entire mission by force and deception. Let alone choosing her own crew and shuffling the rejects around in various Habegger pipelines, as your information indicates. My assignment is to do something about her, and I need your help."

Rance said, "Sure. But just what is it you want?"

Ferrell's brows lowered in concentration. "You lived on that ship; I've never been inside it. Tell me how *you* would mount a raid, stage a coup—and how you'd defend against one."

Rance thought. "It wouldn't be much of a trick for Old Iron Tits to sandbag Habegger's Tush. Fence it in so anyone coming through unsuspecting would be contained, and sitting ducks for an ambush with her memory-zapping stun darts." Before Ferrell could interrupt, he continued. "So if you send anyone in, they need protective clothing against the darts, and equipment to cut or burn through any sort of trap she may have set up."

He paused. "Weapons? You're dealing with only a handful of people, headed by a woman who has some major glitches in her programming—but she's neither a mad dog nor any kind of terrorist. Her secret plans showed she *might* consider killing, but there's no evidence that she's done any. What I'm saying is, this isn't a job for grenades and machine guns."

Dana Ferrell nodded. "But you do recommend a direct raid?"

More thought, taking enough time that Su beat him to the answers: "Why not secure the Habgates on *Roamer* and *Arrow* first—or at least simultaneously? Send crews to trap both ships' *Starfinder* Tushes, the way Rance guesses Irina may have done at her end. So that if she's recycling people through either pipeline, they can be intercepted. Sheep and herders both."

When she had to explain the reference, the pause gave Rance time to organize his own ideas. He broke in, "You'd need dartproof suits there too, of course. And enough people for round-the-clock guarding." He gave a wry chuckle. "Over what might be a long and unrewarding vigil. Because we can't know for sure that she's actually *doing* any of this, and it could take your watchdogs a shipside month or two to find out."

Dana wasn't laughing. "We know a number of people have disappeared and that she's lied about the causes. As far as I'm concerned, the odds are good enough to bet quite a lot of person-hours on the outcome." She peered at Rance. "I don't suppose you brought any of those darts with you? So we could see what it takes to stop one?"

Shrugging, "Sorry; the lady wasn't handing out samples."

"I suppose not. All right; that's it for now. I'll confer with HQ and meet with you again when I have some decisions." She started to raise a hand in gesture, then paused. "Oh, yes; I'll get copies of structural drawings for the ships. And I'll want you, Collier and Teng, to evaluate which types of ambush trap structures might best work in that environment."

Well. The woman certainly didn't waste time getting aboard a situation. Dismissed, Su and Rance left for the galley in rather a hurry. They'd had, Rance felt, quite enough company to last them a while.

Over the next two days, supply ships gathered to dock at the macroGate for personnel evacuation, or hang offboard in position to dock in turn. Among these came three larger vessels, bearing Rike's explosives and the devices needed to detonate them.

All around the big Gate's aft circumference, in the arcs between drive units, cargo was moved to pack the rearmost holds with the deadly stuff. Whatever damage might occur to the Intruder when the proximity fuse went, there wouldn't be much left of that end of macro-Gate Two.

As word of the activity got around, more than a few among the Gate's personnel showed antsy: What if the whole thing went off prematurely? "Ace" Henderson, in charge of the explosives team, laughed and reassured a group in the galley. "This stuff? Hell, stable is its middle name. You could hit it with a hammer, drop it off a cliff, shoot high-velocity slugs into it. Wouldn't even twitch. Nothing less than the concussive wave front of a Two-X electrocap, and *that* won't go without its proper signal."

As Ace left, Rance, for one, felt comfortably reassured. Anne Portaris, though: From the looks of her, he wasn't too sure. Again her thumb rubbed the finger stub, but now harder and faster, more obsessively.

And then the idea Rance had been fishing for, that had hovered tantalizingly and then submerged beyond recognizance, came up and took the bait.

"Annie!" The nickname stilled her hand and brought Rance a cold glare. "No, wait a minute. Listen! Your finger, the way it happened!

"Anne? This Gate's running on twelve *big* Traction Drives."

XXIV

LONG IN DARKNESS

Almost before streaming hues of radiance can be fully seen, farsensor screens dim to black. Instrumentation shows sudden end to all impingement of radiance and particles on Environ. Unable to believe, Seit calls for instrumentators to examine for fault. Yet how can all devices fail at simultaneity? Not happening, not rumored of happening, in all Environ's experience; no avail, then, to consult memory bones.

Consultation is with instrumentators. <Make changes (to discover existing wrongness) in instrumentation adjustments> says Seit. <Discover to me (so soon as may be) what here transpires, that (beyond precedent) ingestion of mattery (by all indication) ceases.>

Instrumentators obey. Receptiveness of farsensors is increased tenfold, then again, and more times—to range at which random thermal flow inside devices almost obscures incoming sensings. Only at this point is particle and radiance impingement at all denoted, and even so, only barely sensed.

Each every farsensor indicates as much. With no volition, expressing no meanings, Seit chirrs palps. Now to indicators of Environ's own workings, it turns. And is horrorstruck. For while ingestor engulfs no matter or radiance—or so little as to add nothing detectable to foursphere's plasma activity—re-creator continues to exude mattery-filled spacetime at maximum rate.

Accomplishing nothing! Far from adding pace, sensors show not even sign of pace already achieved; Environ, so they portray, moves not. Although foursphere, expending from hard-won accumulation, shows energy level dropping steeply.

With mouthsounds breath-strained and palps shaking, Seit orders re-creator activity ceased. Soon this is done, though not before foursphere energy depletes to dismaying extent.

Seit moves its far eyes' gaze one final round through each instrumentation category, takes all indications into mind for ruminance of thought, and lowers ears forward over far eyes to sign that none may intrude.

For now is time every Overwatcher realizes may befall, and dreads: Seit must find a way, where none exists, to save Environ.

As navigationist, Imon numbs with surprise when all observing screens lose outer prospect. Neither Seit's saying nor those of instrumentators bring clarity to its confusion. With no indication from outside Environ, Imon's thought and sense find no hold, and flounder as new youngthon in nesting place lacking weight. Breath comes hardly; palps quiver. Only when Overwatcher commands cessation of re-creator and hoods far eyes for contemplation does Imon calm and follow Seit's example.

Following many cycles in regret and sorrow, grieving loss of breeding node—painful joy and supreme fulfillment never again to be—Imon is again in balance. Like youngthon, now, it must be: living, learning, dutiful as Liij should be and must, with never thought of breeding cycle's stressful reward. Of help are many, and Tesel greatest. Again, as navigationist, is Imon truly fit.

Now, once more as when Crippler construct caused disaster of Environ's loss of pace and plasma energy, Imon waits for Seit to decide and command. So that Imon may obey.

Situation, Seit concludes, is as never experienced by Liij. Even when Environ, uncounted *dre* in past, departed Liij home world with only that world's pace on which to build, spacetime outside Environ provided mattergy to feed ingestor. Now, none appears to farsensors; Environ hangs in dark, empty void—lacking, except in quantity too tiny to be of use, even usual surround of scattered particles and radiance.

Having no past happening to compare, Seit thinks once more, memory bones can hardly add useful knowledge. Emerging from isolation of thought, raising ears to uncover far eyes, Seit commands dutypersons to continue at stations and report all sensings to Dutysetter Persa.

With duty stations instructed, Seit leaves area. Now is time for congress of minds, breeding of new thought.

In search of Chorl, Seit goes to upmost study place.

As anticipated, Chorl has thoughts of concern for new predicament. But none that truly explains nor can be proven. First speculation, that Crippler construct has moved Environ to distant position lacking in mattergy, has no credence. For at any part of spacetime, radiance from other parts may be sensed.

But can more than one spacetime dimensionality exist? Of old, Liij had considered possibility; theoretic of philogenist Huolf, so oldened that even its memory bone has ended function, postulates *necessity* of numerous else-existent spacetimes. Could a given one suffer just such lack as Environ now perceives? And could Crippler device in unknown fashion alter Environ's grasp of known dimensions, shunt it into unfamiliar, unsuspected nexus?

Chorl's palps chirr indeterminacy; from knowledge past and present, no answer is achievable.

<Then what (in light of limitations you cite) is to be

(and in what haste) done?> Fatigue slurs Seit's palp movements.

<Only (but yes, in much haste)> says Chorl <to determine (from knowledge we do have) how best to keep Environ (and Liij) in continued living existence.>

And, thinks Seit, *with surrounding spacetime barren, for what timespan can life be maintained?*

Of Liij convened for studious decision concerning peril to Environ, Imon is among most recently summoned. As such, it heeds much, saying little. Also, designated by Chorl, it records sayings and conclusions of seniors into electrologic integrator.

At end of gathering it proffers records, processed by device to strip away superfluities and redundancies, to Overwatcher Seit for its consideration. But Seit chirrs aside Imon's offer, asking navigationist to state records' conclusions personally.

<We both (being present throughout) have heard all saying> Seit comments. <Tell me (with own mouth and palps) what understanding you derive. Let us discover (here saying) if our (two, each, separate) hearings agree.>

Imon obeys. As Overwatcher and navigationist converse and compare, scope of agreed understanding becomes apparent, and for present moment, what does not agree is put aside.

Undisputed are two inharmonious conclusions. First: For Liij to survive, all action must presume that Environ's surround stays forever barren. Second: For Liij survival to avail in any true meaning, *thought* must be on opposite premise, that at some future, unpredicted time, surround becomes as before.

Seit gives concluding summary. Proper thinking, being matter of will, can be achieved. Action, to maintain Liij life in Environ in absence of notable ingestor input, entails great difficulty, loss, and pain of thought. Possible decisions allow only *choice* of losses.

For with ingestor adding to foursphere's plasma energy, drain for life maintenance throughout Environ is small fraction of total processed. Now, though, without input, normal energy use would drain foursphere in only handsful of *dre.* Had re-creator's thrust ended more promptly, level would be much less depleted, and time span therefore greater.

But as no youngthon can be returned to its shredded nodes, energy once spent cannot be reclaimed. Existing level, then, must not fall more than utter necessity requires—and if achievable means can be derived, must be bolstered as may be possible.

Dominant fact, Seit says—taut, strained muscles of its lips betraying feelings Overwatcher would surely wish concealed—is that mattergy-starved Environ cannot for more than several few *dre* maintain lives of Liij at present number. Or that number halved, or even halved again.

For energy demands of nutriment proliferation, life gas quality, fluid reclaiming, even heat level of nesting and duty places, all reflect numbers of living Liij. And each and every of these demands, Seit tells, must be diminished to small portion of present need.

Decision needed is: how to achieve such diminishment.

Gathering disperses; Seit's thinking finds little hope. Then, as Seit might expect but somehow does not, Chorl suggests source of added knowing. Dron, it states, while still living once said of long-past Overwatcher Paot < From time (so many *dre)* Environ moved between starwhorls. And (so Dron told) suffered (as now) need to diminish Liij numbers. >

Soon as may be, Seit consults with memory bone of Paot. Oldened beyond condition of Dron but not yet so limited as Haef, Paot's saying still holds faint trace of living semblance. < Two lifespans from end of time between whorls > it says < mattergy so sparse, fails to maintain plasma level. To preserve most possible lives, many others must end. >

< How (by what reckoning) chose you those to end? >

< Difficulty was announced to all, and all offered selves. Choice was, those of most value to Environ were not ended. >

With question answered, Seit's thought diverges. < Aside from (most necessary) reduction of numbers, wherefore else (alternative means) can plasma level be aided? > And to full surprise of Overwatcher Seit, Paot limns measures—minor yet perhaps of value—not within Seit's knowings.

As though to living Liij, Seit when disengaging says gratitude. Now, it thinks while leaving, comes greatest distress it could know. For who has flawless judgment of others' merits?

Certainly not Overwatcher Seit . . .

When Liij are told of Environ's direst needs, pain ensues. As in Paot's time, all Liij offer to end selves or be ended before their bodies would by nature do so. But behind those offers Seit cannot but sense, in many, deep fear and regret.

Because early end, before life and learning can be complete, brings great unfairness. Few may continue as memory bones, for few have sufficient knowings both individual to selves and needful of preservation; greatest number can only, simply, end.

Yet now must Overwatcher Seit, in concert with other Liij of greatest responsibilities, choose persons to be ended by assignment. Much pain of thought accompanies all choices; each individual's circumstance and relation with others needs evaluation. Before and after designating each new quota, Seit seeks slumber vainly. As to feelings of those with whom Seit confers, it does not ask.

Customary usage of ended Liij, or of portions remaining when memory bone has been derived, is to become nutriment for growing plants, which in turn nourish both Liij and Environ's few creatures providing scarce meat not grown in bulk. But now are more Liij ended than nutriment proliferation can utilize. Some, then, are placed in designated compartment and exposed to chill of space, to preserve for future use. Others, though Seit deplores inevitability of such waste, go into smaller, inboard maw of Environ's ingestor, each giving benefit to foursphere's plasma activity. But even if all ended Liij were so disposed, energy level would continue ebbing.

As more Liij end, less Environ space and supporting devices are required; Liij occupation of Environ shrinks toward forward areas and median strip extending rearward. In praiseworthy devotion, Liij preparing to end selves, or be ended, expend last cycles of life laboring to consolidate Environ functions for economy of plasma energy. Many facilities—production of nutriment, fluid reclamation, and like operations—are left in place but inactive; hope is, at some time again to use.

Grueling times continue until, by direct means, Liij numbers are three times halved. Still too many for over-all Liij survival—yet now, feel many, further diminishment must occur by other measures. Unsure of own judgment, Imon in unthought feeling agrees.

Most obvious step is curtailment of breeding. Yet before disclosing—perhaps before deciding—what choices are to be made, Overwatcher again calls council. Attending, Imon feels like worldlet in ingestor's path; at each quota for ending, it has expected to be named. Now, surely, its time has come. In Imon is no protest; if chosen, it will obey. Yet learning, discovering knowings new to it, has become such pleasure that it could not easily accept, in wholeness, need for it to cease.

Decisioners convened, first to say is Chorl. It poses necessary conditions for Environ's secure continuation; one is to arrive at smallest number of Liij necessitated to maintain Environ at minimum level to support that number.

Another is ideation all new to Imon: least number to breed over many successive lifetimes, yet conserve full range in variations of Liij heritage. < For if (due to lack of farseeing) our long-to-come Liijlings are less (by insufficient redundancy) than fully Liij, then (no matter the fact of bare survival) we have failed. >

Much discussion follows, biostructionists disagreeing with biochemicians while Seit and Chorl seek to build overview. Comprehending little, Imon waits for conclusions to be said.

But at finality, convening Liij are told only that decisions will be reached by smaller gathering, only of those bearing greatest responsibilities, and disclosed at further time.

Measures to be undertaken weigh heavily upon Overwatcher Seit. No facile choices exist. Decided, herefore, is that all Liij who have birthed or seeded any youngthon, are not now into or entering breeding stage, and have not oldened past possibility of future breeding, shall undergo removal of belly node and underlying matrix.

No specialty of circumstance mitigates; Seit itself must endure excision of breeding function. By condition of oldening, Chorl is past necessity of extirpation.

Over time, these things are done. Now, with regard to grown Liij, provision of future numbers is controlled. Remaining is disposition of youngthons: Which shall breed and which not?

Evaluations begin: determination of desirability of share of Liij heritage carried by each youngthon. Then, based on number of youngthons needed to grow and breed one time each, to maintain Liij at projected level, they are divided into two groups, and those of lesser heritage deprived of belly nodes.

At end of proceeding, Seit's thought struggles under pain. So many Liij, not by any fault of own doing, required to end. Lesser number, though more than half those still living, never in time ahead to breed. Greater part of Environ abandoned by Liij, left cold and airless, shut away from remaining portions where life endures.

But Liij *will* endure.

Diminishment of numbers, lessening use of devices and of Environ space itself, reduces drain on foursphere energy. Still, level always drops, never rises. Trickle entering ingestor could barely power devices that detect it. At present state, Seit knows, Liij and Environ can endure for many *dre*.

But if condition of surround should endure still longer? Simply, Environ would grow cold and Liij would end.

Seit consults. If not so rich in knowings, and skill at adding to them, Chorl would be memory bone with first group to be ended. But oldening aside, living, sensing mind of Chorl has too much value to allow its ending while choice exists.

Now Chorl says to Seit's questions. < Given that Paot (as you report) suggests unfamiliar measures in aid of plasma level, its advice (no evidence being in denial) merits activation. >

Herefore, Seit gathers Liij of greatest responsibility and disseminates instruction. When Environ, in time far past, leaves home whorl, Liij of that period foresee contingency of lengthy passage through place of barren surround, and make provision.

Time comes when that arduous circumstance is realized, and Liij have long forgotten precautionary measure. But Overwatcher Paot, much as Seit now, ideates possibility of aid from memory bone and discovers means of solution.

Packed in Environ's forward reaches, to be reasonably near ingestor's smaller intake, are many, many bars of metal having extraordinary mass in small bulk. Feeding these into ingestor at rate determined by electrological integration can, if not raise plasma energy appreciably, perhaps maintain present level.

< Or so it was > Seit relates < when (in barren surround between starwhorls) Overwatcher Paot performed (or perhaps ordered performed) such integrations. > In truth Paot relied not wholly upon electrologic, since needed parameters were lacking. To obtain those, Paot chose arbitrary number of bars for first ingestion, observed results, *then* resorted to calculation.

Since memory bone of Paot no longer recalls number chosen, Seit can but follow predecessor's same course of action.

Encouraging is that to endure barren passage, Environ consumed less than half original store.

Not so is that between starwhorls Environ yet had great pace, and within farsensor sight, eventual end to barrenness.

Now, in Seit's time, it has neither.

First ingestion of metal bars slows, but halts not, fall of plasma energy level; Seit orders small addition and sees desired result. Now electrologic has parameters and can predict.

Earlier Seit could know, within error margin of only few successions of Liij, how long Environ with energy dropping at present rate might nurture life. Now to that time it adds number of metal bars remaining, multiplied by period, specified by electrologic, between ingestion of one and adding next.

Result heartens: Far, far along time can Liij exist. If parameters do not worsen. If devices do not fail beyond repair. If number chosen to live is enough to carry full heritage, so that over many successions, youngthons are not birthed less than fully Liij.

If. But for Environ's safe continuance, all that Seit can do, Seit has done.

Much time occurs, of little happening. Liij olden, ingestor accepts metal, surround remains vacant. Chorl ends, and later Seit; their memory bones are much consulted. As Overwatcher, Persa succeeds Seit, is succeeded by Tesel; next given that responsibility is Imon. And following Imon is Fahar, birthed by Imon from Tith.

Imon achieves state of memory bone. New condition would be of interest, were memory bone to harbor such attribute.

Many living Liij, notes Fahar, also lack involvement and concern. Because so little happens—*can* happen, in Environ.

Fahar consults memory bone of Imon, its birther. How to cause interest, concern, curiosity, desire to experience? So little necessary duty now exists that Liij too often simply crouch in stillness, waiting for nothing that can occur. How expect Liij to perform duty unneeded, duty set merely to require actions?

<There is (as alternative) study> Imon replies. Yet study of what? Surround provides nothing; cause of barrenness eludes all inquiry. And all Environ is known, familiar.

For memory bone, Imon nears show of impatience. < Radiance patterns (incoming before surround blackened) from Crippler artifacts. Meaning (however incomprehensible) may in them exist. Why have Liij (and I? Was it Overwatching, caught all my heed?) not probed those patterns?>

Fahar feels shock; it is as though Imon, living, rose to batter ears with mouthsounds—and rasp, not chirr, with palps. After thought, Fahar responds < Liij (in my esti-

mation) may by inclination avoid (or ignore) all that
reminds of Crippler world. But you offer (not surprisingly) path toward (possible, at least) solution to severe
difficulty. > Eager to leave and initiate new duty activity system, Fahar yet pauses. Not merely does it say
gratitude to Imon; memory bone or no, Fahar's birther
is promised word of any knowings gained.

Study of Crippler radiance patterns creates interest in
many Liij. Determination of meanings eludes analysis.
Not until four Overwatchers in turn succeed Fahar does
any hint of true pattern yield to discovery.

But slowly, as succession follows succession, *dre* passing like separate breaths of many lifetimes, meanings
emerge. Not with clearness, but seeming to hold con-
gruence with predicaments at time surround vanished.

And if apparent meanings hold even partial truth, Liij
view of Crippler world, its constructs and those who
manage them, must change. This view is given to
Overwatcher Eimn and council by young pattern-comparator named for that Imon who fed Environ's pace by
use of great worlds' spacetime distortions and by ingest-
ment of their worldlets.

But before Overwatcher Eimn, holding council amid
duty stations at place of control, can evaluate young
Imon's theoretic, sensor screens flare bright. Electrologic safeguards reduce sensitivity range by range, scale
by scale, until reaching settings used in far past, before
surround became barren.

Now, outside Environ, mattergy streams as of old.
Crippler world lies ahead, partially aside. Instrumentation shows pace restored to that which was, before disaster, last shown.

Ingestor field no longer flares widely from forward
orifice. Where it should be, near ahead, now rides Crippler construct.

XXV

VIEWPOINTS

Packed with departing personnel, the assembled ships were gone. Evacuation of macroGate Two was near to total. Velocities almost precisely matched, slowly the Intruder crept toward the retreating gate. In Control, empty-seeming with only the few who had stayed, no one said much, and that in hushed tones.

Austen Cohaign commanded a skeleton crew: Arnie Rike the exec; Dana Ferrell for Security; Jeannie Hurd as Gate tech; and four others, including Branson, for general duty. Eight, then, of the macroGate's crew, plus Rance and Su and Anne Portaris.

A small scoutsized ship had been left for them, in case the situation collapsed into last-minute flight. But looking around the place, seeing everyone intent on screens and instruments, Rance Collier doubted the ship would see use.

Because somehow the group was united in a weird

sort of determination—to see this venture through, no matter what.

Seen on the rear-viewing screens, closer and closer came the Intruder's trumpet-shaped, dimly scintillating web. Then, just as contact seemed imminent, the Traction Drives' normal yellow-white emissions changed to surging rainbow spectra, and the Intruder's web shrank and died.

With only moderate impact, macroGate Two seated itself against the rim surrounding the vanished web's central maw. "It worked!" yelled Rance Collier.

Before he could say more, a burst of force flattened him into his seat. Grimly through flashes of blackness he fought for consciousness. Then, suddenly as it had begun, the intolerable strain ended.

Acceleration, it had to be—and definitely the Intruder's, not the Gate's. Rance felt as if every cell in his body had been individually beaten with clubs. Pulling himself upright, he saw Anne and the captain doing the same, while others still sprawled, apparently senseless, in their seats.

Least lucky of all, Rike and Ferrell, standing, had been flattened to the deck.

Unbelting, young Branson moved to help. "Be careful!" The skipper shouted it. "Keep down low, in case it hits again."

Sitting up, flexing a leg and rubbing one shoulder, Dana Ferrell grimaced. "Nothing broken. Nothing that needs a cast, anyway."

Arnie Rike's leg, though, bent in one place too many. As he tried to sit up, his face went pale and he groaned. "Hold still, Arnie," Branson said. "There's splints in the aid kit." He looked around. "I'll need some help. Dana?" The woman nodded.

Anne Portaris's comment ignored the disruption entirely. "Didn't Henderson tell anyone how to turn this mucker *off?*"

Cohaign hadn't wanted to trust the operation to Anne's reflexes "—or anyone else's, and that's final." So the sensor for Ace Henderson's proximity fuse made the crucial decision. When the range narrowed to spitting

distance, that device activated the phase-shifting circuit
Anne Portaris had haywired into the Drives' common
exciter feed; behind the macroGate, twelve huge Traction Drive units ceased to push against space—and
pushed against time instead.

The trouble was, no one had told Anne exactly where
the sensor was hooked into the circuitry. It took her
several additional minutes to find the combination that
put the Drives back to normal. When she did, and they
took hold, the Gate pushed free of the Intruder.

That vast object, it appeared, had lost power. Now, as
near as could be determined, the thing was only drifting.

It wasn't exactly a council of war Cohaign called, after
Rike's leg was set and other, lesser injuries tended;
rather, his objectives were evaluation and decision.
"What do we have here, and what can we do about it?"

Because the Intruder, now without its moon-eating
iridescent web and no longer building speed, displayed
no activity. Except for the onset of several sets of pulses,
typical of range-finder equipment, it was silent on all
bands.

Dana Ferrell cleared her throat. "I don't know if it
means anything, but the X-raydar's blinking an Attention light."

"The what?" Because Rance hadn't the foggiest.

She said, "It's a spectrum analyzer, to determine the
composition of materials. Judging by its aiming coordinates, it's reporting on the rim of the Intruder's orifice
there. And the blinker means there's been a significant
change of some kind."

Spreading her hands, she added, "But what, I don't
know."

Su Teng spoke. "I'm not familiar with this specific
equipment," she admitted, "but I do know analysis
readout codes in the general case. May I look?"

Ferrell stood aside, letting Su slip into the viewing
seat. After looking for a time and fiddling with adjustments, she shook her head. "I don't understand. Normally a starship's hull builds and holds a tiny fraction of
radioactive isotopes, from simple high-velocity particle
bombardment. What with normal decay, activity tends

to build to an equilibrium level and then stay relatively constant. And according to the readout, ten minutes ago this instrument showed the normal condition. What it indicates now is—well, emission is down to practically nothing. And some of those half-lives are *quite* long." She sounded plaintive. "It makes no sense. No sense at all."

Full-voiced, Anne Portaris answered. "The hell it doesn't!"

"What do you mean?" Cohaign asked.

"Hang on," she said, "and let me figure it."

When she announced her results, they brought no immediate comment. At least ten minutes, the misphased drives had "pushed against time." For the Intruder, Anne's best guess was that it had experienced "—well, on the order of twenty thousand years."

She looked stricken. "We've killed them all! Stretched their time so they ran out of food, maybe air. Certainly energy, the way their drive went crazy and then died."

"I don't understand," said Cohaign. "What you did, with the Traction Drive—you just put them on hold, didn't you? I mean, that's what it looked like."

Anne shook her head. "We accelerated their *time* rate. Their energy system has to feed on input: matter and energy both. Say it normally absorbs—oh, fifty billion particles a second. If ten minutes takes twenty thousand years, they'd be getting only about fifty. So although they're back, *now*, to normal rate and normal input, their reserves must be long since gone."

"Maybe not," Cohaign said. "It's a big ship. To find out, we'll have to get a crew out here with boarding equipment. And in any case, I don't see that we had a hell of a lot of choice."

He stood. "First thing, let's have something to eat. Rankin—" He addressed a young woman, one of the four junior officers. "For the next half hour you have the watch; Branson will relieve you."

He moved to support Arnie Rike at one side; Ferrell took the other. "All right, folks. Let's go."

The officers' dining hall, much smaller than the crew's, still dwarfed the group; all ten of them occupied only a sector of it. Rance thawed and heated Irish stew; Su had chicken.

Cohaign ate quickly, left for a short time, and then returned. Seating himself, he said, "I've sent my initial report, just a summary. We should have boarding capability out here before much longer." At Anne's question, he said, "Two days at the outside. Mounting the effort will take some time, but then they'll come out on high accel, in gee suits."

"Not exactly the best preparation for strenuous boarding work, is it?" Arnie Rike sounded skeptical.

"Boarding teams can ride their accel couches the whole way." The captain sounded sure of his facts; Rike argued no further.

With that subject put to rest, Anne Portaris began asking Rance more about events on *Starfinder*. He was trying to explain some of the difficulties of working under Irina Tetzl's regime without getting into the personally embarrassing parts, when the intercom chimed.

"Rankin here. Captain, there's all kinds of signal from the Intruder. I think somebody wants to talk!"

When you thought about it, Rance decided, it wasn't too surprising that the Intruders spoke English. Of a sort. After all, they must have had a great many frantic, pleading messages available for analysis—and if Anne were right, perhaps several thousand years in which to study them.

What did surprise, though, was their attitude. Once the modulation parameters were adjusted, well enough to make incoming signals intelligible, that attitude became quite clear.

"Gratitude, you of Crippler world who restore Environ's surround. Gratitude of Liij who beg you aid. We—"

Oddly flat-toned, the singsong voice went on; slowly Cohaign and the rest began to understand. Weak in numbers, woefully scant of energy, truly the Liij faced dire want. They needed matter and energy for subsistence and to build speed—yet without that speed they had no way to reach and absorb the matter their drive system required. In addition, without more energy they couldn't reestablish the great web, the artifact that enabled their ship to swallow matter in largish chunks.

"And in the short haul," Cohaign said, "there's not a whole lot we can do for them."

For instance, even if the powers-that-be on Earth were willing to chance the consequences of relinquishing Earth's moon, the Liij lacked the means of utilizing it.

Just as well, thought Rance. But what *would* help?

Voice communication had been difficult enough to establish; getting a coherent picture onscreen seemed, for a time, impossible. Juggling parameters early on—modulation frequencies and their ratios, subcarriers, and the like—Rance decided to leave his transmission setups standard, hope the aliens could decipher them, and bend his own efforts to matching *their* output. "Otherwise," he said, "it's like the two people hunting for each other in a big mall. If one of them doesn't stay put, they may *never* meet."

Eventually a sort of picture appeared—flickering, wavering sidewise and flipping frames, color values shifting and displacing like Traction Drive in time phase. Squinting hard, Rance saw *something* that might be a Liij.

Looking over his shoulder, Su Teng said, "Not precisely your run-of-the-mill neighbor, is he?"

As the picture cleared, Rance had to agree. Considering the heavy muzzle with its voracious-looking jaws, the supple tentacles sprouting near their base, what certainly appeared to be a second pair of eyes, and the ungainly, hulking, baboonlike posture, the Liij resembled something out of prehistory.

Someone *else's* prehistory. Not Earth's.

Cohaign might have been reading Rance's mind. "Looks don't matter. What does is changing our thinking—not just here, but the general public's, on Earth. And damned fast."

He gave a brief, rueful laugh. "Less than an hour ago those people were the biggest menace humans have ever faced. Now they need our help. And the trick is to figure out *how*."

.   .   .

Over the next few days, that help took form. Senator Bill Flynn, warming up for a go at the presidency, grabbed the ball and ran with it on the Senate floor. Almost literally, in fact; as a speaker, Rance knew, Flynn was your basic pacer.

At any rate, the Star Visitors' Emergency Act (with Bill's name on it) cleared both houses by too great a margin for the presidential incumbent, Flynn's upcoming target, to risk the humiliation of an overridden veto. Momentum, plus a good strong push by the U.S. delegation, brought the UN onto the bandwagon. So that NASA's first effort, acting on Cohaign's recommendations, was suddenly enriched with new funding and priorities.

Returning from the asteroids to cislunar refineries, an ore carrier was diverted to eject its lumpy cargo through the tube of the yet-to-be-activated Habgate, into the Liij Environ's forward orifice. "That," said Cohaign, "should hold 'em for a while, at least."

Meanwhile the originally requested boarding team, now only a small fraction of personnel rapidly re-crewing the macroGate, had new chores to tackle. When the lately assigned overall team chief, Errol Markey, discussed it with the captain over dinner, Rance listened. "Those Liij haven't been out of that big ark of theirs, near as we can figure, for maybe a half million years— one of their *dre* being about two years, we think—not even in vac suits. Well, they maintain their outside sensors from inside cubbies, same as we do. But they have no idea where the original big loading ports were; not a clue. So we may have to cut us one, with an airlock over it, to get all the stuff inside."

"The stuff," it turned out, was quite varied. Everything from basic chemical components "—their atmosphere and water recycling systems could do with a jump start—" to fusion reactors "—since their matter-energy vacuum-cleaning ramjet isn't much use, just now."

Two uses, those reactors would have. One, to take up some ship-maintenance slack and allow the Liij to reclaim use of more of their Environ. "Designing the adapters between their systems and ours—" Markey laughed. "—could be quite a trick, and in suits, at that.

We can't breathe each other's air, you know." (Rance knew; not only was the Liij version pressurized to several atmospheres, it also carried more than a whiff of chlorine.)

Perhaps more important, in helping the huge craft get up to working speed more quickly, a dozen of the largest available fusion-powered Traction Drive units were being expedited for mounting at the Environ's rear, ringing its exhaust orifice.

"Which all together," Markey said, "makes a pretty good stopgap. Until we can start *really* feeding that ramjet."

"How?"

The answers left Rance more than a little awestruck. The Niflheim probe, macroGate One, was now instructed to bend its iceball-approaching path to intercept from the Oort Cloud's infall as much debris as possible. Meanwhile its receiving gate was being activated and would be brought to replace macroGate Two in station leading the Liij Environ. "So in two years, while the Liij are still building speed slowly, climbing out of the Sun's gravity well, we can start feeding them enough matter to put them on their own again."

Markey grinned. "Whether we get our Traction Drives and reactors back, then, nobody seems to know."

"If they can give us a handle on their conversion system," Austen Cohaign said, "matter to energy and the other way around, we'll be getting more than an even trade. Imagine what we could do with Habgates *and* FTL speeds to spread them around."

For it was no secret that the Liij would be studied intensively by as many teams as could obtain access.

And vice versa? "You'd think so. No one knows for sure, though." The captain didn't sound terribly worried.

So that, it seemed, was that. Or would be. Briefly, Rance wished he had some kind of handle that could get him into the contact end of things. But he didn't.

What he and Su had was a series of conferences lined up. With all the Liij uproar, Rance had almost forgotten the problem of Irina Tetzl. Being reminded wasn't entirely pleasant.

Because the more he thought about the sequence of events on that ship, the less he liked his own part in them. Even the escape, his and Su's: Was it truly the best option he could have managed? Wasn't it possible that if he'd had more staying power and put his mind to it, he might have made a real difference?

Too late now; all he could do was sit with the group from the NASA task force and answer questions. As best he could, Rance tried to give an objective report. But with limited success: When it came to the more embarrassing parts he waffled, covering his ass. Plain and simple, he couldn't help it.

He knew Su understood, because in all the questioning, never once did she correct any of his equivocations.

Even so, he knew the two of them were helping more than a little toward the task force panel's plans to wrest control of *Starfinder* back from Irina Tetzl. "It's our ship, after all, not hers," said Marv Corby, who chaired the panel. Short and ruddy-faced, with a naturally jovial look to him, Corby gave a deceptively easy-going impression. In point of fact, his approach to the situation was deadly serious.

A computer screen showed the area around *Starfinder*'s Earth Habgate—the Mouth, this one was. Slowly, Corby manipulated graphics controls to rotate his view, moving the "observer" so as to look clockwise along the peripheral corridor. "Now from here, it seems to me . . ."

But he had it wrong. Good as the computer simulation was, it couldn't give the *feel* of being on the ship—such as the way the Velcro'd walking surfaces provided a sort of equivalent to gravitic orientation. Trying not to sound like a know-it-all, Rance corrected the man. It went on like that. . . .

Slowly the planning firmed up. Following, more or less, the rough outlines Rance and Su had discussed earlier with Ferrell and Cohaign, the scheme relied on three teams—equipped to build interdicting structures at Habgates or to breach any they found impeding them, protectively clothed against Tetzl's drugged darts, and armed with similar weapons—to Habjump into *Starfinder, Roamer,* and *Arrow.*

What they'd do on arrival depended entirely on what they ran into. As Dana Ferrell stressed, "We don't want to use any undue force. Captain Tetzl, remember, has not been formally charged with anything at all; we are acting solely on suspicions." At Su Teng's glare the Security chief added, "Certain of her activities have been well attested to; what we don't know, for certain, is how far those actions transgress Regs."

Su relaxed somewhat; Ferrell continued. "All I'm saying is, if we use a sledge hammer to swat a gnat, we could regret it."

Rance snorted. "If you go to *Starfinder* expecting a gnat, damn right you'll regret it. But—" hastily, "I agree with Dana that overreaction is just as bad."

At the last meeting Rance and Su attended before the strike teams left, a newcomer gave some input that neither of them understood very well. Dr. Anya Satrov, an elderly Russian woman with UN credentials, spoke heavily accented English.

What she was saying, they decided later, was that the cause of Tetzl's more flagrant behavior could be medical. "Chemical imbalance," Rance said. "Under control, but if she quit taking the medication . . ." He shrugged.

"Maybe," Su commented. "Though it sounded more as if that would curl her up into a depressed lump. But either way, her story about disguising her true aims by using self-hypnosis—?"

"Pure manic bullshit." Even-steven, Rance divided the last of the coffee. "Well, who knows?" Thinking back, he said, "What *wasn't* bullshit was the pride of her, the competence. I'd hate to see that woman brought back in a loony suit."

"If she is, it won't be publicized. We might not even hear about it. Wherever we are, by then."

"Yeah. Wherever." Because neither Rance nor Su had any idea what kind of future NASA had in mind for them now. If they didn't choose to leave and do something else entirely.

He said as much, then stood. "I guess we'd better load

up and hitch a ride back to Earth. And start finding out."

The strike teams had departed. "Containment teams," rather, and in this case, Rance felt, the official euphemism was fairly accurate. Now for Rance and Su came the time of their own leavetaking.

Their transport, a newly arrived Habegger-fueled freight lighter with accommodations for a few passengers, was undergoing turnaround maintenance, so they shared a last lunch with a few of their new friends and some other folk.

Austen Cohaign headed the table. Dana Ferrell was there; and Arnie Rike, who couldn't scratch where his cast itched; and the young junior officer, Hugh Branson. Also present were Marv Corby and several others of his group, plus Dr. Satrov. Rance still understood only a little of what she said, but couldn't see that it mattered greatly.

He felt let down somehow. The Liij crisis had come and—for the most part—gone; much work remained to be done, but he wouldn't be having any part of that. Nor of recouping *Starfinder:* All he could do on that score, he had done. Now nothing was left but to pick up his marbles and start a new game.

Cohaign must have felt much the same way. Ordering up a few bottles of chilled Chablis he raised toasts, which were properly (and promptly) downed, to the Liij solution, to *Starfinder* and *Roamer* and *Arrow,* to the speedy resumption of his macroGate's mission—he didn't stop there, but that's where Rance lost track.

Lunch ended with handshakes all around, and Dana Ferrell surprised Rance with an unexpected hug. His feelings must have shown; she said, *"Starfinder's* problem; you two helped so much."

Stumped for an answer, after a moment he said, "I hope we did." It was about two hours before the lighter's departure, close to time for him and Su to board, so they went back to quarters for their luggage.

Su entered first and stopped so short that Rance bumped into her. Looking over her shoulder, at first he didn't recognize the woman sitting beside the room's small desk.

Then he did. *"Cassie?"*

But she was supposed to be fourteen years older! No—adding in the detour via *Roamer,* make that sixteen, and a bit over. Yet if she'd changed at all, except for maybe a slightly different haircut, he couldn't detect it. "But how—?"

She spoke, and her voice stirred chords of remembrance. "Didn't the senator tell you? I asked him to."

"Tell me what?" Thinking back, it seemed so long ago that Wallin had visited *Starfinder.* . . .

"What I intended to do. What I did."

"No." He shook his head. Then, "Oh, yeah. He said you'd changed your mind. But not what about. So—"

"Damn the man!" Frowning and grinning at the same time, Cassie said, "Why, I decided *not* to age out of your league. To spend most of the time, while you were gone, in transits through the original Habgates at Gayle Tech." With vigor, she nodded. "And I damned well did!"

She stood. "All told, since we said good-bye you've lived roughly fourteen months. For me it's less than two. I *gained* a year on you.

"Does that rate a hug, or what?"

So familiar, her lean warmth, her faint perfume—the hug became a clinch as Cassie kissed him. Confused, Rance backed away and made busy, breaking out from his bag a bottle he'd intended to take along. "This calls for a drink!"

While he fixed three, Cassie sat and talked. Eight times she'd taken Habgate vacations. First-off she'd cleared her personal affairs and set up an investment program. Then at each emergence she took a few days to update that program and catch up on the news ("just the bare bones of it") before her next hiatus.

"Two years ago, when you were supposed to come back but didn't, I wasn't sure what to do. Finally I decided: Take one more Habjump, and perhaps gain *another* two years on you."

Smiling, she accepted her drink and had a sip. "It's worked out all right, anyway. Now we—"

Needing a diversion, Rance said, "How *is* the senator, by the way?" Meaning: Still alive?

"Fine, so far as I know." Unflustered, Cassie rattled on. "He went to *Arrow;* his game plan was to ride that ship, with its twenty-five-to-one time advantage, until two years Earth time before *Starfinder* reaches goal, then go see what kind of worlds it finds." She shook her head. "Talk about curiosity—!"

Su spoke. "Rance? Shouldn't we be boarding the lighter?"

"Oh? You're returning to Earth already?" Cassie seemed surprised. "Then I'd better get my gear back aboard. We won't be too crowded, I expect." Standing, she moved to leave.

Su's look told Rance it was time he said something. "Er—Cassie? You—it's wonderful to see you so—I mean, it's great that you're—but—"

"But you do know that Rance and I are married," said Su Teng.

Brows raised, Cassandra Monlux said, "That shipboard thing, the group marriage? Sure, I know."

But I was here first? Was that what she meant? Her look—somehow *knowing*—told him nothing. Rance shook his head. "Cassie—"

"Yes, Rance? You have something you want to say?"

He did and he didn't. To him their parting was long past, with all of *Starfinder*'s travail intervening. To her, of course, their time together was practically yesterday.

He needed a deep breath, so he took one. "All right. Some things, I'm not good at." Grasping at any straw, he spluttered, "Dammit all, I got us off *Starfinder* safely. Su and me, that is. I even helped save the gahdam *world,* here—a little bit, anyway. But this situation—"

His own drink went in a gulp; for a moment, it choked him. When his throat cleared he said, "I am not and never will be Dink Hennessey." Cassie couldn't know the reference. "I'm not the type to collect a harem." Now she nodded.

He went on. "Cassie—after all you've done—it breaks my heart to turn you down, but I have to." Unable to meet her gaze, he looked down. "So now Rancid gets it with both barrels."

She said nothing. After a time he heard soft sounds he couldn't recognize. He looked up, just in time to see her stifled chuckle break into overt laughter.

"What—?"

Under control again, Cassie said, "Not Rancid. Rancid was the weeble who could never take a stand."

She sighed. "Oh, Rance! You thought I wanted my hooks into you? Well, maybe a little. You did let Habegger twist your tail, and left me to grow old while you didn't. But I forgave you that. Or mostly . . .

"Oh, I was bitter, all right. Poor me! Poor pathetic Cassie." Her grin came savage. "But now I'm not. I'm starting a new life, the same as you are—and on equal terms!"

"You—you have someone?"

"Not hardly. Living in short bursts at two-year intervals? How could I? But now I have plenty of time to, if I choose. And plenty of money to do it with.

"And the meeting I couldn't face, with me old and you not—we've had it, haven't we? And it's not been that way at all."

She stood. "See you on the lighter. You—both of you —can tell me all about space. What it was like on *Starfinder.* "

She left.

"Well!" A bit rattled, Su Teng looked. "So that's your Cassie. I can't say I take to her a great deal."

"She's all right; you'll like her when you get to know her." And, honesty coming not too easily, "She had that much coming to her, don't you think?"

"Maybe. Rance? Money, she said. We should have quite a lot ourselves, shouldn't we? Our shipboard pay, and so forth?"

"Could be. Of course we did leave a few days before our hitch was up, and I doubt they'll credit the extra two years, our unauthorized detour by way of *Roamer.* And who knows what inflation's been doing.

"But we'll make do, all right." He checked his chrono. "I think we really should get aboard the lighter."

XXVI

DEPARTURE

Again, as long in past, Environ builds pace. Although
ingestor finds little grist and foursphere energy growth
is yet negligible, lack is filled by devices affixed to Environ's
after rim. Devices given by not-Liij of Errdt, earlier
cognomened Crippler world, cause Environ's
movement to increase.

Of strange seeming, Errdtans, most unsimilar to Liij,
yet with them Liij find it possible to share labors. First
Errdtan act is to construct admittanceway into Environ.
Entering thusly, they bring needments in great supply:
renewings in aid of fluid reclaiming and life gas quality,
of nutriment proliferation; and most helpful of all, energy
derivers in supplement of highly stressed foursphere.
To aid Errdtans in their efforts, area of Environ
is sealed to become habitat where Errdtans can shed
coverings that protect from Liij life gas.

Saying of Errdtans also holds strangeness. From lack

of palps, only mouthsounds emit. And through coverings Errdtans require when not in own singular habitat, even sounds emerge not as directly produced but with changes of unknown extent due to devices of transmission. And are Liij mouthsounds also altered on path to Errdtans' hearing? None knows. Yet understanding, though of little completeness, is somehow reached.

Pattern-comparator Imon is one who learns Errdtans' sayings. For its abilities, shown by achieving comprehension of non-Liij, Overwatcher Eimn names it Dutysetter-to-become, upon accession of Dutysetter Geren to status of memory bone. And from Dutysetter's place, Imon knows, path may lead to that of Overwatcher.

In long time to come, that result. But yet, if Imon fulfills trust, with reasonable certainty to occur.

Overwatcher Eimn discloses agreement that Errdtans in own habitat construct Habigays, devices puzzling to Imon. By use of these, Errdtan or Liij may move between Environ and Errdt with no sensing of spacetime traversed. Yet, Imon is told, in instant of change, one *dre* elapses. This, Imon will acknowledge when experienced. And to be in Errdt, not in Environ, is desire Imon cannot conceive.

Much more, over time, Imon learns from and of Errdtans. One such, Branzna, tells of differences difficult to credit. Least believable, yet strongly averred, is that Errdtans are seeders or birthers at all times—but each, lifelong, of only one aspect, never other. Since Branzna seems to feel no lack, no desire to experience what it cannot, Imon decides it need not be pitied.

Numbers of Liij still scant, but soon to grow. From time of surround's restoral, even before promise and then provision of Errdtans' bounteous aid, all youngthons remain intact for breeding. In only few *dre* now, increase begins. Already much of Environ is restored of life gas and warming, while inactivated nutriment proliferation units and other devices begin return to operation, preparing to accommodate increased life to come.

•   •   •

In second *dre* since matter and radiance reappeared, Environ receives new source of mattergy. Where earlier was situated device that annulled surround, new circle-shaped construct rides. And through it flows matter somehow taken from vast world, far out from star.

This construct, says Branzna at earlier time, departs Environ to return toward Errdt, when foursphere's plasma level achieves normal. Other devices, though—energy providers inside Environ, units mounted around re-creator orifice to aid Environ's movement—are given to Liij for all time, to use and study and in time reproduce.

In turn, Errdtans are allowed to observe and learn of foursphere, of ingestor and re-creator. With utmost of seriousness Imon tells—and repeats—of perils if foursphere's containment falters of total security. It hopes Branzna and others understand and believe fully; results of foursphere in derangement would be poor return for Errdtans' generosity.

But on these frettings, Imon's thought cannot long dwell. Not soon, but in times Imon will experience, Liij and Environ are to become as of old: filled with life, pacing beyond crawl of radiance. Leaving this whorl—now observed, now depicted in memory bones and other Liij records—to seek another.

XXVII

AND THEN . . .

At first look Earth hadn't changed as much as Rance
might have expected. Styles and fashions were different
—but then, after any given year or two, they would be.
Many young women, he noticed with disapproval, had
revived the messy, uncombed (not to mention, bedrag-
gled) look popular in the latter 1980s.

Politics was an unknown swamp; it seemed prepos-
terous that he'd never heard of the current U.S. president, but so far as he knew, he hadn't. Come to think of
it, though, except where the political scene impinged
on his own interests, he'd seldom paid it much heed.

But what *else* was going on?

Well, as his earliest PR work predicted, Habegger
technology had found use in several aspects of air and
surface transport, including some he wouldn't have
guessed. One surprise was the Habgate application to
ambulances: if a patient wouldn't last the trip to hospi-

tal, it was into the vehicle's Gate—and two years later, a thoroughly prepared ER would handle the case right on sked. (Keeping track, Rance thought, must take some doing.)

He knew private transportation had shifted largely away from internal combustion to alternate means, but the most visible change was the turn to minicars: "overgrown roller skates" built for only one or two persons. By comparison, the four-passenger NASA car that took Rance and Su to quarters loomed like a bus.

Unpacking in their assigned two rooms, Rance checked kitchen cupboards and found materials for coffee break.

"Tomorrow we can report in and see what the drill is."

At NASA, next day and later, things didn't go well. Job promises made more than sixteen years ago hadn't held up too solidly. "You must realize, times have changed. We'll see what we can do."

But "we," nowadays, included UN bureaucrats from many nations; responsibility and authority weren't necessarily on the same page of the book. And Hans Niebuhr, Maggie Sligo's exec who had panicked and tried to abort *Starfinder*'s mission, had somehow become the hero of that crisis, and consequently a top-echelon brasshat. His initials disapproved several of Rance's job applications, and one of Su's as well.

"He won't have forgiven your taking his gun away from him," said Maggie Sligo, thirteen years older but looking durable and moving well. "And he may be worried that you'd undercut his story—though certainly *I've* never bothered to. Still, getting around him may take some doing. I could help, maybe."

"Oh, never mind; it's not worth the hassle. But thanks, Maggie."

So, deciding to bag it with NASA, Rance and Su went to D.C. and looked up Senator Bill Flynn. In the space effort, Bill still cut a pretty good swath. His welcome included putting the two on his own committee payroll, doing liaison.

"That way you'll still have your finger in the pie," he said. "But with no UN strings on you."

. . .

Back, more or less, into the pre-*Starfinder* swing of things, Rance felt pretty much at home. Overall, the starflight program had some surprises for him. *Arrow*'s variant design had proved successful—enough to be followed, with only minor changes, by later ships. *Scout* had left during Rance's Habgate limbo enroute *Roamer;* now, in only a few months, *Falcon* was due to go.

On its roster, in the role of observer-reporter, was listed Cassandra Monlux. So her age-delaying Gate "trips," Rance decided, had more purpose than merely showing *him* what was what. Nosing into the mission's records proved his hunch correct; during one of Cassie's Gate-travel absences, the medical condition that barred her from space had yielded to research.

Along with a copy of the Med Board's entry, he faxed her a note: "Congratulations! Were you betting on a cure, or did you just get lucky?"

She answered: "Thanks. Don't you wish you knew?"

In news reports Rance followed the restoration of the Liij Environ's functioning, and its slow, continuing exit from the Solar System. The installation of Habgates in the Earth-normal life-support area fired his imagination; now, if desired, study groups working on the Environ could rotate duty much the same as crew cadres on *Starfinder* and her sister ships. And although the Liij showed no interest in visiting Earth, a duplicate set of Habegger facilities was being arranged, Liij-normal at each end. Well, hey—better to have it and not need it. . . .

Headlines reported the milestone event when the Tush end of macroGate One stopped feeding material from Niflheim, detached itself as agreed, and headed back in-system to proceed, eventually, with its original program. Fairly soon, now, it would reach cislunar station.

When the job took Rance out to Gayle Tech he looked up Dr. Habegger. Home again, he told Su, "He's in a wheelchair, but his mind isn't. They've made him a something-or-other Emeritus now."

"Was he glad to see you?"

"Who can tell? Chatted right along, though. His current idea is, it wasn't just us hitting the Liij wake, or they ours; there had to be some kind of interaction.

"Mainly, he'd like to get the Liij Environ up past light speed and try it again."

After two disappointing primaries Bill Flynn pulled out of the presidential race ("Wait 'til next time!") and bent his best efforts toward establishing the Liij Foursphere project. Heeding the fervent cautionary advice of Hugh Branson, now promoted to Commander, the Habegger Institute built its facilities in Neptune's orbit, trailing sixty degrees in Trojan position.

When Su and Rance celebrated their third or twelfth wedding anniversary (depending on whether they figured by t or by t_0), she announced that she wanted to get out of the traveling part of their work and live at their main home base, near Mike Flynn's residence in Maryland. And also, "We've never talked much about children. But if we're ever going to—"

"Um, yes." Now that she mentioned it, he liked the idea.

So a few months later, Su was saying she looked like an olive on a toothpick. Twins will do that—fraternal twins in this case. Also, however, Su developed a surprising bust measurement. When, after young Mai and Alex were weaned, she regained her former slimness, Rance wasn't sure whether he felt relieved or deprived. But between shuttling back and forth on business, and learning more than he really wanted to about the grittier aspects of infant care, he didn't have much time to brood, even if he were so inclined.

All in all, Rance Collier had plenty to think about.

So when he'd been on Earth four years and a bit, he was somewhat surprised to hear news of Irina Tetzl.

Benita Torres, looking much the same except for expert makeup and fancy coiffure, was the one who told him; they met unexpectedly outside NASA HQ, where she'd been trying to get her personnel records straightened out, and had lunch together.

"It was the data cap you left us. Margrete and I viewed it and talked things over, and—"

"Wait a minute. First, what happened when the ice melted?"

As might be expected, Old Iron Tits was furious. She couldn't spare anyone to chase Rance and Su to *Roamer* so she made do with sending a message after them. "Didn't do her much good," Rance said, chuckling. "We were on and off that ship in about five minutes."

Tied up or not, Margrete and Benita caught hell for allowing the escape. Which convinced them that Rance and Su were really onto something. "So we checked the cap out. Well, now!" She always did heave an expressive sigh, Rance recalled. "You said to be careful who we let know about it, so we started slow. Fleurine first; we knew *she* was solid. Then Sarge and Ramon, and finally Zsana." Benita grinned. "Well, everyone who wasn't issued a dart gun. And it was okay; nobody spilled anything."

So what happened? Well, as surmised, Irina Tetzl played hell with scheduled arrivals and departures, keeping some past their tours and—as projected in the recorded plan—dumping new arrivals who didn't suit her fancy. "I can't remember just who went where, or most of the names from 2-A. But—"

"Doesn't matter. *Roamer* or *Arrow*, whatever. Long as she didn't kill anyone." His eyes narrowed. "Did she?"

"No. Just the dart gun thing, so nobody at the other end remembered. Or the ones she rejected, either. One of her 2-A recruits took a group to *Roamer*—was supposed to make it a round trip, zapping all witnesses, the way she'd planned. They weren't back yet when I left. And Irina wasn't either, of course."

What—? But she'd only tell it at her own pace; Rance summoned patience.

Finally she did get to the good stuff. Not long after Su and Rance had gone, relief cadre 2-A began arriving. True to her datacapped word, Tetzl interrogated the newcomers under drugs. "Our good luck," Benita said, "she hadn't managed so as to put *us* through it yet."

When she'd finished, the captain had several "rejects" tabbed to send to *Arrow*. Jimmy Hanchett was to take them, put them into that ship's back-to-back gate installation, and return. When Old Iron Tits cut loose with the dart gun, though, her first target ducked, and needed a second shot to put her out.

"But the first dart stuck in a padded chair back. What with all the commotion, while Irina potted three or four others, Fleurine got to it and slapped it into Tetzl's neck. Then she grabbed the captain's gun—and before anyone really knew what was going on, she zapped everybody who wasn't on our side."

"Fleurine, huh?" Well, she'd certainly had enough steam up, to do something. "Then what?"

"She cleaned house." Taking her time, Fleurine Schadel unlocked all *Starfinder*'s Habgates, then chose the group she felt would best continue the ship's mission. "Hayes Morton, the new exec who came with 2-A, was zapped out; Tetzl had him listed for the Habgate merry-go-round on *Arrow*. But he was next in line for captain now, so Fleurine figured he might as well be."

Benita gestured; Rance poured more coffee. "Anyway, she'd rather of just *sent* Irina and some others to *Arrow*, but she said she had to take 'em herself, be sure they went into *Arrow*'s own pipeline. So that's what she did."

Benita shrugged. "What happened after that, at the far end, I don't know. And they debriefed me when I got back, so I don't suppose I should even be telling you about the parts I do know. But—" She grinned. "Any time I don't know who's safe and who isn't . . ."

Oh? Before he thought, "How's Dink?"

"What happened with us, you mean? Well, he was out flat, zapped; Fleurine had him pegged for *Arrow*. And me to stay on and be crew. Hey, no damn *via*, I told her. I'd had enough of sharing him with Irina; sure as hell he wasn't going *with* her. So Fleurine let us both come home. By way of *Roamer*, since the Earthgate switch hadn't been fixed yet, after you bashed it."

Benita grinned. "They kept us on *Roamer* nearly six weeks, more or less locked up. After the way you and Su went through there . . . Anyway, we got home about a year later than you did. Missed all the big Liij scare, but heard plenty about it. I wanted to look you up, but Dink—I think he was too embarrassed."

Rance thought about it. "He needn't be. It's a time

ago." Back to the main point. "And what's he doing now?"

"Right now? He's home taking care of the kids."

"I should look him up. I could use some pointers."

More echoes from the past came the next time Rance had occasion to trade info at NASA HQ. Walking along a corridor, he heard someone hailing him, and turned to see Maggie Sligo.

"Hi, Maggie. What's new?"

"Hans Niebuhr's profile."

"Huh?" The story had to be worth a drink, so they went where he could buy her one.

"So, talk."

"All right." It seemed that Niebuhr didn't like Jimmy Hanchett any better than he liked Rance Collier. Returning not long ago, Jimmy had applied for his own long-promised job and received the same treatment Rance had.

But Hanchett wasn't so easy-going. When he'd figured out that Hans was roadblocking him, he'd confronted the bureaucrat in his own office. ". . . and beat the living hell out of him. Nose all over his face." She lifted her glass. "Here's to Jimmy. I went down and bailed him out, of course."

Probably it wasn't nice to laugh, but Rance did anyway.

One of the perks that came with working for Bill Flynn was the vidphone in his home "office." The circuit cost like a bandit, but the bill went to the senator's account.

Late one evening, the phone chimed and its screen lit, showing a solid-faced black woman wearing a colorful dashiki. It took him more than a moment to recognize Btar Mbente.

She spoke first. "I thought you were going to call me when you got back."

"Well, I—" And how long had it been for her, since they'd said goodbye on *Starfinder?* Seventeen years, anyway. But except for having filled out somewhat, she didn't show it.

Now Btar asked, "What's been going on? We used to

get news of the ship, but about six years ago that all stopped."

Six? Close enough, given the Gate lag. "Well, you see —" On what he did know, he brought her up to date— editing here and there for security reasons, as if those really mattered now. "And you? What have you been doing with your life?"

Still shaking her head over his revelations, she said, "I've done well, Rance. For instance, this is my own phone, not a pay station. At first—" As she'd considered doing, Btar returned to her home village, where for some months she lived the primitive, semi-nomadic life of her childhood.

"Then I went into politics. By now I administer a sector, largely non-industrial, larger than some of your states. My main function, as I see it, is to keep 'progress' away from those of my people who like things the way they've always been."

"Well, I certainly wish you luck. And when we find out what did happen later on *Starfinder,* I'll let you know."

It was Su who got the answers to their remaining questions. Returning from his week at the Cape, Rance found her perusing a classified readout. "Bill's office got this in," she said, once the family's round-robin greeting hugs were done with. "So he let me make a copy. It's not at all clear to me. Here; have a look. See if it makes more sense to *you.*"

Officialese never changes for the better; easy reading, the report wasn't. With persistence, though, the gist of it began to clarify. If, indeed, the timing added up . . .

He said, "Five of them—Irina and Cleve and Jimmy, plus a couple of doubtfuls from 2-A—Fleurine took to *Arrow* and pipelined there. And herself along with them. With t_0/t at twenty-five to one, they'd pop out again in about a month. A short month. She was prepared to keep this up indefinitely, as long as she felt she needed to."

Su nodded. Encouraged, he went on. "One of Marv Corby's containment teams got there shortly before the lot came through the second time. With their protective clothing, Fleurine couldn't zap them, so the merry-go-round stopped. Well over two years ago, that was, by our time." He looked again at the most surprising part.

"Who'd have thought it?"

Partly right, Anya Satrov had been—but also partly wrong. Irina Tetzl had been on medication, all right, but she hadn't been screwing up her dosage. Quite the opposite.

"She'd developed symptoms of depression on *Jovian-Two*," Rance continued, "so the NASA docs changed her prescription. When she drew her berth on *Starfinder*, somehow the medical follow-up got lost. And the new stuff did too good a job: overcompensated for depression. And the side effects made her sort of manic. Not quite the right term, I know; the pathology's not the same. But close enough."

He shook his head. "She always was a horny lady, seems as if—up to then, though, her yens stayed within normal limits. Along with her super-duper ego." He spotted something else in the text. "Things didn't get out of hand until *after* she'd passed the stability tests. And I see she was trying biofeedback for a time; that may be what she described as self-hypnosis, later."

"But there must have been more than that!" Su put in. "She told it, you said, in much detail. Designing a personality to suit the NASA profiles? Mental sets keyed by code words?"

"Maybe she thought up that part retroactively." He shrugged. "Rationalizing can do fantastic things. Or maybe the tests aren't as reliable as the brass likes to think."

"Perhaps. But Rance—you see here, when her medication *was* corrected and she regained a sane view of her actions?"

He looked. "Um, yeah. She insisted on a court-martial."

With no one from the Judge-Advocate's office available, Senator Wallin presided. Tetzl freely admitted the wrongness of her actions. If she had skipped her pills, she testified, she'd have realized she was off track. But as it was, firmly convinced her own rationality was bolstered by the drug, she had no thought to question what she did. "My incapable judgment," she testified, "requires me to resign, under what terms you may set."

"The old boy didn't take her up on it, though." Instead, once stabilized (and retested, to prove the fact), Irina Tetzl was given an interim rating of supernumerary co-exec on *Arrow*.

"If it works out, and no reason why not, Wallin's prepared to recommend that she go to *Starfinder* as leader of relief cadre 4-B, when the ship's neared its goal and gone through decel. And take charge of reconnaissance and exploration."

Su looked disbelieving. Rance said, "When she's straight she's a top organizer; her record proves it. And a qualified medic will be along to see she stays that way."

"So she gets everything she wanted." Su's grin looked wry.

"Well, not entirely. Cleve Rozanski couldn't come up with any excuse for going along with her dipsy-doo, so he did get cashiered—in a face-saving manner, more or less. And Jimmy Hanchett's still hanging around the Cape. Looking for a job, and hoping to reconcile with Fleurine if she ever comes home."

He stood. "So Old Iron Tits is going to have to find herself a new fella. Or more, if she still swings that way."

From another room, shrill sounds came. Rance smiled. "Nap time seems to be over; somebody needs to get the kids dressed."

"And somebody needs to make dinner."

"Flip you for which?"

EPILOGUE

On its way to wherever its none-too-scrutable denizens planned to go, the Liij Environ as seen from Earth dimmed and diminished past most instruments' sensitivity. "Maybe they *are* heading for the next galaxy," said Rance Collier. "Well, when they get there, some humans will be along for the ride." He chuckled. "Maybe even some of our descendants."

He and Su didn't leave Earth again until they took Mai and Alex on extended vacation as a graduation present; for the parents it seemed more like a kind of sabbatical.

Maybe even a pilgrimage.

They all had a great time, though, seeing the sights on Tetzl's Planet.

Neither the tour guide, the younger Colliers, nor any of the other tourists knew why Rance laughed out loud on viewing the matched pair of summits that topped the Iron Mountains.

Su did, though. She didn't let on, but Rance could tell.

STARFINDER

The *Starfinder* class of ships was constructed to a very conservative design, as is evident when we note the magnitude of support provided for crews averaging a mere twelve persons.

Only two of these ships—*Starfinder* and *Roamer* — were actually built, each differing in minor detail from the plan shown here. Both performed well, *Starfinder* reaching Tetzl's Planet and *Roamer* discovering the Triad Worlds.

The initial, in-voyage success of *Arrow,* based on a more powerful drive and wholly different philosophy of crewing, led to a shift of emphasis: *Scout, Falcon*—and *Nomad,* now being constructed in orbit—have each followed *Arrow*'s pattern.

The future holds new expectations. As of this writing, the parameters and possibilities of the experimental Bootstrap combination (alternately termed Boomerang) are kept closely secret by NASA and by the Habegger Institute. As are, we must assume, the more important findings brought back by research teams from the Liij Environ.

But whatever these newer, more complex brainchildren of science may achieve, one fact remains:

First to orbit a habitable planet, other than Earth, was *Starfinder*.

Bowie Fleming Hargis

ABOUT THE AUTHOR

F. M. BUSBY lives in Seattle with his wife Elinor and their two cats: Ivan who is Terrible and Molly Dodd who is calico.

Buz began writing as a serious pursuit in 1971. His previous SF novels include eight in the universe of Rissa Kergeulen and Bran Tregare, *The Demu Trilogy* in Barton's universe, *All These Earths* in the multiple universes revealed by the story's Skip Drive, and *The Breeds of Man* in a possible near future variant of our very own cosmos. His forty or so shorter works, twenty of which appeared in his story collection *Getting Home* and three in *Best of the Year* anthologies, are not readily classifiable.

Buz grew up in eastern Washington and holds degrees in physics and electrical engineering, studies which help him keep his numbers straight. Between college terms and two breaks for Army service he held a number of incongruously assorted jobs before embarking on his first career, communications engineering. With the Army, and later as a civilian, he spent some time in Alaska and the Aleutians, and claims his stories about Amchitka weather to be simple truth; one of these, "Tundra Moss," will appear in the anthology **What Might Have Been**, Volume 3: *Alternate Wars*, late in 1991.

His other interests include aerospace, unusual gadgetry of all kinds, dogs, cats, and people, not necessarily in that order.

Currently he is wrapping up a new novel, *The Far Islands*, of which he says only, "It's different."

He always says that. . . .

What price human peace and freedom?
What price survival?

The Singers of Time
by Frederik Pohl
and Jack Williamson

Earth has been immeasurably changed by the arrival of the "Turtles," who have conquered Earth without a fight. Who in his right mind would oppose the bringers of peace, prosperity, and plenty of trade goods--especially when the Turtles are offering more than a fair price for everything?

Of course, there was a catch. The first things the Turtles bought were Earth's military establishment and space buses. And the Turtles objected to humans like the Quintero twins who did research in physics and cosmology--studies blasphemous to the Turtles' religious beliefs.

Then, in an instant, everything changed. The Mother, the single female of the Turtle species, disappeared. Suddenly the Turtles needed human help--and a space pilot named Krake, the only human who could fly a Turtle waveship. Drafted to convey a mismatched search party on a mysterious journey, Krake takes off on a hazardous mission that will lead him to the Turtles' Mother planet -- and to the most carefully guarded secrets in the universe.

A science fiction adventure based
on the theories of Stephen Hawking,
The Singers of Time
is a fascinating odyssey through space and time

Coming soon in Bantam Spectra paperback.

AN298 -- 8/91

"Banks has given us one of the most dazzling and accomplished pieces of space adventure to appear in the last decade."--*Chicago Sun-Times*

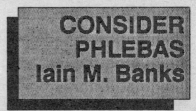

CONSIDER PHLEBAS
Iain M. Banks

"A splendid, rip-roaring adventure by an author who's clearly at home in the genre....Some books will keep you up half the night reading. **Consider Phlebas** is that rarer achievement worth reading again."--*Locus*

In the vast war between the Idrians and the Culture, one man is a free agent--his name is Horza. As a Changer, with the ability to transform himself at will, he works for the Idrians, and it's a fair exchange as far as he's concerned: his work is his most effective means to undermine the smug, sterile, highly advanced Culture that he despises.

Horza's latest assignment is to capture a renegade Culture mind--a form of artificial intelligence well beyond Idrian technology--hiding on a dead planet. Retrieving the mind is the easy part--it's the journey that's the challenge. He'll be facing cold-blooded mercenaries, a cannibalistic tyrant literally out for his blood, and a deadly game of Damage played out to the last minutes on a space habitat about to be blown to bits.

"Imaginative and gripping."--*Kirkus*

Consider Phlebas
On sale now wherever Bantam Spectra Books are sold.

AN328 -- 9/91

Space: the Final Frontier. ™
These are the voyages of the Starship Enterprise. ™....

Star Trek®:
The Classic Episodes

adapted by James Blish
with J. A. Lawrence

In the twenty-five years since it premiered on network television, bringing the voyages of the *Starship Enterprise* into America's living rooms and the national consciousness, *Star Trek* has become a worldwide phenomenon, crossing generations and cultures in its enduring universal appeal.

Now, in celebration of *Star Trek*'s 25th anniversary, here are James Blish's classic adaptations of **Star Trek**'s dazzling scripts in three illustrated volumes. Each book also includes a new introduction written especially for this publication by D.C. Fontana, one of *Star Trek*'s creators; David Gerrold, author of "The Trouble With Tribbles"; and Norman Spinrad, author of "The Doomsday Machine."

Explore the final frontier with science fiction's most well known and beloved captain, crew and starship, in these exciting stories of high adventure--including such favorites as "Space Seed," Shore Leave," The Naked Time," and "The City on the Edge of Forever."

Now on sale wherever Bantam Spectra Books are sold.

AN332 -- 9/91